THE FLOATING LAKE OF DRESSA MOORE

GEORGE ALLEN MILLER

This is a work of fiction. Names, characters, places, and incidents are either the product of the author's imagination or are used fictitiously, and any resemblance to actual persons living or dead, business establishments, events, or locales, is entirely coincidental.

The Floating Lake of Dressa Moore

Cover Art by *Jamie Noble Frier*

Copy Edited by *Robin Fuller*

First Edition, 2025

Trade Paperback ISBN: 979-8-9920996-3-8

Digital ISBN: 979-8-9920996-2-1

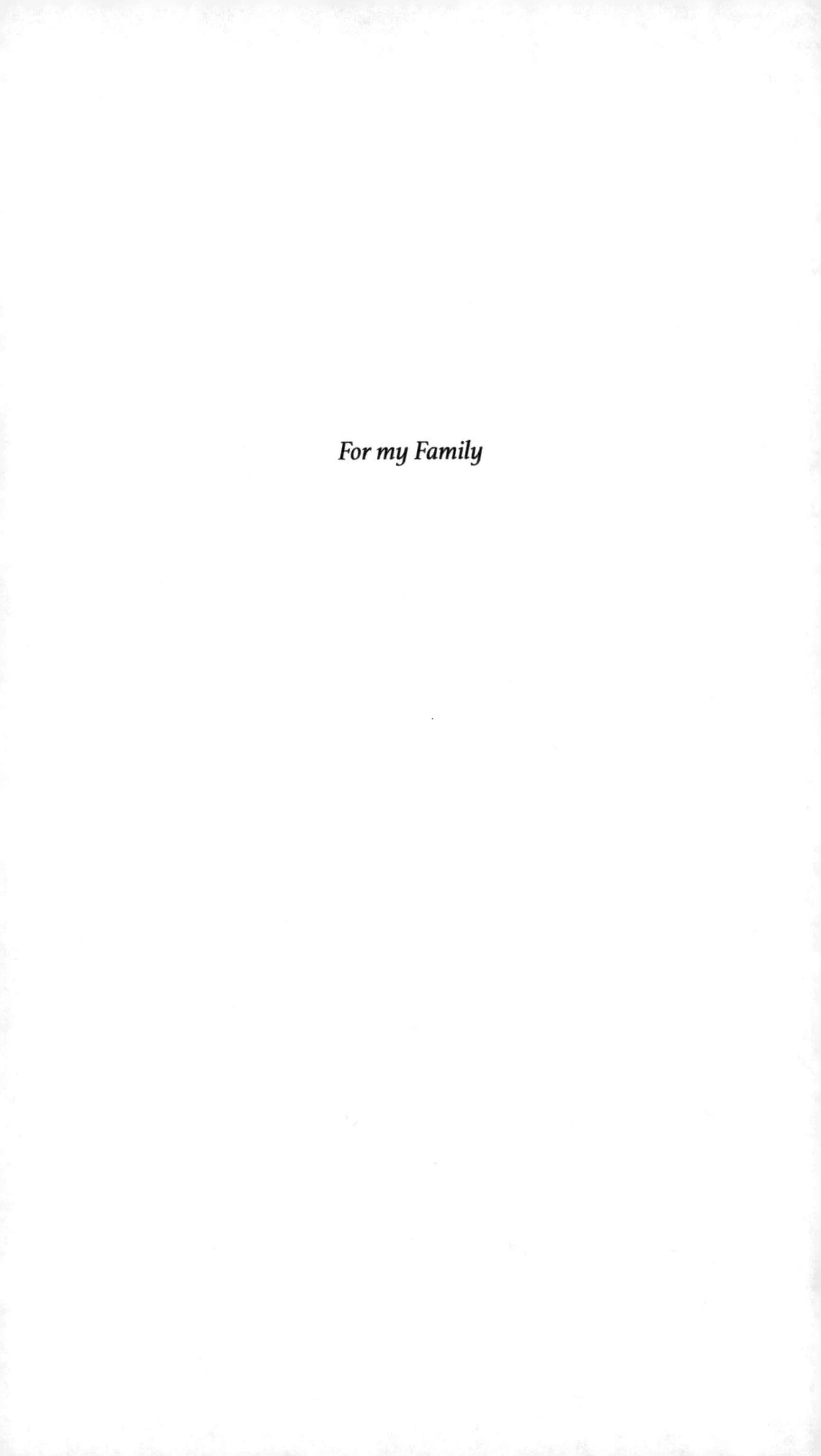

For my Family

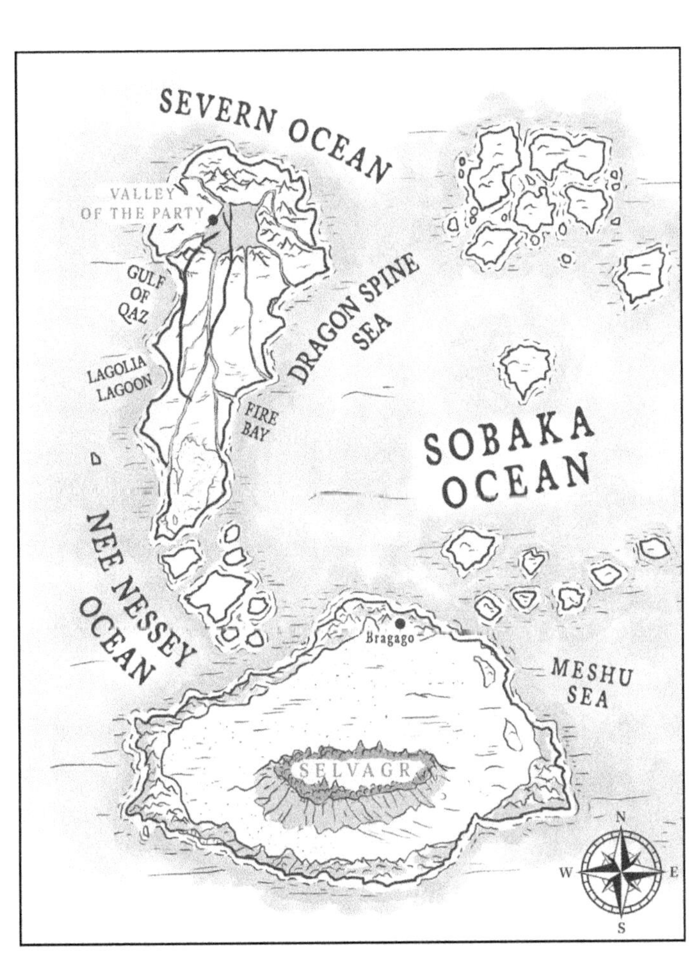

SEVERN OCEAN
VALLEY OF THE PARTY
GULF OF QAZ
LAGOLIA LAGOON
FIRE BAY
DRAGON SPINE SEA
NEE NESSEY OCEAN
SOBAKA OCEAN
Bragago
MESHU SEA
SELVAGR
N
W
E
S

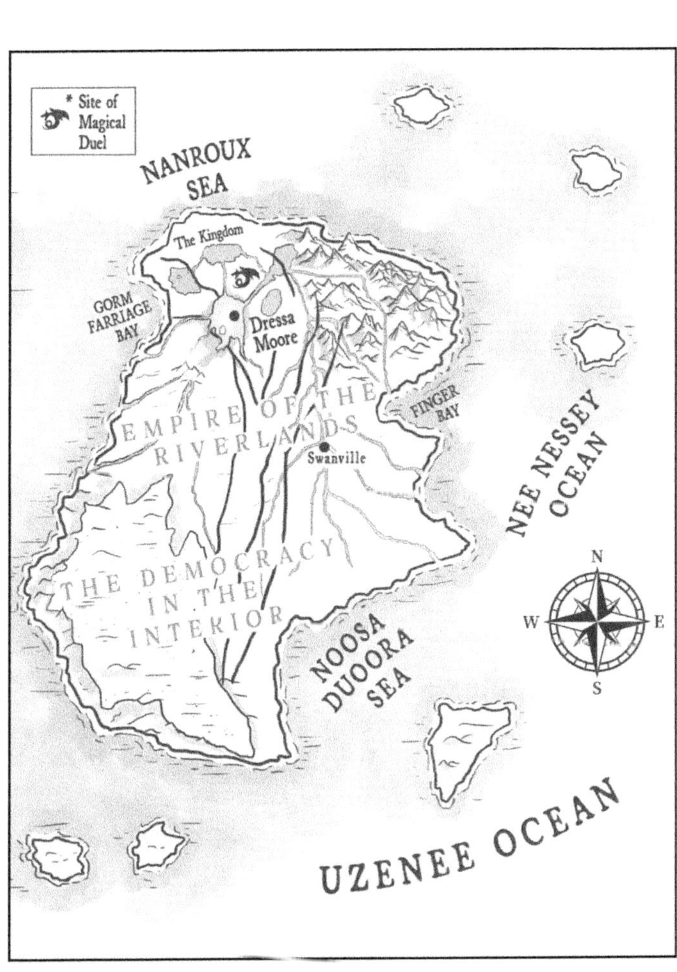

* Site of Magical Duel
NANROUX SEA
The Kingdom
GORM FARRIAGE BAY
Dressa Moore
EMPIRE OF THE RIVERLANDS
FINGER BAY
Swanville
NEE NESSEY OCEAN
THE DEMOCRACY IN THE INTERIOR
NOOSA DUOORA SEA
N
W E
S
UZENEE OCEAN

PROLOGUE

The old man leaned back in his oversized cushioned chair, bones creaking as he adjusted his body to find a spot of comfort—a task that grew more difficult with each passing day. A fire crackled in the hearth. The warmth felt good to the old man. He smiled as the flames licked the bricks set into the wall.

Children flooded into the room. Many of them began to sit at the old man's feet. Some of them danced in joyous circles, only to have their parents guide them to a crisscross-apple-sauce posture on the carpeted floor. The old man smiled at them as they entered. The children of the village always made his heart glow with warmth more than any fire ever could.

From his left, the old man hefted a large book onto his lap. He patted the leather cover once and smiled. This was his life's work—well, the beginning of it, anyway. He opened the leather-bound tome to the first page. Maps of Dressa Moore, the floating lakes, the empire, and the two great continents were painted on the first page with colorful elegance and grace. The old man let his fingers glide across the maps from the great city of Swanville up the Riverlands and eventually to Lake Connell, which floated above the ground below by nearly a mile.

"Can we see the maps?" one of the children asked, a young boy wearing a patchwork sweater that the old man clearly remembered being worn by the boy's older brothers.

The old man smiled and turned the book so the children could see. They all oohed and ahhed and pointed and called out different areas on the maps that they recognized. Several of them began jumping up and down in excitement, while others just smiled and waited eagerly on the carpet. The parents, now all clustered in the back of the room, smiled and shook their heads. They were content to let the old man control the mob of youth. Eventually, the old man turned the book back around and rested the large tome in his lap, much to the chagrin of every child.

"Now, children, do you want to dance, or do you want to hear the story?" the old man said with a smile through his bushy white beard.

All the children backed away, though some more slowly than others. They all sat on the carpeted floor and criss-crossed their legs. Eager smiles covered every face. Each of them rocked as they sat, or repeatedly thumped their feet on the floor, or simply waggled their hands in the air. They had all been waiting for months to hear the story in its fullness, the book only just finished, the last word written this morning by the old man in the chair. And for children of this age, waiting months felt like waiting lifetimes.

"Right, then," the old man said with a smile and nod. He turned the page of the maps to the opening chapter. "This story begins one hundred years before it starts."

One of the children—a girl with red hair and a freckled face—wrinkled her nose. "That doesn't make any sense...?"

A boy with long blond hair rolled his eyes and scoffed. "It's a pre-story," he said with a strong nod.

"What's that?" the first boy's brother asked.

"A story before the story," another girl replied with quiet certainty.

The old man laughed. He held up his hand and flashed them all a stern look before winking. "As I was saying... Our story starts, truly, with the ending of another, as most stories do. Once upon a time, there was a great wizard named Finnian. He was not only great, he was also the last wizard in all the world, all the rest having left our mortal plane."

"Where did they go?" the blond boy wondered.

"They died, silly. That's what it means to leave our mortal plane," his brother explained.

"They died?" a girl asked.

"Ooh, is this a scary story? I don't like scary stories," the girl with the freckled face said.

The old man leaned forward. "I can assure you, my lady, this story is not scary. And though there may be scary parts, I shall do my best to make you all feel at ease."

The freckle-faced red-haired girl smiled.

"What happened to the wizard?" the boy with long blond hair asked.

The old man smiled. "He had the most unfortunate luck, Finnian the Wizard. As he was walking through a valley, he happened to stumble upon the last remaining dragon in all the world."

"The last wizard *and* the last dragon?" said a girl in a makeshift pirate hat, holding a small wooden toy sword in her hand.

"Did they fight?" the blond boy asked.

The old man smiled. "Well, you see, children, wizards and dragons were the greatest of enemies. They had loathed each other since the dawn of time. So, yes, Finnian the Wizard did indeed fight the dragon. But a fight between a wizard and a dragon is no small thing. Wizards and dragons hold vast reservoirs of magic. And since Finnian and the dragon were the very last of their kind, they both controlled all the magic that existed."

"What happened when they fought?" a girl wearing small round glasses asked.

The old man smiled, then nodded. He brought both his hands together into a ball and then ballooned them outward, mimicking a grand explosion. "There was simply too much magic in one place. When their spells touched, they created a magical tsunami."

"What's a soo-nami?"

"It's a big rumble in the ground."

"No, that's a quake. A soo-nami is a huge wave. My dad told me," the freckle-faced girl said.

The old man nodded. "Quite right. But this wave was not made of water. It was made of pure magic."

The children's eyes went wide.

"The magical forces unleashed froze Finnian and the dragon in time, with both of them caught in their final moment before their battle. But that was not all. The magical tsunami flowed outward from them both. It cascaded down the valley where they stood. Just by being next to each other, by being so close, the two most powerful magical beings caused magic to flow out of them and return to the world. It caused whole seas to float a mile in the air. Mountains were cut in half. Whole towns were severed right down the middle. Rivers became waterfalls, miles high. And as the years went on, more magic flowed outward. Some learned how to tame the spells, while others fell victim to their power."

All eyes were wide with wonder. "What happened next?"

"Is that the end of the story?"

"Or the beginning?"

"No, it was the end of the beginning."

"I thought it was the beginning of the end?"

The old man leaned back his chair. "What happened next, did you say?" He opened his book to the first page. "What happened next is where our story begins. And it is quite the story, indeed."

PART I

THE RIVERLANDS

CHAPTER ONE

Morning sunlight cast golden hues on a hundred faces of the myriad of people walking along the docks of the harbor. The scents of fresh fish and stale bread wafted in the air, forming a cloudy mix that rumbled more than a few stomachs. A steady stream of dockworkers crossed the streets next to the harbor to start their day loading and unloading ships. A long line of vessels waited in the waters around the Port of Oyster Piers, the closest port to Lake Connell, the floating lake of Dressa Moore.

Shouts rang out from imperial soldiers. They shoved their way through the crowd and created a formation in front of their superior, walking through the working-class citizens with contempt written on their faces. A beggar fell into the path of the soldiers, only to be met with the butts of their long rifles as they pushed the man out of the way.

William Watts Worthwaddle did his best to ignore the spectacle. He sat down on his large travel trunk, filled with more books and writing items than clothing, and retrieved a small tome detailing the importance of vowels in language.

He opened his book to the chapter devoted to the letter *E*. The thought of racing to the poor beggar's aid filled his mind for a moment, but he quickly shoved the notion away. University professors were simply not built for such encounters.

Before diving into his book, William spared a glance at the lake of Dressa Moore in the distance. Lying where it had absolutely no business being, Lake Connell floated among the clouds. It had been in the skies ever since the magical tsunami a century before, which had sent the lake, the surrounding islands, and a portion of the northern continent soaring into the heavens. Magical forces that no one truly understood kept the lake, islands, and citizens of the few towns that remained floating a mile above the world. But, as William reminded himself, that was exactly why they were here: to unlock those mysteries. Well, at least that was why Jonathan, William's partner, was here. William had just come along for emotional support. He turned his attention to Jonathan, who stood gazing towards the docks.

"Do you see our ship or the tender?" William asked.

Jonathan Braxton, chief magilurgist of the Great University of Learning and Knowledge, foremost expert on magical theory, master of the arts of cookery regarding cured meats, one of the finest dressers William had ever met, and perhaps the most selfish lover William had endured in his short life snorted a response and shrugged. "I don't. And I don't know where they are, William. We were supposed to meet them here at dawn. It's well past dawn, and they aren't here."

"Well, how long do you think we'll need to wait?"

"How could I know that? If you don't want to wait, then you can still return to the university." Jonathan brushed the sleeves of his purple velvet overcoat and adjusted the handkerchief in his breast pocket, lining up the edges to be exactly in line with the hem.

"Is that what you want me to do?"

"Oh, stop it. Of course not. But this is an intolerable situation. Do you think I want to sit here and watch soldiers beat some poor man just because he's poor?" Jonathan asked.

"No, certainly not." William nodded once and went back to studying the letter *E*. He honestly did not know why he was here. Well, he knew, but he didn't know if he really wanted to believe his own reasons. He and Jonathan's affair had been nearing its end. They both knew it. And they both, in their hearts, didn't want it to end. So, when the opportunity had arrived to travel to the most exotic location in the world, with the promise of wild adventures and unknown discoveries, William had decided to join Jonathan in hopes of rekindling their love. Why not take the chance? But sitting here in the muck, with his oak travel trunk sinking into gods knew what, William admitted that he'd perhaps romanticized this journey a tad much.

"You, there! You seem out of place." A soldier with a few more flashes of regalia on his shoulder had noticed Jonathan and William's argument and walked over to them.

"Hello, Lieutenant, is it?" Jonathan pointed to the adornments on the soldier's coat. "My apologies, my military heraldry isn't what it used to be."

"Lieutenant Swanson. Merrick Swanson."

"Wonderful to meet you, Lieutenant. I am Jonathan Braxton, of the Great University of Learning and Knowledge. And this is my companion, also of the university, William Watts Worthwaddle, linguist."

"Ah, from Gulk, are you?" Lieutenant Swanson said.

William cringed at the mention of the commoner's name

for the university. He'd chaired a panel with the express desire of renaming the college, but his efforts had fallen flat. The university president simply hadn't cared. Rumors swirled that the only reason he'd been allowed to form the panel was as a gift to Jonathan on William's behalf.

Lieutenant Swanson turned to William. "You're a what? A lingist? What is that?"

"Linguist. I study language," William clarified.

"You mean a grammatist?" the lieutenant said.

"No, not quite," Jonathan said, his back straightening and his jaw clenching. "A grammatist studies the rules of language—nouns, verbs, structure, and such—while a linguist scientifically studies the core of languages."

William loved when Jonathan defended his field of study. Yes, it was odd; why study languages when there was just the one in the entire world? But William felt in his soul that there was a need. How could so many societies develop across the globe and all of them speak the same language? It made no sense. And yet, the world thought William mad. All but dear Jonathan. Well, maybe he did as well, but it warmed William's heart that, though Jonathan didn't understand the choice, he did support and even defend William's desire to study language. It was perhaps one of the few reasons they were still together.

"Languages? Isn't there only the one?" the lieutenant said.

"Well, yes..." Jonathan started.

"But there could be more that we haven't discovered yet," William said from atop his trunk. "More people who speak something other than the classic tongue."

"Where would these people be, then? The empire covers the whole continent. We have relations with the Democracy in the interior, and when we did have relations with the kingdom on the other side of the floating lake a century ago, there was never talk of another tongue," the lieutenant pointed out. "We've even had excursions to the second continent, and the primitives there speak the same language as we do."

"Yes, I do realize. But there could be undiscovered peoples. And even if there aren't, I find it odd that only one language has ever developed. Even in peoples who were separated by centuries, still they spoke the same language." William rested his book on his knee, a brief bit of excitement creeping up his spine. It wasn't often that he got to speak of his field of study.

Lieutenant Swanson nodded. "Right. So, you're like a philosopher, then? Wondering about things that don't exist."

"No, I'm not a philos—" William began before Jonathan cut him off.

"Is there anything we can help you with, Lieutenant?" Jonathan said.

Lieutenant Swanson gave William a pointed stare before turning his attention back to Jonathan. "Yes. You can tell me what two university professors are doing in this nothing of a town."

Jonathan shrugged. "What does that matter?"

"Everything that happens here matters to the imperial navy. And you and your grammatist—"

"Linguist," William whispered.

"*Shh,*" Jonathan shushed.

"—are both out of place," the lieutenant continued. "The nearest university classroom is one hundred miles away. That's your place. Which means you are out of place. And I don't like things out of place."

Jonathan nodded once and pulled an envelope out of his pocket. "We have been allowed to come, I assure you."

Lieutenant Swanson snatched the envelope and read it from top to bottom. "Magilurgist? You're a magilurgist?"

"That's right."

"And you're headed to the Aquirren River to enter Lake Connell, the floating lake? Is that right?"

"Quite."

"Right. Well, travel to the Aquirren River is restricted. I'm afraid you'll have to return to the university, gentlemen."

Jonathan cleared his throat and did his best to maintain a smile. "We have formal approval from the regional governor, Lieutenant." He tapped the letter in the lieutenant's hand where the governor had applied his seal.

The lieutenant gritted his teeth, his jaw clicking as his molars ground together. "Why would he do that, then?"

"Scientific investigation of magic at the source is long overdue. Both the regional governor and the imperial commandant have approved."

"At the source."

"Yes."

"The source of magic," the lieutenant ground out. "You are going to the actual source of magic?"

"The very place."

"Last time the military sent a ship anywhere near the source of magic, the crew came back with extra limbs, some of them made of broccoli. One poor bosun grew a second head and argued with himself for the rest of his life."

"We are aware of the dangers. But we do still have permission to go."

The lieutenant straightened his already straight shoulders and squinted his eyes at Jonathan. "If this has the backing of the military, why not travel on a military vessel?"

"My understanding, Lieutenant, is that there is the desire from the highest levels of government to keep our expedition secret." Jonathan straightened his back to match the lieutenant's. "Which is being jeopardized the longer we speak. Don't you think?"

Lieutenant Swanson scowled. He looked around and nodded in acknowledgment to the increased stares latching onto their conversation. He let out a sound somewhere between a huff and a growl, handing the letter back to Jonathan. "Have a fine journey," he muttered. Without waiting for an answer, he stormed off, with his contingent of soldiers following him. They pushed and shoved the nearest people away from them, regardless of whether they were in their path or not.

"Well, he was a joy," William said.

"At least he's gone," Jonathan replied.

"Is what he said a concern? I mean, I don't know how I feel about either of us growing extra pieces."

"It'll be fine, William. We are prepared. Scientifically so."

"Excellent, we can get back to waiting, then." William opened his book and proudly began reading of the intonation habits among coastal peoples of the letter *E*.

Captain Marta Agnes Rhia Bartolome planted her leather-booted foot on the wooden dock of Oyster Piers. She nodded once to herself and waved her crew to follow. She hadn't been to this town in years and had no desire to be here now. If it weren't for the fact that she'd stumbled onto her first real chance to reclaim her island home and reverse her own curse, she wouldn't ever have come to this oyster-filled, rat-infested miserable place. After getting a well-timed tip from Sylvia, a young girl Bartolome had helped once, and then using that tip to pirate a travel barge in

Dressa Moore, Bartolome was able to convince the captain of that barge to give the contract to her—and by "convince," shee meant "threaten." When Bartolome read the details of the contract, and confirmed that the path would take them to the Wizard and Dragon, the source of all magic in the world, her choice had been easy. This was her first real chance to undo what had happened two decades ago. Her first real chance to go home. And the buckets of money the university would pay for the transport was a nice bonus.

Now all she had to do was find the two university professors. How hard could that be?

The aromas of cooked meat and baked bread floated on the air, accompanied by the sweetness of sugar. Most likely cookies, Marta thought. She hated cookies. And cooked meat. And boiled vegetables, and fresh fruit, and just about everything else this town offered. But with luck, she wouldn't be here more than a moment.

"Smells lovely," Anton said.

The ship's cook heaved himself out of their rowboat and onto the dock, an action that Marta had to admire. Anton wasn't a small man by any measure. He stood over six-and-a-half feet with a roundness just as impressive as his height. His clothing, mostly fabric except for his leather boots and jacket, hung loosely on his frame, another fact that Marta found impressive. She could probably hide in clothing that large.

"It smells lovely to you and you alone, Anton," Marta replied.

"Well, yes, of course, to me—considering I'm the one that said it."

"Don't be crass."

"Yes, my Captain. Are you sure you should have brought so many of the crew?"

Bartolome nodded. "The contract said there would be luggage. Lots of luggage. They'll be fine as long as I don't get distracted."

"Right. I'm off to resupply the galley, then," Anton said.

"Be back fast. You know what's at stake here. For both of us. For our people."

"Indeed. Of course, the money we'll earn isn't bad either," Anton said with a wink.

"Money never is. Besides, we must maintain our reputation."

"Indeed!"

"Off, and don't get any ideas."

Anton smiled. "Never would consider it!"

Marta watched Anton walk off into the town. He gently moved crowds out of his way as he waded through them. She hoped he wouldn't find trouble. Despite the bulk of his belly, most of his clothing covered thick bands of muscle that Anton knew how to use in a fight. But she knew he would keep his head; he had just as much on the line here as she did. Her success meant his people would be safe as well.

"Alright, the rest of you scalawags, let's find our passengers and get out of here." Marta waved at the other crew members that had joined them on their skiff. "And stay close. No wandering."

A chorus of grunts affirmed her directive.

Marta nodded. So far, so good. Keep the crew in line and Anton out of trouble, restock the provisions, and pick up passengers. And then back to where the empire feared to follow—which suited Marta just fine.

"Fresh meats!"

"Bread fresh baked today!"

"Day-old bread—cheaper than his!"

A wide swath of people walked in a dozen directions. Some held the smell of the salty sea, others of the fish that swam in the waters, and still more of spilled beer from the night before, none of which Marta found foul. In her heart, she loved the sea and loved the denizens that were often found here. But her home was on Lake Connell in Dressa, not the Riverlands below.

Marta came to a stop where the dock ended and the dirt roads began. She sighed, placed her hands on her hips, and tilted her head to one side. How was she supposed to identify these two travelers, exactly? Perhaps she had been too hasty in leaving the captain of the travel barge drifting in a dinghy. The contract didn't mention what the professors looked like.

"Span out. Look for someone who doesn't smell like anything else."

Her crew grunted in confusion.

"Just go, yes? And don't get any ideas!"

Her crew shambled off at a slow pace while Marta scanned the crowd, looking for people out of place. Two chaps from the university should stand out like sore thumbs, shouldn't they? Honestly, she wasn't sure. Marta had never seen someone from the university from Swanville, the imperial capital.

In a flash of torn leather and with a slight limp, a figure Marta recognized darted through the crowds. The captain of the travel barge, who should be sitting in his dinghy floating on Lake Connell, walked with a fast pace toward something or someone just out of sight. She clenched her jaw and shook her head. The barge captain had not only found his freedom, but beat her to Oyster Piers. The audacity...

The barge captain turned around, made eye contact with Marta, and increased his pace twofold.

"Oh, that's just rotten." Marta shook her head again and marched toward her former almost-victim. "You just can't trust people you pirate anymore."

JONATHAN BRAXTON ADJUSTED his purple jacket and smoothed the lines running down his tailor-made form-fitting linen pants. He found a single loose thread and quickly plucked it free, while also maintaining the integrity of the hemline with ease. Jonathan often thought that if his expedition to Dressa were to fail, he could always focus his energy on clothing. He could open a shop near the university and weave such threads as to make the faculty swoon.

"It's nearly lunch," William said.

Jonathan nodded and turned to William. His lover, friend, and confidant, whom Jonathan cherished, sat on his trunk in a pair of cotton trousers and smiled. Threads dangled from Williams's pants like forgotten spiderwebs. A button-up shirt hung loosely on his frame with a food stain on the bottom right sleeve covering his light brown skin. Frankly, Jonathan thought silently to himself, William was a mess. But he was Jonathan's mess. Though their relationship had been rocky these last few months, Jonathan felt there was still a chance for things to improve. And unlocking the secrets and mysteries of the world together was just the thing to rekindle their flame ... or if not rekindle it, then perhaps just stoke it a tad.

"Shall we buy some fresh meat, do you think?" William asked.

Jonathan looked at William and nodded. The one thing that drove him crazy was William's absolute obsession with food. "We could. But are we certain that the food here is safe?"

William chuckled. "Well, we'll have to eat, eventually."

"I suppose we will."

For two university professors who had hardly left their academic-focused town, with local pubs, bakers, and butchers offering food that both Jonathan and William had eaten for years, traveling to never-before-visited towns with questionable meats was both an adventure and a gamble. It didn't help that their friends and colleagues had filled their minds with many bizarre or downright insane magic-filled stories of what awaited them in Dressa Moore.

Jonathan walked over to a local vendor and purchased two large turkey drumsticks. He kept them at arm's length from his clothes for fear of the grease staining his coat. He handed one to William with an approving nod. "I'm reasonably sure this can only be what it looks like, don't you think?"

William grinned, his stomach grumbling at the rich smells of the roasted meat. "Reasonably."

"Excuse me. Are you the visiting professors?" said a man wearing a dark grey cloak.

Jonathan nodded, nearly choking on the chunk of turkey he had just bitten into. "Yes, indeed. Are you our transport?"

"Indeed. Now, we must hurry. Our ship has to leave port in just under half an hour due to port fees."

"Well, that's fine. Where is your crew? We'll need help with our luggage."

"Luggage?"

"Yes, luggage. What, do you think we would travel halfway across the continent without luggage?" he snapped.

"Well, you don't need it. We can provision you with new

clothes. Probably need new ones anyway. Sometimes foreign fabric turns into birds in Dressa."

"I'm sorry, what did you say?" William said.

Jonathan swallowed down his disgust at the concept of buying clothing in a backwater town. "We also have scientific instruments with us. If you are suggesting we abandon our luggage, it's just out of the question."

The man turned around as if he were looking for someone, turned back to Jonathan, sighed, and shook his head. "Fine, let's grab it. Is it just this trunk, then?"

"Yes, and those as well," Jonathan said, pointing.

The man turned to see a dozen more trunks stacked in a pyramid several feet to the side. His eyes grew wide, and sweat beaded on his forehead. "What in the name of the thirty-seven gods of the fifth pantheon is in there?"

"Scientific equipment."

The man shook his head. "Well, do you need it all?"

"If we are going to be conducting science, which is the entire point of this journey, then yes, we do." Jonathan folded his arms while also brushing dirt off his sleeve.

"I just have some books," William said.

"Well..." The man turned in a circle and wiped his forehead. "I can't possibly carry all of that."

"Where is your crew?"

"On the bloody ship!"

Jonathan's eyes went wide. He hated when things went against plans. Why have plans if people didn't stick to them? Jonathan had been quite meticulous about the instructions he'd sent to the transport ship. He'd counted every single piece of luggage and even included their dimensions and weights. Why was this man being so obtuse? Jonathan screwed his face into his fiercest glare—the kind he reserved for first-year students who dared challenge him on some elementary particle question of basic magilurgy. He gave William a quick glance and noted that his face was buried in his book, but Jonathan doubted that William was reading through the commotion.

"Now, listen here—" Jonathan began.

Just then, a hand fell on the cloaked man's shoulder, and his eyes widened with shock. Genuine fear etched its way across his face. The man's body became as still as an ancient petrified tree. Jonathan felt that the man knew whose hand it was.

"Hello, my good sirs. I'm Captain Marta Bartolome. I see you've met my dear colleague. There's been a bit of a mix-up, it would seem. You'll be guests on my ship, *The Knotted Wood*. My crew here will take care of your things." The captain nodded back toward her crew. As one, they ambled forward toward the luggage.

"Very good, then. This is what I would expect. But I should warn you the luggage is quite heavy," Jonathan advised.

The crew didn't acknowledge him. Each member, with little effort, grabbed two pieces of luggage and dragged them through the dirt. Jonathan marveled at the sight. It had taken two men each—per side—to unload every single trunk from their transport. Now one man alone easily handled two trunks at once. Clearly, the university had gifted them with a strong crew on a well-run ship. Jonathan nodded his approval.

"What about mine?" William said.

Captain Bartolome turned to William and nodded. She swung her head around and counted her crew. Frustration flashed on her face. "It appears I didn't bring enough crew with me. I apologize. Would you two be able to carry the last piece on your own?"

William let his shoulders sag, but nodded. "Come on, then, Jonathan."

"Hold on... The university paid for porters to help," Jonathan said.

"And they *are* helping. But you've overburdened us. I beseech your mercy." Captain Bartolome winked.

"Let's just go, Jonathan. Yes?"

Several loud shouts and a scream erupted from somewhere down the docks. Captain Bartolome rolled her eyes and sighed. "And there goes the cook..."

"The who?"

"I'm afraid we must be going." Bartolome nodded to her crew, who had already dragged Jonathan's trunks a hundred feet towards the docks.

"Come on, Jonathan," Willian urged. "Let's just get on the ship."

"Fine. But this does not bode well for what we have in store."

Together, Jonathan and William grabbed either end of William's trunk and heaved it after the crew of Captain Bartolome.

"I'll be just along!" Bartolome shouted from behind.

Jonathan turned and nodded. He noticed that the cloaked man, who hadn't uttered a word or moved a muscle since she laid a hand on him, stood shaking as Jonathan and William left. The whole spectacle was more than odd. But as long as Jonathan was moving forward, towards Dressa and the source of magic, he had to admit to himself, he didn't care about local squabbles. All that mattered was the science.

〜

BARTOLOME WATCHED her crew haul the luggage towards her ship. She could feel her control of them waver slightly. This far from Dressa, where the magic was weak, her abilities were lessened. Still, she could maintain her hold on her crew long enough to board her ship and get out of Oyster Piers; of that she was certain. She knew it had been a gamble to come here, but it was well worth taking. But before she could go home, she did have to deal with one last little loose thread still dangling from her finger.

"You have some nerve, don't you?" Captain Bartolome said, turning back to the captain she'd pirated on Lake Connell.

"What would you have me do? You took all of our supplies, and you took our next paying job."

"So, you rushed to Oyster Piers and beat me here and take him back. Well done, I have to say."

A surge of bodies rushed from one end of the dock and ran towards the streets leading back to the town. Several military men, their guns loaded but lowered, rushed forward toward the commotion. Captain Bartolome, one hand still holding steady on her prey, grabbed a running peasant and brought her close.

"Is there a large man with arms the size of pythons and a stomach that looks pregnant with triplets at the center of all this?"

"Yes, madam." The young woman looked like fear had rooted in her face and decided to make a home there. "There's a fight over the price of fish."

Bartolome rolled her eyes and let the girl go. Couldn't she trust Anton for a single moment? He was a stubborn as a mule, but also as large as a mountain bear, which made him quite the danger.

Suddenly, pain shot up Bartolome's leg. Her eyes went

wide with shock as her hands went to the knife in her thigh. The pirated captain standing in front of her had dug his pocket blade into the fleshy part. The man stumbled backward and shook his head, his mind swimming in obvious fear.

"What is wrong with you?!" Bartolome shouted.

"Me? What's wrong with *me*?" The man fell backward as he retreated. "You pirated my vessel, stole my contract, and threatened to make me one of your monster crew, and you ask what's wrong with *me*?!"

Bartolome tilted her head to one side and shrugged. She had to admit, the man had a point. She pulled the dagger out of her thigh and winced. Her thoughts ran to her crew, and she realized, with a sense of dread creeping up her spine, that she couldn't quite feel all of them on the dock. It only took a moment before the taste of flesh filled her mind. One of her crew had broken free of her control and bitten a local peasant.

"This day is becoming quite bad," Bartolome muttered. She marched forward and grabbed the captain, lifting him single-handedly and giving him a shake. "You ruined my trousers!"

The man shook in her grasp as the screams from the dock intensified. Bartolome knew they weren't coming from Anton's fight this time. She closed her eyes and concentrated, the pain from her knife wound still clouding her thoughts, but it was futile. There were already half a dozen going through the change. Once they turned, the whole town would be lost. Even in Dressa, it would be a challenge to control an entire town, but here, in Oyster Piers, it would be sheer folly.

"This is not a good start to saving the world," Bartolome said.

"Saving the world? You're mad!" the captain cried.

"More than you know." Bartolome lowered herself to just inches from his face. "Never again try to steal from me what I've already stolen from you. Got it?"

The man nodded.

"Good. Away with you. Now. I don't have the time." She bored her eyes into the man's face.

The man shook his head and dug his hand into his satchel. He pulled something out and thrust it towards Bartolome. "They must have this! It's part of the charter. The church will know if I don't give it to him!"

Bartolome glanced down to see a book clutched in the man's hand. "Is that enchanted? Do you take me for a fool? I give that to them, and you can track them all over Dressa. That will come nowhere near my vessel. Now, go—and fear the day when I do."

The captain shook his head in confusion. "What? Fear the day when you what?"

"Have the time. Fear the day when I have the time! I was referring to my previous sentence... Oh, never mind. Go!"

Once released, the man hesitated for a second before darting forward without caring for his direction. Marta smiled at the retreating man, but also cursed her timing. She really needed to work on her threats. It was good to instill a little fear and let them live. That was how rumors spread.

She turned to the town. This city was about to explode into chaos, and there wasn't anything she could do to stop it. Yes, it was her fault—though technically it was the fault of the pirated captain who had stabbed her. Granted, he never would have stabbed her at all if she hadn't pirated him, but she'd only pirated him because that was her job as a pirate, after all. And since she was really attempting to save the world from an even bigger threat, it was all justified—in an odd pirate kind of way.

Yes, people will die today, but eventually, that's what everyone does.

Bartolome closed her eyes and took a long breath. She tried to feel her way through the crowd, but her abilities were just too weak. She shook her head clear and ran after her crew and her new guests. They needed to find Anton and get as far away from this now cursed place as possible.

COMMODORE THOMAS WILKES stood in his office, his hands clasped behind his back, his eyes darting between faces on the docks three stories below. He sighed with boredom and contempt. Not for the masses of people; they were mostly kind souls going about their day and earning a fair living. Granted, there were robbers and scum among them, though Thomas always felt confident that his men would arrest those unsavory souls, but the majority were just people living their lives and feeding their families—the very people the empire was sworn to protect. If not for the people, what would the empire be?

No, his contempt was for his chain of command. He had no desire to stay in this end-of-the-world town and be the magistrate for all things coming from and going to Dressa Moore, but that was the fate the admiralty had decided for him. If he could, the commodore would set sail this very day for Dressa Moore. He knew what he desired most awaited him in those waters. Yes, there would be mysteries, and of course, magic. Well, mostly magic—which was the reason the admiralty didn't want imperial ships sailing into Dressa in the first place. But Commodore Wilkes thought that not going into Dressa was poor planning. One could not be afraid of what one didn't understand.

The door to the commodore's office opened, and Lieutenant Swanson walked into the room.

"Hello, Merrick," Thomas said.

"Commodore."

"Anything of interest happening out there?"

Lieutenant Swanson crossed the room and stood at parade rest. "No, Commodore. A few too many beggars and vendors with rotten meat."

Commodore Wilkes nodded. "What does a man do when he has nothing?"

"Sir?"

"Nothing, Lieutenant. I thought I saw a pile of travel trunks outside the station this morning. Any idea what that was about?"

"Ah. Yes. Two professors from the university are here."

"Professors?" Thomas's curiosity was piqued. "From the university? What would professors from the university be doing here?"

"Traveling to Dressa Moore, sir."

Thomas twisted his head over his shoulder so fast that he could feel the muscles in his neck tighten. "What? To Dressa?"

"Yes, sir."

"I take it you stopped them from finding passage."

The lieutenant's eyes shifted ever so slightly from the commodore's stare. "No, sir. They already have passage."

Commodore Thomas Wilkes spun on his heel and took a step towards the lieutenant. "Travel to Dressa is restricted."

"They have special permission, sir. From the regional governor, and it would appear from the admiralty."

"What?"

"I saw the seal myself, sir."

"Did you? And you don't think that would be something out of the ordinary?" The commodore's voice took on an edge.

Lieutenant Swanson shuffled his stance and cleared his throat. "Well, I suppose it is, sir."

"I would suppose as well. Considering that the ordinary circumstance of this town does not include visiting professors with permission from the admiralty and the governor to travel to the restricted seas of Dressa Moore."

"Yes, sir. I see your point."

"I would hope."

Shouts from below reached the commodore's office. He turned back to the window in the room's corner. On the streets below, crowds of people pushed their way away from some commotion happening near one of the butcher shops. He scanned the growing maelstrom and spotted a man attacking another and biting into his very flesh.

"What is happening down there?!" Wilkes demanded.

"I don't know, sir."

Thomas's voice caught in his chest. The man who had been attacked just moments ago rose from the ground, only to grab a random passerby and bite them on the neck. Blood spurted out from the wound, followed by the screams of the new victim. The commodore's hands unclasped from behind his back and went to the weapon at his side. Without thinking, his eyes left the dock and scanned the ships in the harbor. He found the vessel almost instantly.

"My gods," Thomas said. It was there—right there. The vessel he'd seen many times before. The vessel he'd know at a hundred leagues. He'd spent every morning of the last six months surveying the faces of Oyster Piers. He'd grown so accustomed to the act that he'd neglected the ships in harbor. And now, there it was: *The Knotted Wood*. The ship he'd pursued for a decade now sat idly in the very harbor the commodore commanded. How could he be so negligent? And because of his oversight, a thousand could die—the entire town.

"Sound the alarm."

"We don't have an alarm."

The commodore turned to the lieutenant. "What?!"

"It broke last August, sir."

Frustration filled the commodore's mind. "Just gather your men, Lieutenant. Cordon off the docks below. Only allow those not acting feral to leave." He took a step toward the lieutenant. "Do you understand me, man? Anyone acting feral!"

"Feral, sir?"

"Anyone trying to bite anyone else. If you see someone doing that, you are to shoot them in the head. You are to stab them in the head. And if they are still successful in taking their bite, you are to do the same to the victim. Do you hear me, Swanson? There are flesh-eaters in our port. If we don't act quickly, we will lose the entire town!"

"Sir?"

"Go, man! Don't think, go!"

Swanson turned on his heel and quickly left the room. Thomas could hear the shouts of the men echoing through the halls seconds later. He spared a moment before joining them to look out to the harbor. His anger built in his chest as his eyes settled on *The Knotted Wood*. How dare that woman bring that ship to his shore? No matter; her foolishness would only lead to her own long-overdue death.

At long last, Commodore Thomas Wilkes would have the one thing he'd wanted for years.

CHAPTER TWO

"All aboard!" Bartolome shouted.

Her crew lifted the professors' luggage across the dock and onto the tiny skiff, which sunk lower into the water with each piece. Marta halted the loading and gave one trunk a tug. Whatever they carried, it weighed more than the skiff could handle.

"What in the name of the seven gods of joy is in here?" Marta demanded.

"Scientific equipment. And every single piece is vital to our success," Jonathan said.

"Many things are vital to our success, Professor."

"Chief among them is in these trunks."

A scream cut through the air behind them. A mass of bodies surged forward from some unseen event happening on the far side of the dock. Vendors clutched their wares and closed their shops and stalls. More shouts and screams joined the first, which only caused more panic to rifle its way through the crowds.

"What is happening?" William asked.

"Probably some locals fighting," Jonathan replied.

"Anton!" Marta waved at the large man approaching the ship.

"Sorry, Mum. Seems to be a bit of an event happening."

"Did you start a fight over fish?"

Anton shrugged. "His prices were an insult."

Marta sighed. "We're missing one of the crew."

Anton looked at Marta and frowned. "The continuing ruckus is one of the crew? You lost control?"

"I was stabbed," Marta countered.

"I knew coming here wasn't worth the risk," Anton muttered.

Marta stared hard into Anton's eyes. "You know what happens if we fail."

"And what if you're wrong?" Anton shot her a look filled with concern.

"Just get to the ship," Marta said. She gave Anton a lingering stare, but he eventually nodded and moved forward. She cursed the skies that her entire plan to reclaim her island home was nearly in shambles, and her chief ally was questioning everything.

Anton stopped at the dock, looked at the skiff, then back to Marta. "How do I get to the ship, exactly? Whose trunks are these? They're taking up the entire skiff."

"They belong to me, and they are essential," Jonathan said.

"Throw them over," Anton said.

"What? You mustn't!" Jonathan declared.

"Marta, we have to go," Anton insisted.

"I know, Anton!" Captain Bartolome bit her lip and spat out a tiny drop of blood. Maybe she had overextended herself. What was she thinking, coming down to the River-lands? On thinking things over, she could have always pirated the travel barge after it had picked up the professors, sparing her from coming down to Oyster Piers entirely. The thought made her wince. She simply had to spend more time on planning in the future.

Marta shook the thought from her head. She still could make this work. All she had to do was get these professors onto her ship and get back to the safety of Dressa Moore. If she kicked the trunks over the side, she would likely lose the payment from the university, creating a scene with the professors and jeopardizing the entire endeavor. Considering how much the professor with the immaculate clothing wanted these trunks, if they were lost, he'd likely just go home. But if she kept the trunks, then there was no way they would make it back to their ship—which meant she needed another skiff. And she only knew one way to get it.

Marta drew her sword. Her crew followed their captain and drew theirs. Fishermen on the dock nearest them— those not already scrambling to understand the commotion happening down the docks—backed away from Marta with their hands raised.

"I apologize, good sirs, but we're in a rush, and you don't have a sword or a sidearm. So, if you don't mind, we'll be borrowing your boats to get to our ship at anchor in the harbor. We'll leave your boats there for you to claim." Marta lowered her sword and waved at the fisherman nearest her. "Agreed?"

Nods from all the fishermen answered her.

"Splendid. Shall we?"

"Are we stealing something?" William said.

"I don't believe we should be party to theft, Captain," Jonathan said.

"We aren't so much *stealing* as we are *borrowing*. And they have all agreed." Marta again floated her sword in the air around the fishermen's heads.

They nodded again.

"See?"

"Now, listen here, Captain—"

"No, *you* listen, Professor. Your university has hired me to take you to a certain place. I shall do so. You shall not ask how it's done. You shall have your scientific equipment in good order as well. Good? Yes? There appears to be some things happening here that we don't wish to be part of. A local fight has broken out, it seems. Quite common in these fishing towns. Shall we?"

Increased shouts caused both William and Jonathan to look around even more nervously than just moments before. They both spared a glance at each other and nodded quickly to Captain Bartolome.

"Excellent!" Marta sheathed her sword, gave Jonathan a pat on the cheek, and directed her crew to split the trunks between their small fleet of skiffs.

"What about our missing crewman?" Anton said.

Marta nodded. "Get to the ship. I'll find him."

Commodore Wilkes grabbed the collars of two civilian men and pulled them forward. His men, led by Lieutenant Swanson, formed a barrier between a growing mob of men and women in the throes of total madness.

"Weapons down!" the commodore bellowed.

Soldiers holding the line lowered their rifles with bayonets attached. Several hesitated a moment, but a thump from Lieutenant Swanson steadied their nerves. In front of them, several feral men and women lunged towards those fleeing. Wilkes watched as one woman, her eyes wild with rage, dug her teeth into a man twice her age. The man screamed a horrible cry as blood stained his clothing.

"What is happening?" one soldier demanded.

"He bit her!" another said.

"It's magic! It must be magic! Magic is here!" said another.

"Hold the line!" Commodore Wilkes commanded from behind them. He'd been in this situation before, years ago. And now, as destiny had commanded—or at least suggested, or perhaps just implied—he found himself here again. In his mind, that meant it was time to take the fight to Dressa Moore. It was time for him to find the one thing in this world he wanted most. But first, he had to survive this outbreak.

"Let those fleeing through. Kill the mad ones! It's too late for them," Commodore Wilkes commanded.

A man lunged for one soldier between the raised bayonets. The knife on the end of the gun plunged into the man's shoulder, but he continued to push himself forward, digging the soldier's rifle through his body.

"Help!" the soldier called.

The soldier directly next to him raised his rifle and fired at the deranged man. The bullet pierced the man's chest and sliced through his heart. Yet the deranged man still pushed himself forward, his teeth chomping as if he hadn't eaten in a hundred days.

The commodore ran to his soldiers, drew his sword, and plunged his rapier's blade into the crazed man's skull. The man gurgled once, slumped forward, and remained motionless.

"In the head, boys! Do you hear me? Aim for their heads!"

The soldiers nodded, emboldened by their commodore,

and their grip on their weapons tightened, as did the steel in their eyes. As one, the line of soldiers strengthened. They let out a loud war cry and took a bold step forward.

MARTA SCREAMED.

She could feel the blade pierce the skin of her crewman. The attack scrambled her mind. Searing pain tore through her body, and she dropped to one knee. She checked her body for wounds, but found none. The damage she felt came from one of the growing horde in the town. This far from Dressa, she could only feel their pain and desire. She had no control over their actions. That meant this town was already lost.

Heavy hands grabbed her under her arms and heaved her to her feet. "You need to get out of here," Anton said.

"So do you. Get them to the ship." Marta waved Anton off and took a step away. Her hand rose to her forehead and felt smooth skin just beneath the brim of her hat. She was physically fine, but her crew member was gone. And that hurt. Not as much, however, as seeing the owner of the sword that plunged into his brain.

Commodore Wilkes was here.

The fact sent twin feelings of relief and fear down Marta's spine. The commodore knew how to deal with her crew, and the children of her crew, and he knew how to deal with her. On one hand, that meant the town might not be lost, but on the other, it meant he could stop her from achieving her goal. Now that the commodore knew she was here, he would chase Marta down to the ends of the world to find what he thought Marta had taken from him. Unfortunately, she didn't have it.

"The crew member is gone. Let's go." Marta turned from the dock and jumped on one skiff. "Are you coming or gawking?"

Anton nodded, then smiled. He heaved a bag filled with consumables over his shoulder and boarded one of the fishermen's skiffs, along with the two university professors.

"Heave off, you scallywags!" Marta cried.

Her crew pushed off from the docks and each grabbed one oar on the small skiffs. They pushed farther into the harbor, toward *The Knotted Wood*, and away from the growing collection of flesh eaters and military men, both readying for a battle that Marta wanted nothing to do with, even though she was indirectly responsible.

COMMODORE WILKES SURVEYED the chaos with a sense of pride. His men had handled the initial salvo of flesh-eaters with discipline and courage. A testament to the lieutenant's command, to be sure. But their work was far from done. Wilkes counted over the shoulders of his soldiers—at least twenty savages still chomping away at their victims. That meant soon their numbers would be nearly doubled.

"We must charge them, or we'll lose the town!" Wilkes called out.

"Sir, their bite appears to be infectious," Lieutenant Swanson declared.

"Indeed, it is, Lieutenant. But if we don't charge now while they feed, their numbers will overcome us."

Lieutenant Swanson nodded. "You heard the Commodore: charge!"

A chorus of battle cries erupted from the line of imperial soldiers. They charged forward in unison towards the mob with controlled chaos. The few unscathed civilians who had so far avoided the grasp of the horde passed through their ranks to safety beyond.

"Remember, lads and ladies, aim for their heads!" Commodore Wilkes joined the ranks of his soldiers, his sidearm drawn in one hand and his rapier in the other.

The first of his men reached the mob and targeted the heads of the maddened populace. Once their bullets or bayonets pierced their target, the crazed creature fell to the ground, dead.

"For the empire!" screamed a soldier.

Wilkes smiled at their tenacity. He made a mental note to commend the chancellor of training when he returned to Swanville, the capital city of the empire. Considering, however, that that could be years from now, perhaps he'd send a raven. And in the event that he didn't survive, perhaps the grave man could write it on his tombstone.

"Keep pushing!" Wilkes shouted. "We can't give them an inch of ground!"

"You know much of these creatures, Commodore," Lieutenant Swanson observed.

"I have fought them before, Lieutenant. I fear this may only be a diversion. We must dispatch these things and turn our attention to the harbor."

"The harbor, sir?"

"Yes, there is a ship there—a ship from Dressa Moore itself. That ship brought this blight to Oyster Piers."

Gurgles and growls came from the crowd in front of the soldiers. A dozen more of the flesh-easters, once victims, now rose from the ground and grasped at the legs of the soldiers. They, like those who had attacked them, chomped their teeth, desperate to bite the nearest man or woman they could.

"Watch the flank!" shouted a soldier.

Commodore Wilkes turned to see three flesh-eaters emerge from an alley off the docks next to a fish market. He raised his revolver and fired, dropping one beast. But his shot didn't deter the other two from charging forward into his ranks. Wilkes attempted to fire again, but his gun jammed. He watched helplessly as one beast sunk their teeth into his soldier's hand just as the soldier was about to strike with the butt of his rifle.

"Fall back! Hold the line on the retreat!" Wilkes declared.

"Fall back!" cried soldiers on the line.

Five more flesh-eaters burst out of a market shop, their ages ranging from an adult man to several children. Wilkes cursed the gods. The entire family had turned. Now his men had to strike down the young. These soldiers had never faced an enemy like this. No one in the empire had. These creatures could only come from *The Knotted Wood* and its cursed captain. But if their line fell, then the town fell. It had only been moments, and yet Wilkes counted nearly twenty who had been infected, and possibly now one of his own men.

Still, the brazenness didn't add up. Why bring these fiends here? What purpose did it serve that woman? Yes, the town might fall, but the empire had resources at its disposal —even magical ones—and she knew that. So, why try to take the town at all? ... Unless taking the town had never been her goal.

"Thievery! They're stealing my skiff!"

"And mine!"

Wilkes spun on his heels. With a quick scan of the shouts, he located three overloaded skiffs rowing to the harbor. This was a distraction. The attack was just to keep him and his men occupied. The vileness required to kill dozens of souls for a mere distraction so she could work some manner of evil was unthinkable. Wilkes spat on the ground and cleared the chamber of his revolver. He turned back to the line and unloaded three rounds into the family of flesh eaters that emerged from the market shop. Several of his men recoiled in horror, but now was not the time to educate them on just how dangerous the situation was becoming.

"Steady! Do not trust your eyes! Trust your training, trust your lieutenant, trust me! These are no longer the citizens we would protect!" The commodore moved behind his men, shouting encouragement and firing his revolver at anyone he felt he alone should dispatch.

"For the empire! For the commodore!" The lieutenant charged forward, his revolver and rapier both at the ready, and dispatched a flesh-eater that charged the line.

Wilkes nodded. The man was determined. A soldier screamed to Wilkes's right, and he looked in terror as the private bitten only moments before turned on his fellows with hunger and crazed eyes. Wilkes rushed forward, grabbed the flesh-eater soldier by the coat, and spun him around, away from others in the line.

"Fight it, man! Fight it!" Wilkes demanded.

The soldier snarled and snapped at the commodore, and Wilkes could quickly tell there was no humanity left in the man's eyes. There was only hunger, only madness. Wilkes raised his revolver and put the muzzle on the man's forehead. His finger began to squeeze, but he stopped. He knew this man—Connor. He was a good man. Commanders should never execute their own soldiers.

Wilkes stared into the soldier's eyes, desperate to find some slice of humanity still alive. But all he could find in

Connor's eyes was an animalistic need to feed. He wasn't a man anymore. Wilkes pulled the hammer back on his revolver, but try as he might, he couldn't find the strength to pull the trigger. This was his man. This soldier depended on Wilkes for his life. And yes, soldiers died in war, but never at the hands of those they trusted to bring them home.

A silver blade pierced through Connor's skull from the side and jutted out the other. Wilkes stepped back in shock and followed the blade to see it end in Lieutenant Swanson's hand. His second-in-command put his boot on Connor's shoulder and kicked the soldier off his sword. He wiped the blade on some cloth he found on the ground and sheathed his rapier at his side.

"Are you bitten, sir?"

Commodore Wilkes stared into Swanson's eyes. The lieutenant had done the right thing, Wilkes knew. Despite that, something in the act felt cruel. Swanson didn't seem to mind having to dispatch his own soldier. Not even a moment of hesitation. Perhaps it was just battle rage and the desire to protect his superior officer that drove Swanson.

"No, I'm fine."

Lieutenant Swanson nodded. "We're making gains, sir. The monsters are becoming less aggressive for some reason. Look there."

Commodore Wilkes looked to see several of the monsters feasting on the dead. They became lethargic in their movements and seemed to care less about the living around them. He had no idea why they would do so. He hadn't witnessed this on his last encounter with this sickness.

"Have the men press the attack, Lieutenant. Finish them off here. I fear this was all just a distraction."

"A distraction, sir?"

"Yes. Take three men, and come with me to the docks, quickly!" Wilkes charged forward and reloaded his revolver.

"Aren't we on the docks now, sir?"

"Just follow me!"

Soldiers rallied along the docks, firing into the crowd and digging their bayonet-tipped rifles into the growing mob of victims of her crew member. Marta shook her head at her own stupidity. She should have killed that travel barge captain in Dressa; then she never would have lost her grip on her crew. If the military didn't get things in order, the entire town could fall. Honestly, it made her sick to her stomach.

Marta used every ounce of her strength to get control of the townspeople who had turned. She stopped the horde from growing by making them feed longer than normal. She slowed them, made their movements take longer. Her mind nearly broke under the weight. But it proved valuable, as the soldiers gained an edge. And they needed it. With luck, the soldiers could stop the horde before it grew too large.

Marta felt the last of the horde on the shore go silent, thankfully. The commodore's men, under his instruction, and with her help calming them, had made short work of them. But now that meant he could turn his attention to her. She tilted her head to the side and squinted through the noonday sun. Someone of rank pointed at her with his rapier and commanded the soldiers near him towards her and her crew. Soldiers ran down the dock and raised their weapons. She had to give the commodore some credit: the man was persistent. The ranking soldier lifted his revolver directly at Marta. She smiled back. There was no way he could hit her at this range.

A puff of smoke rose from the muzzle, followed by the blast of gunpowder. Marta's shoulder jerked backward, and she nearly spun off the skiff, saved only by one of her crew, and one of the professor's overloaded trunks, which jostled from the blow and tipped over the side of the skiff.

"No!" screamed Jonathan from one of the other skiffs. Marta ignored him. She looked at her shoulder, a slow molasses-like stream of blood oozing down her leather vest.

"Argg!" Marta shouted. She rose and stood on the end of the skiff. "It took me three months to find the perfect-sized vest! Do you know how much pirating I had to do?!"

The man on the dock fired again, but this time his shot went wide left. Marta squinted to get a better look, but she didn't recognize him. Another man ran up next to the officer, and this one Marta did recognize. Commodore Thomas Wilkes stared at Marta while one of his soldiers handed him a rifle. The commodore had saved the town, a fact that Marta was glad for, but now he was coming for her.

"Faster! Take us home faster!" Marta shouted at her crew. She spared one glance over her shoulder at the commodore before pouring her attention into getting as far away from him as possible.

COMMODORE WILKES FIRED two more shots, but both went wide. Swanson, an excellent shot, had struck her once. The commodore had seen her fall. But he knew she would rise again, cursed sea witch that she was. An evil, cruel, slave-running, love-stealing sea witch. But now she was here, not in Dressa. And he had far more at his disposal than the last time they had met.

"Lieutenant!" Wilkes called.

Swanson appeared at his side, his sidearm drawn, and pointed at the departing skiffs.

The commodore put his hand on the lieutenant's to lower his aim. "She's too far out."

"Who is she?" the lieutenant asked.

"The vilest creature to sail the seas. And the cause of this attack."

"So, she's responsible for Connor, then?" Lieutenant Swanson said.

Wilkes turned to his second and locked his eyes on Swanson. Good—the man cared. For half a heartbeat, he had questioned any commander who could so easily dispatch one of his own.

"She is, Lieutenant."

The lieutenant nodded, his face turning to stone.

"Ready *The Swan*. Tell the men we shall give chase."

"Which *Swan*, sir?" the lieutenant asked.

"What? How many are here?"

"*The Crimson Swan, The Opaque Swan*, and *The Morning Light Swan* are all in dock, sir."

Wilkes sighed. Why did the emperor have to have such a fascination with swans? And why had the admiralty told him the renaming of ships was in his purview? Everything was in his purview, of course—he was the emperor, after all —but he didn't have to know that.

"Crimson," Wilkes said.

"Sir!" The lieutenant turned and ran down the docks.

Wilkes watched the sea witch shout commands to her crew. She knew he was here. She would run hard. But that was fine; he would just have to run harder.

"Fly, cursed bird. But you shall not fly fast enough."

Wilkes turned and ran down the dock to *The Crimson Swan.*

CHAPTER THREE

Marta grabbed the rope ladder hanging down from the side of her ship. Behind her, she could hear the shouts of soldiers running along the pier—no doubt heading towards her and her crew.

"Raise anchor! Stow the trunks and professors and prepare for battle!" Marta screamed as soon as her legs swiveled over the banister of *The Knotted Wood* and onto her deck.

"I'd best be getting to the galley," Anton said.

"Eat fast!" Marta commanded.

"Isn't he already round enough?" William said.

Anton took a large bite from a hidden turkey leg that he retrieved from his pocket, winked at William, and left the deck for the recesses of the ship through a door near the stern.

"You dropped my trunk overboard! And I don't even know what was lost! We are not going anywhere until you retrieve it!" Jonathan insisted.

Marta ignored the professor and ran to the wheel of her

ship. She surveyed the harbor and shook her head. Sure enough, the commodore was running down the docks and would soon give chase—probably in an imperial warship. *The Knotted Wood*, though a fine and strong vessel, was no match for a military frigate, either in speed or cannons.

"Hurry with those things!" Marta told her crew who were handling the professors' remaining trunks.

Shots riddled the side of her ship, fired from soldiers on the docks of the port. Luckily, at this distance, they were more of a nuisance than a danger. Still, she needed to get out of the harbor.

"Pull that anchor and raise the sails!"

"Are they *shooting* at us?" Jonathan asked, his face going pale.

Marta turned and smiled. "Of course not. Why would they do that?" She patted the professor on the shoulder and moved past him.

More members of her crew rushed on deck. Several went to the sails, while others joined the two at the anchor. Out of the corner of her eye, Marta saw Jonathan stride onto her bridge with a level of audacity that made her blood boil.

"Those look like rifles."

Marta sighed. She didn't have time to deal with the professors' angst. She turned to face them and realized one wasn't there. "Where is your fellow professor?" Marta spun the wheel of the ship towards the mouth of the harbor.

"He went to our quarters."

"How does he know where they are?" Marta demanded.

"William is quite good at these things."

Marta's face twisted in confusion. "What things?"

"Navigating the intricacies of assigned accommodations, of course."

"I'm sorry?"

Jonathan shrugged. "William has his charms."

"Right."

Jonathan shook his head, body taking on a tense stance. "We lost a trunk overboard. And I must have it back, Captain."

More shots rang out from the shore, and one lucky soldier struck a member of her crew in the hand. Fortunately, her crew member still had one hand wrapped around one of Jonathan's trunks as it was being raised from the skiff. Unfortunately, the hand that was shot had been holding steadfastly to *The Knotted Wood's* railing. The crewmate and the trunk fell off the ship from the open railing that led to the skiffs below at water level. Marta cringed as she heard the trunk impact the skiff, followed by the distinct sound of wood breaking. She ran to the side of her ship and sighed.

"I really think they're shooting at us," Jonathan said, his eyes fixed on the soldiers along the pier. Just as well; he hadn't noticed another of his trunks going overboard.

"Nonsense." Marta winked at him. "Tie up the fisherman's skiff to replace ours!" Marta returned to the wheel and looked into Jonathan's eyes. "Good thing we're pirates, eh?"

"You're *what*?" Jonathan's eyes grew wide with shock.

Marta faked a laugh. "Just a jest, my good man." She rushed past him back to the wheel.

Jonathan turned to count his luggage. "Wait—another one is missing! Did you lose another one?!"

Marta sighed. "I'm sure whatever we lost, we can replace in Dressa."

"Those are delicate scientific instruments! You can't replace them with pig farmer's shovels or crow wands!"

Marta frowned. "What the hell's a crow wand?"

"It would take far too long to explain. I simply must have my equipment, or this trip will be canceled!"

Marta tightened her grip on the wheel and let out a long breath. She was a passenger ship now, not a pirating vessel, she silently reminded herself. Besides, she was tied to the professor's fate. If he failed, she would fail. And she couldn't fail.

"I assure you, kind sir, we shall replace your valuables. There are many more things available to us in Dressa." Marta turned to Jonathan and nodded. "You have my word."

Jonathan nodded. A look of calm briefly passed over his face. "Fine. If it was only the lead suit, then that is easily replaceable. However, the magonmeter is not. And didn't one of your crew fall overboard with my trunk?"

Marta closed her eyes and concentrated. "They're fine."

"They're dead!"

Marta smiled. "Oh, you have no idea. Now, if you'd kindly get off my bridge, or we'll be joining them at the bottom!" She nodded towards the imperial frigate in the distance. The portside gunports were open, and several guns had been moved into position along the side. She was readying for battle.

"Right. Why are they doing that, exactly?" Jonathan asked.

"You are booking passage to a place the empire wants to isolate. How you got as far as you have is a mystery to me— which is something we should discuss as well, yes?" Marta knew their destination, but it suddenly struck her that she hadn't thought about how the empire would have let them come this far at all. The thought that she'd just stumbled into something greater crossed her mind.

Jonathan nodded. "But we can't leave if the trunk that fell contained my magonmeter."

Marta scowled. She shook her head, then nodded. "Well, we can't stay if we don't know it's lost. Yes? Why don't you go check your remaining trunks for it, and if we have it, we can set sail? Good? My crew shall take them below for you to examine."

Jonathan looked stunned for a moment, but nodded at the logic of Marta's plan. "As long as you won't leave until I've made sure it's here."

Marta nodded. "Wouldn't dream of it."

"Splendid. I shall do just that." Without another word, he left the bridge and found his way through the crew to the lower decks. Her crew followed him, carrying each piece of his luggage, which suited Marta just fine. She didn't have time to bother with this now, anyway. Not with her ship about to be attacked.

Marta watched him leave the bridge and thanked the twelve gods of anger that he did. She didn't have the patience to remind the poor man that she'd already set sails and raised the anchor. So, in a sense, she wasn't technically *leaving* Oyster Piers, as she'd already begun to leave. Besides, she was a pirate, and lying was not only allowed, it was expected.

COMMODORE WILKES CLIMBED aboard *The Crimson Swan* and marched his way to the bridge, his lieutenant and a contingent of his men fast on his heels. Shouts rang out among the crew, followed by several salutes, all of which Wilkes returned. Discipline like this was crucial. They would soon ask these men and women to travel to the magical lands of Dressa. They would need to count on the steel of their commanders.

"Captain Bridgewater," Wilkes said with a nod.

"Commodore. Is that your men firing recklessly into the waters of the harbor?"

"Indeed, their aim is practiced and precise, and their target is *The Knotted Wood*."

"Splendid. Have them stop, will you?"

Wilkes, startled by his candor, eyed the captain with a hard stare. "Is that meant to be a request?"

Captain Bridgewater sighed, closed his eyes, took in a breath, reopened his eyes, and smiled. "Would you, sir, at the request of the captain of *The Crimson Swan*, the empire's flagship in the Aquirren River, signal your men to cease firing? Though I am quite convinced of their training and skill, the smooth-bore rifle becomes somewhat unreliable the farther the aim of the soldier. And since I know you are about to command us to give chase to the vessel that is the target of your well-trained men—"

"And women," said one soldier beside Lieutenant Swanson.

"I hadn't finished. And women..." Captain Bridgewater nodded to the soldier. "I'd rather not have our ship and my crew..." The captain's eyes turned hard and returned the commodore's stare. "... come under fire."

Commodore Wilkes looked into the captain's eyes. Bridgewater was right, of course. Any thoughts of laying into him faded instantly. "Of course, Captain. Lieutenant."

Lieutenant Swanson nodded and instructed one of their accompaniment to signal the shore to cease firing.

"Good?" Commodore Wilkes said. He had known Marcus Bridgewater for years. He was a strong captain who cared more for his men than for imperial dogma. In fact, if the rumors that swirled around were to be believed, Bridgewater cared little for the emperor and hated swans. But the admiralty were loyal to their own, a sentiment that the commodore fully supported. Although, truth be told, Wilkes found swans to be majestic.

Bridgewater nodded, and his face softened. "Thank you, Commodore. Your orders, sir?"

Commodore Wilkes raised his arm toward *The Knotted Wood* and locked his eyes on her stern. "That ship is behind the riots that just erupted in Oyster Piers."

Bridgewater's face turned hard in an instant. "Is it?"

"Yes, their captain is villainy incarnate. It hails from Dressa Moore."

"Surely not."

The commodore turned back to Captain Bridgewater. "It does indeed."

"You know this vessel, Thomas? It's the one you've dealt with before?"

"It is, Marcus."

Bridgewater nodded. "Sails! Cannons! Crew! Prepare to give chase!"

"Sails! Raise the bloody sails!" Marta screamed. Her crew were loyal, but godsforsakenly stupid. "The rope on your left!"

The crewmate reached for the wrong rope and pulled. The sail did not rise. That only caused the crewmate to pull on the rope with increasing levels of frustration and anger, which caused Marta to nearly lose what was left of her mind.

Behind *The Knotted Wood*, one of the *Swans*—who could tell which—unfurled her sails. That ship had a compliment of two hundred souls, and likely more with the commodore's men. Marta's paltry crew of thirty—minus those she'd lost—would be overwhelmed easily, even if her crew was ravenous.

Just as Marta had the thought, a hand clasped the side of her ship. The crewmate who had fallen overboard heaved himself over the rail and coughed.

"Man the sails!" Marta screamed at him.

He turned, grunted, nodded, and walked over to the wrong rope.

"Idiot! The one on your left!"

He grunted and moved to another wrong rope.

Marta gritted her teeth and squeezed the handles of the captain's wheel. Her crew was rattled and hungry; she could feel it. Normally, without the stress, they could be directed with ease. That was her greatest strength. And if she were to survive this, she would need that strength.

Marta let her anger go. She let her frustration dissipate. She closed her eyes and gave herself a moment to gather her thoughts. With practiced effort, she extended her mind to her crew and gave them her thoughts. She pictured the right ropes for the sails. She imagined *The Knotted Wood* riding the currents of the Aquirren River to Lake Connell of Dressa Moore.

Grunts from her crew spread across the deck. Marta opened her eyes. The one next to her had found the right rope for the forward sail. The other crew found ropes and pulled. Fortunately, most of them were the right ones. Even more joined the effort, and soon *The Knotted Wood's* sails rose to catch the wind.

"That's how you do it!" Marta called down from the bridge. Her ship lurched forward, which brought a smile to her face. A sea dog belonged at sea with a strong wind and the smell of salt in the air. If only she weren't being pursued by a warship.

The Knotted Wood swung around and pointed her bow at the harbor's exit. Marta didn't have time to watch for smaller vessels. If they were in her way, then they'd best get out of it. She glanced behind her to the frigate. That ship's crew were much more practiced and skilled. Sails were already out, and the ship was already moving. Bad news. *The Wood* was fast, but Marta was sure on the river that the frigate would best her speed. But that also meant the frigate would get close to *The Wood.*

"You! To the stern!" Marta shouted at one of her crew. She had one more surprise for the dear commodore—one she had been saving for an encounter just like this.

Commodore Wilkes folded his arms and gritted his teeth as he choked back his anger. He did his best to put aside his feelings. No commander should allow emotion to control their behavior, but it was difficult. There was no final tally on the deaths in Oyster Piers, but even one was too many. And for this to happen under his watch and protection... Bartolome would pay.

"We'll catch her easily enough," Captain Bridgewater said.

Wilkes nodded, realizing that his mood was so easily picked up on by the captain. "Thank you, Captain. She's wanted for crimes beyond this port."

"Oh, I'm well aware. I have been briefed about that vessel."

The Crimson Swan lurched forward on a gust of wind, the sails billowing. The crew took to their ropes and stations as the ship swung around to give chase. Lieutenant Swanson, on the lower deck with the commodore's troops, had them line up along the rail, out of the way of the crew, but still able to take aim at *The Knotted Wood.*

"We have much bigger guns, you know," Bridgewater said. "Swanson's men won't be needing to shoot. They'll miss anyway."

Commodore Wilkes nodded. "I'm aware." He looked at Bridgewater. He knew he had to say something. Having a superior office on your ship had meaning on the sea. "Marcus, I respect the rule of the sea. She's your ship. I have no intention of assuming command."

Bridgewater nodded. "We'll catch her, Commodore. Rest assured."

"I've no concern that we won't, Captain. My concern is that we will."

Bridgewater nodded, but remained silent.

The commodore looked back out towards *The Wood.* Most of the navy knew about what Wilkes had witnessed in Dressa. The reports he had filed had become the stuff of legend. In fact, the existence of *The Knotted Wood* was one of the reasons why travel to Dressa was restricted in the first place.

"She's left the harbor!" called the watchman in the crow's nest high above the bridge.

"Fast ship," Bridgewater said.

"Very. And the captain knows a spell or two."

"Does she, now?"

Wilkes nodded. "Won't work here, of course. The magic in the air is far too weak. But once she reaches the river channel leading to Dressa, and the magic thickens, it will."

Bridgewater nodded. "Well then, we'll just have to catch her before she makes it. Boson! Ready the claw!"

"Claw?" Wilkes frowned in confusion. He'd never heard the term.

"Well, the admiralty named it 'the webbed swan foot,' but that hardly instills fear."

In the ship's bow, the commodore noticed a small contingent of Bridgewater's crew arming a front-facing cannon. They inserted a spear into the front with a chain attached to the end. The chain extended out of the cannon and was wrapped into a large coil on the deck.

"A harpoon?"

Bridgewater nodded. "It's quite effective in pursuit on the river channels. The chain is attached to an auxiliary anchor on our bow. There's a cap on the tip of the spear with a small amount of gunpowder. Once it penetrates the hull, the cap explodes, and the ends will blossom out into a webbed fan. It should catch on the inside of their ship and pull the anchor off our hull, and then they will drag the anchor."

"I've not seen anything like this."

Bridgewater smiled. "One of our crew came up with it. Well, he *was* one of our crew; transferred to Oyster Piers just today. Quite a smart lad. We showed the claw to Admiral Becket last spring."

"Does it work?"

Bridgewater smiled. "We'll find out shortly."

"Can't we just shoot them with a cannonball? I mean, we know that works as intended."

"Creates too much drag for us. Cannonballs are quite heavy. Our primary charge is to catch ships before they reach the falls at the end of the Aquirren."

Wilkes nodded. "Well then, let's see if this webbed foot of yours works, Captain."

"We'll know soon enough. Once they're farther out into

the river, we should be close enough to fire without risking any of the locals."

In front of them, *The Knotted Wood* had a lead that Wilkes estimated to be nearly half a mile. The exit of the harbor fed into a tributary which itself fed into the Aquirren River. Once they swung both ships around the jetty and entered the river proper, they would be just a few miles from the surge of the Aquirren River that would propel them via magical currents straight into the lakes of Dressa Moore. If Bridgewater's webbed foot contraption didn't work, then the commodore would have to face the decision of pursuing them into Dressa, which all naval captains were ordered never to do, or letting *The Knotted Wood* go. His rank of commodore granted Wilkes the authority to give the order to pursue only in extreme circumstances—which was exactly what he would do, considering what had happened in Oyster Piers. An attack on an imperial outpost by a renegade ship was a high crime of the sea. No matter what Bridgewater's objections would be, considering the stakes, and what that vile woman represented, Wilkes already knew what command he would give.

JONATHAN KNELT beside one of his trunks that the crew had placed in the cargo hold next to a large cache of canned fish and beans. All but two of his trunks were present—a fact that he tried his best not to let anger him too much. He mostly failed.

"What are you doing down here?" William's voice came from behind Jonathan. "It's rather dank in here, wouldn't you say?"

"I'm checking to see which trunks were lost."

"My books made it alright, in case you were wondering."

"I wasn't."

William sighed.

"Oh, not now," Jonathan snapped.

"Not now what?"

Jonathan looked over his shoulder at William. "Look, I'm quite happy you have your books and can endlessly study the use of conjunctions and their origins in the one and only language of the entire world. However, everything I have been working towards for a decade is in these trunks. If the wrong one went over, then we might as well jump overboard and find a nice bed-and-breakfast to spend the winter in, because this trip will be quite useless. Alright?" He turned back to his trunks and opened two of them at once.

William nodded. Of course, Jonathan was right. This was his life's work. To have some piece of his equipment lost now, when they were finally on their way to the mysterious magical lands of Dressa, would be devastating. Still, did he have to insult William's life's work? Yes, granted, being a linguist when there was only one language in the world was an academic pursuit that commanded little interest and even less respect. But honestly, couldn't others in academia see the oddity in only a single language existing? Did that not merit research? How was it even possible? William had documented a dozen remote societies, some separated for nearly a thousand years, and still they barely had any noticeable difference in their dialects. Language should evolve, just as societal customs did. And yet it hadn't. At the very least, Jonathan could at least not ridicule him as much as he did.

"It's here!" Jonathan exclaimed. He pulled a large black metal box out of one trunk with a wand attached to the end.

"Oh, good. What is that again?"

Jonathan set the box on top of one of the closed trunks and attached a metal arm to the back end. He gave the handle a few cranks, and a light on the box came to life. He stood and waved the wand around in a large circle.

"Very impressive," William said.

Jonathan scoffed. "I described this to you before. It's a magonmeter. It measures magic."

"Ah, yes. I do remember now."

"Appears to be working, though, as expected; nothing to detect here. When we reach the Aquirren, we'll know for certain."

"Know what?"

"That the magonmeter is working."

"Right. So, what was in the trunks you lost?"

Jonathan's expression turned into a frown. "I believe I lost several pieces of the anti-magical suit."

"Oh, that's dreadful," William said.

"Not entirely. Of course, it's only theoretical. I've only had a few magical particles to experiment on back at the university. I believe I can replace the lost pieces if we find a quantity of lead."

"Did you say lead?"

"Yes, of course. What else could I have said?"

"What?"

Jonathan sighed. "Doesn't matter. At any rate, I believe we can proceed even with the loss of the two trunks. Though I may have to reduce the amount paid to our host."

"She lost some of her crew, didn't she? I mean, not exactly the circumstances to demand a rebate."

"Is that *my* fault?"

William shrugged. "I suppose not."

Jonathan smiled at William and placed his hand on his shoulder. "I apologize to you, Will. I don't mean to belittle your field of study. I was just anxious regarding what was lost."

William smiled. "It's alright, Jon. I know this is a stressful time. And I want to support you. I would just like the—"

Jonathan's eyes went wide. "Support! I have to check to see if the support harness is still here. That will be difficult to replace."

"—same," William muttered under his breath.

ON THE BRIDGE of *The Knotted Wood*, Marta directed her crew to the sails to get the most speed from the wind that her ship could muster. *The Wood* cut through the river waters like a knife through butter. Every second, she seemed to gain speed. From here, they were only a few miles from the Aquirren Falls, and once there, they would be home free. *The Swan* wouldn't dare follow them, and even if they did, Marta would have access to magic, and she knew more than a few spells to throw at them. But as she glanced over her shoulder, fear grew in her stomach. *The Swan* was fast as well—and it was gaining on them.

"Going to be close," Marta said under her breath. "Pull the sails! The port sails!"

Her crew fumbled with the ropes, one of them stumbling over his own feet. Eventually, they found the right rope and pulled the sail tight. Marta cursed under her breath. She really didn't have the patience to direct them properly—not with *The Swan* and the commodore so close. Her crew, it seemed, just didn't work well when magic wasn't in the air. Once they rode the currents of Aquirren closer to Dressa, they should all snap back into better shape.

Marta glanced over her shoulder again at the imperial

frigate behind her, and then to the bow of *The Wood* and the lakes of Dressa in the distance. They were going to make it. It was a judgement based on speed and distance, but she felt it in her gut. She smiled to herself and allowed herself a quick nod. Maybe she wouldn't need to sacrifice another crew member after all. She'd already lost one in the town. Losing one more would mean she'd have to replace them—something she found no pleasure in doing.

A boom sounded from her stern. Marta turned to see a small puff of smoke from the bow of *The Swan*. Her jaw dropped, and laughter billowed out of her stomach. They had fired a cannon from the bow? What madness was that? Even if the shot hit *The Wood*, which Marta thought practically impossible, the recoil from the cannon would only slow *The Swan* down. And she could already smell the salt and magic in the air from Dressa. They were nearly home.

WILLIAM SAT on a wooden stool while Jonathan dug through his trunk, searching for the support harness. William knew this research operation meant everything to Jonathan, but still, couldn't William mean everything just once in a while? But then, he felt he was being too harsh. He didn't need to always be the center of attention. Just more than occasionally would be nice.

Jonathan's face lit up as his hands lifted a series of leather belts from his trunk. As he did so, without warning, a three-foot-long black spear burst through the hull of the cargo area and embedded itself in a wooden beam in the center of their room. Both William and Jonathan jumped at the sudden minor explosion that followed seconds later.

"What in the heavens is that?!" William said.

Webbed spines along the side of the spear exploded outward, and the spear dislodged itself from the wooden beam. The strange item hit the deck of the cargo hall and rested on two of the webbed spines.

"Is that an umbrella?" William said.

"It looks like an umbrella," Jonathan replied.

"It's quite big. Who needs a six-foot-long umbrella?"

"And there's a chain on the end."

"A chain? Where does it lead?"

Jonathan turned to William, and a look of confusion passed over both their faces. Together, they walked to the end of the umbrella and followed the chain to the wall of the cargo hold, where it exited the ship through a small hole.

"That's odd," Jonathan said.

"Very."

"Do you think it's a bad thing?"

William nodded. "I can't imagine how it could be beneficial."

Suddenly, the chain sticking out of the hull tightened, causing the umbrella to lift off the deck. Jonathan's eyes went wide. He pulled William back from the small hole in the hull. Seconds later, the umbrella jerked backward and slammed into the wooden frame of *The Knotted Wood's* cargo hold. The ship lurched backwards, sending Jonathan and William slamming into the hull. They both landed on the deck and rolled to their sides. Above them, the umbrella had secured itself tightly to the frame of the ship, and they could both see that an extreme amount of force was pulling backward on it.

"Yes, I do believe this could be considered quite bad," Jonathan said.

"What do we do?" William stood and grabbed the umbrella.

Jonathan leapt to his feet. "What are you doing?!"

"Whatever this is, I have every confidence that it's meant to prevent us from reaching your goal."

Jonathan smiled briefly at the thought of William's first motivation being to protect his research. They did fight, and often, but they also shared a deep love—which, Jonathan was proud to acknowledge, was bolstered when they both showed empathy for each other's projects. Of course, that also sent Jonathan into a moment of guilt, as he had often ridiculed William's research. But frankly, it was silly. Linguistics? Really? Of all the fields William could study? Quite like the anti-magic movement that refused to acknowledge that magic was real. Sorry, but that was simply fantasy, and Jonathan had offered frequently to take the anti-magic university community chapter to a small village on the Aquirren River where magic was present, because of tidal forces, and prove the existence of magic via a woman in the village who knew one spell: turning goats into pigs. Of course, it had the unfortunate side effect of displeasing many other villagers, as they had strict rules against eating pigs. But it would prove magic's existence unquestionably.

"Can you not daydream right now?!" William exclaimed.

"What? Oh, sorry."

"Fetch the captain! I'll try to release it here!"

Jonathan nodded and kissed William on the cheek, which caused him to flash a smile.

"Now! Go, Jonathan!" William screamed.

Jonathan went.

∽

From somewhere beneath Marta, a loud thumping echoed through the hull, soon followed by a tiny blast—both of which she thought to be quite odd.

"You there, go below and see what that was!" Marta shouted to one of her crew, who grunted, nodded, and shuffled to the lower decks.

Moments later, with the Aquirren River nearly in sight, the ship lurched backwards with enough force that Marta almost impaled herself on her own wheel.

"What in the name of the seven hells was that?"

Behind them, *The Swan* surged forward as *The Knotted Wood's* speed slowed nearly in half.

"Captain! Something came through the hull!" Jonathan ran to the bridge, panting. "A large, well, umbrella—or something, with a chain sticking out of the hull!"

Marta turned to the female crew member next to her, grabbed her hands, and stuck them on the wheel. She ran to the stern and peered over the edge. A black chain extended from inside her ship and stretched backward toward *The Swan*. The metal links dipped below the water and appeared to sink into the depths of the river.

Marta whistled. "Now, that is clever. Jonathan, take some crew and go below deck. Do whatever you have to do to get that off my ship!"

"But I'm not—"

"Just go!" Marta turned to her ace-in-the-hole crew member. "Looks like you're taking a trip after all."

William dug his fingers into the webbing on the metal spikes of the umbrella, or whatever it was. He tried to dislodge the thing from the hull, but whatever pulled on the contraption with the chain held a strong grip, which he could not budge.

"Help!" William screamed. Of course, he had no idea how much of a danger this item was to their ship, but he was relatively certain that most ships didn't have exploding four-foot-long umbrellas bursting through their hulls. Just a guess, of course.

A grunt came from behind, and William turned to see one of the crew standing at the base of a ladder leading to the higher decks. The man tilted his head to one side and sniffed the air.

"Help me, man!" William said.

The crewman looked up the ladder and then back to William. He tilted his head to the other side and sniffed the air one more time.

"What are you doing?!"

Eventually, the crewman nodded and walked toward William. The mate's face held a blank stare. William didn't know his name or recognize him from his brief time on deck. He sniffed the air several more times before his eyes landed on the slight cut on one of William's fingers. The crewman's jaw moved slightly, almost as if he had just taken a small bite from something inside his mouth. All of this made William question every choice he'd made for the past three weeks.

"Pull this, man! Here!"

The crewmate shrugged, nodded, tilted his head to one side, and shrugged again. After a long, uncomfortable silence, and a large portion of that spent staring at William's cut finger, the man eventually grabbed one of the metal spines and pulled.

To William's great surprise, the metal spoke of the umbrella bent with the force of the crewman's hands. Then again, these men had carried all Jonathan's luggage with ease. Whatever the cook was making for this crew must be quite hearty.

"William? Are you still down there?" Jonathan called from the deck above through the ladder hatch.

"Yes! One of the crew is down here helping me. He's making quick work of this thing!"

"Excellent, I have more crew with me. The captain sent us more members. We're coming down," Jonathan announced.

MARTA GRABBED one of her crew by the collar—she didn't bother looking to see who it was—then planted him in front of the ship's wheel and pushed the crew member manning the wheel to the side. She pointed her arm toward the Aquirren River and told the crewman to steer straight down the middle once they enter from the tributary. She then dragged the female crew member, who looked exactly like the person Wilkes wanted, to the stern and commanded several other crew to ready the ropes and prepare the catapult.

She took a step back and held the girl by the shoulders. "Right height, right size, even your hair color and eyes are like hers." Marta frowned and tilted her head to one side. "Still, you'll not be very frightful looking like that."

Marta sniffed the air for the scent of magic on the breeze. She frowned. Being this close to Dressa, she'd hoped there'd be a whiff or two, but there wasn't so much as a puff of the stuff in the air. It didn't matter, though. The imperial frigate was getting a little too close, and she would have to send the girl overboard. Of course, that meant if she ever tangled with the commodore again, she'd have to find another replacement—which wasn't a walk in the park.

Another of the crew brought a harness made of leather straps. Marta grabbed them and began wrapping them around the girl's body, at which the girl gargled once and chomped her mouth.

"Easy now, love. You'll be just fine."

The girl half smiled and rolled her eyes.

Once the straps were wrapped around her body, Marta attached a hook to the back of the harness behind the girl's head and gave it a quick tug. She then looked deep into the girl's eyes and whispered a single word.

"Feed," Marta commanded.

Her undead crew member grunted. She opened and closed her mouth half a dozen times before growling. Her eyes went wild with sudden hunger, and she raised both her hands, looking for something to grab. Marta smiled and patted her once on the head.

"Good girl. Now, go get him."

Marta walked to the side of the bridge and grabbed a lever. She'd never actually used this contraption other than in testing. But the mechanics seemed sound, as did the math. She caught herself and chuckled. She did not truly know if either was sound at all. But Sylvia, the girl who had given her the tip to pirate the barge captain, the very same girl who had built and installed the massive slingshot cata-pult, seemed to know what she was doing.

The Knotted Wood jolted to port, pulled by whatever was at the other end of that chain sticking out of Marta's hull. But she couldn't worry about the commodore's crazy weapon right now. She had to focus on the task at hand. She looked up to the rigging to make sure the lines of rope were set properly. If not, this thing could rip her crew girl right in half.

Marta nodded in satisfaction and looked behind her. *The Swan* was gaining—fast. But they weren't quite close enough to launch her crew member over the side. On the river, she saw small waves with a rainbow shimmer coming from *The Wood's* wake. She looked to the port to see they had finally entered Aquirren River from the tributary. Even with the harpoon anchor, or whatever it was, *The Wood* still pulled at least five knots. This part of the river, because of the Aquirren's strong currents, had a very smooth silty bottom that prevented most anchors from finding purchase, which was now working in her favor.

"Let's give them something to see, shall we?" Marta smiled and whispered the one-word spell she knew by heart. "*Moass.*"

The girl's face instantly melted. The illusion of flesh gave way to her true, mostly skeleton form. True, she had more meat on her bones that most of her crew. Marta had kept her fed for just such an occasion. Hopefully, she would distract the commodore long enough for her crew and the professors to remove the chain from her hull and let them sail the Aquirren to freedom.

WILLIAM NODDED towards Jonathan descending the ladder. There were four crew members with him, more than enough to help, William thought. He turned back to the crewman already working on pulling the metal umbrella off the hull. But where the crewman had been just moments ago, something else altogether now stood in his place. William's heart nearly stopped in his chest, and his jaw fell open. He backed away from the crewman, tripped over a bag of rice in the cargo hold, and fell onto his backside with a thump.

The crewman turned to William and snarled. The skin of his face melted away, leaving half his jaw exposed. The flesh on his body curled and shrank. Several of the man's bones showed clearly through now tattered and ripped clothing. The man's hair grew into a long, stringy, unkempt mess that jostled like loose cobwebs when the crewmate turned. The man gurgled something, opening his jaw wide, only to bite down with force and turn his attention back to the umbrella.

From the ladder, Jonathan let out a loud scream and fell into the cargo hold. William shook his head clear and rushed to Jonathan's side. Above them on the ladder, three more of the crew, all of them with fleshless patches on their bones and exposed muscles, calmly climbed down the ladder. Once in the hold, they walked casually to the umbrella contraption and assisted their fellow crewmate in pulling the spines back that held onto the interior of the hull.

"What in the name of any god that would listen is going on here?" William demanded.

Commodore Wilkes stood behind Captain Bridgewater on the deck of *The Swan* with his hands clasped behind his back and a slight smile on his face. They had her. Bridgewater's insane gadget had worked. *The Wood* was snared. She must have lost at least five knots of speed, maybe more. There was no chance that that blasted woman would escape him this time. Not one.

"Here, have a look." Bridgewater handed Wilkes a spyglass and pointed to the stern of *The Wood*. "You can see your captain scrambling on her bridge."

Wilkes brought the spyglass to his eye. There she was, Captain Bartolome. She looked over the side of her ship to see the chain coming from inside her hull. Amazing—that thing had worked!

Wilkes ran the spyglass over the bridge—and stopped on the woman at the helm. His heart skipped a beat. Could that be her? Did Bartolome really travel with her? It would make sense, considering that Bartolome had come to the Riverlands. She would want some kind of insurance.

On the deck of *The Wood*, Bartolome grabbed the woman at the wheel and dragged her to the stern. She wrapped her in some kind of harness and then attached her to ropes that hung from the rigging.

"No! Abigail..."

"What?" Bridgewater said.

Wilkes lowered the spyglass and called down to the lower deck. "Lieutenant, tell the men to hold their fire!"

"But sir!" Lieutenant Swanson sputtered.

"Why?" Bridgewater asked.

"I'll explain later, Captain."

"I'd prefer you explain now, Commodore. I doubt *The Wood* will hold her own fire the closer we get."

"They have civilians on board. Two university professors, at the least."

"Yes, we know that. Those civilians, however, did board that ship after the attack on Oyster Piers, which makes them suspects in the attack."

"The ship may also possibly have my wife on board."

Bridgewater turned to Wilkes and gave him a confused stare. "Your wife?"

Wilkes nodded. He brought the spyglass up to his eye to see Bartolome pull a lever on the stern of her ship. Ropes pulled and twisted in the rigging of *The Wood*. The ropes whipped around the rigging. Wilkes spied a large spool of rope unwinding with force. He brought the spyglass towards the deck to see his wife, Abigail, get yanked off her feet and into the air toward the bow of the ship. Wilkes jumped forward and tried to follow the movement, but all he could find were twisted ropes.

"They're launching something!" cried the crewmate in the crow's nest above.

"Is that a body?" Bridgewater said.

Wilkes lowered the spyglass and followed the outstretched hands of the crew, pointing at a body in the air. The contraption aboard *The Wood* had flung Abigail over the port side toward the bow and then back along the starboard side to finally release her and send her sailing into the air toward *The Swan*.

"Abigail!" screamed Wilkes.

"Savages!" Bridgewater declared.

The woman sailed through the gap between the two ships, which had now closed to nearly four ship lengths, thanks to the harpoon anchor. *The Swan* had taken a position directly behind *The Wood*. As a result, and due to the angles used in the contraption on *The Wood*, *The Swan* was in a perfect position to catch her in her sails ... which was exactly what happened.

"Abigail!" Wilkes ran from the bridge to the lower deck. The woman had hit the sails, but they did not tear from her weight. She slid down the canvas and got tangled as one rope wrapped around her foot. She dangled just above the deck, her arms waving wildly.

"Cut her down!" Bridgewater commanded from the bridge.

"No, wait, we have to be sure!" Wilkes said, but he was too late. One of the crew cut the rope holding Abigail, and she fell to the deck with a thud.

"Abigail?!" Wilkes ran to her side and waved at the crew to back away.

The young woman on the deck snarled. Then she gurgled and turned her face, half of which wasn't there. The girl lunged at the commodore with her mouth wide. One of the crew jerked her backward from Wilkes, but she then lunged at the crewman, desperate to find something to bite.

"Don't let her bite you! She's one of them!" Wilkes cried.

One member of the crew kicked at the woman, while another threw a rope around her torso. She lunged again with her mouth wide, but again the crew kept her at bay.

"What the devil *is* that?" Bridgewater said. "Strike the sails! Slow us down!"

"What are you doing?!" Wilkes demanded.

"We're not going near that ship until I understand what is going on here! Is this really your *wife*?"

Wilkes knelt down by the woman and examined her from a few feet away. She looked like Abigail, though half her face was gone. Her body was the right size, but Wilkes stared into her eyes and shook his head. "No, this isn't her. Abigail's eyes were a different shade."

"There is some rot there, sir," one crewman pointed out.

Wilkes turned to the man and shrugged. "So?"

"Just saying, sir. When things rot, they can change color."

"That's enough, crewman. Commodore, I do still think some explanation is in order."

Wilkes nodded. "Nothing much to explain. My wife traveled to Dressa many years ago on a church-sponsored humanitarian mission. She was visiting an island when a magical quake occurred. She was caught in the blast."

"And this happened?"

"Yes, something like that."

"And that woman was involved?" Bridgewater pointed to *The Knotted Wood* without looking.

"Yes. Which is why I would like to have a talk with her."

Bridgewater nodded. "I knew Abigail was missing, but gods on the mountain, Thomas, I had no idea."

Wilkes stood from the crew member and looked to where *The Knotted Wood* should be. It was with no small amount of anger that he saw *The Wood* now several boat lengths away, sailing at great speed, the chain attached to her stern gone.

"What happened?!" Wilkes shouted.

"Sorry, sir. We were watching this creature-thing," one of his men said.

Wilkes bit his tongue and looked up. Sure enough, the crew in the crow's nest were staring down at the deck and not at the river. One sharp look from the commodore, however, and all the crew high above the deck looked out in various directions.

One of them cupped his hand over his mouth and shouted, "The ship is off the chain!"

Bridgewater grunted in frustration. "She's gone, then. No chance we can catch her now." He kicked one leg of the woman on his deck and jumped back when she tried to bite him. "Not sure we want to, though."

Wilkes stood. "We want to. And we will."

"How's that?" Bridgewater said.

"Captain, raise your sails. We are pursuing that ship into Dressa Moore."

"Commodore, I don't think—"

"I don't care what you think, Captain. That ship attacked Oyster Piers, it is directly responsible for deaths in the township, and it may carry kidnapped imperial citizens. Raise your sails to full!"

Bridgewater remained silent. Wilkes could almost feel the tension racing through the crew. If he took command, which was within his rights, it didn't mean the crew would follow him. Some would, but all? And would they follow him with absolute loyalty? Sailing into Dressa was not for the faint of heart. He would need them to be steadfast and obey commands.

Finally, Bridgewater nodded. "Raise sails! Prepare to give chase into Dressa Moore!" He turned without addressing the commodore and returned to the bridge.

That went well, Wilkes thought. He looked down at the woman on the deck. She was just another distraction. Bartolome knew what Abigail looked like. That vile woman had risked every man on this ship, just like she did at Oyster Piers, just so she could escape. No matter whether he found Abigail or not, Wilkes swore he would deal with Bartolome once and for all.

CHAPTER FOUR

Daniel Desun ran through the quad like a young man whose life depended on reaching his destination. And though his life didn't, his blooming academic career probably did. He reminded himself nearly every day at dawn, breakfast, lunch, snack time, teatime, and dinner that this path was something he had chosen. It was indeed a great honor to be the assistant to the chancellor of the Great University of Learning and Knowledge, the greatest university not only in the Riverlands, but perhaps the world. Although, to be honest, reports from the second continent were quite murky.

Students strolled along the spiderweb-like walkways through the quad. Some yelped, while others used profane language as Daniel darted between them. Without a backward glance, he continued towards the building in the center of the sprawling network of paved walkways. At the end of each of the central spokes sat one of the university's main buildings of study. Behind each of those, as the university had had to expand over its five centuries of existence, auxiliary buildings that housed additional classrooms and experimental labs spread outward for a mile. Behind those, the great city of Swanville, capital city of the empire, surrounded the university like an enormous spider, always patiently waiting for new students to pop into her web as they began their humble careers.

At the center of the various paths on the quad, the administrative building stood like a beacon to the arts, to knowledge, and to all things worthy of being known in the world. Daniel burst through a side door into the administrative hall and ran down a long corridor to the chancellor's office. He darted and skipped between students and faculty, fortunate not to knock into any of them. He apologized in passing for his rudeness, but frankly, it was justified. The letter he held was of monumental importance. In essence, the chancellor's entire plan was endangered, and Daniel knew the chancellor's wrath would spill over to every underling even remotely involved. And since he was currently the only assistant involved, that would be a great deal of wrath coming in his direction.

Four twists and two turns through the mazelike structure of the administrative building found Daniel standing outside the door to the chancellor's office. To his right, a small delegation of men and women stood in the reception area. They all had dark black skin and wore long, colorful robes. Daniel recognized them instantly as representatives from the Democracy, the government located in the deep interior of the continent. He gave them all a smile and a wave. He then turned to the chancellor's door and opened it just an inch to peer inside. His eyes went wide, his mouth drying up in seconds. The admiral of the imperial navy and the archbishop of the church were in there. This would be far more than an awkward interruption. Their glares had sent much stronger men than Daniel to their knees. But he knew he had no choice.

Daniel pushed the door a quarter inch more before stopping. No, this wasn't the right time. Spontaneously opening doors during a conversation between powerful people was a practiced skill—and Daniel had much practice in this. So instead, he put his ear to the door and listened for the perfect moment to enter.

CHANCELLOR DUNNINGHAM SAT BACK in his leather-cushioned mahogany chair and tilted his small flute of morning champagne to his lips. The sweet taste and slight fizz brought a moment of joy to his face, which within mere seconds dissipated back into the depths of his subconscious.

Looking out the window, her hands clasped tightly behind her, her long blonde hair neatly and precisely tied into a bun, her uniform crisp and recently pressed, the admiral waited patiently for the chancellor to gather his thoughts. Or perhaps she waited to pounce on the next thing he said. Or just to be crass and brutish, as she often was—behavior that made the chancellor question this bizarre union of the university, the admiralty, and the church. Yet here they were, in this together now, for good or ill or whatever else might come. At the very least, the chancellor had an admirable supply of port, which should allow him to get through this business in one slightly inebriated piece.

"Any word from your people?" the admiral asked.

"No, of course not. They have no means to give me word, even if they had word," the chancellor replied.

The admiral sighed. "I am aware. I was speaking to the archbishop."

The chancellor nodded, shrugged, and took another sip of port. Standing in the back of the room in the shadows cast by the sunlight through the open windows, the archbishop of the True Religion of the Gods stepped forward into the light, a large robe with an equally wide cowl covering his body and head, both of which obstructed any view of his face. Honestly, Dunningham had almost forgotten the archbishop was even here. The chancellor always thought the archbishop's manner and actions were a tad melodramatic. Did he intentionally *try* to be so creepy?

"Not yet, Admiral. The university professors have not yet reached Hogkarta. Have you heard from the military in Oyster Piers?"

The admiral shook her head. "Not yet."

"Well then, drink, anyone? Champagne? Port?" the chancellor offered.

"You realize it's barely noon," the admiral admonished.

"Oh, my word, you're quite right! Almost time for afternoon scotch. No harm in having a snort a little too early."

"Smelke, the great god of drink and merriment, would find your devotion to his ways a form of worship," the archbishop said dryly.

"Would he, now? Perhaps I'll convert."

"I would prefer you to be clearheaded for the days to come." The admiral turned from the window, her hands still tightly clasped behind her back, and took a step towards the chancellor.

"What for, exactly? I mean, what would be the rationale there? Our professors are nearly a thousand miles from here by now. It's not as if my clear or clouded head can influence anything at this stage."

"We can communicate with them using ravens, Chancellor," the admiral said.

"Indeed, but I won't be writing them personally, will I?"

"But you still have influence here, Kyle."

The admiral's use of the chancellor's first name startled him. Granted, they were involved in a minor conspiracy of sorts, though the chancellor somewhat doubted that description. The university wanted to study magic, and the admiralty had a vested interest in Dressa Moore. Of course, no one knew what the religious people wanted. They were the biggest mystery of all. They had churches throughout the Riverlands and had been making inroads with the emperor himself. Still, why care about magical research? Why help fund an expedition to the source of magic? True, they weren't the most empirical of thinkers, so seeking the university's help in this matter was warranted, but why attempt it at all?

"I'm not sure what influence you think I have, Sus—" The chancellor started to use the admiral's first name, but a hard stare and gritted teeth from her made him recalculate. "... Admiral. Our professors are quite free in their scholastic pursuits."

"What if they discover something?" the admiral said.

"Sorry, but that is the goal, isn't it? Of research, I mean. To discover things."

"The admiral means, if your professors do discover something, then they must proceed with the university's discretion on how it should be made known," the archbishop said.

"Jonathan knows what's at stake here."

"And the other one?"

"You mean the linguist?" Chancellor Dunningham let out a stifled laugh. "Who cares? We have quite a few in academia who study subjects on the fringe. Are you worried he'll decipher a new use for the word *magic*? Perhaps he'll uncover an unknown vowel..."

Both of them glared at the chancellor. Clearly, neither the military nor the church had any semblance of a sense of humor. With more effort than he would have liked, the chancellor stood from his chair and walked to the scotch shelf in his office. He grabbed a tumbler and gave himself two fingers of a pour. A little more than he should before lunch, but this entire business was just turning his nerves into jelly.

The door to the chancellor's office creaked open, and he, the admiral, and the archbishop turned to see who would be bold enough to disturb the chancellor during a meeting of this magnitude.

Daniel, the chancellor's long-time assistant, entered the room and flashed a brief smile—an act that the chancellor found a bit more perplexing that he would have liked.

"Something you need, Daniel? Is there a new joke going around from the School of Comedic Thought that you'd like to share?" Chancellor Dunningham said.

"Sorry, sir. We've just received a raven from Oyster Piers with news."

The admiral marched over to Daniel and snatched the letter from his hand. She nodded to the door and turned her back without waiting to see if Daniel would leave.

Chancellor Dunningham sighed. "Thank you, Daniel."

Without a word, but with relief on his face, Daniel left the room and closed the door.

The door then popped open again, causing the Chancellor to grow frustrated. "What is it now?"

"I just wanted to inform you, sir, the delegation from the Democracy is waiting to see you," Daniel said.

Chancellor Dunningham rolled his eyes, nodded, and waved Daniel away. The door closed with a small click. "The Democracy. Can you believe they even exist? They vote—all of them. On everything." The chancellor shook his head in disgust. "What does the average commoner know about matters of state? Madness. I wonder if they'll vote on which one gets to speak to me?"

"Can we focus, please? What news, Admiral?" the archbishop asked.

The admiral read the note over twice before folding it neatly and placing it in her pocket. She walked back to the window and clasped her hands behind her back.

"Well, what is it? Good news, or bad?" Chancellor Dunningham sipped his scotch and touched it up to a full three fingers from the decanter.

"Your professors have made it to Dressa Moore."

"Excellent news," Archbishop Santos said.

"Yes, thankfully, the first leg of the journey is complete."

The admiral nodded. "And there has been an attack on Oyster Piers."

"An attack? By whom?"

"The creatures you mentioned to us, Archbishop. The undead."

"What? The undead? What does that even mean? How is someone undead?" Chancellor Dunningham sputtered.

"A ship full of them, it seems. Dozens dead at Oyster. I thought they had traveled on a travel barge? This note says the ship was *The Knotted Wood*, captained by someone named Bartolome," the admiral said.

"Dozens dead, or 'undead'?" Chancellor Dunningham demanded.

"We did hire a travel barge, Admiral. I don't understand how *The Knotted Wood* has gotten itself involved."

"You know the ship?"

Archbishop Santos nodded. "Everyone in Dressa knows the vessel of the dead."

"And one of our commodores has taken a frigate, *The Crimson Swan*, with thirty cannons and four hundred souls, in pursuit."

"That is distressing to hear, Admiral." Archbishop Santos retreated to the shadow by the window and stood by a bookcase.

"Wait... You said the professors made it to Dressa? Did they avoid this attack?"

The admiral let out a long, tight breath. "Our commodore sent word back to Oyster Piers. His lieutenant reports that since your professors boarded the undead vessel, they have been labeled co-conspirators in the attack."

"Madness. Impossible." Dunningham drank the full three fingers of his scotch and poured another. "Neither Jonathan nor the linguist would ever do anything of the sort. You must recall your commodore at once."

"That will be difficult. We don't have an outpost to receive ravens in Dressa, and he's at sea."

"But Jonathan had your signed letter granting them passage! How can they be chased?"

"Did you already forget that there are dozens dead in Oyster Piers caused by the ship on which they fled? My letter did not grant them permission to commit murder."

"Which I am insisting they did not!"

"That doesn't matter now. Once Commodore Wilkes catches them—and he will—this endeavor will be over. Worse than that, the collusion between the university, the military, and the True Religionists of the Church will be revealed."

Sweat beaded on the chancellor's brow. If the board found out he had colluded with the military on a scientific endeavor funded by religious zealots during his tenure, his chancellorship would be effectively over. Why on earth had he let Jonathan talk him into this madness in the first place? It seemed like a splendid idea for the university—the first exploration of the magical source of Dressa. Thoughts of celebratory dinners, of accolades, of foreign wines and cheeses evaporated from the chancellor's mind. He poured another finger of scotch and collapsed into his chair.

"We may yet salvage this," the archbishop said. From within his cloak, he pulled out a large crystal cube attached to a chain around his neck.

"How do we do that? And what manner of religiousness is this?" Dunningham said, slurring several of his words.

"I can send word to the church in Hogkarta."

"And how do you do that? With a crystal on a chain?"

"There is much you don't know of the world," the archbishop said.

Chancellor Dunningham laughed. "I'll bet there's a tad more that I do!"

"Regardless, we have a substantial amount of force we can leverage in Dressa. More than you know."

The admiral spun her head on her shoulders and stared daggers at the archbishop. "If you mean to threaten my ship or my officers, we will have a larger problem here, Archbishop."

"Nothing of the kind, Admiral. We can distract your commodore long enough for the professors to complete their research."

"Wilkes won't give up. Ever. Not after what happened in Oyster Piers. That happened on his watch."

"All either of us care for is the research. Let them conduct it, and then the commodore can have them. The church can survive any revelation that may come. As can the admiralty," the archbishop said with confidence.

Chancellor Dunningham snorted. "Excuse me? Hello? Still here, you know. Are you actually saying to abandon my professors and embarrass the university—and myself?"

An uneasy silence settled over the room. The admiral looked out the window, her fists clasped behind her flexing arms.

"Do it," the admiral finally said.

"You can't be serious!" Chancellor Dunningham protested.

"Don't fret, Kyle. We'll navigate this."

"And my professors?"

The admiral shrugged. "Casualties of war are a tragic thing."

Chancellor Dunningham sat back in his seat and wiped more sweat off his brow. This was a step too far. Glory and fame were worth a price, but this seemed far too steep. He could no more abandon his professors than he could his own children. Of course, he had none, but if he had, he'd never trust their fate to these two vipers.

Dunningham stood from his chair and walked to the door of his office.

"Where are you off to, Kyle?" the admiral asked.

The chancellor stopped at the door, his hand grabbing the handle, his heart hammering in his chest. "Since this is decided, I have other matters to attend to. I'm sure you heard that delegates from the Democracy are just outside." Without another word, he opened the door to his office and abandoned the admiral and archbishop, both figuratively and very much literally.

Daniel sipped on a lovely cup of tea and kept his shoulders high and tall. He'd weathered a battering from the chancellor and even stood toe-to-toe with an admiral, and he had come away unscathed—a fact that he had just revealed to the assistants surrounding him in the administrative building employee cafeteria. Most notable among them was, of course, Vanessa Renee Laurent Aimee Vaillancourt, a beautiful new assistant this semester working with professors of rigorous debate. Daniel had met Vanessa accidentally. He'd knocked over her morning coffee on his way to some errand for the chancellor ... which allowed him the excuse of buying her a fresh cup a few days later.

"Tell us again, Daniel. Did the admiral really thank you by name?" Vanessa said.

"As did the archbishop?" added Ryan, another assistant.

Daniel let the moment linger for just a tad longer than it should. He sipped his tea, winked at Vanessa, and nodded. "She did, indeed."

"That's quite impressive, really. I've heard she never speaks to underlings like us," Ryan said.

Three other assistants in the room hovered over the table, all of them staring at Daniel, their eyes filled with admiration and awe. That suited him just fine. Assistants didn't often get to have any glory at the university. Most students despised them for being the bearers of hard tests and poor grades, and all the faculty used them as gofers and servants. So, why not take a little pride in such a small thing as delivering a letter? Daniel couldn't muster a tall tale as large as being of any actual use in a meeting as important as the one he had just come from, but he could at the very least claim to have received a modicum of respect from the highest of ranks. And that was more than enough glory for the assistants of the university to dote on for a full semester, at the least.

"There's a party tonight at the Dunhill Fraternity, for graduate students. Are you coming, Daniel?" Vanessa asked.

Daniel practically beamed. He had asked Vanessa out on multiple occasions, only to be toyed with, like a cat playing with a soon-to-be-dead mouse. And now here she was, inviting him to a party. Oh, how the tables turned when a little glory landed in one's lap. Never underestimate the effect of bragging rights, after all.

"I would love—"

Then the door to the assistants' dining room crashed open, and the chancellor stormed inside. He clutched a table to prevent himself from falling and took several large, full breaths before speaking. His face was quite flushed, which caused Daniel to look for a clock on the wall to check the time. He was sure scotch didn't start until after lunch.

"Out! All of you, out! Except you, Daniel."

The other assistants, whose faces had gone from admiration of Daniel to utter shock and fear, nodded and moved to leave as quickly and quietly as they could. No one made eye contact with the chancellor for fear of being ended on the spot, which he did with impunity and a little too much frequency—especially after lunch.

"Daniel. We have a problem," the chancellor said after the room had been vacated.

"Is the delegation from the Democracy still voting on lunch?"

"What? No. They settled on the roast chicken. A fine choice."

Daniel's heart jumped in his chest, and he grabbed the corners of his chair. Had the chancellor heard him bragging? Lesser offenses had sent assistants packing their bags, doomed to teach remedial grammar in some distant corner of the Riverlands. And possibly even in the interior—a thought that made Daniel's blood turn cold.

"Well, what's the problem, then, sir?"

"It's the expedition."

"Oh, thank goodness!"

"*What* did you say?"

Daniel squirmed in his chair. "I mean, thank goodness you came to me, so I can help you correct the matter, Chancellor."

Chancellor Dunningham huffed. "Whatever. Come with me. We have to get to the rainbow crow's nests."

Daniel's head lowered, and his shoulders sank.

"What is it?"

"I haven't finished my lunch, sir."

"Bring it, then! The entire university's reputation is at stake!"

Daniel nodded, grabbed his food, and hurried after the chancellor. Together, they ran through the winding corridors of the administrative building and up several flights of stairs. They rounded a corner and then two more before coming to a locked door, which the chancellor hastily unlocked with his master key. Once inside, he relocked the door and threw down the wooden bar to ensure that no one could gain entry.

"Our professors are in great danger," Chancellor Dunningham announced.

"Well, didn't we know that when they went to Dressa? I mean, I do recall that being mentioned quite a few times..."

"Yes, indeed. But now they are in *extra* great danger."

"Extra great danger?"

"Yes. Very much so. Very much extra, and very much great."

"Sounds extra dangerous, I suppose," he offered uncertainly.

The chancellor turned and eyed Daniel hard. "Don't be sarcastic, now, Daniel."

"No, of course not, sir."

Dunningham led them up a final flight of stairs to the roost where the messenger crows lived. The birds were magical creatures, smuggled here through subterfuge and no small sum of gold coins. These creatures were secret to all but the highest ranks at the university. Of course, most of the senior assistants knew of them; rumors were always terribly hard to control. Dunningham bringing Daniel up here was a bit of a promotion, without actually being a promotion, but the events clearly called for drastic actions. At least, that's what Daniel imagined.

Despite their mundane surroundings, the magical birds had retained their unique properties, most notably their bright plumage of every color of the rainbow. The cages were filled with birds with wings of sapphire, crimson, and violet. Beaks of yellow plucked at the doors to their cages, while iridescent green feet clutched their perches. These birds knew how to fly to one location and that was the one place Dunningham's professors were traveling to in the next few days. And the fact that the birds could travel a thousand miles in mere hours, another benefit of their pure magic nature, made them beyond useful. Word should reach Hogkarta before Jonathan and William drank their first ale in the city.

"Why are we here, Chancellor?"

"We have to send a message."

"Yes, that much I gathered. Has something happened to Jonathan and William?"

"Who's William?" The chancellor stopped and cocked his head to the side.

"The linguist."

"Oh, him. Yes, both are in danger. Apparently, the journey to Dressa wasn't without its surprises. There was an attack on Oyster Piers, and the professors are being blamed."

"What? Neither of them knows how to hold a sword, let alone lead an attack!"

Chancellor Dunningham nodded. "Yes, I'm aware." He led Daniel through the roost to another locked door on the far side. Again, he opened it with his master key and walked inside.

"Is this a storage closet?" Daniel asked, his tone full of uncertainty.

"Hardly. There are things I keep even from you, Daniel. We have to get word to Jonathan, and quickly. They are already in Dressa."

"Oh. I see. Well, we have an outpost a few miles from Oyster Piers."

Dunningham shook his head and waved Daniel into the small space. In a row of cages, five of the rainbow-colored birds squawked as the two entered. Though Daniel had indeed heard of the magical messenger crows, he had never seen them before. They were incredible to behold. Their feathers were rainbow-colored, with dots of what looked like diamonds in the bands.

"Last year, in secrecy, I sent one of our professors to Dressa to start an outpost campus. The archbishop himself, Santos, formally requested the outpost and asked for Samson to lead it personally. Quite the honor, I have to say."

"In Dressa?" Daniel's shock filled every syllable.

"Yes. Didn't I just say that? Anyway, it worked. Well, it *is* working. Samson has several students enrolled and has even asked for additional resources. At any rate, he's able to communicate with us with these."

"Rainbow ravens?"

"Yes, quite. Except aren't they crows...? Well, whatever. They fly fast—very fast. We need to get a message to Samson that Jonathan is in trouble."

"And William?"

"Yes, of course, the linguist as well."

"I can't believe we've set up a university campus in Dressa!"

"We have. With substantial support from the church, of course. But don't speak if it. It's top secret. We must make sure it's successful. So far, Samson has kept it quiet, even from most of the locals. He's billing himself as the foremost authority on magical forces in Hogkarta."

"And the church is okay with that?"

Dunningham looked at Daniel and tilted his head to one side. "That's quite a good point. You know, I've never thought it through. The church is the foremost authority on magical forces in Hogkarta. That's their selling point, really. Why would they allow Samson to claim it?" He shook his head. "No, no time to think about that now. It doesn't matter, Daniel. Ignore that. It's not important. We must get word to Samson."

"I see. Yes, sir. Do you need my help crafting the message? Deciding how best to describe the danger? Should we include any coded ciphers to fool anyone who should find it?" Daniel could feel his chest bulge. If him being given respect by his betters had garnered affection from the other assistants—most notably Vanessa—how much would actually helping the chancellor in his direst hour do for him? Of course, in telling them, Daniel would have to say nothing about the secret parts, but he felt he could handle that trick. Especially since the core of it would be true.

"What? Help me craft the message? No, you imbecile! I need you to write while I dictate, attach the message, and send it. My hands are too shaky from the events of moments ago."

"Are you sure that's not from the afternoon scotch, sir?"

Dunningham shook his head. "No, that only happens after three."

Daniel's shoulders slumped, and he nodded. Of course; the chancellor could barely write his own name after three. And frankly, it was mostly downhill for the day from there.

"Are you ready, boy? I don't have all day to sit here with you."

Daniel pulled out his pen and parchment, equipment he always had at the ready in case the chancellor required a spontaneous dictation. "Ready, sir."

"Right. 'Samson, comma, there is—"

"You don't need to say when to input the commas, sir."

"What? Are you certain?"

"Very much so, sir. One of my degrees is in grammar."

"Like the linguist?"

Daniel did his best not to sigh. It was frightening how poorly the chancellor understood the schools of his own university. "Not quite."

"Whatever. Begin again, and scratch the word 'comma' out."

Daniel had, of course, never written it down. "Done, sir."

"Right. 'Samson, distressing news. Two of your fellows, Jonathan Braxton and…" He waved his hand in the air.

Daniel knew the gesture well. He dutifully wrote William's name next to Jonathan's.

The chancellor nodded. "'... are in Dressa on a research mission. The religious fanatics and our own military intend to do them great harm. Warn them to avoid both. Use your contacts, resources, and as much university funds as needed. Save your fellows.' Done. Don't write that last word."

Daniel nodded. "Very good, sir."

"Now, fetch one of those rainbow birds."

Daniel curled up the note into a tight tube and opened one of the bird cages. He unceremoniously grabbed one colorful bird and opened a window in the storage closet roost. He started to attach the note, but the chancellor barked at him to stop.

"Wait, you daft boy! You have to say the word."

"What word, sir? I thought you could just throw them out the window, what with their wings and all..."

"No, these birds only fly fast if you say the magic word."

"Magic word? I thought magic words didn't work outside of Dressa. I mean, I know the birds are magical, but I didn't think you had to cast a spell." Daniel's face went pale. "Are we casting a spell?"

"No, we are not. We're telling the birds to go home. And stop thinking so much, Daniel. I do not keep you around for you to incessantly think," the chancellor snapped.

Daniel didn't think his shoulders could slump any lower. Yet they did that very thing.

"Magic isn't here, but creatures touched by magic can exist outside of Dressa. These birds were touched by magic, and it changed them forever. They can fly all over the world. Now, you have to hold the bird, just as you are, and say this word." Chancellor Dunningham handed a small piece of paper to Daniel. "The bird will then fly directly to Samson in Dressa at great speed. He may very well receive this message within the hour."

Daniel took the piece of paper, but didn't recognize the word. "What word is this?"

"What? I don't know, Daniel. Just say it."

"But it's not a word."

Chancellor Dunningham huffed, which caused him to enter a brief bout of coughing. "Just sound it out, man!"

Daniel looked at the letters written on the note. They did not form any kind of word that he had ever encountered. He recognized each individual letter, but could not fit them together in his mind in any reasonable way. Fortunately, beneath the word was a phonetic spelling of how the word should sound. William had showed Daniel the technique once, for use with those really long words that no one liked using.

Daniel sounded out the syllables as best he could. *"Doudony...?"*

The bird in his hand cawed twice, then bit his finger, and he released it at once. In a whirl of vibrant colors, the crow rose to the window and darted out into the sky in a flash of red and blue light.

"Well done."

Daniel smiled, raised his hand—and realized the message that the chancellor had just dictated to him was still held in his fingers.

The chancellor looked at the message, then at Daniel, and finally at the remaining birds in the rainbow crow coop.

"Do I need to speak at this moment?" Chancellor Dunningham growled.

Daniel's hands shivered with fear. He took a deep breath, grabbed a new crow, attached the message, and said the word again. The second crow cawed loudly, bit his hand like the first, and flew to the window. In another blinding flash of color, the bird disappeared in an instant into the overcast sky.

"Excellent. Perhaps I can be saved from this fiasco after all."

"You, sir? You mean Jonathan and William?"

"What? Oh, yes, of course. Both will be safe now. Good work, Daniel. Despite the lost bird... But no matter, I'm sure Samson will send another."

Daniel breathed out a quiet, slow breath of relief. At least he had gotten out of this chaotic encounter mostly unscathed.

He tilted his head to one side as the name on the dictated message suddenly jarred something loose in his mind. He remembered Samson: the previous chief magilurgist of the university. The one Jonathan had replaced. Daniel hadn't known that Samson had been directed to go to Dressa to lead a new outpost of the university. He smiled at the honor given to Samson. Though he had never really liked the man much, Daniel wished him well.

"Doesn't Samson hate Jonathan? Considering that the latter took over the former's role at the university?" Daniel asked.

The chancellor tilted his head as Daniel did and let out a loud grunt. He let out two more grunts in thought and finally shrugged. "I'm sure it will be fine."

ARCHBISHOP PHILIP SANTOS left the chancellor's office and walked through the hallways of the great university. He twisted a ring on his finger, one of the many magical artifacts the Church of the True Religionists possessed. The church had many such artifacts, talismans more ancient than the world itself, each with unique miraculous abilities, created eons ago. Although magic—the casting of spells—only worked within the borders of Dressa Moore, growing more potent the nearer one came to the Wizard and Dragon at the source, such magical artifacts, as well as the abilities of magical creatures, worked anywhere in the world.

A shimmering energy surged around Archbishop Santos. The spell imbued in the ring granted him an aura of invisibility. It wasn't quite the same as the magic of the bracelet he wore, which allowed him to merge with shadows, but the result was similar. Santos weaved his way among students who couldn't see him, bumping into elbows and slamming himself against a wall. But at least this way he didn't have to bother with them asking him about Dressa, which was always a bother. Santos ducked into his office and closed the door, to the shock of a student standing in the hallway who was sure no one had entered.

"What a mess," Santos said. "Years of work, ruined in an instant. What was the purpose of partnering with the empire if the empire was going to pursue them anyway?"

All the plans Santos had spent years developing were unraveling in his mind. For the gods to be free, the professors would need to travel unhindered to Dressa and cast a spell at the foot of the Wizard. Of that, he was certain. But now that mission was in jeopardy, which meant Santos himself would have to travel to Dressa and ensure its success—a task he did not look forward to, as he already had tickets to the School of Comedic Thought's next show.

Santos shrugged. "Perhaps I can make it back in time to fix this." He went to his desk and opened a drawer. Inside sat a crystal cube engraved with runic symbols, attached to a silver chain. The crystal was nearly identical to another that

Santos wore around his neck. The crystals were part of an ancient artifact that a junior priest had accidentally shattered into a dozen pieces while cleaning the rectory in a small church on a lonely street on the far side of Hogkarta. No one in the church at the time had known the secrets of that artifact. Only after it was shattered (and the junior priest demoted to church congregant) was it discovered that the shards could do two miraculous things. First, by simply holding one of the crystal shards, the bearer could instantly send their voice to the location of any other shard, no matter where it resided. The second ability, it was soon discovered, was that this transfer between shards wasn't limited to voices. While holding a shard, if a person spoke the location of another shard, they could teleport to that location instantly. These magical talismans had become the bedrock of the church's influence around the world, allowing instant communication and effortless travel for high ranking-dignitaries, of which Santos was one.

Santos patted the crystal in his desk twice and left it where it sat. He locked the drawer and pulled it to make sure it was secure. If anything were to happen to the crystal he left in this room, Santos wouldn't be able to use the one around his neck to travel back here. He knew he should return it to the church here in Swanville, but for the past year, Santos's business had been here at the university. Besides, purview over the crystals had been his for quite a few years now, Santos being the one who had discovered their unique properties.

From a table behind his desk, Santos grabbed his OUT OF OFFICE sign. After he'd placed it on his door, shooing away a curious student, he went to the center of his temporary office at the university and clutched the crystal around his neck.

"To Dressa," Santos intoned.

The ceiling blossomed with a rainbow of lights, shifting and swirling and dancing around the room. Santos's skin became translucent, his entire body merging with the patterns of the rainbows racing around him. In a flash, he'd joined the swirling colors. As one, the river of lights dived into the crystal cube that now hovered alone in the room. Then with a sharp crack, the lights, Santos, and the crystal vanished.

CHAPTER FIVE

Samson Oswald Sutter III sat at his desk, reviewing the submissions from the town's latest group of university hopefuls. Of course, he wouldn't call them that. They were just academic students, riffraff from Hogkarta that didn't deserve to set foot on the university's grounds. Still, every credit they earned was a valid credit at the Great University of Learning and Knowledge and moved them one step closer to a degree. What they would go on to do with said degree—given that the university's presence in Dressa was minor, and no such degree could actually be issued in Hogkarta—was no concern of Samson's. If the locals wanted their degrees, they would have to trek a thousand miles to Swanville. Why would anyone do such a thing? Perhaps for bragging rights.

Three more papers into his stack of fifteen, Samson took a little break to have a cup of ginseng tea. Being from Dressa, it was a special cup of tea in that it not only quenched one's thirst, but also made the world smell like cinnamon and cherry, which Samson thought was a nice touch.

Just as he was about to dive back into his grading, a rainbow-colored crow flew through his window at an astonishing speed, lodging itself beak-first into the wood siding of his office. As Samson wasn't expecting any correspondence from the chancellor until next month, he approached the bird with curiosity piqued.

"What, no message?" Samson sighed. "Is it lunchtime at the university already?"

Moments later, another rainbow crow burst into his office, this time nearly impaling his arm. Fortunately, with his reflexes sharpened by the tea—another unusual benefit of the magical herb—Samson dodged without so much as a scratch.

"Definitely after lunch," he said with a smile. Samson walked over to both birds, made sure they were both unharmed, and detached the message tube from the second bird's neck. He then went back to his desk and sat.

The note was only a brief paragraph, but it carried weight. Jonathan Braxton was coming to Dressa. The implications were staggering. Jonathan, the very person who had replaced Samson at the university in Swanville, was coming here to do research in what was now Samson's backyard.

"Jonathan is here doing research into magilurgy?" Samson reread the note three times before crumpling it into a ball and throwing into the wastebasket. He then quickly retrieved it, unfurled it, and reread it yet again, before finally cutting it into tiny pieces and setting it on fire. Without thinking, he whispered a word of magic, and the flames leapt from the burning paper and did a spin, two tumbles, and a pirouette in midair before disappearing into a puff of smoke.

"Jonathan!" Samson downed his tea, then stuffed an ample portion of snuff into his nose to block out the smell of cherries. Jonathan had previously been his assistant for nearly four years, and now it seemed he was tasked with doing important research on the very source of magilurgical matters in the heart of Dressa, while Samson remained in this godforsaken outpost under the thumb of the church.

"The gall. The unmitigated gall!" Samson roared. He stood forcibly from his desk and walked over to the window overlooking a major thoroughfare of Hogkarta. It was Samson who had convinced the board and the chancellor to take this chance of establishing a school here, with prodding and support from Archbishop Santos. It was Samson who had created new territories, forged new alliances, and established a bond between the True Religionists and the Hogkarta government. Granted, the locals didn't know of Samson's affiliation with the university, but that was trivial —a deliberate oversight so he could entrench himself in the hearts of the leadership here. And now Jonathan was to just swoop in and claim all the credit for himself? Would he be made chair of the Magilurgical School of Thought as well?

"Scandalous!" Samson shook his head and tried his best to quiet his nerves. What else did that note from Dunningham say? Did the old fool say the admiralty and the True Religionists were a danger? And why would that be? No, something seemed off to Samson. The note had clearly been written in haste; that was why the drunken chancellor had botched the sending of the first crow. That meant there was a far greater likelihood that the chancellor's own skin was on the line—a fact that suited Samson just fine.

He could just ignore the note, of course. Let whatever happened to Jonathan be his fate. But that would leave things to chance—always a fool's choice. If Jonathan was here to research the source, that meant he must travel to the

Wizard and the Dragon. And that was a danger to Dressa Moore—possibly to the entire world.

A plan unfolded in Samson's mind. His needs were really quite simple. He needed to placate the chancellor and stop Jonathan from getting anywhere near the source, and by so doing, save Jonathan from the admiralty and the True Religionists. If he could also manage to claim some fame for the university's campus in Dressa, then he would win in every respect.

And as it just so happened, he was friendly with Hogkarta's chief administrator. Who else had more to fear from disturbing the Wizard and Dragon than Hogkarta itself? The last time anything had happened with those two magical beings two decades ago, with a mere puff of smoke emitted from the Dragon's nostrils, an entire island was reduced to a mob of undead beasts, ravenous to feed upon the flesh of the living. Yes, that would be enough to send shivers down even the iciest of spines.

Without another thought on the matter, Samson gathered his things, graded all of his remaining papers with a C, and ran out of his office to find the chief administrator of Hogkarta. He must inform him of the disastrous impending doom.

SAMSON KNOCKED TWICE on the door of Alfred Streckenbach, chief administrator of Hogkarta. The rustling of papers and moving of furniture sounded from behind the door. Samson heard the distinct voices of both Alfred Streckenbach and Ludwig Schmitt, assistant to the administrator. Normally, citizens of Hogkarta couldn't just waltz their way through town hall and demand an audience with the administrator. But considering how much the Great University had donated to Hogkarta, Samson had greater access than most—which, today, was especially important.

The door opened with a groan. Ludwig smiled wide and held out his arm for Samson to enter. A large wooden desk sat against the far wall of the office of the administrator. Sunlight filled the room from ample stately windows. Paintings depicting historical events of Hogkarta lined the walls. Samson recognized several battles fought between the citizens and the old kingdom centuries ago. Small tables lined the walls of the grand room, which sprawled to take up the entire corner of the third floor of town hall. Bottles of various multicolored liquids, which Samson assumed were alcohol or magohol, covered the tables.

"Well, Mr. Sutter, can I get you something to drink? Perhaps a spot of the licorice root?" the administrator offered.

"No, I'm fine. Thank you for seeing me on such short notice."

Alfred smiled. "Yes, certainly, anything for a donor of your esteem."

"Indeed," Samson said with a tight smile. "We're happy to donate to the city."

"Oh, yes, yes, greases the wheels, so to speak," the administrator said. "I mean, it's not a bribe, of course, but, well ... perhaps close."

Ludwig cleared his throat and shook his head.

Samson tilted his head to one side. "I'm sorry...?"

"I mean, I have thought of limiting donation sources. Of course, limiting incoming funds isn't exactly a popular topic to bring up at party lunches." Alfred laughed once and continued. "Frankly, the other side would never agree. But that benefits you, doesn't it? Now then, what can I do for you?" Alfred raised his eyebrows, imploring Sutter to get on with it.

Samson sat there for a moment with his mouth agape. He looked at Ludwig and then back at the administrator. Shaking his head, he dismissed the administrator's weird rambling and cleared his throat. "So, two of my colleagues have just arrived in Dressa. And they mean—"

"There's two more of you?" Alfred interrupted.

"Well, yes, two more professors."

Alfred nodded slowly. "How big of a school are you planning, exactly? I mean, it's all well and good if you're teaching comedic thought. But isn't your specialty magery?"

"It is indeed." Samson adjusted himself in the chair. He did detest coming here. Dealing with the administrator was always such a chore.

"Well—and I mean this in the nicest of ways—I'm not sure we need a small army of any more mages running about. It was bad enough when one of the school children discovered a new spell that causes pigs to float. Do you have any idea how sad they were?" Administrator Streckenbach fumbled around his desk for something, didn't find it, and gave up.

"The children?"

Streckenbach looked at Samson as if he were mad. "No, the pigs! They have no concept of floating. Completely unnatural."

Samson nodded in understanding—and wished he hadn't. "I can imagine that they were very confused."

"Precisely. The butcher had a terrible time getting them back. A special net had to be made." Streckenbach looked at Ludwig. "Isn't that right?"

Ludwig nodded dutifully. "Yes, Administrator."

"I can assure you, Administrator Streckenbach, that at the school in Dressa, we aren't teaching spell work."

"What are you teaching, then?"

"Magical theory," Sutter said.

Alfred looked at Ludwig, who only shrugged and then looked back at the teacher. "What's the difference?"

"It's ... complicated. But it doesn't matter—"

"Tell that to the butcher and his pigs."

"—the larger point is, more of my colleagues have arrived. They aim to do magilurgical research."

Streckenbach shook his head and started to brood. "I really don't think there's a market for teaching magilurgical research in Hogkarta, Professor."

"They aren't here to teach, Administrator."

"You said they're your colleagues. What else do the colleagues of professors do but teach?"

Sutter sat back in his chair and let out a breath. "Well, yes, that's right, they are from the Great University."

Alfred shook his head and rubbed his temples. "I'm confused, Professor Sutter. Isn't that what you called your school? The Great University of Dressa Moore?"

"Yes, well... No, but... I mean our school here in Hogkarta does intend to become a university."

"I thought you were already a university?"

"Well, no, not yet, but ... in time. And we're actually part of another university. A much larger one."

"I'm sorry... So, you're not a university, but you want to become one, and in fact you are already part of one? And I rather doubt that you are part of another university, Professor. Hogkarta isn't that big. I would have noticed another university somewhere on our island."

"No, Administrator." Samson pinched his leg to hold back his frustration. "The Great University of Learning and

Knowledge is in the Riverlands, not in Dressa. There are hundreds of faculty, thousands of students."

Alfred leaned back in his chair and nodded his approval. "Well, that's impressive. Yes, I know about the Gulk in the Riverlands. But I thought you were making your own university here in Hogkarta?"

"The school here in Hogkarta is an outpost campus. So we can bring the education of the Great University here."

Streckenbach's eyes shot up, and he leaned forward. "Is that right, then? Like the School of Comedic Thought?"

Sutter nodded.

"And the School of Gastronomical Science?"

"That as well."

Streckenbach practically beamed. "I had the honor of visiting both one summer in my youth." He leaned back in his chair and smiled to Ludwig. "A mastery of song, a delight of the palate, a wonder of merriment... Ludwig, my good man, even you might have cracked a smile."

"Indeed," Ludwig said, without so much as a twitch of his mouth.

"Well, this conversation is going far better than I could have hoped. I had thought you, Professor Sutter, nothing but a shyster, like those men who run after healing carts with promises of compensation for their injury. But I believe you're not!"

"... Thank you?" Samson said.

"I can see an entire section of Hogkarta devoted to the higher studies. Why, we could become the central hub of fine dining and comedic pursuits in all of Dressa Moore. Oh, yes, this has possibilities..."

"Right," Samson said.

Streckenbach sat forward in his chair and gave Samson a proper nod. "Well, this changes things, I think. What do you need, my good sir? Shall we dispatch some of our vessels to your two colleagues to assist? Will they need provisions? Where are they going in Dressa?" Streckenbach again fumbled across his table. Ludwig took a quick step to hand Streckenbach a piece of parchment, an inkwell, and a pen.

Samson nodded. Then he shook his head. He held up his hands and silently cursed. How had this conversation gone so wrong? "Oh, no. My apologies... I don't want you to *help* them. I want you to stop them."

"I'm sorry, what?" The administrator's face flipped from joy to confusion.

"What they are researching is dangerous. You see, my former apprentice is going to the source of magic, and he wants to conduct research and experiments."

"The source?!" Ludwig sputtered, boring his eyes into Samson.

Samson looked up at Ludwig. Something about the man scared Samson to his core. Ludwig was fiercely intelligent, and diligent to the point of mental illness. Every single document was always in triplicate, and sometimes a fourth copy was made "just to have it."

Samson nodded and tried to smile. "Yes, the source. To the Wizard and the Dragon themselves."

Ludwig nodded once, but didn't speak.

"Well, we certainly can't help them with that," Streckenbach said. "The only safe passage to get anywhere near the Wizard is through the Insanity Cliffs, at least by boat. I suppose they could venture overland, but that is some rough travel indeed. And the magic is as thick as soup there. You don't want to go stepping in magic that rich! My cousin did once, and his leg turned into a wheel. It wasn't as helpful as it sounds."

"But you could stop them from getting to the cliffs?" Samson said.

"Oh, no need. The Anti-Religionists control the passage, and they hate everyone. They just hate the True Religionists even more."

"This could be quite dangerous. If they get close to the Wizard... Well, may I remind you of what happened on Bedrich Island?" Samson said.

Streckenbach nodded slowly. "I see your point." He looked up at Ludwig, who nodded in reply.

"Thank you for your time, Professor Sutter," Ludwig said. "I can assure you that the administrator and the council will take up this matter with the utmost urgency." He moved to help Samson up from his chair and direct him towards the door.

"I can assist, if you need. I can—"

"No need at all, kind sir. We shall manage." Ludwig's face became set in a smile that promised anything but joy to anyone who got in his way.

Samson gulped and nodded, then stood and headed for the door. Ludwig put his hand lightly on Samson's shoulder, at which he shuddered. Did Ludwig have some kind of intimidation spell at work? Or was the man just naturally that intimidating?

The door slammed behind him as Samson exited into the hallway. Something had set them off.

Samson turned in a fast circle. Seeing no one, he then cast a hearing spell on the closed door. Sounds from the room beyond grew. He cast another spell to reduce the sound. He then cast a third spell to direct the sounds to his ears only. The hearing spells were one of Samson's prizes. He'd discovered them in a used tea ware shop on the far side of Hogkarta when he first arrived.

"Thank god that's over," Administrator Streckenbach's voice sounded in Samson's ear. *"But I must say, having the Schools of Comedic Thought and Gastro Sciences in Hogkarta would be thrilling. Thrilling! The fine dining would be astounding. And our current comedians are horrid. Who on earth would think throwing a perfectly good pie into someone's face is funny? Don't you agree, Ludwig?"*

Ludwig didn't answer.

"My stomach just grumbled. Can you order some bread, or perhaps a lamb chop? I believe I have time before the next meeting," Streckenbach said.

Ludwig sighed with enough force that Samson could hear his chest deflate. *"I believe the professor is correct, Alfred."*

"Is he, now? About what?"

Samson heard the distinct sound of feet walking towards a window. Eventually, they would wonder why he hadn't left the building. But Samson would have to risk it. He needed to know where these two stood.

"We can't let the professors reach the source of magic."

"I thought we'd covered this? The Anti-Religionists will do the job. If they aren't worshiping that fool hamster of theirs." Streckenbach snickered.

"I believe it's a guinea pig, sir."

"Is it?"

"Indeed. However, perhaps we can stop them before they reach the Anti-Religionists."

"Why expend the energy?" Streckenbach said. *"Even if they do manage to reach the Wizard and the Dragon, and even if they do manage to do something monumentally stupid, Hogkarta is surrounded by the magical dams. That's what has protected us from magical forces for a hundred years. We'll be fine."*

A long pause filled the room. Footfalls sounded with a clop on the hardwood floors. *"I don't know that I share your* certainty. *I do feel it is in our best interest to stop them, Alfred,"* Ludwig said.

"Are you sure?"

"Yes, I am. What if what happened to Bedrich twenty years ago happens again? To another of the many islands in Dressa Moore? Or if the magic spills out to the Riverlands below? Or the kingdom over the cliffs...?"

Streckenbach sighed. *"Fine. Call the constables. We'll have them sort this out."*

Samson yelped with glee. They were going to stop them! Success!

"What was that noise?!" Streckenbach said.

Samson snapped back to reality. Quickly dispelling the magic hearing spells, he sprinted down the hall and turned a corner just as Ludwig opened the door to Streckenbach's office. Samson held as still as a statue against the wall until he heard the door close. Letting out a long breath, he practically skipped his way out of the building, whistling a jaunty tune.

In the city of Hogkarta, deep within the floating lake of Dressa Moore, Archbishop Santos sat in his large wooden chair in his office in the great Church of the True Religionists. His magical crystal cube had deposited him next to his oak desk. The whirlwind trip always seemed to make his head wobble just a bit, but he shook off the feeling. Now was not the time to succumb to weakness. Now was the time to act.

Santos lifted the cube around his neck into the air. The crystal flashed with a multicolored light, indicating that someone wished to communicate with him. Santos lifted the large crystal toward the sky and beseeched the gods to grant him the message.

A white light grew in the center of the crystal, and the voice of a faraway member of the True Religionists Order of the Gods filled the room. Santos could *feel* the words as much as he heard their message. He immediately responded to the cardinal who had called him. After their conversation ended, Santos lowered the crystal and frowned.

"Was it Sylvia at the Anti-Religionists?" asked Bishop Renaldo Cupo, an aide to Archbishop Santos.

"No, it wasn't. A cardinal in Bragago—the church's outpost near Selvagr, the mountain home of the Gods—wished to speak with me."

"What did the cardinal want?"

Santos let out a frustrated sigh. He turned towards a window that overlooked Hogkarta below. Multistoried buildings filled the vista, some a thousand years old. On the horizon, mountains touched the sky. Lake Connell, just visible, glistened in the noonday sun, its surface hovering a mile above the landmass far below. "The cardinal wanted to speak to her mother."

"Not exactly a divine use of the gods' gift, is it?"

Santos shrugged. "It is for the church to decide how to use the gifts of the gods. Besides, what harm could it do? Her mother has been ill for weeks."

Bishop Renaldo nodded. "Of course, Your Grace." Walking over to a side table along the far wall near the door to the wider halls of the great church, Renaldo grabbed a pitcher of sweet tea and poured a glass for the archbishop. Santos's eyes lit up, and he took it greedily, sipping on the crisp nectar with the enthusiasm of a child.

"Oh, that's quite good. How I love sweet tea."

"Of course, Your Grace."

Santos walked over to a cushioned leather chair next to his bed and sat down. The dealings with the empire and the university made him terribly nervous. And now that things had gone wrong, the whole endeavor was in jeopardy. The whole matter had been the idea of the DemiGod of the church. Why did she need to hasten the gods' return in the first place? It was the church's mission to spread the word of the gods' imminent return, not to make it come faster. And yet, here they were, caught up in intrigues that the church simply had no business being involved with.

"Perhaps you should inquire with the DemiGod?" Bishop Renaldo suggested.

Archbishop Santos let out a gruff laugh. "And give that woman the pleasure? I think not."

"But we are to assist the professors once they reach Dressa."

Santos sat back in his chair, unsure of what to do. Even now, in this very moment, an imperial frigate was in the waters of Dressa Moore. For a moment, Santos forgot about the journey to the Wizard and thought about the implications of the empire sailing up the Aquirren River onto Lake Connell and into Dressa Moore at will. What if they failed, and the gods did not return? The only thing keeping the empire out was the rumors of the dangers of magic in Dressa and the dangers of being on Lake Connell. Granted, if a spell got out of hand, it certainly could wreak havoc. But on the whole, Hogkarta and Dressa was quite a safe place to live. People thrived in Dressa, as did the church. In fact, it was thanks to the generous donations of the citizens of Dressa that the church enjoyed its wealth and status. That wealth had allowed it to expand its influence throughout the Riverlands and into the interior. They had even established churches on the second continent, where not even the empire dared venture! But now the empire was in the church's backyard. And if they learned that their ships and soldiers could survive here just fine, it could change the very balance of power in Dressa Moore. Santos wondered why he had ever agreed to this.

The archbishop took a deep breath and calmed his nerves with a prayer to the goddess of calm and her fifteen sisters. Or was it fourteen...? He could never keep track.

"Summon the Order of the Magi."

Renaldo's face turned white. "The Magi?"

"Yes. Do it quickly. Things have gotten out of hand."

"Already? Haven't we just begun?" Renaldo protested.

"Yes, Renaldo. We've just started—and already, things are dire. Now, summon the Magi!"

"Most are with the cardinals, Your Grace."

Santos shot a look at the bishop. "What? Where?"

"Cardinal Rossi took a contingent on a pilgrimage to visit the DemiGod in her mountain retreat. She took with her a good number of the Magi."

"So, there's none left?" Santos spluttered.

Renaldo shrugged. "There are the reserves, of course, but they are, well ... reserved. For a reason, shall we say."

"I don't care, just summon them!"

Renaldo nodded once and ran from the room.

The only option now was to send a message to the empire. They had to know that Dressa was not welcoming to them, not safe. They had to believe in all the stories about Dressa—which was precisely why the Order of the Magi had been created. Santos would have to juggle carrying out the mission with the empire's help, and making sure they never came back here again to see the fruits of their endeavors.

CHAPTER SIX

William held onto a rope that was part of the rigging of *The Knotted Wood*. His eyes were wide open, and a smile larger than he'd ever felt spread across his face in astonishment. Below them, as far as the eye could see, Lake Connell of the great lakes of Dressa Moore stretched to the horizon as it floated nearly a mile above the ground. Sunlight that both shone through the nearly five-hundred-foot-deep lake and angled from the edges of the water illuminated green valleys and lush landscapes beneath the floating waters.

The university was, of course, filled with stories, paintings, and magical photographs of Lake Connell. One such painting, *The Travels of Juno the Jester*, a pioneer of the Comedic School of Thought, was William's favorite. It depicted Lake Connell floating gracefully over the lands of Dressa Moore, with Lake Ellise and Lake Branan both still attached firmly to the ground in the distance. Though he loved that painting, along with all the images of the magical lake he'd ever seen, no artist's rendering could do justice to the thrill of riding on waves that floated on an ocean of air. The sensation was a mix of awe and terror. *The Knotted Wood* should be crashing spectacularly to the earth on a waterfall of millions of gallons of Lake Connell. And yet, here they were, floating serenely on these enchanted waters.

"I still demand to know what happened to our original charter!" Jonathan's voice rose to dangerous octaves behind William.

"What does it matter? You're here now. I'm your charter, and I will take you wherever you wish to go. Just point. Yes?" Captain Bartolome said.

Jonathan let out a tight, angry sigh. "How would I know where to go?! First, we need replacement materials for the items lost. Second, it was our charter captain that knew the location! I know nothing of Dressa Moore!"

Bartolome shrugged.

A crewman, half his face rotten, his jawbone and teeth clearly visible through his greying skin, ambled by them with a low growl. A dozen more crewmates of *The Knotted Wood* tended to their sailor's duties with precision and focus. Something, William noted, had quite improved since they had arrived in Dressa.

"Not to mention, your entire crew is dead!" Jonathan cried.

"Undead," Bartolome corrected him. "And perfectly harmless to you."

"So you say..."

The entire crew stopped what they were doing and instantly turned to Jonathan. As one, they all let out a loud growl and stomped their feet on the wooden deck. Jonathan took a step back, away from Bartolome.

"*Exactly* as I say. I am their master. They obey me."

"How does that work, exactly?" William asked with genuine curiosity.

"Not now, William," Jonathan admonished.

William sighed. Jonathan's temper was the reason they'd broken up six months ago. Afterward, he said he'd spent the summer in therapy, sucking on stones and only looking at things that were pink. Despite that, whenever his anger got the best of him, Jonathan was as intolerable as ever.

Bartolome winked. "Look, it's quite simple. And all jests aside, I'm your charter captain now. I know where you're going and how to get there. And I'm the best captain in all of Dressa Moore, so relax. Yes? You have nothing to fear here."

"Then what happened in Oyster Piers?!" Jonathan's face turned to a mix of fear and anger. "I heard people screaming! Did you order them to do that? Seems the people who live there had plenty to fear!"

Bartolome lowered her gaze to the horizon and nodded slowly. "No. I didn't order them to attack anyone in Oyster Piers."

William watched her face and noticed the pain in her eyes. She meant it. Whatever had happened back at Oyster wasn't her doing. At least, not directly. William was sure of it. He'd seen that look many times—mostly when the school janitors had thrown away papers they had no business throwing away.

"Then what happened?" Jonathan demanded.

Bartolome let out a long breath. "The farther I am from Dressa, the less control I have over my crew. And then I was stabbed, causing me to lose my grip on a crew member. You deserve to know that much. But since we're staying in Dressa, where magic is plentiful, it won't happen again. I give you my word."

"Your word? The word of a pirate?" Jonathan spat.

"Stop it, Jonathan. We can trust her," William cut in.

Jonathan wheeled on William, and their eyes locked. "Can we? And you just *know* that, do you?"

A moment passed before Jonathan nodded once. He might have the temper of a two-year-old, but he trusted William's judgement. One of his most redeeming qualities, William thought.

"Fine. We trust you." Jonathan folded his arms and checked the lines of his suede early afternoon pre-dinner jacket.

"Excellent. Now, I believe you are bound for the source of all magic, correct?" Bartolome said.

"How did you know that?" Jonathan asked, his eyes squinting in suspicion.

Bartolome looked at Jonathan as if he were mad. "It's in the charter, Jonathan."

"Right. Of course, it would be. I see."

Bartolome turned back to the horizon. "We should be able to sail quite close. There's a lovely cove where we can drop anchor, and you can take in the source for as long as you like. Great view of the Dragon's wings."

"No, Captain. You must have misread the charter. We are going to the source. Directly *to* it. As in, I shall set foot on the ground," Jonathan insisted.

Bartolome took a step back and shook her head. "Are you mad?"

"Certainly not."

"Debatable," William interjected.

Jonathan shot him a glare.

"Come here. Next to your fellow." Bartolome took Jonathan by his arm and hauled him to the side of *The Knotted Wood*. She extended her arm over the side and pointed below. "Do you see that ground down there? If you set foot on that ground, you'll likely turn into a swarm of beetles. Do you understand? And even there, we're miles away from the Dragon and the Wizard. The magic from those two—what you call the source—is strongest on the ground. It spreads from them like waves on a pond, and it was strong enough to push this entire lake and these lands more than a mile up into the sky!"

"I can assure you, with my equipment, I can very much set foot near the source," Jonathan said. "However, you are quite right that I couldn't set foot directly below us, or anywhere else beneath the floating lake in Dressa. I can only set foot on a precise location, as determined by magilurgical principles."

"Magi... What?"

"He means he's calculated a spot where the magical forces from the Wizard and the Dragon cancel each other out," William explained.

"And you end up in a location with negative magic," Jonathan concluded.

Bartolome nodded slowly. William saw something flash in her eyes for a second. Then a smile darted across her face, as if the captain had heard something she quite approved of. William had seen such expressions at the university when one professor thought they'd gotten another one over a barrel. An icy chill ran up his spine when he wondered just what kind of barrel this captain would put them over.

"Well, you're wrong. There's no place in Dressa where magic doesn't work," Bartolome said firmly after a brief silence.

Jonathan smiled widely. "Oh, yes, I know. It would only be in a location close to the ground. Close to both of them. Very close."

"Perhaps a location stranger than the rest?" William suggested.

"William, please," Jonathan snapped.

"Just trying to help."

"Well, don't. This is serious science. 'Strange' means nothing."

William nodded and looked back out over the side of the ship. "Sorry, Jonathan."

Bartolome snorted a laugh. "Done, you two? And how would you get there, precisely? Down to the ground, I mean. We're over a mile in the air."

Jonathan shrugged. "You would lower me down, of course. That's what my equipment is for."

Her brows shot up. "Lowered over a mile? How?"

"Other interested parties have assured us that there is a location, a ravine or waterfall, where we can reach the surface. Just above the Dragon and Wizard."

Bartolome took a step forward and narrowed her eyes. "'Other interested parties'? You never mentioned other interested parties, and neither does the charter."

"Yes, well, we have sponsors for this expedition."

"And who might they be?"

Jonathan lifted his head in the air and crossed his arms. "Sorry, I can't reveal that. It's quite confidential."

"Oh, I'm going to have to insist." Bartolome's hand rested on her rapier hilt, and her face turned hard.

"The Religionists and the empire," William offered.

"William!"

"Oh, who cares, Jonathan? If that's what she needs to know to get us to your precious source, then so be it. The sooner this trip is over, the better."

Bartolome removed her hand, turned around, and walked away. She then stopped mid-deck, turned in a circle, and let out a stifled laugh. "The Religionists. And, I'm sorry —the *empire*? You realize they were the ones chasing us, right? None of this is mentioned in the charter."

"I can't speak to that," Jonathan replied. "At any rate, now you know. I can't imagine why this is of such concern to you. The True Religionists want us to succeed. Why shouldn't we go to them for help?"

Bartolome's stifled laugh turned into a thunderous roar. "*Help?* That lot wants only what benefits them! I expect once you've completed whatever it is you think you're doing, they will be done with you."

"That isn't the agreement as I understand it," Jonathan said.

"Oh, I'm quite certain there are a great deal of things you don't understand about what is happening here." Bartolome kicked wooden side of the ship and shook her head. "But fine. A charter is what is agreed upon, and a charter is what I shall provide. Doesn't matter, anyway. Hogkarta is the largest city in Dressa, on Lake Connell. If we are to replace your supplies, we'll have to do it there."

Jonathan nodded once. "Splendid."

"Now then, about my fee..."

"Fee?" Jonathan's eyes went wide. "What fee?"

Bartolome frowned. "My fee for bringing you to Dressa, of course."

Jonathan shrugged, then shook his head. Then he shrugged again. "It was paid. The church paid the barge captain to ferry us to the source of magic. I have no money for you."

Bartolome closed her eyes, then smiled. "Good on you, captain of the travel barge." She shrugged at Jonathan. "Well, my mistake for not pirating him quite enough. Still, I must be paid. Can't have rumors spreading that I'm in the business of doing favors for traveling professors. Next thing you know, I'll get a stream of you beggars. Can't have that."

Jonathan's face went red. "And how am I supposed to pay you?"

Bartolome shrugged. "More importantly, how are you supposed to pay for your replacement gear?"

"But you're the one who lost it!"

"Risk of traveling on the high seas, I'm afraid."

Jonathan huffed. Stomped the deck. Turned in a circle and put his hands on his hips. He checked the hem of his coat at the sleeve, and his collar just below the neck. After a good long time, he finally nodded. "Fine. We'll go to Samson, in Hogkarta. I can secure your funds there. The chancellor said to go to Samson if things went wrong, and I think this qualifies."

Bartolome clapped her hands together. "Excellent. We have an accord! Good thing we're already going to Hogkarta; cuts down on time at sea, yes?"

A bell rang out from below decks, and all the crew turned their heads at the sound. Captain Bartolome nodded once, and the crew, as orderly as any William had ever seen even on a military vessel, proceeded calmly to the lower decks.

"What does that bell mean?" Jonathan asked.

"Feeding time," Bartolome replied with a wink.

"Oh, good. I'm famished." Jonathan took one step forward, but William's hand landed on his shoulder and stopped him cold.

"And what exactly does your crew eat, Captain?" William asked.

Bartolome just smiled.

∾

COMMODORE WILKES STOOD on the bridge of *The Crimson Swan*, his jaw clenched tight, his hands sweating from the anticipation of what was to come. The ship sat less than a hundred yards from the rising falls of the Aquirren River, with the spray shooting upwards at a forty-five-degree angle. A mile above them, Lake Connell floated peacefully in the sky, as if it were meant to be there. As if the world, when it was created, had decided that a massive lake that defied the laws of gravity would be a splendid addition to the scenery.

"Are we sure about this?" Captain Bridgewater said.

Wilkes clenched and unclenched his hands behind his back a dozen times. Honestly, was he sure about this? Of course not. No part of his mind was sure of this. Imperial reports from Dressa were filled with stories of undead creatures, of ravenous fishermen, of magical tide pools that shifted and morphed with the daylight to create fantastical events, of blooming starfish flowers that crystalized and changed into fireflies. Snails the size of dogs. Cats with spiked tails. Birds that flew so fast they were a blur. Those stories and a hundred more that everyone from the Riverlands had known since childhood cycled through Wilkes's mind, and he could see the same stories dancing through the minds of the crew. The weight of those tales, half of which he knew to be true, filled him with dread, informing his rational mind that he was very much *not* sure about proceeding.

But he knew he must.

Lieutenant Swanson had taken his men, along with a handful of crew who didn't wish to go to Dressa, on a skiff to Oyster Piers to inform the admiralty of the commodore's decision. Wilkes knew the admiralty would support him— if, of course, he and his crew survived.

"Commodore? It's now or never. Sails are at quarter

mast. We can turn back now and beat the current, but any closer, and the Aquirren will take us into Dressa, with or without sails."

The commodore nodded. He walked to the edge of the bridge that overlooked the deck below. "A crime has been done to the empire, an attack by the most fiendish of means. And now, we shall bring these criminals to justice. Nowhere in the world can they hide, even in Dressa Moore. We go together. We go as one. For the empire!"

"For the empire!" the crew cheered as one.

"For the emperor!" Bridgewater said from behind the commodore.

"For the emperor!" the crew returned.

"Captain Bridgewater, raise sails."

The Crimson Swan turned to port and caught more of the current's pull flowing to the Aquirren River. Men and women were lashed to the deck throughout the ship. The angle they must take could easily send a crewmate overboard.

The ship lurched forward when the current hit the stern. In seconds, *The Swan* pitched upward from the bow, boards creaking under the alien strain, the sails even at quarter mast filled with the chaotic magical wind that blew along the Aquirren.

Shouts from the crew along the deck drew Wilkes's attention. Some were excited by the thrill of riding up the flowing falls of the river, while others were clearly terrified that their feet were leaving the earth while still on the deck of *The Swan.*

Over the edge of the ship, Wilkes watched the land retreat from him in such a way that he had only witnessed once before. Trees that towered to the sky soon became mere dots on the ground below. Behind them, Wilkes could see Oyster Piers in the distance. Moments later, the spirals of New Backbury, the capital city of this district, came into view. That city was nearly a hundred miles from Oyster Piers. Some part of Wilkes's brain strained under the impossibility of what he was witnessing. His military mind couldn't help but calculate the advantage any fleet would have from this height. They could see an armada coming before it even left port.

"Even more amazing than the first time," Wilkes said with awe in his voice.

"The mainmast is breaking!" someone screamed.

Wilkes looked up to see the mainmast cracking under the weight of gravity. Several crew members did their best to get to the sail to lower it, but the angle of the Swan prevented them from moving.

"We've got to lower that sail, or we'll lose the mast!" Bridgewater yelled over the roar of the wind and the river.

"Will it hold long enough to reach Dressa?" Wilkes yelled back.

As if in answer, a frightful tearing of canvas sounded above them. Seconds later, another sail ripped free of its tie-down and flapped in the mighty winds of the Aquirren falls. Ropes swung wildly over the deck. The torn sails ripped even faster with the added wind. Several smaller pieces of the rigging snapped under the strain.

"We'll lose the sails!" Bridgewater screamed. "I'm having a hard enough time steering in these currents. If we veer too much to port or starboard, we'll sail right off into the skies and plummet to the ground!"

Wilkes untied himself from the line tethering him to the deck and clawed his way to the starboard mast. Once there, without a second thought, he flipped himself onto the side of the ladder that leaned into their assent. Now gravity was working for him. He climbed upward towards the torn sail, and within seconds, he was able to secure the sail back down.

"Hold tight!" Bridgewater called.

Wilkes looked at the bow. The end of the falls was approaching frighteningly fast. He knew he couldn't make it back to the deck before they crested the rise, so he lashed himself to the sails, sending up a fervent prayer to the old gods that he'd make it through.

The mast continued to crack. If they didn't get out of these fierce winds soon, they'd lose the ability to sail home, let alone chase *The Knotted Wood* through Dressa.

Just as the thought crossed Wilkes's mind of becoming stranded in a dangerous land, the ship rose above the water, flung from the fast-moving current and carried by their sails at quarter mast. Wilkes could see *The Swan* hovering above not only the earth, nearly a mile below, but the waters of Lake Connell as well.

It was the longest thirty seconds of Wilkes's life as *The Swan* hung in midair. Eventually, the wooden vessel crashed back into the waters of Lake Connell. The crack in the mast grew, but the wood held fast. That meant they could limp to port—or even to the Alpine River, the sister river to the Aquirren that flowed downward toward the Riverlands—and back to Oyster Piers if they must.

Regardless, the commodore took a moment and thanked the old gods for his life. He rested on the wood of the mast high above the deck and closed his eyes. They'd made it.

At least, if you could call this making it.

JONATHAN RECOILED in terror at the macabre scene, while William stood his ground in shocked horror. Below deck, in the galley of *The Knotted Wood*, the undead crew of Captain Bartolome feasted on raw flesh. Nearly every crew member held a human limb in their hands and dug their teeth and nails into the meaty muscles. Thick red blood congealed at their feet and stained the floor a deep crimson. The reek of iron and butchered meat coated them in a sickening stench.

Jonathan scanned the undead, who all sat calmly at tables throughout the galley, and became mesmerized by the scene. Their flesh was regrowing before his eyes. With every bite the crew took of the severed limbs, some patch of decayed flesh replenished or regrew over the bone. Muscle grew in their jaws and on their arms. Their shoulders rose and their backs straightened with each bite.

"What in the name of goodness have we gotten ourselves into?" William whispered under his breath.

"Sacrifices," Jonathan declared. "We must make sacrifices. In life, and in death, for that which we want most."

"This is a bridge too far, Jonathan. How can we be party to this?"

"We aren't party to anything."

"We are complicit in murder! What do you think they feast upon?! It's men! Women! Children! We cannot—"

"Greetings!" Anton's voice cut through the air like a knife through meat chutney.

"Anton. Good day. We were just leaving," William said, taking a step backward.

"And we aren't at all hungry," Jonathan added, looking green.

Anton's face screwed into a wicked grin, and he lowered his head. "Are you certain? The menu is still fresh."

Neither Jonathan nor William spoke. Both held a look of

utter conviction that neither would survive the next few minutes. Jonathan's hand reached for William's, and they shared a moment together. It was perhaps the finest moment they had shared since coming to Dressa. With only a squeeze of their hands, both conveyed the true love at the heart of their recent arguments. Desires had become priorities, and priorities had become duties, and soon love had drifted beneath it all to become nothing but a fond memory of simpler times. That very thought and feeling leaped between them through the clasping of their hands. A lone tear fell down William's face, and somehow, without looking, Jonathan felt it fall. He turned to William and rested his forehead on his lover's.

"Oh, stop it, Anton. They're scared enough," Bartolome said.

Anton bellowed out a laugh and shrugged. "Have to have some fun every now and again, Mum. Strangers rarely get to see the crew eat."

William and Jonathan barely moved. Neither felt that the jesting was anything but a distraction. Soon the cleaver would fall, and their lives in this miserable world would end. They shared the quickest and most passionate of kisses that either of them had ever felt.

"You two want to go to your room?" Bartolome said, quirking an eyebrow.

Jonathan turned from William and eyed the captain with contempt. "Kill us. Or take us home. This instant. We want no part of this."

"Part of what?" Bartolome said with a shrug and a smile.

Jonathan turned and kept William behind him. He raised his hand and pointed at the limbs being feasted on by her crew. "Where did those come from? Are heads the next course? There must be thirty bodies that those belonged to when they were alive!"

Anton let out a stifled laugh. "Shall I?"

"Oh, please do."

"They're not eating limbs from the dead, lads. Or even from people."

"Sorry, how's that, then? They clearly *are* eating people," William said from behind Jonathan.

At that moment, both William's and Jonathan's eyes instinctively scrutinized Anton's body. He had two arms, both the left and the right, and no extras. However, he no longer had a full, bulbous stomach.

Following their gaze, Anton lifted his shirt and revealed small wounds all over his torso, as well as tiny bumps of flesh growing in other areas. He patted himself on the tummy and gave a wide, toothy grin. "We didn't kill a soul, lads. The crew are eating *me*."

CAPTAIN BARTOLOME SAT BACK in her chair in the captain's office and puffed on a pipe of tobacco. Jonathan sat in the chair opposite her desk, while William paced the back of the room. Both of them were a bit jarred, to say the least. It was certainly a macabre sight. But once the men understood what was happening, Bartolome hoped they would settle down.

"He's a *what*?" Jonathan said.

"A tree-man. Or maybe a man-tree? It's hard to explain... Part of the oddness of Dressa."

Jonathan shook his head in confusion. "You're telling me you didn't kill anyone?"

Bartolome took a long pull on her pipe and shook her

head. "Even though I am a master of the undead, and even though I'm a pirate, I do value human life. I never take one without good reason."

"And the limbs just grow from his torso?"

Bartolome nodded. "That's nothing. Anton is a few years away from planting himself. We'll pass through a grove on the way to the fjords, and then you'll see what I mean."

"The what?"

"Our eventual destination. Well, your original destination. The Madness Fjords. Or, as some call them, the Insanity Cliffs. I've never been, myself. It's controlled by the Anti-Religionist movement."

"The what?"

"Are you going to keep saying that? A splinter group from the True Religionists. They control the passage to the Madness Fjords. I suspect that's the location where the True Religionists want to send you. It makes the most sense. Through the straits, there's rumored to be a waterfall that touches the ground just near the Wizard."

"I take it the Anti-Religionists don't get along with the True Religionists?"

"Not in the slightest."

"Then how did they imagine we would get there?"

Bartolome let out a long plume of smoke and nodded. "There's a letter, in the charter. From the True Religionists to the Anti-Religionists. It's magically sealed, so I can't open it. But I'm sure it's some offer of gold or something to allow us to sail through the straits."

"Sorry—can we get back to the matter of your crew devouring human limbs?" William said. "I still don't understand what's happening."

She huffed. "They are Anton's *dead* limbs. They would

have fallen off anyway. He's not ready to plant. It's a perfect union: man-tree and undead crew. Get it now?"

William nodded and sat back in his chair.

Jonathan turned to William, who was still quite shaken from the grisly sight in the galley, then back to the captain. "Well, I suppose if you're not *murdering* anyone to feed your undead crew..."

"It happens. I can be quite ruthless if need be. But no, my crew does not routinely feast on the flesh of mortals."

Jonathan nodded and smiled weakly.

"All good, then? Ready to continue our journey? Best that you found out now, at any rate." She took a contemplative puff of her pipe. "Of course, to replace your gear, we'll need to travel to Hogkarta. A slight detour from the fjords. But as per our earlier conversation, we must go there to secure my fee, regardless. So, even though a stop in Hogkarta was not part of your original itinerary, we're adding it. But be warned, that city holds its own surprises and dangers. You're in Dressa now, gentlemen. Things are quite different here than in the rest of the world."

"Of course, Captain." Jonathan stood and took William by the arm, leading him to the door.

The poor linguist, if that was his title, had been really shaken since the galley—not that Bartolome really cared. How could she? This was her life. Both of the professors needed to trust her if they were to achieve their goal. Bartolome had given her word that she would see them to the end of their journey, and by the eight gods of wanderlust, and the three gods of lesser travels, she would. Everything depended on it.

Their goal was her goal after all. This would be the first visit to the Wizard and the Dragon in twenty years. The last time someone went there they'd cast a spell, created a magical quake and shook all of Dressa Moore to its core. She'd lost her island kingdom on that day and the dead rose from the ground. If Jonathan could set foot on the ground near the Wizard, then she could as well—or at least, she could cast the spell that would reverse what was done twenty years ago and allow her to go home. Maybe even let the dead rest. Not to mention curing Anton's people of the blight that had stricken them for the last twenty years.

All doubts over having pirated the barge captain of the original ship meant to take Jonathan and William into Dressa fled from Marta's mind. Truth be told, Bartolome hadn't even been sure if Jonathan was going to try to set foot on the same ground as the Wizard until he'd just confirmed it. Yes, Sylvia had suggested as much, but how could Marta have believed it? No one was stupid enough to try that—except Jonathan, it would seem. But now that it was confirmed, and this little folly of an adventure actually had a chance of making Marta's dreams come true, the world felt all the brighter.

Bartolome smiled. Things had started off terribly, but the winds had turned in her favor. Her thoughts turned to the poor souls of Oyster Piers. She had felt them—every one of them—turn when her crew bit them. She had felt their minds recoil in terror, and she felt each of them as they died and took on the false life of the undead. Bartolome took a long pull from a bottle of whiskey and shut her eyes as tight as she could. The pain from those poor souls would haunt her for the rest of her life. She hated that it had happened. She blamed herself for the whole event, even if she hadn't ordered it herself. *Casualties of war,* she told herself in a selfish desire to take the pain away. Of course, it never did.

"Well, we'd best get some rest. Come on, Jonathan," William said.

Jonathan nodded and rose without another word. Exhaustion finally taking hold of the man.

Bartolome's eyes followed the professors out of her cabin. She wondered if they'd both make it through what was to come. They would all find out soon enough. But again, she told herself, it didn't matter. With a shrug, she reached into her pocket and pulled out a finger from one of Anton's extra limbs. Then she plopped the pudgy digit into her mouth and gave it a good chew. The flesh was meaty and filled her with a calmness. She smiled as a tiny scratch on her hand healed as she swallowed.

From her desk drawer, she pulled out a large square stone and passed it back and forth in her hands. This stone, a magical artifact that could repeat phrases, was the key to her success. This was how she would sail back to her home island of Bedrich and reclaim her rightful place. Bartolome pressed the sides of the stone. Magical words flowed out of the repeating stone in reverse order. A neat trick Bartolome had learned a long time ago: if you wanted to undo a spell, you just said it back to front. Most of the time, that is. The particular spell this repeating stone always repeated was meaningless here. It would do nothing. But at the feet of the Wizard, where this same spell had been uttered once before in the proper order, this repeating stone could possibly do a great thing indeed. It could free Bedrich, end the curse of the undead, and heal Anton's people. And finally, Bartolome could go home.

COMMODORE WILKES WALKED across the deck of *The Crimson Swan,* helping the crew to their feet. On the other side of the ship, Bridgewater directed several crew members to strike the sails. *The Swan*, for the most part, seemed to miraculously have made the journey in one piece. Yes, the main mast was badly cracked, as well as some smaller pieces of wood above, but that was minor compared to how bad it could have been.

Wilkes joined the captain on the far side of the ship. "Captain."

"Commodore. In one piece?"

Wilkes nodded. "How is the crew?"

"Bruises and bang-ups here and there, but mostly fine."

Wilkes nodded, his eyes turning to the masts and rigging above. "Can we give chase?"

Bridgewater shook his head. "'Fraid not, Commodore. At least, not at speed. The aft sails are in tatters, and the mainmast is nearly snapped."

"How do we repair it out here?"

"Nathan in the crow's nest spotted what looked like a village when we crested the Aquirren into the air."

"A village?"

Bridgewater nodded. "So it would appear."

"I thought the only habitable place in all of Dressa was Hogkarta."

"That is what the True Religionists have told the empire —and our spies as well. Of course, most of our spies were supplied by the Religionists—perhaps something we should rethink now that we know there's more here. We've confirmed nothing that they've told us."

Commodore Wilkes frowned and nodded. "Very well. Let's see what it is."

Shouts from below deck sent the crew scrambling. The undead creature sent from Bartolome broke free from her bonds below deck and charged a crewman. She wrapped her hands around the man's neck and pulled him into a vicious bite.

"Stop her!" Commodore Wilkes screamed.

Bridgewater ran to the woman just as other crew members yanked her off and threw her to the deck. The captain drew his sword and lifted it to plunge it into the undead thing's head, but he was stopped by one of his own crew pulling on his arm.

"Don't need to do that, sir. She's not dangerous," the crewman said.

Wilkes marched over, his eyes holding a crazed look. "Not *dangerous*? Are you mad? The woman who sent this creature here is a mass murderer! She'll kill us all!"

The crewmate shrugged. "Don't think so, sir."

"What do you mean, man?" Bridgewater said, bewildered. "You'd best have a good reason for stopping me, or you'll be on double duty for a week!"

The man nodded, worry crossing his face more from his captain's scrutiny than the commodore's. He lifted the woman up from the deck and turned her so that she faced the captain and commodore. He then unceremoniously stuck his hand in the undead creature's mouth, turned to the captain, and smiled.

"Ain't got no teeth, sir."

The undead woman, who resembled Wilkes's wife, Abigail, gummed on the man's hand with frenetic desire, but never pierced his skin—which only made her chew on the crewman's hand even more. The crewmate let out a giggle at the sensation, then straightened his back at the captain's stare.

"Let me see your hand, son," Bridgewater said. He examined the crewman's hand, but could find no puncture nor wound. "Hold her. Open her mouth."

Several crew members grabbed onto the undead woman. The captain looked into her open mouth, but could only see smooth gums, rotting in a few places.

"Why would a mass murderer attack us with a harmless weapon?" Bridgewater turned to Wilkes and examined the commodore with scrutiny.

Wilkes seemed to pick up on the stares and steeled himself. "I wouldn't know, would I, Captain?" He turned and left the lower deck to reassume his place on the bridge.

PART II

DRESSA MOORE

CHAPTER SEVEN

Archbishop Santos walked down the long pier on the docks of Hogkarta. Bishop Renaldo and several of the Order of the Magi followed just a few steps behind. Ahead of them along the docks, the constables of Hogkarta, the foremost experts on matters of security and generalized law keeping, stood several feet away from Administrator Streckenbach and his assistant, Ludwig. Their presence made the archbishop's heart skip. The likelihood that Streckenbach and Ludwig were here for any other reason than the professors departing for the source of magic was extremely low. But how had Ludwig found out? Santos had long known that Ludwig ran Hogkarta. Regardless of who the administrator was, Ludwig was always there, pulling strings and directing the flow of power. Ludwig's spy network was well known. But did his reach extend all the way to the empire?

"We need to name the things, I think. It's past time we did so." Administrator Streckenbach's voice, loud and booming as always, carried over the wind as Santos approached.

Ludwig, standing next to Streckenbach, nodded.

"After all, having a clearly recognizable name that describes exactly what these people have become would be essential, especially if they are sending raiding parties throughout Dressa. It simply won't do to just call them 'the undead.' Undeadies...? No, that wouldn't do either. Creepers? No, that means something else..."

Archbishop Santos approached the contingent of constables and the administrator. He cleared his throat and pointed to the side where the Magi should stand. The last thing he wanted was for the Magi and the constables to get into a scuffle. Just last week, groups of both had launched a magical temper tantrum in the town center over who had bought the last of the sausages from the sausage vendor. It was one thing to have an argument in public; it was quite another to launch magical missiles at each other across a public square.

"Philip, good to see you," Administrator Streckenbach said as he turned towards Santos.

"I do wish you would use my title in public, Alfred."

The administrator smiled. "Oh, yes, of course—*Archbishop*." He threw in a nod of respect following the formal title. The administrator wasn't a member of the church; in fact, he was not very religious at all. But as Santos knew quite well, Streckenbach attended quite a few of the church's Sunday brunches.

Several of the constables next to the administrator loudly shuffled their feet and stiffened their grip on their weapons. Santos turned to his Magi and gave them a solid look of a warning. It didn't sit well in Santos's gut that one of the Magi was absently admiring a butterfly on the pier. He'd have to have a talk with Renaldo later.

"What brings you out on this fine warm day, Archbishop?" Ludwig asked.

"We have official church business that the Magi must attend."

Ludwig frowned. "Do you mean attend to or be present for?"

Santos frowned back. "What? Both of course."

"Seeing your magi off personally, are you? Nice touch." The administrator smirked.

The archbishop flashed a quick smile. "And you? What brings you out to the docks with a full contingent of constables?" Santos hated having to play this game. Ludwig knew exactly why Santos was here, and Santos knew that he knew. Not to mention, Santos knew what Ludwig was doing here, and he knew that Ludwig knew that he knew. It was all very dizzying.

"Oh, some nasty business we must attend to," Streckenbach said while waving his hands in the air.

From behind, Ludwig tugged on the administrator's sleeve, but Alfred shooed him away.

"What business is that, then?" Bishop Renaldo asked.

"Well, as it happens, there's a plot afoot."

"A plot, you say?" Renaldo said, raising a brow.

Again, Ludwig tugged on the administrator's arm, but Alfred pulled back and gave him a stiff glare. "Not now, Ludwig. These are high-level conversations. It is beyond your capacity to understand the nuances involved." The administrator turned back to Santos. "We have it on good authority that the university in the Riverlands, and the empire itself, have dispatched a team to do some sort of research at the site of the Wizard and the Dragon. Can you imagine the audacity? Sailing into our waters and poking about in our things? The sheer vanity of it!"

Ludwig let out a loud, frustrated cough and brought his lips inches from the administrator's. Just before the administrator could turn and beat the man about the face and neck, Ludwig whispered something into Alfred's ear that caused the administrator's back to stiffen. He frowned and turned to look Ludwig in the eye. "The church is part of the plot as well? Is that right, then?" Alfred said.

"Yes, Administrator," Ludwig sighed in a weak tone.

"Ah." Administrator Streckenbach turned to face the harbor and made a quick glance at the archbishop. "So…"

"So," the archbishop agreed.

Several moments passed without a word being spoken. Administrator Streckenbach rolled on his feet a few times and gave a few nods to passing citizens. The Magi and the constables seemed to pick up on the tension, and both groups gripped their weapons and ropes just a slight bit tighter. Santos did his best to stifle a laugh as Ludwig's clenched fingers turned white.

"Well. Bit awkward now, isn't it?" Administrator Streckenbach offered.

"I can assure you, Alfred, our only interest is study," Santos said.

The administrator nodded violently. "Yes, yes, of course. But you understand, we can't have people just venturing about to poke at the Wizard. Do you want us all to become groulies?"

All eyes shifted to the administrator.

"What?" the archbishop said, lost.

The administrator shook his head at Ludwig. "Definitely not the right name." He turned back to Santos. "I simply mean, we don't know what could happen if there's another magical quake, do we?"

"The gods will protect us, to be sure," Renaldo said.

"Well, they didn't protect the island of Bedrich from becoming ... whatever they have become."

"They were unbelievers."

"And now they are un-*alivers*." The administrator smiled to himself at his clever turn of phrase. He motioned for Ludwig to write something down.

"Gentlemen..." Ludwig emerged from behind the administrator and stepped in front of the Religionists. "We simply wish to ensure the safety of all of Dressa Moore. Perhaps a joint engagement? We shall ensure safety, and you shall ensure that research is conducted."

A few grumbling nods from the True Religionists, followed by one from the administrator, calmed everyone's nerves. Several of the constables nodded as well, as did a few Magi, though not quite all.

"And, of course, maritime law is still in its infancy." Administrator Streckenbach flashed a nod and a smile at the chief constable.

"We know what ship they are traveling upon and where they're headed. Let's just work together to resolve this, yes?" Ludwig said with haste.

"Yes, indeed. A wise choice, Ludwig. *The Knotted Wood* is the name of the ship. I know her well. Comes to port here every now and again," Streckenbach said.

"That is our understanding as well," added Archbishop Santos.

"A fine ship, indeed. Sturdy bow, three masts, and nearly ten canons, as I remember. Or was it twelve? They used knotted wood along parts of the hull, hence the name." Administrator Streckenbach smiled as he described the old ship.

"Is that right, Administrator?" Archbishop Santos said. "Must have been hard to construct. A real sight to see."

"Yes, yes. They even worked a knot of driftwood that sits prominently on the bow—in the form of a cluster of grapes, I believe. Bedrich was widely known for very good wine," Administrator Streckenbach said with a strong nod. His eyes drifted to the ships in port.

Santos followed his gaze. Several ships sat in the harbor. Most were fishing trawlers, crab catchers, or sea spine stealers. Through the inlet that led into the harbor, a new vessel was coming into view. It was a fine ship, and Santos got a good look at her profile. Three masts strong, and six gunports on the starboard side. The ship turned to point towards the dock. Santos frowned. A curious design of knotted driftwood adorned the bow. He tilted his head to the side and couldn't help but notice the distinctive cluster of grapes. His mouth fell open just an inch as the captain of the ship came into view. She took off her hat and gave a strong wave as *The Knotted Wood* sailed lazily past the congregation on the dock.

"Oh, yes, looked quite like that, in fact." Administrator Streckenbach waved to the passing ship. "Almost exactly."

All eyes followed the administrator's wave. A stunned silence fell over the small group. The Magi turned to the archbishop. The constables turned to the chief. Everyone seemed to shrug at the turn of events. Even Ludwig seemed in a bit of a daze at seeing *The Knotted Wood* herself pass them in the harbor.

"Perhaps an armistice, then," Ludwig said.

"Yes, until maritime law can be applied," Streckenbach concluded.

Archbishop Santos shook his head and nodded. "Yes, fine. While they're here, I think we can all agree it's in our collective best interest to ensure that they aren't here for very long."

CAPTAIN BARTOLOME STEERED *The Knotted Wood* towards the harbor of Hogkarta. Smaller ships, mostly fishing vessels, passed by on both sides. Some of the crew waved, while others, knowing *The Wood* by reputation, averted their eyes and turned away. That suited Bartolome just fine. *If you can't win them over with love, then terrorize them with rumors of fear.* It had seemed to work for her so far.

"I can't believe this is here," Jonathan said.

"What's that, then?" Bartolome replied.

Jonathan waved his arms in the air and pointed at Hogkarta. Hugging the harbor, beyond the wooden docks, a city that rivaled some of the biggest in the Riverlands stretched out before them. Buildings of stone and wood reached heights of nearly five stories in some places, some in such tight quarters that only a small alley separated them. Along the shoreline, an open colonnade of imposing pillars of stone surrounded the entire town, each standing a few stories tall.

"Nearly fifty thousand souls call Hogkarta home. It's the largest of all the cities in Dressa Moore," Bartolome said.

"This, I mean... This is a true city. This could rival cities in the empire!"

Bartolome beamed, though she did not know why. "Yes, it's quite impressive. Hogkarta was the capital city of Dressa, before magic returned and cut the island continent of Drenall in half. 'Course, the kingdom is cut off from Dressa now. Nothing but sheer cliffs. We've had little contact with them for the last hundred years. Just a bunch of free towns throughout the lakes now."

"But I had no idea it was this big! Samson never said it was this big." Jonathan shook his head with no small amount of disgust. "He was clearly keeping it a secret. If the university knew the true size of Hogkarta, they would have sent more professors. Assistants. We would have rented whole blocks, purchased buildings... Made a true expansion, not just some three-classroom hovel next to a bar."

Bartolome shrugged.

"My word, this is extraordinary!" William said as he popped up from below deck. His eyes went wide with wonder. "Jonathan, this is amazing!"

Bartolome smiled as William ran to the rail of the ship and watched the city stretch out as *The Knotted Wood* sailed into harbor. She wondered how the locals would treat them on this trip. She had a long-standing agreement with the chief of constables that she could come to Hogkarta, but her crew had to stay on the ship and be under constant guard. That suited Bartolome just fine. Being back in Dressa, she held a much firmer grip on her crew, could feel their every urge and desire, and she could direct them from afar. But still, they were animals at their core. Some fresh meat with an open wound, and they could go into a frenzy.

The Knotted Wood eased into the harbor, and Bartolome directed her crew to lower the sails. Standing on the dock, a full contingent of constables, and a group of Magi with what looked like an archbishop of the church, all gazed up at her with looks of surprise plastered on their faces.

"This should be a fun trip," Bartolome muttered. She raised her hand and waved to the group on the dock. Only the administrator, whom she recognized from previous trips, waved back.

"HELLO, CHIEF CONSTABLE," Bartolome said from the gangway as she departed her ship.

"Bartolome. You know the rules: only you are allowed off. Don't care who or what you bring on," the chief constable said. He was an older man, hair greying hair at his temples, with a scar on his right cheek from the corner of his mouth to his ear. The powerful smell of wilderberry, and the black stains that came with it, covered his hands as he pointed to the undead on the ship.

"These two are chartered guests, not crew," Bartolome assured him.

Jonathan and William stood behind her, both with wide grins on their faces for the adventure to come. Bartolome could almost smell their excitement. She didn't know why it brought her some degree of joy, even pride to see them nearly dancing in place at the thought of exploring a city where magic flowed as freely as air.

"Sorry, they are on your ship, so they aren't coming off."

"Now, listen here, good sir—" Jonathan began, but Bartolome waved him off.

"I can assure you, Chief Constable, they are not part of my crew. Our agreement regards my crew only."

The chief stubbornly shook his head. "They are on your ship; therefore, they are members of your crew. I cannot allow it."

Bartolome shrugged and turned to Jonathan. "Looks like you two may have to stay here, I'm afraid."

Jonathan's face turned red, while William's shoulders sagged. "Absolutely not! May I remind you, Captain, that your payment is for our travel throughout Dressa Moore. That includes Hogkarta. How am I to secure your funds without actually going into town to secure your funds? Not to mention I must buy replacement items for my lost luggage!"

Bartolome nodded once. "Right, those things. Forgot about that." She turned back to the chief constable. "They need to come ashore."

"Not happening." The man's face turned hard, and his eyes squinted.

Along the railing of *The Knotted Wood*, the crew lined up menacingly, their mouths open wide. A collective low growl began, and all of their eyes fixed on the chief constable.

"Gentlemen!" the chief constable said. Behind him, a dozen constables raised long staffs and pointed them at the crew along the deck of *The Wood*.

"Are those just sticks? What are they going to do with sticks?" William asked.

"*Eloush!*" one constable shouted.

Without warning, a white ball of fire burst from the end of his staff and launched towards one of the crew on the rail. The undead's head burst into flames, and within seconds, his entire body was reduced to ash that lightly drifted away on the wind.

"Gods!" William shouted in horror.

Bartolome let out a long, hard sigh. "You just killed one of my crew." Her hand came to rest on her rapier.

"Can't kill what isn't alive, can you?" the chief constable retorted. "They try to set foot on my docks, they go up in flames." He pointed at the professors, then crossed his arms.

"I suppose we're going to have a disagreement, then," Bartolome muttered.

The chief constable grinned. "It would be my delight."

"Stop!" Ludwig Schmitt marched forward between the constables and pushed his way in front of the chief. Bartolome knew the man well. Ludwig was the brains behind Hogkarta—and typically, Ludwig allowed Bartolome to dock and enter the town. Hopefully today would be no exception.

"They aren't coming here," the chief constable insisted.

"She speaks true, Chief Constable. Those two aren't members of her crew. They are guests of the administrator and the archbishop," Ludwig explained.

The chief constable shook his head and rubbed a hand over his hair. "I can't—"

"You must keep the peace." Ludwig motioned his head farther down the docks to where the Magi stood, each with their hands firmly inside of their robes, their eyes like daggers pointed at the chief. They all muttered something under their breath that no one could hear.

The chief constable swung his head back to Ludwig. "You know what those things are, man! You remember what happened three summers ago."

"That wasn't me," Bartolome said from behind them.

"Doesn't matter if it was or wasn't. Those things aren't setting foot in my city streets."

Ludwig sighed, then nodded. He swung his head around to the citizens who had gathered around them to watch. His eyes landed on a young boy, and he beckoned him forward. "You, boy, are you bleeding?"

The boy approached and nodded. "Yes, sir. Cut my hand on a rusty knife."

"Does it hurt?" Ludwig asked.

The boy shrugged. "Yes."

Ludwig marched up to the boy and snatched him up in his arms. The father of the child stepped forward in protest, but the constables held him back. "Don't worry, sir, the boy will be fine," Ludwig said as he carted him toward Jonathan and William.

"Hold your hand out," he ordered the boy.

The boy did.

"Put your face near his hand," Ludwig said to the professors.

Neither of them moved. They both looked at each other, then at Ludwig, then at Bartolome, and back at the boy.

"Just do it!" Ludwig commanded.

"Go ahead, lads. Ludwig is the brains around here," Bartolome said.

Jonathan was first to nod and move forward. He wrinkled his nose, but placed his face in front of the boy's bloodied hand. After several seconds, Ludwig turned to the chief constable, who nodded and then motioned for William.

"You next," Ludwig said.

William brought his face near the boy, puffed his cheeks, and grinned widely. Shouts from the constables behind them and from the Magi not far away startled William. He looked up and noticed the commotion. He then screwed his face into a weird grin.

The chief constable reached for a weapon at his belt at William's sudden shift in expression.

William held up his hands, his eyes going wide. "I was only trying to humor the boy."

"See? They're not my crew, they're just idiots," Bartolome said. "Blood would drive any of my crew to at least snarl and take a bite. Can we go now?"

Ludwig let the boy down and turned to the chief. "They are indeed guests, and not of the undead."

The chief constable nodded slowly and moved out of the way. "We'll have a guard posted here around the clock. They stay on this ship. Got it?"

"Our existing agreement shall not be violated. I wouldn't

have it any other way." Bartolome smiled and led the two professors off her ship and onto the docks of Hogkarta. Ignoring the stares of the constables and the Magi, they entered the streets of the city.

"That was eventful," Archbishop Santos said.

Ludwig nodded. "Didn't see you were still here, Archbishop."

"We do have a vested interest."

"Quite."

"What's yours?" Archbishop Santos asked pointedly.

"Sorry?"

"Please don't dance around your sword, Ludwig. If you wanted to stop them, you could have done so right here—just let that madman of a chief constable incinerate those two professors and be done with it. But you didn't. Why?"

"Is it really so strange to want to keep the peace? If the constable were to have done as you say, then your Magi would have attacked."

"Yes, they would."

"And then we're back to another incident." Ludwig turned to the archbishop. "I don't want another incident. And I will ensure that the administrator doesn't want another incident, and that madman of a chief constable will not let there be another incident. *That's* my vested interest, Archbishop."

The archbishop nodded. "Then we are in agreement, it would seem."

"So it would." Ludwig smiled.

"I know you care a great deal for Hogkarta, Ludwig.

Believe me, so do I. I would never let anything happen to our great city."

"And yet, I must ask, do I believe you?" Ludwig said.

Santos squinted. Were he and Ludwig about to speak plainly? "You will have no choice, I'm afraid."

Ludwig smiled. "We all have choices, Philip."

Santos let the statement hang in the air. "No, Ludwig. We do not."

"Fine. Then we all have our duty." Ludwig's face turned hard.

Santos nodded slowly. He felt the unspoken threat in his chest. "In that, we are in total agreement."

Ludwig shrugged his shoulders. "So many agreements today. I wonder what tomorrow will bring."

Archbishop Santos nodded. Then he turned and left without another word, Renaldo and the Magi following behind him. Ludwig's intentions were quite clear: let no harm come to Hogkarta, and the church could do whatever it liked. With the magical dams around the city, which had protected Hogkarta from magical quakes in the past, it was no wonder that Ludwig's concerns rarely went beyond its borders. Still, the man was no fool. Magical dams or not, they couldn't hold back the power of the gods once they returned to the world. And if Santos was successful, that was exactly what was going to happen.

CHAPTER EIGHT

Captain Bartolome walked the streets of Hogkarta with a small but swelling sense of pride. Behind her, the two professors pointed, gawked, exclaimed, and commented on nearly everything they saw. From the floating apples at the magical fruit stands to the singing dogs at the local pubs to the miniature carts driven by mice and pulled by rats, Hogkarta held more spectacles than the greatest circuses of all the Riverlands.

The streets twisted and turned their way through the city, some wide enough for horse-drawn carts, and others so narrow that only two people could walk comfortably side by side. Small shops offering elixirs—some of which actually worked, and others promising eternal youth (none of which did)—lined the streets. All of it made Bartolome smile even wider. Though this city wasn't the place of her birth, these were the streets of her youth. She recognized various corners, alleyways, and shops, and even some merchants who had endured these many years, and to all of them, she nodded and waved. Some even waved back. A rare few turned their heads and walked in the opposite direction.

At a large intersection of several streets and sidewalks, Bartolome came to an abrupt halt, Jonathan and William nearly crashing into her from behind. Neither of them seemed to care. Both pointed at a large painting floating above the street that shifted and changed from moment to moment.

"What in the name of the Riverlands is that?" William asked.

"That belongs to an old man who's lived here for years. Forgot his name... But he's a local who learned a spell to make floating paintings that change."

"So many things float here," Jonathan observed.

"Yes, well, floating spells are quite common. Everyone knows a floating spell, so lots of things float. Like Lake Connell, and the land on which Hogkarta lives."

"That makes sense," William said.

Bartolome winked. "Now then, I have some business I must attend—ship business. You two must be on your own for a time."

"What?!"

"But ... we'll get hopelessly lost!"

Bartolome shook her head. "Nonsense. Your university outpost is right there..." She pointed to a nearby building with several books in one window. "And I thought you, my good sir William, would love to tour one of the local churches." Bartolome directed his gaze down the street to a large stone structure with a majestic tower that soared into the sky. "And here's a magical map of the city. Shows where you are at all times. I only have the one, though, so please don't lose it. I've also marked a metal shop where you can buy your replacements for the lost supplies."

"My word," William said.

"Indeed. There's a tavern called Redbeard's Hall, just around the corner there. Meet me there by sundown."

"And where will you be going?" Jonathan inquired.

"I told you, ship's business." Bartolome nodded one more time and turned without looking back.

She crossed several streets, ducked down alleys, turned corners, and doubled back on her path just to make sure neither of them followed her. They hadn't—which was quite a good thing. The last thing she needed was either of them knowing what she was up to. They had been scared to death when they found out her crew was undead. How would they feel if they discovered how she found new recruits to serve on *The Knotted Wood*?

Bartolome rounded one more turn and stopped cold when she came upon the Hospital of the End of Life, where those who had no chance of survival by medical or magical means spent their last days. These poor souls would only find death waiting for them at the end of their "convalescence." It was from this sorry group that Bartolome allowed herself to find new crew members, and the only time she willingly offered her own bite upon others' flesh. And even though she was only killing those already all but dead, every time she did, it pained her soul a little more.

JONATHAN STOOD on the street and watched as Bartolome departed down a side alley. He wasn't sure he trusted that woman. Her uncanny control over her crew certainly required more scrutiny. One thing was for certain, however: magic here in Dressa was far more powerful than he had previously thought. No one at the university or in the empire—except Samson, perhaps—knew just how big

Hogkarta was. Or how easily magic flowed. And that demanded the question, why hadn't Samson told anyone?

Next to him, William took a step towards the university outpost. Jonathan quickly grabbed William's arm and pulled him backward. "Where are you going?"

"Oh, I thought it would be nice to visit the outpost and see Samson. Perhaps there's interest in expanding the linguistic department."

"William, please. You know only a handful of souls are interested in your fascination with language." Jonathan regretted the words as soon as he said them. He didn't know why he could sometimes be so cruel to William.

William nodded. "Yes, but if I could simply sit down with others and tell them of the intricacies..."

"You've done that with me, and I don't find it interesting," Jonathan snapped.

"Do you have to always be so belittling?"

Jonathan closed his eyes and nodded. He turned to face William, his hands immediately going to William's collar to adjust it. "I'm sorry, love. I am. This trip is just so stressful. It's my only chance—perhaps the only chance in a generation—to come here and do this. Besides, I don't want to see you wasting your brilliant mind on such a silly subject."

"It isn't silly." William shoved Jonathan's hands off his shirt and looked away.

"No, of course it isn't. I apologize. For now, however, I would like to talk with Samson alone. We have important university matters to discuss. And then I must find a metal shop and have them hammer out lead pieces and have them delivered to *The Wood*."

William gritted his teeth and let out a sigh. "I am part of the faculty as well, you know."

"Indeed, but this is a matter for the magilurgical department. You understand. I mean, there are no other departments here."

William nodded once and kicked a stone on the ground. "Fine."

"Excellent. I'll meet you at the tavern, alright? I do think you may find the church quite nice. I hear their architecture is lovely. And afterward, we shall dine together, and you'll tell me about your studies of pronunciation."

"*E*-nunciation. And you don't want to hear about it."

Jonathan combed William's hair with his left hand. "I do indeed, and you shall tell me."

"Stop it," William said, but smiled and pushed Jonathan's hand away.

"Tonight, then?"

William nodded.

Jonathan smiled at William. "I love you, you silly man." He leaned in and kissed William on the cheek, at which William smiled.

"What was that the constables said?"

"What?" Jonathan turned around in the middle of the street and shrugged. "What do you mean?"

"They said something before fire burst from one of their staffs. What was that?"

"It was magic, of course."

"That's different from when other magic is done, isn't it?"

Jonathan nodded. He tried his best to humor William. Perhaps his lover would grow an interest in magilurgy and change his discipline. "It was a spell—nonsensical sounds that elicit a magical response. Why?"

William shrugged. "Sounded almost like a real word."

Jonathan rolled his eyes, but tried his best to hide his disdain. "Well, it wasn't. How could it be? Perhaps it was a mis-enunciation?" He smiled and tilted his head.

William frowned. "Cute."

"Tonight, you can tell me all about it." Jonathan turned and marched towards the university, knowing William was staring at his backside. After all, his matching pants, made with twice the stitching of his walking pants, fit him nicely to the bottom.

For once, Jonathan felt good about their relationship. It had been quite rocky back at the university. Everything they did seemed to grate on each other's nerves. And there were elements of that here, for certain, but it felt like their old relationship was coming back—a thought that made Jonathan smile. But he couldn't focus on that now—not with his opponent only steps away.

Jonathan approached the door of the outpost and gave the handle a firm and angry turn. Wood and metal creaked as he pushed through. Inside, a woman sat at a desk with a pen in one hand and a stack of paper hovering just by her ear. Her hair was a striking black, and she wore a purple shirt. As she nodded at the paper, she whispered a magical spell, and a new sheet came down to rest on top of the first.

"Hello," Jonathan said.

The woman looked up and smiled. "Good day, sir. Are you here to inquire about university training?"

"No... Well, I suppose, in a roundabout way. I'm *from* the university."

The woman's face took on a look of confusion. "Oh, I don't think so. We only have one instructor."

"No, I mean I'm from the university in the Riverlands."

"Oh, yes. Mr. Sutter said we might expect one of his subordinates."

"*Peers*," Jonathan said through a forced smile.

"A peer? Oh, no, he was quite clear. Subordinate."

"I'm sure he was. Could you fetch him, by chance?"

The woman shook her head and raised her eyebrows. "I don't take instructions from subordinates, I'm afraid."

"Madam..." Jonathan said, but the woman had already turned her attention back to the papers on her desk.

"Have a seat, Mr. ...?"

"Braxton. Jonathan Braxton."

The woman smiled. "Splendid."

Jonathan let out a huff. He put his hands on his hips and spun in a circle, looking for something he could point to and complain about. He found nothing. Eventually, with all the patience he could muster, he nodded once and took a seat in a chair by the window. After several deep breaths, he thought he could feel his temper lowering.

More than half an hour passed before the woman calmly lowered her writing instrument to the desk and stood. She never looked at Jonathan as she rounded her desk, passed within just inches of his leg, and walked through a doorway on the other side of the room. After a few more minutes, she returned, rounded her desk again, and sat down, all without saying a word.

Jonathan's face reddened. "You just told him I'm here, didn't you? After *thirty minutes* of me sitting here?"

"Yes."

"You could have done that earlier, couldn't you?"

"Yes."

Another quarter of an hour passed before Samson strode into the office, a bright, wide smile on his face, his long purple university robe billowing behind him, the sleeves embroidered with the sigils of his rank and the degrees that he held.

"Jonathan! What a surprise."

Jonathan slowly stood and reached for Samson's

outstretched hand. "Samson. Good to see you. May we talk somewhere private?"

Samson shrugged. "Of course. Follow me." He nodded once to the woman at the desk, whose name Jonathan still didn't know, and left the room the same way he had entered.

"Thank you for your kindness and promptness," Jonathan muttered to the woman.

She raised her head from her papers and lifted the corners of her mouth into the smallest of smiles.

Samson led them through several twists in the corridors of the outpost before entering a room that Jonathan assumed was his office. Samson's degrees were displayed in elaborate frames around the room, along with several paintings of the university. A large wooden desk with ornate carvings sat at one end of the room. On the wall opposite his desk were several bookshelves, all of them stuffed with manuscripts.

"So, what brings you to Dressa?" Samson walked behind his desk and took a seat.

Jonathan was momentarily stunned by his colleague's question. "What do you mean? You know why we're here!"

"No, I was only told you were coming, but not why."

"I see. Well, the chancellor likes to keep his secrets. We are here on a research mission. To investigate the source of magic."

Samson nodded slowly.

"Why didn't you tell us of this place?"

Samson's face screwed up into a look of confusion. "What do you mean?"

"This city is immense! It rivals any city in the Riverlands."

"Oh. Yes, it does, doesn't it?"

"Indeed! So, why keep it a secret?"

Samson shrugged. "Perhaps I didn't want anyone coming here to steal the glory of bringing the university to this city."

"What? What kind of reasoning is that?"

"Well, I mean, you're here now. Aren't you?"

"Samson. I'm here to do research. I am the foremost expert on magilurgy at the university."

Samson huffed. "Only because I left!"

"Are we really going to do this now?"

"Do what, dear Jonathan?"

Jonathan let out a long sigh and rubbed his temples. Of course, infighting at the university was rampant, as department chairs were quite limited and held onto with an iron grip by those who sat in them. The magilurgy department was no exception. There was a long-running rivalry between Samson and Jonathan. But Jonathan had always thought it was professional, even cordial. Samson was no more Jonathan's enemy than any professor at the university. Did Samson harbor more jealousy than Jonathan knew? Of all the times to find that out, Jonathan thought, this was perhaps the worst.

"I don't want to do this. I really don't. You chose to leave."

"I chose to accept a sponsorship to bring the university to Hogkarta. And you chose to follow me. Can't even let me have Dressa, can you, Jonathan? And for the record, I was *invited* to come here—by the Religionists themselves. Clearly, they felt I would be the superior choice to build a true magilurgical school of study."

Jonathan rolled his eyes. This again. Yes, indeed, Samson had been invited to come to Hogkarta by the True Religionists several years ago to start a university. Yes, they had felt he would make the better instructor. But what did the church know about the quality of professors at the university? They could have just as easily picked Jonathan. Frankly, however, he had always been glad they didn't. Jonathan had had no desire to come here, and even now, seeing this great city for what it was, he really had no desire to stay. His life was at the university in the Riverlands, not in Dressa Moore.

"I have no desire to stay here," Jonathan said.

"No. You just want to come here, do research with university funds, and take all the credit once you sail home."

"Samson."

"Jonathan."

Jonathan tilted his head to one side and let out a sigh. He would get nowhere here. But it didn't matter. Once he got back to the Riverlands and word spread of the true size of Hogkarta, other departments would want in on the action. Let Samson become the lord of magilurgical studies in Dressa, if that was what he wanted.

He cleared his throat, cutting to the chase. "Fine. I need funds to pay for the expedition, as well as replacement items, and then I'll be on my way."

"Sorry, what was that? Replacement items?"

"Oh, please. Don't you dare."

Samson shrugged, a smug smile spreading across his face. "I'm afraid I have no funds for you, Jonathan."

"Be very sure about this, Samson. Chancellor Dunningham assured me you would provide me with aid. He stated that he regularly sends you additional funds with those rainbow crows of yours. Albeit a few coins at a time…"

"Did he, now? Well, I'll have to check the roost, won't I?" Samson spread his face into a wide smile, but didn't budge from his desk.

Jonathan crossed his legs and folded his arms. "Yes, I believe you will. And not to worry. I can wait."

WILLIAM TURNED from walking toward the church and watched Jonathan march across the street and enter the university outpost. He stood there for several long seconds, staring at the now closed door of the building. Why he put up with that man made his head spin. Yes, he loved Jonathan, but the man had no respect for William's research. Not really. And it showed. Yes, he defended William to others, and the gesture was heartwarming, but why couldn't he just believe a little in the study of language? Jonathan had not one iota of confidence in William's theories of deeper roots of language that should have existed, but simply didn't. How could the entire academic world just accept that only one language had ever evolved on the entire planet? It made no rational sense at all—especially considering that the ancient peoples had had little contact with one another.

With a long sigh, William turned from the university outpost and took a step towards the church down the street. He let himself get lost in the majesty of the stone tower that rose above the city skyline, hoping that the architecture would chase away his anxiety over this trip and his growing confusion about where things stood with Jonathan.

Small crowds of locals passed him on the street as William walked toward the church. Many wore clothing quite similar to the styles of Dressa as recorded a hundred years ago, with minor alterations. Wool pants and thick overcoats for the men, and long, modest dresses for the women were the main fashion trends he noted. Many of the women augmented their dresses with bright colors of red and purple, while most of the men's clothing ranged from dark blue to grey or black. If he was being honest,

William found the styles a little drab, especially for a magical city.

Several horse-drawn carts and carriages, both for goods to be sold and people to buy them, passed by on the street just in front of the church, and William waited for them to pass before crossing. A large archway at the front of the church framed two enormous iron doors. Several worshipers—at least, that was what William took them for—walked through the open doors and into the church. Without hesitation, he followed them inside.

A small vestibule greeted him upon entering, lined by little red couches. On the other side, a pair of wooden doors opened on a large chamber. Next to doors stood a small table bearing a stack of books.

"Hello," said a smooth, calm voice.

William turned to see a woman standing just inside the wooden doors. "Hello," he replied.

"I've not seen you before. Would you like to join the church? Inquire of the gods?"

William smiled and shook his head. "No, I'm just a visitor. I thought I'd take a look at the architecture."

The woman smiled in return. "Of course. Please, take one of our books. It holds all the truths of the universe. You are free to explore any part of the church as you like."

William took the top book from the stack and flipped it open. Symbols covered the pages, none of which William could decipher or had even seen before. That was quite odd, considering that he'd been to the local church in the River-lands. His frown grew as he turned each page. Many depicted images of gods. The most prominently featured was Yelke, king of the gods. He stood nearly seven feet tall, with long blond hair and blue eyes. His wife, Neltzy, equally as blonde and tall, stood by his side. As Jonathan turned more pages, more gods were depicted. He stopped seven pages in as the clusters of blond gods began to make his eyes ache.

"Why do they all look the same? They don't look anything like any priest I've ever met. And what are all these symbols?" William asked.

Met with silence, he looked up—but the woman was already gone.

"Odd." He pocketed the book, entered the church, and noticed immediately that the same symbols adorned much of the walls, paintings, and tapestries throughout the grand hall. Of course, many cultures throughout the Riverlands, the interior, and the second great continent had their fair share of odd symbols. Even the university loved squiggly drawings and had many etched into the stone of the ancient buildings. Still, something about these symbols was especially unusual, a fact that William found most intriguing.

Archbishop Santos stood with Bishop Renaldo and watched the professor from the university tour the capital church from behind a two-way mirror several flights above the main hall. The professor walked among paintings and sculptures, each time noting the strange symbols and intricate designs that decorated them. Several priests, none of whom knew anything about the greater plans going on right in their midst, wandered to and from various alcoves and nooks.

A woman walked into the archbishop's office and gently shut the door. She lowered her head and took a step to the right of the entrance, placing both hands in front of her.

"Does he have the book?" Bishop Renaldo asked.

"Yes, Bishop. I placed the sacred text on top of a stack of simple hymnals."

"Splendid. Pure chance that he walked in here. And did he suspect anything?"

"No, Bishop."

A long silence settled over the room. Archbishop Santos knew Renaldo was waiting to see if he had any last words. He did not. After several long minutes, the bishop dismissed the woman and shut the door behind her.

"Another step completed," Renaldo said.

Archbishop Santos snorted and shook his head. Another step, indeed, in the DemiGod's insane plan to unleash the gods. Giving their most sacred of texts, a document meant only for the eyes of archbishops and Her Holiness the DemiGod of the Church, to a nonmember, a nonworshiper, someone who didn't know one god from another in the pantheon... This lowly nobody now held their dearest secrets in his pocket—and thought nothing of it.

"You are vexed, Your Grace?" Renaldo asked.

"Vexed is hardly the word. If he hadn't come into this church, how would he have gotten the book? They weren't supposed to be in Hogkarta at all. Your charter captain failed miserably to give it to him."

"He was pirated, Your Grace. And the charter stolen."

"Indeed."

"Are you having doubts now, Your Grace?" Renaldo questioned.

Santos shrugged. "I had doubts when the DemiGod suggested this insane plan five years ago. Honestly, I thought she'd given up by now. I'm amazed it's gotten this far. And for this man to just stumble into the church and play the part of the unwitting pawn... Just shocking."

"And yet, it happened. Perhaps the gods are smiling on us for our endeavors."

Archbishop Santos loosened the collar around his neck and coughed. Just what was he even doing? The impossibility of this, of actually freeing the gods... Was he insane? How did he agree to this? All of the plans for the last few years came crashing into him. The professors were never meant to come here. Was it worth the risk of bringing the empire to Dressa? The church had been trying to free the gods for a century, and not once had they come even marginally close. Finnian, the ancient Wizard, still lived, locked in battle with the great Dragon itself. They were no closer to killing Finnian than they were to freeing the Dragon—unless one counted when they had coaxed smoke from the Dragon's nostrils twenty years ago. Of course, the poor priest who had managed that was currently locked in the basement, eating spoons with seven mouths made of steel.

And gods, what if the DemiGod's plan actually worked? What if these professors from the university could actually decipher the book, sail to the Wizard, and unlock the spell that had frozen the Wizard and the Dragon in their eternal fight? What if the Magi that followed actually accomplished the impossible and killed the Wizard? The gods would return. But who knew what foolish ideas they'd have been stewing on for centuries? The idea of having to report not only to the DemiGod of the Church, but also to an entire cadre of overly powerful, self-indulgent gods...? A shiver ran down Archbishop Santos's spine. He shook himself free of the thought. Had he not thought this through enough? Why was it getting so hot in this room? Was he having chest pains? Were the walls closing in on him?

"Are you alright, Your Grace?" Renaldo asked.

Archbishop Santos nodded. "Yes, of course. And yes, the gods smile on us as we smile on ourselves. Have the Magi follow him. Make sure our sacred text doesn't leave him." Perhaps he could muster a means to thwart this whole mess. A local thief stealing the book out from under the Magis' noses? Yes, that might work. The DemiGod's authority would be lessened, and this mad obsession for many in the church of breaking the spell over the Dragon would end. Archbishop Santos would guide the church through this mess and emerge on the other side as the new DemiGod of the Church. The thought sent another shiver down his spine. Yes, of course. Why bring the gods back now, when he was a lowly archbishop? Why not do it when he was the DemiGod? Then he would have true power in the world.

"The priest cast a binding spell as soon as the professor's hands touched the book," Renaldo assured him. "It will not leave his presence."

Santos nodded and ground his teeth. Renaldo, ever the thorough one. Fine. There was more than one way to wreak havoc. Which reminded him: he had a dinner planned with the administrator. Perhaps it was time for a more formal union between them. If the administrator and the constables could intervene here, then Santos could still find a path to victory.

COMMODORE WILKES LOOKED up at the rigging of *The Crimson Swan* and marveled as the local villagers swung themselves around the masts with the ease of birds in flight. Of course, it helped that most of them had an extra set of limbs around their torsos—something Wilkes couldn't quite get past.

"Extraordinary, aren't they?" the village leader said. One set of his arms—those lower on his torso—was clasped behind his back, while the pair at his shoulders pointed at the villagers swinging between the sails.

"Quite," Wilkes said uncomfortably.

"We've never had guests from the Riverlands before. Well, few, anyway. Most run in fear when we wave."

"It was a bit jarring," Wilkes said cautiously.

The village leader laughed. "No question. No question."

"Is this the one?" Captain Bridgewater walked onto the bridge from the lower deck, holding a large piece of orange-and-red fruit in his hands.

"Ah, yes, it is indeed. Don't allow any of your people to eat that, or in a few days' time, they begin to grow a second set of limbs." The village leader clapped both sets of hands together before returning them to their previous positions.

Bridgewater nodded and turned to leave. "We need additional provisions, but how do we even know what's safe to eat in this mad place?" He left the bridge and hurried down to the deck.

"Dressa is certainly full of surprises," Wilkes observed.

"You have no idea," the village leader said with a grin.

"But at least some of it is benefiting us. I've seen nothing like what your people can do." Wilkes looked up to the splintered mast as the wood continued to reshape itself. In several places, the wood had knitted itself back together, and not a single member of *The Swan* could tell anything was ever amiss.

"Well, we are a lakeside village, aren't we? My great-grandfather learned that nifty little spell shortly after the upheaval a hundred years ago."

Wilkes nodded. "Amazing." He turned from the mast and walked to the rail of *The Swan*, overlooking the village on the shore, which in truth looked more like small town. Wilkes guessed it must hold a thousand souls, perhaps more, stretched along the shoreline and up into the hills and thick forest beyond. "We also didn't know Dressa was still so full of life."

"And we didn't know you didn't know. Our local church —though I admit I'm not much of a worshiper—has long warned against our traveling to the Riverlands. Of course, with our unique physiology, few of us villagers would dare. We're quite shunned in Dressa; can't imagine the loathing we'd be subject to in the Riverlands."

Commodore Wilkes smiled. "Nonsense. The empire welcomes everyone. There are quite a few differences among imperial citizens."

"That's fine to hear. Just fine!" the village leader said with a wide smile.

Wilkes nodded. He knew these moments would be crucial for the empire. They could establish a beachhead right here in this village, just a short sail from the Aquirren River and close to the Alpine River, whose waters flowed downward back to the Riverlands. This village, as the village leader called it, was nearly as big as Oyster Piers. These people could provide the empire with vital intelligence they would need if the emperor and the admiralty came—and Wilkes was very confident that they would.

But that was for the future. For now, he had more pressing matters. "And Hogkarta—you know how to navigate there?"

The village leader nodded and laughed. "Oh my, yes, we do! Though we never go. No, no. Well, we ferry the True Religionists who live in our town to Hogkarta when they have need to go. But, well, four-armers don't set foot there."

He shook his head. "No, no, we'd never set foot there, that wouldn't go over very well."

Wilkes frowned. He detested such prejudices. "The people of Hogkarta don't welcome you there? Just because you have four limbs?"

The village leader frowned, then smiled and shook his head. "Oh, no, no, nothing like that." He touched his nose. "Well, not *only* that. I mean, we aren't prohibited, just frowned upon. And frankly, we don't like the stares. It's intrusive. Plus, our sense of smell is fantastical. And, well ... Hogkarta smells horrid, frankly. Just too many people. *Thousands* of them, all clustered together. And all those floating pigs... Do you have any idea where floating pigs use the toilet while they're up in the air?"

It wasn't often that Wilkes was stunned into silence, but this was one of those times. He blinked away the village leader's statements and nodded. "But you could direct us there?"

"Oh, why, of course! We are a friendly lot, no question. No question. But, if I may, why do you want to go? Our village has everything you need—everything. We also have a fine assortment of non-magicalized fruits and foods that your crew will love. Just love! And our taverns are filled with the finest whiskies, aged in oak barrels for decades. Decades!"

Wilkes smiled. He was really taking a liking to this man. "We have business in Hogkarta. But I assure you, if you would have us, the empire would love to establish more of a relationship with your town."

The village leader's eyes lit up, and his brows rose. "Splendid! Just splendid. Yes, yes, of course we would. Very much so."

"Then perhaps some of your men will join us for the navigation?"

"Oh ,yes, fine. Just fine. But if it's all the same to you, we'll sleep in the rigging. And we won't set foot on any shore." The village leader wrinkled his nose and took a step back.

Wilkes nodded. "No problem." He turned back to *The Crimson Swan*. She would be shipshape in no time. And now they had navigators to take them to the heart of Dressa. Wilkes would finally bring Bartolome to justice, once and for all. And then, perhaps Wilkes could find the only thing he really cared about in these waters.

No. Wilkes shook his head. He *would* find her. No matter the cost, Wilkes would find Abigail—or die searching.

CAPTAIN BARTOLOME ENTERED the hospital of the dying. Solemn-faced attendants with their heads lowered and faces covered walked by without lifting their eyes from the floor. Three long corridors stretched from the main entrance, one directly ahead and one to either side. Bartolome picked the right-hand one—not that it would matter. The dying were everywhere in this cursed place.

"May I help you? Here to see a loved one?" a woman asked.

Bartolome shook her head. "I'm looking for volunteers."

The woman nodded with a sad smile. "Do you have anything to offer their families?"

"A gold piece each. No more."

The woman nodded. "What ages?"

"What?"

The woman sighed. "You're not the first to employ the

dying or the dead. And it's not my place to judge. Anyway, it frees up a bed for another."

Bartolome nodded, shivering at the thought. Who else was buying the dying? And dear gods, what did they want with them? At least Bartolome offered them a release from their pain. That was what she told herself, at any rate. "Middle-aged or young adults are fine."

"Genders?"

"Doesn't matter."

"This way." The woman led her through the corridors of the hospital to a large room with twenty beds, ten to each side, so close to one another that the frames nearly touched.

"So many," Bartolome said.

"There was a fire three nights ago on the west end. A shame that no one has figured out how to heal with magic. At least, not injuries this grievous."

"Maybe one day," Bartolome said dejectedly.

The woman nodded, then turned to address this room. "This woman has need of..." She turned to Bartolome. "How many?"

"Five will do."

"... five souls to accompany her. A gold coin to the families of all those who come."

Without hesitation, six bodies rose from their beds, while another three raised their hands.

Bartolome let out a sigh and took out her money pouch from her pocket. She didn't really need this many, but she could find uses for them. She picked out nine gold coins and placed them into the outstretched hand of the woman. When the woman did not pull back her hand, Bartolome retrieved one more coin for the hospital and added it to the other nine.

"Take your time. Though not too much." The woman left the room without another word.

Bartolome shook her head sadly. This was the part she hated the most. But she needed more crew. One had been lost in Oyster Piers, another had gone to fend off Wilkes and the trigger-happy constables, and she'd lost three more when she attacked the travel barge. She reminded herself to tell Anton to feed himself well the next few weeks.

The first bed she reached held a man in his thirties, half of his face scarred badly from a fire. Bartolome sat on the edge of the bed and placed her hand on his chest. His ragged breaths came fast, but he locked his eyes onto Bartolome.

"My ... family?"

Bartolome nodded. "They have been paid."

The man nodded and looked up at the ceiling. "I ... can't walk."

"You will." With that, Bartolome took the man's hand in hers and lifted it to her mouth. She bit gently into his skin, drawing a small amount of blood. The man jerked his hand back with a yelp.

It only took moments for the effects of the bite to spread through his body. His eyes rolled back in his head, and he let out a quick but forceful grunt. His teeth snapped open and closed, and he started sniffing loudly, causing several others in the room to look their way with concern.

"Settle," Bartolome said quietly. She whispered the one spell she knew by heart and cloaked the man in an illusion that gave him the look of his former living self.

The man calmed, now completely under Bartolome's control. She nodded once in grim satisfaction, then approached each of the other eight volunteers. They were all too weak to have seen Marta take a bite out of the first man. And they were far too devoted to helping their families to change their minds even if they had. One by one, Bartolome welcomed the dying men and women to her crew. Once the act was done, each of them dutifully rose from their beds and formed a line behind her. She led them through the hospital, where not one eye rose to mark their passing, and out into the streets of the city.

Outside, where no one would recognize them, Bartolome altered the illusion spell to make them all appear healthy, with no signs of injuries on their bodies. She also added a few cosmetic changes here and there to fool any family that might happen to pass them. Bartolome then marched her new crew through the streets to their waiting ship, where she knew the constables wouldn't stop them. The constables were under orders to prevent her crew from disembarking, not to prevent anyone from boarding. Thankfully, constables weren't the type to misinterpret orders from their chief.

Once that task was done, it was on to the tavern to get paid by the professors and then embark on the last leg of this trip.

CHAPTER NINE

Jonathan stormed into Redbeard's Hall with a foul attitude and a deep thirst. The tavern was filled with wooden tables and chairs, with a bar lining the back wall. Oversized glass beer mugs were stacked in a precarious pyramid on one end of the bar. Jonathan surmised that just one of those mugs could hold enough beer to keep him in a drunken stupor for the day—which, at the moment, sounded pretty appealing. Tantalizing smells of hot sausage and fresh-baked bread filled the room. As it was barely noon, only a scattering of patrons were seated in the bar. But each of them held one of the large glass mugs, most of them about half full.

A barmaid with long blond pigtails and wearing a white skirt gave Jonathan a smile and a nod. She motioned for him to sit at one of the many empty tables. Jonathan nodded back in a curt and quick manner. He picked a table, yanked the wooden chair across the floor, and sat down hard. The barmaid met him at the table. She smiled wide and held a pleasant enough demeanor.

"Everything alright, love?" she asked.

"No, it's not, as a point of fact. Nothing is alright. It may never be right again."

"One of those days, is it, love? Not to worry, Shelly has you now." The barmaid patted him once on the shoulder and went behind the bar. She returned in short order and placed a large mug of blonde beer on the table.

"What's this? I didn't even order anything," Jonathan said.

"It's called a pilsner. It's quite good, love. We have sausages and sauerkraut as well, if you like. And pretzels— really big ones, in a variety of shapes. Our chef is experimenting with putting cheese inside a ball of a pretzel dough and baking it until the cheese melts. It's delicious!"

Jonathan nodded, then frowned as a question popped into his brain. "What does the name Redbeard's come from, then?"

The barmaid nodded to the bar. A mountain of a man— the barkeep, Jonathan assumed—stood nearly seven feet tall, a long bright red beard hanging down his broad, muscular chest. Noticing Jonathan's gaze, he folded his arms, both the size of small tree trunks, across his chest and gave him a very firm, borderline threatening nod. There was no anger in his eyes, but Jonathan felt intimidated just by the big man looking his way. Some people just had that kind of gift.

"Right." Jonathan nodded back and quickly remembered just how much trouble his own anger could create.

"Don't worry, love. He looks mean, but he's gentle as a cub. Unless you have a bit too much and go about breaking things... But even then, he'll just escort you out with a gentle pat. Some people's bark is worse than their bite. Unless your hands find a place where they aren't invited... Then his bite can be fierce."

Jonathan smiled. "No fear of that, I assure you."

The barmaid's face took on a hurt expression. "Sorry, love? What's that supposed to mean?"

"Oh, no, sorry, not what I meant. I just ... prefer other company." Jonathan smiled and shrugged.

A puzzled look flashed on her face for a fleeting moment, but then she nodded and laughed. "I understand you now, love." She winked. "Not to worry. I should say, some places here offer an open invitation." She nodded to the red-bearded man and bumped Jonathan with her hip as she left.

"Perhaps there are some redeeming qualities to the place after all," Jonathan said to himself with a chuckle. He downed a large gulp of his pilsner, readying himself to finish the glass. He would need a few after what had happened today—and more for what was undoubtedly coming tomorrow.

"You're swine, Samson. Pure swine." Jonathan downed the rest of his glass—a feat he found himself quite proud of, considering the size of it—and waved to the barmaid for another.

"No right, Samson. None whatsoever," he muttered. "When the chancellor hears of this—"

"Hears of what?" Captain Bartolome sat down across from him and plopped her hat on the table. "You got my money? I've had a recent expense."

Jonathan adjusted himself in his chair and half nodded, while shaking his head at the same time, a move he'd perfected over many years. It was the best way to offer both a positive and negative response in one fluid motion. At the very least, it bought him a few moments for the barmaid to refill his glass. Getting assaulted by the pirate captain, which he knew could very well happen, would be best suffered when inebriated.

"Good. Your treat, then." Bartolome asked the barmaid for a drink of her own.

"Did you finish your chores, Captain?" Jonathan asked, doing his best to not let his voice break.

"Yes. New crew. More than I wanted, but probably less than we'll need, considering where we're going."

Jonathan gulped. "Where exactly do you find new crew? Considering they're ... you know ... dead?"

Bartolome smiled. "Oh, here and there."

The door to the tavern opened, and William walked inside. He took one look around the room, saw Jonathan, and smiled. He walked over to the table, but then his eyes found the window in the far wall, and his head tilted to one side.

"You can see the harbor from here! How's that possible? Is it a magic window?" William asked.

Bartolome turned to the window and then back to the table. "No, we're just on a hill."

William nodded. "Ah. That makes sense."

"Not everything is magical here, William." Bartolome smiled and reached for her mug of beer from the barmaid, who had also brought another for Jonathan.

"Want one, love?" the barmaid asked William.

"Please."

She looked at Jonathan, nodded towards William, winked, and bumped William with her hip. She then walked back behind the bar.

"What was that about?" William asked.

"Oh, nothing. Did you find the church enjoyable?"

"Oh, yes, quite. I mean, the architecture is older than

that of any church of the True Religionists in the Riverlands, but many of the paintings and sculptures are similar. But the church here had some odd scribblings of symbols everywhere."

"Quite fascinating." Jonathan took a sip of his beer and wiped sweat from his brow.

"Everything alright?" William asked.

Bartolome leaned forward and squinted her eyes. "Yes, is everything alright? You seem nervous, Jonathan."

Jonathan let out a shaky laugh and shook his head. "Oh, yes, fine. Fine. Just a contentious meeting with my colleague."

"Oh, yes, how is Samson?" William asked.

"How, indeed?" Bartolome said.

Jonathan looked at Bartolome and turned his attention to William. "He's alright. Very comfortable here. Didn't like the fact that the university sent me to research the magilurgy, but, well, that's what happened."

"He's always been a bit of a crass, hasn't he?" William said. He shook his head, stuffed his hands in his pockets, and leaned back in his chair. Before Jonathan could answer, William pulled out a small red book from his pocket, and his face took on an expression of shock.

"What's the matter, William? What's that?" Jonathan asked, relieved to change the subject.

"I put this back! I could have sworn I put this back as I left," he muttered. "On the stack of other books in the church."

"Looks like a hymnal, love. Thinking of converting?" the barmaid said as she brought William's drink to the table.

"No, I was just exploring." He opened the book and flipped through several pages.

The barmaid looked down at the book as she set down his glass of blonde beer. "That's odd, isn't it?" she said.

"What?"

"Don't look like any hymnal I've seen before. I'm a regular at the church—lots of folks in this part of the city are. The Sunday brunches are to die for! They have pastries and ham. Free to all." She smiled and walked back behind the bar.

William's face twisted in confusion as he looked back at the book and flipped through the pages. Jonathan leaned over the table to get a look, but Bartolome's stare pushed him back down into his seat—a stare that he realized had never left his face.

"About my fee..." Bartolome said.

Jonathan smiled and took another drink.

"Jonathan," Bartolome said, her voice dropping a full octave.

Jonathan sighed. He didn't know what else to do but be truthful; he was a terrible liar. But at that moment, his stomach reminded him to eat. And though he might be a terrible liar, he fancied himself a fantastic delayer.

"Everything is fine, Captain. But I'm starving. Can we eat and discuss this later?"

Bartolome sighed and nodded. "Fine. But we aren't leaving here until I'm paid, as per our agreement. Yes?"

"Agreed," Jonathan said, followed by a gulp. He felt a sudden pang of fear bubble up in his chest. He certainly didn't want to make payment by becoming one of Bartolome's crew.

"Barmaid? Three meals, please. Sausages and sauerkraut, and those cheese things," Jonathan said.

"Make it two, Shelly," Bartolome said. "Not my kind of fare." She winked at Jonathan.

William looked up. "'Cheese things'?"

Jonathan nodded. "Melted in a pretzel ball."

William's eyes went wide with hunger. "That sounds wondrous!"

The barmaid nodded and whisked away.

"How do you know the barmaid?" Jonathan asked Bartolome.

Bartolome frowned. "I've been here many times, Jonathan. I belong in Dressa." She winked. "You're the ones who don't fit in."

Jonathan nodded and turned back to the bar. "And keep the beer flowing!"

COMMODORE WILKES STOOD on the bridge of *The Crimson Swan* and marveled at the city that stretched out across the horizon. This was far greater than anything the empire knew existed in these waters. The audacity of the Religionists in keeping this a secret for so many years astounded him. This was the type of betrayal that caused wars, and he had little doubt that the emperor would shy away from any sort of confrontation.

In the harbor, people pointed and shouted at the imperial frigate. Wilkes watched bodies run along the dock and soon spotted what could only be a militia gathered around a ship, which he recognized as soon as his eyes landed on her knotted hull.

"She's here," Wilkes said.

"And has company," Bridgewater added.

Wilkes nodded. "And look there—next to them is a True Religionist. I recognize his cloak."

"Spies tell us they can work magic here. Powerful magic, at that."

Wilkes snorted a laugh. "Yes, but those same spies couldn't tell us that a city of this size existed at all. How can we trust anything they say?"

Bridgewater grunted. "Granted."

The Swan lurched backward, and Wilkes quickly grabbed hold of the railing. An enormous wave—nearly five feet tall—slammed into the bow and pushed the entire vessel backward. Shouts rang out from the crew, and one man fell from the rigging, only saved from a collision with the deck by his foot getting caught in the ropes.

"What was that?" Bridgewater asked.

"Seems your spies may have been right. Look there." Wilkes pointed at the True Religionist who had walked forward on the dock and raised his arms in the air.

"Is he really raising the water to push us backward?"

Wilkes could only guess. "I would assume so."

"Bosun! Introduce that man to the empire!" Bridgewater called down to the lower deck.

"Are you sure about that?"

Bridgewater looked into Wilkes's eyes. "What I am sure of is that magic or not, if we show weakness, we've already lost."

Wilkes nodded. Bridgewater was right, and Wilkes knew it. But they were far from home, with no way of getting reinforcements. If the True Religionists here could do more than just move water with a spell, then they could be in some very real trouble.

On the bow of the ship, one of the crew brought out a long rifle and attached it to the railing. He let the ship settle before taking a long, steady aim. Seconds passed before a shot of gunpowder exploded with a puff of smoke. Wilkes stared in disbelief as the man on the dock clutched his shoulder and fell. The shot was by far the best he'd ever seen in his career.

"How...?"

"Best shot in the fleet, bar none."

Back on the dock, the militia came to arms and lifted rifles to their shoulders, but did not fire. They also did not help the fallen True Religionist, which Wilkes found to be quite peculiar. Perhaps this militia worked for the government of the town ... and perhaps they were more open to talks than the True Religionists.

"Bring us into port, Captain. I think it's time this city was introduced to the military of the empire, don't you?"

"Yes, Commodore ... though I feel they just were."

Archbishop Santos folded his arms across his chest, then moved his hands behind his back. Then he placed both hands on his face to squeeze his eyes shut after what he had just witnessed. From his office high in the church's tower of Hogkarta, he was afforded a view of not only the city, but the nearby port and harbor—which was where he had just witnessed, for the first time in the history of Dressa Moore, an imperial frigate from the empire of the Riverlands sailing leisurely into the waters of his majestic city and actually docking. In *his* city—a city of which the empire wasn't even supposed to know the true extent.

"Disastrous," the archbishop said.

"Perhaps this isn't as bad as you think, Your Grace," Renaldo offered.

Archbishop Santos shook his head and fumed. "Well,

you may be right there. As I now believe, it may be quite worse than what I had thought just hours ago."

"How is that, Your Grace? We knew the empire was here in Dressa."

"In Dressa, yes—on the sea, chasing Bartolome and those two professors. Not in Hogkarta, for the gods' sake!"

"Is that such a distinction?"

Santos turned on Renaldo and shot daggers into the man's eyes. "Are you a fool? Once the empire knows the size of our great city, that Dressa is not a dead and dying country, that there is an economy at play here, that they could be a force here, then they will want a foothold."

"What does it matter if the DemiGod's plan comes to fruition?"

"And if it doesn't? We've tried for years to do what this professor is supposed to figure out immediately." Archbishop Santos turned back to the window and shook his head. "I've spent years in the empire, at the university, and crisscrossing the Riverlands, spreading the exact rumors needed to keep this from happening. This entire plan is falling apart at the seams. The church is in grave danger."

"Danger?"

"Can you not reason, Renaldo? I have lied to the empire for years on the state of affairs in Dressa. Bribed their spies, deceived their admiralty, and made their emperor look the fool. This could not be worse."

"Perhaps we should—"

"Conduct a prayer! We must pray to the gods for guidance! Call the nuns, call the priests and all the bishops. Call them all to the great hall. Now!"

Renaldo bowed and left the room.

Archbishop Santos took one last long look out of his

window. He truly did not know what to do. The administrator would welcome the empire, thinking they could manipulate them with their economic policies and even win concessions and victories. But the emperor would be furious with the church. The Magi would protect them for a time, but the empire had numbers. What good would fireballs and magical waves be when ten thousand soldiers landed on their shores? Besides, the empire would learn spells in due time. All they had to do was listen to the Magi cast them, and they could do the same. Once they figured out how magic worked in Dressa, the church would be doomed. Their only hope now was for the gods to answer their prayers—which made Archbishop Santos even more concerned.

THE LARGE HALL of the great church of Hogkarta filled with nuns, priests, bishops, and reservist junior magi, several of which were still hastily adjusting their robes and garments, and quite a few more were finishing their afternoon snack. It was with great pleasure that Archbishop Santos noted less than a handful swaying from too much mead. He really needed to make an official statement about mead at some point. Yes, there was a god who loved mead—seventy-two of them, actually. Yes, that many who loved it, and most of them liked it, so each drink was something like a prayer to the gods, in a roundabout way. But the clergy couldn't all be praying at the same time. It just wasn't practical. Not to mention that much "prayer" also ended in swearing, fighting, cursing, and fornicating—which, to make matters worse, were in fact all forms of prayer to other gods in the pantheon.

As the organist played triumphantly, Archbishop Santos

took his place at the front of the great hall behind a podium on a raised dais. Behind him, the images of the 12,297 gods of the pantheon stared down at the gathered crowd, some having a larger visage than others. Under each likeness of a god was written their name and generalized area of godliness. From war to peace and famine to feasts, every god had a specialty. At the very top sat Yelke, lord of the gods, first of the chosen—he who commanded lightning and thunder, who ordered the cosmos to spin, the great god who had conquered the dragon horde and brought peace to the world. To him was devoted the utmost prayer and sanctity. Morning and evening prayers were always directed to the lord of gods.

Beneath Yelke were other faces of his immediate family and consorts, each with their most celebrated prayers. At the very bottom of the large stone mural of images, which stood nearly twenty feet tall, sat those gods that were just sort of, well ... there. There hadn't been enough room to include their signature prayers, but their images and names were captured forever. One day, all the world would know them too. Which was a good thing, Archbishop Santos always thought, as the True Religionists didn't know who they were. Beneath those, in even smaller print nearly too tiny to read without aid, were the remaining lesser gods known only by name—most of whom, Santos wasn't sure if they were actually gods, or just human spouses of gods. But considering how far down on the list they were, worrying about insulting them wasn't exactly a hot-button item in his mind.

He cleared his throat and began. "Gathered, we have come to a time of great concern—"

Somewhere in the crowd, someone loudly hiccupped.

Archbishop Santos sighed. "... and we must now enter into prayer and beseech the gods for aid."

Mumblings from the crowd grew. Many of them nodded and whispered quiet prayers.

"We must do this tonight, as one. Enter with me, children of the gods! Enter with me, worshipers of the divine! Come with me—"

Another loud hiccup, followed by a burp and a cough, erupted from somewhere else in the crowd.

Archbishop Santos ignored the priest or nun or whoever couldn't hold their drink and raised his hands to the ceiling. "Come with me and beseech the unseen!"

Everyone in the crowd—well, most—did the same, rising from their seats. But more than few remained seated, some clearly no longer conscious. Less than a handful stumbled while attempting to stand, which Santos took as a good omen.

A cloud of grey mist formed in the ceiling, followed by tiny flashes of little bolts of lightning. The nuns were the first to say their part of the summoning spell, followed immediately by the priests.

"We beseech thee for guidance! What is our path?!" Archbishop Santos shouted.

The junior Magi stood and cast their part of the spell, and a sudden wind formed a whirling vortex in the center of the church. The Magi's words and chants merged, becoming a river of intent. Then a flash of brilliant white light erupted in the ceiling, and an image of a distant mountain formed—the great mountain of the gods.

"Lord Yelke! Give us guidance! What is our path?!"

A voice came from the ceiling like a clap of thunder. "Proceed..."

Archbishop Santos twisted his face in a slight bit of confusion. "Proceed with what, great lord?"

"With your path…"

"Yes, that is our question. What is our path?" Santos called. He had the distinct impression that more was said, or yet to be said, or was trying to be said. He shook his head and waited, but nothing else came.

The grey skies in the room unceremoniously dissipated as quickly as they had formed. Nuns and priests patted each other on the back with congratulations on the prayer session. The Magi uttered another spell, which announced pastries in the antechambers, at which the crowd cheered.

"I really don't know why I bother," Archbishop Santos muttered to himself. Yes, the gods answered, but often it was uselessly cryptic, the meaning quite subjective. Usually, he could twist it into something he favored. This time, it was clear to Santos, would be no exception.

"Renaldo. The message is obvious! We must stop them at once." He turned to find Renaldo, but the bishop was nowhere in sight. "Renaldo…?"

No matter; he'd find the bishop later. The word of the gods was always open to a bit of interpretation. Santos took comfort in the knowledge that he could easily spin the message to mean the gods were speaking to him directly, and that his path was to stop the professors and make sure the empire left Dressa Moore. Yes, that would play nicely. He left the podium quite confident in his next moves.

Jonathan savored his last bite of pastry and promptly finished his fourth pint of pilsner. His head swam and his vision wavered, but he still had his senses about him—

enough to know that throughout his dinner, not once had Captain Bartolome stopped staring at him.

"That was quite good," Jonathan said.

"Yesses, the melted cheese was divine!" William hiccupped and giggled.

"Thank you, love," the barmaid said as she swooped around the table, gathering up dirty plates. "Our cook has fine skills and knows a bit of magery to enhance the flavor."

"There're spellses for foods?" William slurred.

The barmaid nodded. "Oh, yes, love. There're spells for everything under the sun, if you know how to cast 'em."

"And how d'you cast thems, exactlies?" William asked, placing the book from the church in the spot where his plate had been.

Jonathan rolled his eyes, but let William ask his questions. Besides, the beer was hitting Jonathan as well, and he always found inebriated William to be quite amusing.

"Just say the spell with intention and feeling, is what I was told by my mum. 'Course, I never could cast much. I know a few, but they always fizzle out. Not my forte." She left the table with a smile and returned to the bar to deposit the used plates.

"You could ask me, you know. I am a magilurgical scholar," Jonathan said.

"And be ridiculed for the askings?" William said.

Jonathan felt a drunken anger bubble up in his chest. "Oh, I can't with you. Not now."

"And I can't with you," William snapped, himself on his third glass.

"Well, I can. With both of you," Bartolome said. "Now, about my payment, then?"

Jonathan fumbled with his hands. His eyes went to his coat sleeve—and a look of terror crossed his face. He'd lost a button! Not just any button on any coat either. This was his special purple travel coat—the one he'd had made especially for this journey. He held up a woozy hand to Bartolome and dug into his right-hand coat pocket, where he found his emergency travel sewing kit. Jonathan turned the bottom portion of his coat inside out to find the spare button attached to the fabric. He took out a very tiny pair of scissors from his sewing kit, but his hands trembled too much to make the cut precise.

Tears welled in his eyes. "I can't do this. I can't do anything! I'm losing my research, losing my buttons, and I'll probably lose my life soon!" Jonathan slurred half the words and mumbled through the rest.

"Oh, no worries, love, Shelly's got ya." She came to stand next to Jonathan, leaned in close, and whispered into his ear, *"Po Lo Meh Sut."*

Instantly, Jonathan's head miraculously cleared. His watery eyes dried up, and his hands became steady. He looked at Shelly, who winked back.

"What did you just do?"

"As I said, love, I only know a few spells, like that one—the one I just gave ya. Reverses all effects of magohol."

"Of whats?" William said, stuffing another pretzel cheese ball into his mouth.

"This isn't alcohol?" Jonathan asked, holding up the beer mug. "Not beer? Mead? Wine?"

Shelly shook her head. "No, love. It's magohol. Smells, tastes, and feels just like alcohol—with the added benefit that all effects can be reversed with the casting of a spell." She leaned into the table. "Great for business, innit? Folks get a bit too much on the stuff, and then just reset themselves to a clear head." She winked.

"That's quite the business model," Jonathan said.

Shelly nodded, took a look at William, and leaned into his ear. William waved her off and jerked his head away. "I quite like the effectses, thank yous," he said through a mouthful of cheese.

"Just let me know if you want to start fresh, then," Shelly said.

Jonathan turned his attention back to his missing button. With a now steady hand, he removed the extra button from the interior of his coat and began preparing it to be added to his sleeve. He glanced up occasionally at Bartolome, flashing her a smile each time.

"Jonathan, an agreement is an agreement. Before we leave this tavern, I'll have my payment in hand, as agreed. Yes?"

Jonathan threaded a needle and knotted the end. "I'm working on it."

"Any luck, then?" Bartolome asked.

Jonathan smiled. He finished attaching the button to his coat sleeve. Only once he was certain the knot would hold and it was attached correctly did he close up his emergency sewing kit and place it back in his pocket. He sat back in his chair and just shrugged. Samson hadn't given him a dime— not one gold, silver, or copper coin. Nothing. His former instructor and now clear nemesis was playing hardball, but Jonathan had no idea what the stakes were. It felt like Samson wanted to withhold the funds just to prove that he could. Well, that wouldn't go down well when they got home. That, at least, was very certain.

"Is that a no?" Bartolome asked, her expression turning into a frown.

Jonathan let his shoulders slump. "I don't have it. I have nothing. Samson is playing games. University politics. I'm sorry—please don't feed me to your crew!"

"Samson is doing whats? He can't do thats! How does he think he can do thats?" William said.

"He can, and he did. Or rather, he can't, and he won't give us any resources. He is the authority here in Hogkarta." Jonathan's eyes darted to William and back to Bartolome, who only nodded once.

"So, no money. Do I have that right?" Bartolome asked.

"No, not at all. No money *right now*. But I promise you— I give you my word as dean of the magilurigical school of the great university of the Riverlands—you shall have your money."

"But not right now."

Jonathan shrugged and nodded at the same time. "Not right now."

Bartolome sighed. "You are putting me in quite the predicament, Jonathan."

Jonathan exchanged a stunned look with William. "Are you going to abandon us?"

Bartolome returned a shrug of her own. "This is a business arrangement—and you've just told me you can't keep up your end of the agreement."

"No, I can. I can!"

Bartolome held her hand up. "However, as it happens, our interests beyond business do somewhat align."

"They do?" Jonathan asked, taken aback.

"Still, I must maintain some semblance of a reputation. There are eyes on us, even though no heads are turned this way. I can't just give you free passage. But since you have given me your word that payment will come, I suppose I can be talked into taking that."

Jonathan's eyes lit up. "Yes, yes indeed! Guaranteed!"

Bartolome smiled wider and tilted her head to the side. "But, I'm afraid I'll need a down payment of some kind. Just to prove to all those watching eyes that we can't see that I haven't lost my edge. A pirate who loses her edge soon loses far more, if she's not careful."

Jonathan frowned.

William belched. "Wha's that mean?"

Bartolome looked at Jonathan's pinky finger. "A finger will suffice."

Sweat beaded up on Jonathan's head, and he shifted in his seat. "Madam! I shall do no such thing!"

"But you must. As I said, our interests are aligned. I'm your means to get to the source, and you're my ticket to the same place. And as I can't do a thing for free..." Bartolome shrugged, smiled, and drew a small dagger from her belt.

From behind him, Jonathan could hear the red-bearded man shift in his seat behind the bar. He was growing very interested in the heated exchange at their table. William put his hand on Jonathan's, but could offer nothing but a gentle shrug.

And this, thought Jonathan, was what it had come to: sacrificing a finger to save his career. He nodded. There were worse things it could have been. He thought for a moment of refusing, of finding a new charter ship and demanding that Samson give him money for it. But what if he failed? All of his research and equipment would be lost. It wasn't his fault that Samson was chosen to come here, and it wasn't his fault that his theories of magilurgy were revolutionary. Not Randolf, Theodore, or Mary, not one of the other professors had even been considered for the honor of coming to Dressa to study the source of magic. Only Jonathan. First choice, only choice. And now he would return in a body bag, or as digested mush, and be nothing but a laughingstock. Tears formed in his eyes and flowed freely down his cheeks. He nodded at his fate and could only shrug. Then he placed his hand on the table and extended his pinky finger. With his other hand, he clasped onto William's, hard. He bored his eyes into the mess of cheese and pretzels that had taken over William's face. Hopefully, the pain would be quick. Perhaps he'd even find a spell to regrow his pinky. He honestly didn't need the thing. Or did he? Would his remaining fingers be deft at sewing?

Just as Jonathan was about to close his eyes and surrender, a large bag filled with coin slammed onto the table. A man dressed in robes took a seat next to the captain. He then reached across the table, grabbed one of the mugs of beer, and took a long pull.

"Paid in full, madam," the robed man said when he finished his drink.

Jonathan, William, and Bartolome stared at the strange man for a long minute. The robed man turned to Shelly, who nodded and smiled back. Seconds later, a fresh mug of magohol was brought, as well as a delicious-looking pastry.

"And who are you, exactly?" Bartolome asked at last.

"Renaldo. Bishop Renaldo."

Bartolome's eyebrows shot up. "The *church* is financing this expedition?"

"Didn't I tell you we had sponsorshipses?" William slurred.

Renaldo nodded. He closed his eyes and took a sip of his large pilsner, then shook his head. "No. To answer your question, the church isn't financing anything. I am not even here."

"But you're right theres," William said.

Renaldo stared at William for a good minute and then said, "You're not the smartest, are you?"

Bartolome snatched the coins from the table. "He's had more than a few of those." She tucked her small dagger back in her belt. "Payment in full accepted. Finish your drinks, lads, and we can be off. Or would you rather sleep here at the tavern's inn and leave in the morning?"

"I'm afraid that won't be possible." Renaldo pointed to the window overlooking the harbor.

Bartolome followed his finger to the window. "That's *The Crimson Swan*?"

"I'll have you knows I'm a sitting professorship at the universities—the greatest university in ... well, everywhere there's a place for universities to be." William forcibly nodded. "And I shant be besmirched or whatever's happening heres." He stood from his chair and threw the little red book at Renaldo. "And this is yours."

Renaldo caught the book, placed it in his pocket, and offered a smile. "Apologies, dear sir. I meant no offense. I didn't mean to say you're not smart. Little time has me on edge. But some things that can be said, I can't really say. And some things that I should say, well, I just won't. There are factions of the church that no longer support your expedition, you see. Secrecy is a must."

William nodded. "I sees." He wobbled his way back into his chair. "I'm not quite sure I followed thats, but apology accepted."

"What do you mean, factions that don't support our expedition?" Jonathan squinted his eyes.

Renaldo sighed. "I serve the church, and the DemiGod."

"Wha's that? DemiGod?" William said. "That's a sillies names."

Jonathan huffed. "No more drinking for you on this trip." He waved for Shelly to come over and reverse the magohol effects on William.

"The supreme leader of the church—her title is Demi-God. I serve her. And she wants this to happen. However, some have lost their way and no longer wish to see you succeed. Or perhaps they do? I'm not sure... Frankly, the archbishop can be confusing."

"Seems a bad place to be an employers," William said with a hiccup. Shelly arrived next to him, whispered into his year, and gave him a bump on his shoulder with her hip as she walked away. William shook his head, his face going red from embarrassment at realizing how inebriated he had become.

Renaldo stared at William for a long moment before looking at Bartolome with urgency in his eyes. "We have to go. That is the ship that pursued you, I'm afraid."

"Which I can only imagine prompted you to help us?" Bartolome asked.

"Quite." Renaldo threw the rest of his mug of pilsner down his throat, along with his pastry, and stood. "I can get you to your ship, but then you're on your own. You weren't even supposed to come to Hogkarta."

"We weren't supposed to come here?" Jonathan said.

"No, not at all. The barge captain was already paid for. Not by the church, of course." Renaldo winked at William. "But someone had to intervene." He glared at Bartolome.

Bartolome smiled and shrugged back at him. "A scorpion can't change her nature, Priest."

"It's Bishop."

"My equipment! I still need to purchase replacement pieces for my equipment!" Jonathan said in an excited tone.

Renaldo let out a long breath and nodded. "What kind of equipment, exactly?"

"Lead pieces. A breastplate and a helmet."

"Is that all?"

"Yes, the two trunks lost only contained those items and

some clothing. A double-stitch knitted wool knitted head-scarf and a twill jacket with perfect-length sleeves."

Now Renaldo looked at Jonathan for a long moment.

"But I can make do with my overcoat," Jonathan added.

Renaldo nodded. "I'll make sure to deliver replacements for your lead items to *The Wood*. We have leaded suits of armor in the church, as it happens. We've long known the anti-magical properties of lead. Then you sail for the Anti-Religionists. They were the original destination."

"Wait—did you say Anti-Religionists? What does that mean, exactly?" William asked.

"They are anti-us. As in, they don't agree with our philosophies. But they control the passage that will take you to the source. So, your arrival there is required."

"Why would they let us through?"

"We have an agreement with them. Unusual times calls for unusual bedfellows. You'll have a task to perform for them. There should have been a letter to them in the charter."

Bartolome nodded. "I have that."

William huffed and shook his head.

"Problem?" Renaldo asked.

"Just seems an odd name. I mean, if we were to break down the language. Your lot are theists, as in, you believe in the existence of gods. Wouldn't that make them anti-theists, since they don't believe in your gods?" William said.

Jonathan smiled. It was just like William to push back on someone who had offended his intellect. He rarely did it in academic circles, for fear of having his funding pulled, but with the general public, he could be quite ruthless.

Renaldo and Bartolome, along with Shelly and the red-bearded man, all came to stare at the table, their heads all tilted to one side, a look of confusion on their faces.

Jonathan felt that worried feeling creep up his spine again, as if they had just landed themselves in more trouble—and only after being miraculously saved from trouble just moments before.

"What? What are you all staring at?" William said.

"They don't worship gods because they *believe* in them, William," Bartolome said.

"No, love. We worship them because they're real—and we're terrified of them," Shelly said.

"They're scarier than a thorned behemoth bear in heat," the red-bearded barkeep added gravely.

YELKE, lord of the gods, master of magic, king of the great mountain continent, conqueror of dragons, first to tame the forces of the ancients and bend magic to his will, architect of the great spell that would usher in a new age of gods, looked out across the vastness of the world that was his.

And screamed.

His fists balled into hammers of stone, and flames burst from his mouth. From the depths of his soul, he summoned the essence of magic itself and commanded it to rain down from the heavens. Flashes of green and red lightning erupted in the sky over the mountain of the gods. White-hot bolts of force crashed through the air above their prison, but the great spell that held them there refused to even acknowledge the tantrum of the lord of the gods.

"Done with your morning tantrum, husband?" Neltzy said. She crossed the marble patio and stood a few feet behind Yelke.

"Never!" A blast of purple light erupted from his chest and met the lightning that rained down from above. The two forces stopped several yards apart before meeting, then both the lightning and the purple force from Yelke slowly withdrew.

"And now?" Neltzy said.

Yelke turned, never once looked at his wife, and strode with anger and contempt back into his golden home. Lesser gods—those Yelke kept as his attendants—ran to find a shadow to hide within for fear of his wrath. He could still snatch one from the darkness and torment them for a year if he wanted to. He was their lord, and all the power of the world flowed through his very fingertips.

"You broke my statue! Again!" Neltzy called from the patio.

Yelke ignored her. Once they were free to roam the world, he could command an army of statues to be made—a thousand for every god on the mountain. Well, maybe just for his immediate family. And perhaps a few friends. No reason to get carried away.

Through the twists and turns of the golden keep, Yelke stalked, destroying another statue or work of art. What did it matter? Artisan gods needed something to do to pass the eons of time, after all—and eons were exactly what they had to spend. All because of that bumbling Wizard, Finnian, and that insufferable Dragon, Qaz. Couldn't one of them have just died? Just one? Oh, no—both had to be stubborn, find each other in the world's vastness, and attack each other with the same spell, causing them both to be frozen in time for eons. Ten thousand years' worth of planning, all poured down the drain in an instant.

Grey clouds filled the hall of prayer. Yelke waved the smoke away and walked up to the podium, where Fulte, the answerer of prayers, stood with clenched teeth and balled fists. She banged on the podium and screamed into the grey clouds that spread out over a round sunken floor below her.

"No, not just that. Say everything I said!" Fulte shot a dozen stone darts from her eyes, each passing harmlessly through the grey cloud to collide with the marble floor below.

"What is happening?" Yelke asked.

"That dimwit Archbishop Santos held a surprise invocation to ask for guidance." Fulte turned to Yelke and shook her head. "Do they think I have nothing better to do than wait around for them to invoke me for guidance? I was in the middle of pruning!" She pulled out a pair of garden shears and tossed them into the sunken pit below.

"Were you able to answer?"

"No! Of course I wasn't. Not really. Without time to prepare, the spell only allows one-word answers. Not that I've ever been able to give more than a sentence, anyway. Though I did manage to get three words in at the end just now."

Yelke fumed. If only they could tell these True Religionists exactly what to do, when to do it, and how they could free themselves from this mountain prison... But the great spell cast by both the wizards and dragons of old that held them here also blocked them from communicating with anyone outside of the mountain in anything more than one or two words, or perhaps the occasional sentence, which was infuriating in a thousand—no, ten thousand ways. All ways!

"Try harder. I will help."

Fulte nodded. She turned to the pit and raised her arms in the air, but immediately lowered them as the grey smoke around the sunken floor dissipated. She spat once where the smoke used to be and jumped down to the marble to retrieve her shears.

"What happened?" Yelke asked.

"They left. Stopped praying."

"What did you send them?"

"I told them to proceed with their plan, but to kill the Dragon first. They still think they need to kill Finnian. I even gave them the spell to release the Dragon and Finnian both."

Yelke nodded. "And what did they hear?"

"'Proceed.'"

"That's all?"

"Yes, great lord of the gods. And we both know Archbishop Santos will twist that in a hundred ways."

Yelke stomped his feet on the marble, which cracked under his might. "You would think after hundreds of years, you would have made some progress with this."

Fulte turned and gave her brother a wicked stare. "Oh, yes, blame me. I had this working twenty years ago, I would remind you."

Yelke nodded. "Yes, and how did that turn out?"

Fulte shrugged. "Message got across, didn't it? And the Dragon let some smoke out of his nose, didn't he? Not exactly a fireball, but it was something."

Yelke turned without another word and marched out of the room. He slammed his hand into a stone wall and screamed in frustration. The entire world was sitting there like a ripe fruit for them to claim and rule, but even with all their magical might, they could do nothing but wait and watch as humanity bumbled their way forward. At least that Bishop Renaldo had the right idea. But he needed help. And clearly, Fulte wasn't the one to provide it.

Deep in the lower levels of the golden palace, Yelke

entered a large room lit by a thousand flickering candles. Tables filled the space, each covered with a dozen instruments and experiments of Borke, the tinkerer of the gods. He could build devices that channeled magic, funneling it into a contracted form and exact power ten times what could be gained otherwise.

"Borke," Yelke said as he entered the room.

"Hello, Yelke. How are the little ones?"

"Why do you always ask me that? They're fine. They've been fine for three thousand years."

Borke shrugged. "It's what you ask when a friend visits."

"Just tell me about your progress. Fulke has failed. Again."

"You should be easier on her, Yelke. She is your sister."

Crackles of lightning flashed in Yelke's eyes, causing Borke to grab several instruments from his table. Yelke smashed a table next to him with one blow of his hammer of a fist. He shot a bolt of lightning out of his eyes, carving a long scratch down the length of the stone wall.

"If you could not smash the table to your right, that would be a good thing," Borke said.

Yelke snarled, turning to the table with his hand raised high in the air, but he came to an abrupt stop when he saw the two rainbow crows in a small cage that sat on the table. Both birds looked at Yelke and opened their beaks, but no sound emerged from either.

"What is this? How are these here?" Yelke asked.

Borke smiled. "I managed something wonderful, Yelke. Or rather, I found something wonderful."

"Why are they not making any sounds?"

Borke let out a long sigh. "It's a very annoying caw, to be honest. So, I put them in a cage where no sounds can escape."

"Tell me what you found. Now!" Yelke commanded. A tiny thundercloud formed over his head with small flashes of lightning inside.

"A loophole in the great spell between wizards and dragons."

Thunder rolled above them, and Borke quickly nodded. "Borke..."

"Fine, so much for suspense. You used to like suspenseful announcements, but I see those days are over."

"Borke!"

"Right. I found a hole in the spell that blocks escape from our mountain prison. Tiny, nearly invisible, but there."

"Impossible. I wrote the great spell with the dragons. There was no allowance for a hole."

Borke nodded with a smile. "There actually is. A recluse of a wizard made an allowance for a hole."

"What wizard?" Yelke's eyes sparkled with lightning.

"He had a long beard and a pointy hat and carried a staff. I always thought the look was silly for a wizard, to be honest. What's the point in walking around with a staff all day when your legs work just fine?"

Yelke frowned. The look was familiar, but he couldn't place it. He recalled every wizard on the mountaintop, and not a one had carried a staff or worn a pointy hat. In fact, there was only one wizard that Yelke had ever met who wore a pointy hat. But that Wizard, a blight on all the gods, was currently in the valley and frozen in time, standing in front of the Dragon.

Yelke's eyes suddenly went wide with shock. "You're not serious...?"

"Finnian loved birds, that old Wizard. Knew so much about them. Migratory patterns, gestation periods, flight times..."

"Get to the point, Borke."

"Well, the Wizard added to the pact before the dragon king sealed it. An allowance that the great dragon king permitted for a migratory path of a specific species of bird, the rainbow crow—which he had a hand in making, actually—to pass through the protected mountaintop on a cliff on the far side."

"Nonsense." But Yelke doubted himself as soon as he said the word. That pointy-hatted fool of a Wizard's face came crashing back into his mind. Yes, the bird man. Wanted to be the god of birds, and no one else did. Had he really added such a frivolous amendment to the great spell? The casting of it had taken a year, with dragons and wizards reciting the pieces constantly. The blood of the lord of gods boiled at the thought of one of his minions jeopardizing the grand plan just to maintain the lives of some stupid birds.

"Finnian," Yelke muttered. Thunder cracked outside, and flashes of lightning lit the heavens on fire. Even mentioning Finnian's name boiled the blood in Yelke's veins. That fool of a wizard had mucked up millennia of planning. The gods were imprisoned in their own mountain until the battle between Finnian and the Dragon concluded—and that day was a lifetime away.

"Finnian did this? That imbecile added something to the great spell that could destroy everything we've worked to create?!"

Borke shrugged. "It was a quite ingenious addition. The hole technically doesn't touch the mountaintop, only the cliffside where the birds roost. I've reviewed the great spell, and it's still intact."

"Wait... What are you saying? Can we use this?"

Borke nodded. "With Finnian's addition and some tinkering, we can, at very specific times of day matching the tides, using the caves in the mountain, allow passage through to the world beyond."

"This is astounding!"

"... For birds."

"What?"

"Only birds, specifically of this species..." Borke pointed to the two birds in the cage. "... can pass through."

Yelke looked at the cage and tilted his head to one side. Plans formed in his mind. There was a way he could leverage this, he was certain. This could be the key that turned the tide. They could use this hole, this portal, a gateway to the world beyond, and free the Dragon once and for all.

"You could send a full message to the True Religionists with this. Direct them precisely on what to do," Borke said. "Well, you'd have to train them to fly to Hogkarta I suppose. Not sure how we could do that, to be honest. Perhaps with seeds?"

"Oh, I have a much better plan in mind."

SELKE and Fjorn sat on the balcony of the magnificent palace of the gods. Their feet rested on the marble railing that overlooked the vastness of the world below. In each of their hands sat a mug filled with the finest mead that all the gods of drink could ever have brewed. Ham sandwiches, each with a slice of cheese and tomato, were held in their other hands.

"What shall we do today, Selke?" Fjorn asked.

Selke shrugged. "Don't know. Same thing we did yesterday?"

"What did we do yesterday, then?"

"Same thing we're doing now," Selke said.

Fjorn nodded.

They both sighed.

Frankly, being a god wasn't as fun as Yelke had made it sound all those thousands of years ago. Sure, one day they would rule the entire world and could even create passageways to other dimensions of existence. Yon the Traveler, the only god not on the mountain and not stuck in an eternal battle with a dragon, had showed them all how it was done. Of course, he had never returned, but that wasn't really the point.

What was the point? Fjorn shrugged as he lost his train of thought and drank another cup of mead.

"You know, being a god isn't all it's cracked up to be," Selke said.

"Yes! That was it, Selke."

"What was it, Fjorn?"

"My train of thought. You found it, Selke."

"Did I?"

"Quite."

Selke smiled. "Didn't know I was looking for it."

"Being a god... It's terribly boring."

Selke nodded. "And repetitive."

"And dull."

Selke took a sip of her mead and looked at Fjorn. "You already said that."

"Did I?"

"Well, you said it's boring. Same thing as dull."

Fjorn nodded. "Well, it deserves to be said twice."

Selke sat forward in her chair and pointed to a spot far below in the world of humankind. Fjorn looked where she pointed and shook his head in frustration. Below them, in the great valley of celebration on the second continent of the world, a mass of people—a thousand, perhaps more—were gathered to have a party. Not just a minor affair either. By the looks of the amount of celebration already underway, this party was going to be quite the event, perhaps even becoming legendary. And neither Selke nor Fjorn could attend.

"Least we can watch," Fjorn said.

"I'll get more mead."

Before Selke could move from her chair, the door to the balcony burst open, and Yelke strode onto the patio. He followed Fjorn's gaze to the valley far below and placed his hands on his hips. The king of the gods remained silent for a long moment before grabbing Fjorn's mug of mead and downing the drink in one gulp. Yelke tossed the mug to the patio, grabbed Selke's empty cup, and tried to down that too, then gave Selke a side glance and shook his head.

"I was going to get more. Should I get you one, Uncle?" Selke asked.

"You two have been drunk for a thousand years," Yelke muttered.

Fjorn shrugged. "Fine way to pass the time, if you ask me. I mean, not a lot more we can do."

"Would you like something more to do?" Yelke asked.

"Are you asking to be vague?"

"What?" Yelke said in genuine confusion.

"Fjorn means you're not asking for our permission. You clearly have something you'd like us to do," Selke said.

Yelke nodded. "I do indeed."

"I'm not fixing any more statues, if that's what you want. You can turn me into a pig and roast me for supper if you like. I've fixed over ten thousand statues for you, and I just can't anymore," Fjorn said.

"Is that how you address the god of gods?!" Yelke's voice thundered in the air.

Fjorn rolled his eyes. "It is today."

"Sorry, Uncle. He's melancholy today. But then, we all are."

Yelke let out a long sigh and nodded. "I understand your pain, children."

"And that's another thing. We've been here nearly the longest—died when we were just teenagers. Do you know the frustration of being a teenager for three thousand years? No one here on the mountain respects us. No one cares what we offer to godhood. They just want us to fix statues all day long."

"I said, I understand. But my patience with you is not eternal."

"But our stay on the mountain certainly is." Fjorn slumped his shoulders with a sigh.

"Enough!" Lightning erupted from the Yelke's eyes. From the heavens beyond the mountain, thunder clapped, responding to the great god's call. Fjorn shrank in his chair and looked down at the patio. He could only push Yelke so far. Fjorn and Selke had done much for the gods and had little reward, but Yelke was always sympathetic to them. But push the lord of the gods too far, and things could turn. Truth be told, Fjorn had no desire to be made into a pig and fed to other gods. Since they were all under the power of the great spell, he would just return to existence back on the mountaintop on the Plain of Returning, but it wasn't a very pleasant experience.

"Sorry, Yelke. I'm just in a foul mood."

Yelke's hand rested on Fjorn's shoulder. "Which is why I offer you something that no other god will be offered."

"What's that, Uncle?" Selke returned to the patio.

Neither Yelke nor Fjorn had seen her go. She returned with a cup of mead in each hand and a third pressed against her body.

"You shall both return to the world of men."

"And women," Selke added.

Yelke nodded. "Yes, and women. The world of men and women. And once there—"

"What do you mean, return? We can't leave the mountain," Fjorn protested.

"We have found a way. And once there—"

"You did? Was it Borke? I knew if anyone could do it, it would be him," Selke said.

"Do you think we'll make it in time for the party, Selke?" Fjorn asked.

Yelke's voice grew in thunder. "Once there—"

"Oh, I don't think so. I mean, it's probably something where we have to be birthed or something, Fjorn," Selke said.

"Reincarnation? Not that again. That's never worked."

Selke shrugged. "It kinda worked."

"Oh, I just can't with you two!" Yelke snapped his fingers. A flash of white magic burst onto the patio. When it left, both Fjorn and Selke had been transformed into birds with brightly colored feathers and iridescent feet—the exact kind whose migratory patterns allowed them flight via the cliff-side along the mountaintop. Yelke snatched both the birds before they could fly away and marched them to Borke, who waited outside the patio with a cage.

"Take them, Borke. Send them back to the world."

"They may not remember they're gods at first. We're in uncharted territory."

"Nothing is uncharted for me. I am lord of all!"

"Have you ever done this before, Yelke?"

"No, of course not."

Borke half shrugged. "Then, really, by definition—"

"Just do it, Borke! Send them to the world of men."

One of the two birds cawed loudly in anger.

"... And women. The world of men and women. They shall be the first gods to walk the earth. They shall direct the Religionists to kill the Dragon, end that imbecile Finnian, and free the gods once and for all!"

"It may not work, Yelke. I just must inform you now. It's really only theoretical at this point."

Yelke shrugged. His eyes drifted to the cage holding both birds. He flicked the metal bars, closing the door and plunging the occupants of the cage into silence. He then shrugged. "Yes, well... We'll have not lost that much then, now, will we?"

CHAPTER TEN

Commodore Wilkes walked down the gangway of *The Crimson Swan* to the docks of Hogkarta. Confidence carried him with every step, as well as the line of his military along the railing of the ship, and the fact that every cannon on *The Swan* was primed and ready to let the citizens of this city know that the empire was here —and that the empire demanded respect.

Behind him, Captain Bridgewater and a contingent of armed soldiers walked down the gangway. They fanned out behind the commodore once he reached the dock. In front of him, two groups had formed on either side of *The Crimson Swan's* gangway. One group, with crisp uniforms and standing at attention, looked to be of the same steel as Wilkes's own soldiers, while the others, with long grey robes down to their ankles and black cowls covering their heads, were clearly of the True Religionists' order. Two men, one from each group, walked forward to stand just in front of their respective military and priest. The one from the militia looked like he'd been in a few fights in his life and carried himself in a manner that said he wasn't the type to take much verbal abuse. The other, Wilkes knew personally—though he had no idea how Archbishop Santos, standing there with his long purple robes and fine golden jewelry on his fingers, could possibly have gotten to Hogkarta so fast. But it didn't matter. Wilkes had to focus on the here and now.

"Gentlemen," the commodore greeted them.

"Get back on your ship, raise your anchor, and get out of my port. Now. Or we'll send you to the bottom," the military-looking man said.

Archbishop Santos stifled a laugh before speaking. "I'm Archbishop Santos, of Hogkarta."

"Aren't you supposed to be in the capital? At the Great University?"

Santos shrugged. "I was needed here."

"How'd you get here so fast?" Commodore Wilkes asked.

"The church has its ways. And I wanted to welcome you to our city personally."

"It's not a welcome, 'cause he's leaving," the other man said.

"May I have the honor of knowing your name, sir?" Commodore Wilkes asked.

"I'm chief constable of Hogkarta, supreme authority of the law and protector of the city. And I'm telling you to get out of here."

Archbishop Santos shook his head. "He doesn't have that much authority."

The chief shot the archbishop a wicked look, but twisted his attention back to the commodore. He let out a long sigh of frustration. "Well? Are you leaving?"

Wilkes shook his head and returned the hardness of the chief's stare. "No. We are pursuing a fugitive. And we're not leaving without her."

"Fugitive?" The chief's eyes squinted.

"She attacked Oyster Piers in the Riverlands, a town under the jurisdiction of the empire."

"You know who she is?"

Wilkes nodded. "The captain of that ship." He pointed to *The Knotted Wood*, floating not a hundred yards away, moored to the dock.

The chief constable nodded. "Well, in that case, if it means I can be rid of that one sooner, you have my permission to stay, as long as you get her out of my city. Agreed?"

Bridgewater started to say something before Commodore Wilkes raised his hand to silence him. "We don't need your permission, Chief."

A long silence grew between the three men. The archbishop smiled politely, while the chief constable and the commodore locked eyes in a sudden battle of wills. All three groups—the empire, the constables, and the reservist Magi of the church—tensed at the silent confrontation unfolding in front of them.

"Doesn't matter if you accept my permission or feel you don't need it. I'm giving it." The chief constable turned from the commodore and took a step towards his men.

The men behind the commodore let out a silent sigh— one he shared. "Thank you, Chief—"

"But, just so you know where you are..." The chief constable turned on a dime and pointed to the central mast of *The Crimson Swan*. "Fire!"

White balls of flame shot out from a dozen staffs held by the constables behind the chief. The fireballs blazed a path to *The Crimson Swan* and slammed into the mainmast. Wood shattered into splinters. Shouts and screams sounded immediately from the unexpected attack. Men along the rail raised their rifles and took aim at the constables on the dock.

"To arms!" Bridgewater shouted.

Commodore Wilkes watched the next few moments as if in slow motion. He calculated their next moves with lightning-fast efficiency. They could fire a cannon into the city, but they would kill dozens, if not hundreds of innocent people there. They could fire on the constables, destroy the docks, and send them a mile down to the ground below. Or they could engage in hand-to-hand combat and show these Hogkarta men what imperial soldiers could do.

The words of an old admiral came to him in that moment: *"The empire is above this."* There was only one option to take—one option to secure Bartolome and let these people know what it meant that the empire was here. Wilkes held up his arm and balled his hand into a fist. "Hold!" he called out to the crew of *The Swan*.

The chief constable regarded the commodore with a mix of confusion and curiosity.

"Captain Bridgewater," Wilkes said.

"Sir!"

"Have our men report casualties and begin repair of *The Swan* at once."

"Sir...?"

"These men will accompany me to capture our fugitive." Commodore Wilkes approached the chief constable and came within inches of his face. "If any of my men were injured by your reckless and pointless attack, you shall answer for it."

The chief constable smiled. "Shall I? And yet I'm not."

"The empire does not respond to the tantrums of children," Wilkes snapped. "But we punish those who do us harm."

The smile on the face of the constable vanished. "Those sound like very strong words."

"Oh, I assure you, they are."

"Hold! Hold! Stand down! Back away this instant!" a voice called out from a crowd of gathered locals.

Wilkes turned to see a portly man charging towards them, his fine silvery clothing billowing as he ran, his stomach bouncing with the pounding of his feet. He stopped near the chief constable and put a hand on the man's shoulder while he gasped for air.

"And you are...?" Wilkes said.

"I am Administrator Streckenbach of Hogkarta. Supreme authority is mine."

"No, it isn't," the chief constable said.

"Your guard dog needs a tighter leash," Archbishop Santos observed wryly.

"Philip, please." The administrator turned to the chief constable. "And yes, my authority is the highest! Stay out of this, Chief Constable!"

"Well, Administrator Streckenbach, your men attacked my ship without provocation."

"Yes, I'm aware. The entire city is aware."

"And what shall be done about this?"

The administrator removed his hand from the chief constable's shoulder and took a long, deep breath to gather himself. "Let us retire to my official office, where we shall discuss matters of state. You are the very first imperial ship to visit these shores in over a hundred years. The honor is ours."

Wilkes nodded. His eyes darted between the chief constable and the administrator. There was clearly a power struggle of sorts here, the depths of which he couldn't determine. But a meeting of state was his duty as the highest-ranking officer in the empire, so he simply couldn't refuse.

"Fine. Captain Bridgewater will accompany me," Wilkes said. "My men shall stay here at the dock. For a showing of goodwill." He shot the chief constable a glare, which wasn't returned.

"Splendid. Archbishop, perhaps you should come as well? You are the leader of the church in Hogkarta, after all."

"The DemiGod is the most sacred and highest of the church and—"

"Yes, well, no one has seen her in a year. So, you'll do. Follow!"

The administrator wrapped his arm around the commodore and led him from the docks into the city proper. Bridgewater followed, along with the archbishop, while the three groups of military and religious soldiers were left to stare at one another. All of them, Wilkes noted, kept a tight grip on their respective weapons.

COMMODORE WILKES SAT in the office of Administraor Streckenbach. Next to him was Archbishop Santos of the church. Ludwig and Bridgewater stood behind them in the back of the office. On the other side of a large oak desk, Streckenbach leaned back in his chair, more out of habit than intent. He smiled at the commodore, then at Santos. "Well then, welcome to Hogkarta, Commodore Wilkes. What brings you and the empire to our fine city?"

"And more importantly, how long will you be staying?" Archbishop Santos added.

Wilkes smiled. "We are here to capture a fugitive. Captain Bartolome of *The Knotted Wood* attacked Oyster

Piers. Those who attack our people soon learn that there is nowhere in this world that they can hide from the justice of the empire."

"Splendid. And so, you have no other business in Hogkarta, is that right?" Streckenbach said.

"None. Though I must admit, the empire is quite surprised to see such a flourishing society in Dressa, a place we had thought was broken by magic." Wilkes shot the archbishop a glare.

"Yes, well, we are quite a hearty people," Administrator Streckenbach said.

Archbishop Santos gritted his teeth and shifted in his chair. "So, you shall leave, then? As soon as you find your fugitive?"

Wilkes shrugged, in a way that held far more suggestion than it did an answer. "Though, perhaps, given the extent of commerce in Dressa, it's in our interest to establish ourselves here. As friends, of course."

Streckenbach looked at Ludwig, who had kept his face still and silent. The message, Wilkes hoped, was clear: *Now that the empire knows that we can come here, we will come back.* Which meant everything in Dressa would change soon. But Wilkes knew their changes would be for the better, for both Hogkarta and the empire. Truth be told, Wilkes was still in shock at the size of this city. He, and the empire, had thought there were nothing but small villages in Dressa since the magical tsunami, as it was called, one hundred years ago. Not to mention the event that had claimed his wife two decades prior. But Hogkarta had survived both and thrived. There was opportunity here—opportunity for the empire to grow.

Wilkes noticed Streckenbach sharing looks with Ludwig behind him. They were having some kind of silent conversation. Perhaps it was even of magical nature? What the empire could do with such magic… Of course, magic only seemed to work in Dressa Moore—with the exception of magical items, as Santos could attest—but perhaps that was more than enough? Wilkes imagined magically imbued vessels commanding the Riverlands. They could chase down any pirate that dared run from imperial ships. He shook his head. There would be time enough for such things later.

"Again, I insist, we would only be here as friends. But being friends with the empire can be a very good thing." Wilkes took out a small bag of gold coins from his pocket and placed it on Streckenbach's desk. It was customary for capital ships to carry quantities of gold for just such occasions.

Administrator Streckenbach reached for the bag, then counted the coins. He looked up with the grins. "I agree! Wholeheartedly."

"You *what*?!" Archbishop Santos's face exploded with rage.

"Dressa Moore would love to welcome a contingent of the empire to stay here. We can even afford you a barracks house—have to clean it up a bit first, of course. I believe the building I have in mind is an abandoned fish house. But I'm sure you can make it a home."

"Alfred," Archbishop Santos growled, "this is going too far."

"Oh, nonsense, Philip. We have our spies in the Riverlands—"

Ludwig let out an audible groan from the back of the room.

"—and they assure us that the empire would be quite beneficial to the interests of Dressa."

Wilkes sat back in his chair and turned to look at Bridge-water, who nodded and shrugged.

The commodore turned back to the administrator. "That is most hospitable of you, Administrator."

Streckenbach nodded, retrieving three tumblers and a bottle of port from his desk drawer. "Every good negotiation should end with a drink, wouldn't you agree?"

"Are we concluded? What of my fugitive?" Wilkes asked.

Streckenbach shrugged. "Have her? She and her crew of un-alivers scare the daylights out of everyone, anyway."

Archbishop Santos burst from his chair and loomed over the desk. "The church does not approve of this course of action, Alfred!"

"The church has no say in it."

"Is that right?"

"Oh, Philip, stop being so dramatic. It was inevitable that the empire would come here. We might as well benefit from it." Streckenbach took a sip from his glass and refilled it.

Archbishop Santos shook his head, his face turning bright red, both his fists clenched into tight balls. Without another word, he turned and stormed out, slamming the door behind him.

"Don't mind him. He's never been a fan of the empire," the administrator offered.

"Why is that?" Wilkes asked.

Streckenbach offered glasses to Bridgewater and Ludwig, who both stepped forward. "I don't really know, honestly. Ludwig?"

Ludwig took the offered glass and let the administrator pour him a drink. "Archbishop Santos is a complicated man."

"Of that, we can all be certain!" The administrator raised his drink and offered a toast to the room.

BARTOLOME KNELT behind a large sack of potatoes and an even larger bin of freshly caught squid, some of which had tiny little hands they used to wave at her as she knelt. Only one of them could speak. Behind her, Jonathan and William huddled together, waiting for whatever other instructions she or Renaldo would give. Marta took the time to give Jonathan a quick stare. She had revealed to him that her motives were more than just money. But what choice did she have? She couldn't have just walked away from them. This opportunity to sail through the straits, access to which was strictly controlled by the Anti-Religionists, and on to the Madness Fjords was just too good to let slip through her fingers. But now Jonathan knew Bartolome was up to something, which complicated things. What if he prevented her from throwing the repeating stone over the falls to the Wizard and Dragon below? What then? All would be lost.

"There's your ship," Renaldo said.

"Yes, sitting next to *The Crimson Swan*, with our gangway surrounded by Magi, constables, and imperial soldiers."

Renaldo shrugged. "I said I could get you here. I didn't say I could get you on your ship."

"Actually, that's exactly what you said." William plunged his hands into his pockets and sulked.

"Well, I can't. As you can see, it's surrounded. Your supplies arrived, at least, in those trunks by the dock. See them?" Renaldo said.

Jonathan nodded. "That was fast."

"Like I said, we had leaded suits at the church. As well as other items."

Bartolome turned to the priest and almost struck him in the face. "Are you always like this?"

"Like what?"

"Filled with half promises and an equal amount of disappointing news?"

Bishop Renaldo nodded. "Comes with the job."

"So, what do we do now? This is simply intolerable," Jonathan said.

"For once, I agree. We can't sit here with the squid," Bartolome added.

"You can, you know," the one squid that could talk said. "You could also tip us over and free us from impending doom at the hands of your merciless brigades of white-hatted madmen."

"Did that squid just talk?" William asked, eyes wide.

"It did. And no, we can't. Sorry, friend," Bartolome said to the squid.

"Who said we were friends?" the squid snapped.

"This is a strange place you've taken us to, Jonathan," William said.

Renaldo rose from his crouch and backed out of their hidden nook. But Bartolome was faster and grabbed him by the collar to pull him back down to her side. "Where are you going?"

"I am already missed. There are quite a few intricacies at play here. Far more hands are at work than we had planned for," Renaldo said.

"Who's 'we'?" Bartolome asked.

"Even that takes too long to explain. Suffice to say, I am already missed, and though getting you here was paramount, so is me returning to the archbishop."

"But how do we get to my ship?"

Renaldo shrugged. "You're resourceful, Captain. I'm sure you can think of something."

"Can we expect help from your Magi?"

"No, I'm afraid not. They are under the command of the archbishop."

"Isn't that who you work for? Didn't he send you to help us?"

"Well, yes, and no, in the order of your questions. I must go." Renaldo stood and looked at William. "Best of luck to you, good sir."

"It's me," Jonathan said. "It's me you should wish good luck too. I'm the magilurgist."

"Yes, you are indeed." Renaldo smiled to Jonathan and nodded again to William. He rose from his position and calmly walked from their secluded spot into the throng of people.

"That was cryptic," William said.

"To say the least."

"Hey, he pocketed that book back to me!" William plucked the book out of his pocket and thumbed through a few pages. "Why would he do that?"

"That is a question we don't have the luxury of answering right now," Bartolome said. "I'll have to create a diversion. When I do, you two board the ship."

"Won't they recognize us?"

Bartolome turned to them and nodded. She whispered a magical spell into the air and moved her hands over both Jonathan and William. Within moments, their clothes changed color and style. Jonathan's face grew long with a thin beard, and his stomach grew to the size of a beach ball. William's hair changed to red and grew to five times its length. His cheeks moved high, and his jaw squared. Two large overcoats formed over both their shoulders, the exact size and color of the red overcoats worn by the imperial soldiers.

They pointed at each other. William pulled a few times on Jonathan's coat.

"This is brilliant! We can just walk aboard now, can't we?"

"It won't fool the Magi. They know this spell," Bartolome warned.

"Then what do we do?"

Bartolome smiled. "We give the soldiers exactly what they want and hope the Magi get distracted."

Bartolome watched her newly created doppelgänger walk toward the dock, the girl's hips swinging proudly from left to right as she walked with the confidence a few gold coins in her pocket provided. It wasn't a good plan, but it was all she had: use her illusion spell to transform a nearby barmaid's likeness into Bartlome's and send her to the docks. She'd be fine, eventually, and have enough money for months. No risk, no reward in this life, after all.

Jonathan and William rounded the docks from the other side, nearer to *The Knotted Wood*. Once the commotion started, if it started at all, they should be able to slip onto *The Wood* with the imperial guards none the wiser.

On the dock, the barmaid reached the imperial soldiers, who stopped her at once and took her forcibly by both arms. The Magi nearest them approached the girl, then shook their heads and snapped their fingers. The disguise folded in around itself and disappeared. The soldiers took the girl away anyway, probably to question her about Bartolome, but still left most of them near *The Wood*.

"Well, that failed terribly," Bartolome remarked.

"It was a stupid idea, really," the squid said. He had lifted himself out of the tub and looked over the side to the docks.

"You have any better ideas?"

"Of course, but it'll cost you," the squid said.

Bartolome sighed. What choice did she have? "Fine. What's the plan?"

"Throw us in the water, and we'll do the rest. Simple."

"Not much of a plan. What are you little things going to do?"

"Trust me, woman," the squid assured her.

Bartolome shrugged. What could it hurt? She dragged the drum of squid near to where the water lapped at the dock and tipped the entire thing into the harbor.

Moments later, an angry shop owner appeared and raised his voice in alarm and shock. Bartolome immediately offered him payment, but the man wanted more justice than gold could buy.

"Help! She's stolen my squid!" the man shouted.

Soldiers, constables, and Magi on the dock several hundred feet away turned at the shouts of the shop owner. One of them pointed at Bartolome and yelled. All the imperial soldiers, most of the Magi, and three of the constables rushed in her direction—which accomplished at least half of her goal.

Bartolome pushed against the shop owner, dodged a rolling cart of rotten fruit, and dived through the alleys of Hogkarta.

RENALDO REACHED the church just as shouts from the city streets alerted him to something amiss near the docks. Archbishop Santos could see the bishop hesitate before entering. He wondered what Renaldo was up to. Had the DemiGod gotten to him? No matter. Santos rushed down the stairs to the front entrance, grabbed Bishop Renaldo's robe, yanked him inside, and slammed the door closed.

"Closed for services!" Archbishop Santos shouted through the closed door.

"Yes, Your Grace." Two priests came to the front door and locked it tight.

"Where have you been, Renaldo?"

"Church business, Your Grace."

"Nonsense. I *am* church business, and I didn't send you anywhere."

Renaldo didn't answer. Archbishop Santos glared at him, but soon waved him away. Let him have his secrets. Santos led them through the church, up the stairs, and to his office that overlooked Hogkarta and the docks. He went to the window and breathed heavily for a moment before shaking his head.

"We are doomed. The church is doomed," Archbishop Santos said. "I never should have set this in motion."

"How so, Your Grace?"

"That fool Alfred has invited the empire to stay. Even giving them their own barracks!"

"Is that advisable?"

Santos huffed. "Of course not! They have no idea what the empire and the emperor can do. Once you let them in, the results will be dreadful. I've seen it!"

Renaldo nodded. "Then we have to succeed."

Santos turned to him, his eyes wild with shock. "Succeed? With the DemiGod's mad plan to kill the Wizard?"

"Yes, Your Grace. We must succeed now. I fear you're right. Even with our knowledge of magic, the empire will learn it soon enough and annex all of Dressa," Renaldo said.

"Fool's folly. We had the entire resources of the church last time we went to the source, and we only ended up creating an entire island of monsters." Santos took out a set of beads and began counting them. His dreams of becoming the DemiGod were slipping through his fingers. He'd always suspected this plan would fail, which would allow him to challenge the DemiGod for leadership of the church. But, if they succeeded now, his plan would be lost, and the gods would return to the world. And there's no telling what that lot would do. That said, succeeding now would be better than the empire staying in Dressa. Of that, Santos was certain.

"With grace, your grace, but why did you put this plan in motion if you weren't sure of its success?" Renaldo said.

Santos fumed. "Don't question the actions of your superiors, Renaldo."

"Yes, your grace. I will say, we have the professor now, and he has our holiest book. So, this time is different than twenty years ago. The book contains a litany of spells just waiting to be used," Renaldo said.

"That we can't decipher. What makes you think it will do them any good?"

Renaldo smiled. "The DemiGod feels that the linguist offers a unique perspective. You yourself sent reports that he studies language. Perhaps he can see things we can't. He just needs the artifact the Anti-Religionists stole."

Archbishop Santos snorted. "Sylvia."

"She has the second book."

Silence fell over the office of the archbishop. Santos tilted his head to one side. "And you are confident we can trust her?"

"Aren't you?"

"Perhaps. But I haven't spoken to her in some time."

"We must try again."

Archbishop Santos nodded. "Of course."

"What matters now is that the empire must not stop the undead captain from taking them to the Anti-Religionists. If they do, and Bartolome fails, then we will have lost. And if we lose now—"

"The empire wins."

"Yes, Your Grace."

Archbishop Santos nodded forcibly. "Unleash the Magi. Provide Bartolome our complete support."

"Right away, Your Grace." Renaldo turned on his heels and left the office of the archbishop. He rushed down the stairs and out the door to the docks.

Hopefully, this can still be controlled, Santos thought. *And done without blowing up half the city.*

CHAPTER ELEVEN

Bartolome jumped over a stall of fresh fish and dived beneath another filled with root clams and mussels. Shouts from the owners followed her as the three separate groups of militarized forces chased her through the docks of Hogkarta. The hands of imperials soldiers wrapped around her collar and yanked her backwards. Bartolome fell to the ground, rolled onto her back, and kicked upward at the man who had caught her. Both her feet found a home in the soldier's stomach, and he flew backwards into three more of his comrades.

Behind the soldiers, a Magi raised his hands to cast a spell. Bartolome grabbed the nearest piece of fish and flung it at the man's face, hitting him square in the eyes, breaking his concentration and stopping the spell from being cast. With a triumphant shout, she spun and leapt to her feet, running behind the shops to the alleyways.

Footfalls from the soldiers soon sounded off the brick walls surrounding her. They weren't long delayed from an attack by her counter-kick. She turned to a random door and kicked her way through. Before she could enter, a rifle fired behind her, and the lead ball pierced her left shoulder, sending her forward into a heap.

Bartolome screamed in anger and pain, but quickly jumped to her feet. In front of her, the small family whose house she had burst into sat around a table that barely contained them. The father pointed to the front door and went back to eating his meal, as did the rest of the family. Bartolome threw them a silver coin, apologized for the door damage, and ran to the front.

On Main Street, a small but steady stream of Hogkarta citizens walked calmly to and from the docks. Without second-guessing herself, Bartolome ran for the docks instead of leading the soldiers deeper into the city. If there were only a few soldiers on the docks, perhaps she could overtake them, or call on her crew to scramble down the blank and overwhelm them, though that was an option she was loath to take. Her crew's only weapons were their teeth, but their bite carried a death sentence.

Bartolome heard more shooting behind her, and at least half a dozen voices, and she thought for a moment that her plan might yet work. She rounded a corner and launched herself onto the wooden planks where the docks of the harbor began and the streets ended, only to come to a dead halt. Standing in front of her, a dozen Magi glowered behind their cowls, with Renaldo in the front of them, a bizarre smile across his face.

Jonathan leaned against the side of a building and peered out as inconspicuously as he could—which, considering he currently looked like a soldier from the empire, was not very inconspicuous. The stares from passersby on the docks, through the various fish markets, and back behind them towards the city proper were many and growing.

"I think these symbols aren't just symbols," William said.

"What? What are you talking about?"

"The symbols in the book from the church."

"Why do you still have that thing? It's just silly drawings and prayer scribbles."

"No, I think there are patterns here."

Jonathan shrugged and shook his head. "Patterns in a painting? You don't say."

Behind him, he could hear William sigh with frustration. "You really are quite trying, do you know that?"

"Well, I'm sorry, I'm trying to get us—"

The sounds of a commotion erupted from the docks in front of *The Knotted Wood.* Jonathan peered around the corner. Several of the Magi and a few constables ran down the docks toward someone who looked a great deal like Captain Bartolome.

"William, put that book away. This is our chance."

William came to stand beside Jonathan and peered around the side of the building. "Are you sure? There are still those local constable people in front of *The Wood.*"

"Bartolome said they would ignore us. The constables only care about people coming off the ship, and the soldiers have all left."

William nodded. "Well, alright, then. I suppose."

Jonathan nodded once and walked with confidence onto the dock. Several more people looked their way, all of whom he ignored. All that mattered was walking up the gangway to *The Wood* and then rushing to their quarters and hoping the crew weren't hungry for a snack. They reached the constables at the end of the walkway and gave them both a steady nod.

"Hang on—where are you two going?" one constable demanded.

"Onto the ship, of course," Jonathan replied.

The two constables who were still standing guard exchanged looks and shuffled their feet. "We aren't supposed to stop anyone from boarding," one said.

"Yeah, true, but are we allowed to allow them to board? Wouldn't that be an incident?" the other said.

"Whatcha mean? Like that time with the Magi? The bar fight?"

"Yeah, like that."

The first constable shrugged. "Don't think so. I mean, we haven't had one with these imperials before, have we, now?"

"Yeah, well, the imperial soldiers haven't ever been here before, have they?"

"That's a good point." The constable turned to Jonathan. "Should we have an incident with you?"

Jonathan shrugged. "No...?"

The constable nodded several times. "The man makes a good point."

"That's not a point. That's an opinion."

"Is it?"

Footsteps behind them sounded on the dock, and someone came within a few feet of Jonathan and William. The chief constable's voice echoed a single-syllable spell. The illusion that surrounded Jonathan and William faded away, and their normal professor selves were revealed.

"They aren't soldiers!" one of the first two constables said with shock.

"What did I tell you both about thinking?" the chief constable snapped.

"Not to do it?"

"Quite." The man put one hand on Jonathan's shoulder and spun him around. The chief constable stared into his eyes with contempt and pity, as if to say, *"Nothing that is about to happen in the next few moments is up to you."* Jonathan felt he agreed.

"Hello, Chief Constable."

"Word from the top is that that I am to detain both of you for the imperial soldiers," the chief constable said.

"Is it? Well, there must be some mistake. The empire commissioned us."

The chief constable nodded once. He folded his arms across his chest and examined both Jonathan and William for a long time. Eventually, after a stare that sent both of them into a tailspin of worry, he nodded.

"I would agree." The chief constable pointed to the gangway of *The Knotted Wood* and turned around.

"Does that mean we let them on?" one constable asked.

"Yes, it does. And stop thinking," the chief constable snapped.

"Right," the two constables said at once.

Jonathan grabbed William by the arm and dragged him onto the wooden plank that led to *The Knotted Wood*. They scrambled on board, dodged several crew members, and made it to their quarters in under thirty seconds. Jonathan slammed the door closed and let out a long sigh. He turned to see William sit down on their bed and reopen the red book from the church.

At least there was one consistent thing in his life.

～

BARTOLOME STARED at Renaldo and waited for the hammer to fall. Or for the rescue to happen. Or for any of a hundred other things other than the bishop just standing there and staring at her. Behind them, soldiers from the empire came into the street and pointed in a dozen directions, as they hadn't spotted her yet.

"If you're going to help, then do something," Bartolome said.

Renaldo whispered something under his breath that Bartolome assumed to be a spell, which was quite typical of the church. They knew more spells than anyone in all of Dressa, but they kept their secrets very close. Whenever they uttered a spell, it was in hushed tones and whispers.

Light shimmered to Bartolome's right. She turned to see a figure taking shape out of the essence of magic that Renaldo had cast. Shouts from the soldiers informed them that they too had seen the figure. Their footfalls on the cobblestone street could already be heard echoing off the brick buildings.

"So, that's it, then," Bartolome said. A fine life, or death —or un-death, perhaps. She had enjoyed being captain of her own ship well enough. She worried about what the town and the empire would do to her crew. Their fate was practically sealed. Without her commanding them, they would embrace their most basic instincts. Her crew would feed.

"The end is only a beginning," Renaldo said. He pointed to the magical figure now standing next to Bartolome and smiled.

Bartolome turned to the figure and laughed—and the magical being mimicked her laugh exactly. She felt that if she concentrated hard enough, she could do far more than make the being laugh.

"Well, aren't you and the church a bunch of cheeky buggers?"

Renaldo giggled. "Cute. Now run!"

Bartolome bolted through the Magi, who parted for her and then closed ranks. She spared a glance behind her to see the magical being Renaldo had created running in the opposite direction toward the soldiers. She turned back toward the dock and her ship in the distance. Honestly, she had no concept of what was going on here. Renaldo had just stated that the church and the Magi couldn't help, and now the Magi had done just that. She was quite certain they had helped with Renaldo's spell. Something of this complexity required multiple casters focused on the same goal. The only thing remaining was to make sure the professors were secure.

COMMODORE WILKES RAN out onto the street from the administrator's office and immediately heard the shouts of his men close by. He bolted toward their shouts, with Bridgewater fast on his heels. The chief constable and the archbishop had left the building earlier, and both of them caused Wilkes a great deal of suspicion. Of course, the archbishop's reaction was obvious. Santos was fearful of the empire taking over Hogkarta. And he should be.

As for the chief constable, he just didn't enjoy having another rooster in his henhouse. Wilkes knew how to handle men like that and had been in those situations dozens of times. There was no question that the empire could navigate him easily enough—especially considering the surprise welcome from the administrator. That would make the empire's future in Dressa go very well.

Wilkes turned a corner and ran into a cluster of his men running toward a wall of Magi. The warrior priests—at least, that's how Wilkes thought of them—were chanting something in whispered tones. Through the dense collection of bodies, including average citizens of Hogkarta walking down the street, Wilkes glimpsed Bartolome.

"Bridgewater, get to the ship, and get more men to surround the docks!" Wilkes commanded.

"Sir!" Bridgewater turned another corner to make a run for the docks.

"Soldiers, to me!" Wilkes ran in front of the soldiers, who came to brief attention while also running. Three of them nearly tripped with the effort.

In front of them, Bartolome smiled and ran towards them before ducking down an alley. She even threw a salute in total mockery of the empire. The saucy gesture made Wilkes's blood boil. He drew his sidearm and charged forward, knowing full well that his men followed. The Magi collectively smiled but neither gave chase nor impeded the soldiers. That suited Wilkes just fine.

"You two stay here if she doubles back. The rest of you, with me!"

Wilkes ducked down the alley and through the open doorway Bartolome had gone through. He burst out onto another street and ran toward overturned carts and startled citizens. The undead captain turned a corner and threw a bottle of wine into the street, causing the owner to explode with colorful language. Wilkes charged forward even faster and rounded another corner, only to find Bartolome standing with her hands raised and two of his soldiers in front of her.

"Well, at long last." Wilkes approached Bartolome, put his hands on her shoulders, and spun her around. The undead captain said nothing. She swayed back and forth on her legs and smiled.

"Nothing to say? You have much to answer for. And you have much to tell me. Where is my wife? Where is Abigail?"

Bartolome smiled and continued to sway on her feet.

"What's wrong with you? Did you hit her?" Wilkes asked his soldiers.

"No, we just stopped her."

Wilkes brought his face within inches of the captain's. "Well, how hard did you stop her, exactly?" He focused his attention on Bartolome. "Hello? I've got you! You will tell me where—"

"Commodore!" Bartolome suddenly said.

Wilkes, startled by the sudden outburst, backed away from her and raised his gun to her chest. "Very funny, Bartolome."

"What's funny?" Bartolome asked.

"Enough with the games. You're coming with us. Your ship and crew will be burned. The professors, if they are not already infected, will come home to the empire to stand trial."

Bartolome shrugged with that same infuriating smile on her face. "Sounds fair, Commodore."

Wilkes squinted his eyes suspiciously. Something was off here, which made him want to question her now. "Where is she, Bartolome? Where is my wife?!"

For the first time, the smile on the captain's face faded. "I don't have her, Commodore. I never did."

"You're lying! Where is she?"

Bartolome's face reverted to the dull smile for half a heartbeat before it faded again. "Sorry, hard to command this thing and my crew and raise anchor."

"What?"

"Look, what happened in Oyster Piers was a mistake. I didn't attack you. I didn't attack the port. I lost control. And yes, that was my fault, and I take responsibility for it. And I am truly sorry that I brought my crew there. But there are far bigger things and more lives at stake now."

"What lives? Where is my wife, you undead thing?!"

"She's on the isle of the dead—the island known as Bedrich. My home. I'm sorry, Commodore. I truly am, as well as for the lives lost in Oyster Piers. But for now, our time together is at an end."

Wilkes laughed. "Oh, no, I don't think so—"

He stopped mid-sentence as Bartolome faded into thin air right in front of him.

"I hate this place," Wilkes muttered. "To the docks!"

SAMSON OSWALD SUTTER III, first of his family to attend the Great University of Learning and Knowledge, and the quickest man to ever become the head of a department, leaned back in his custom-made leather chair, puffed on a large cigar, and smiled. Today had been a delightful day. He'd thwarted a challenge to his claim of being the dean of a new branch of the university here in Dressa. That wasn't exactly what Jonathan was doing here, but the ramifications of him discovering ancient truths and being the face of magilurgy at the university could not be understated. The university board would surely award Jonathan all of Dressa as a prize, so that he might set up what could be an entirely new branch of magic. The implications and the stakes were quite clear.

At least, they would be clear until Samson took action and thwarted Jonathan's plans.

Of course, there would be consequences. Samson had already sent a letter via rainbow crow to the university, informing them of recent events. Always best to plead forgiveness rather than ask for permission, after all. Yes, the chancellor would inevitably have an enraged meltdown and likely take it out on his assistants, but so what? They would give Jonathan's research—and more importantly, his money —to Samson, and he would carry out the expedition and experiments himself. As it always should have been.

Shouts from the street below briefly interrupted Samson's good mood, but he closed his window to muffle the sound. Magi and constables probably getting into another scuffle. Why they couldn't just get along was astounding. Didn't matter—once Samson stole the truth of the Wizard, he would bring them all to heel.

The door to his office opened, and his secretary walked in. She placed her coat on the rack and threw a quick smile at Samson. She sat down in the chair opposite his desk, took out a nail file, and whispered a word into the air, and the file flew to her fingers and began working on her manicure.

"Shouldn't you be out front?"

She looked up and shook her head. "This is my break."

Samson nodded. Normally, he'd chastise the woman for taking her break in his office. She had said previously that she liked the view of the docks and the smell of the salty sea. But today was different. Today, the world could do no wrong.

"We're going to be quite busy in the future, you know. Quite busy."

His secretary nodded.

"No, I mean it. Very busy. Triple the students. More faculty. You'll need your own assistant."

A dozen more shouts sounded in the street, and Samson

stood from his desk to look out the window. "What is going on out there?"

"Soldiers went after the undead captain and her passengers."

Samson's smile grew wider. "Excellent. Chase them right out of Dressa."

"And take their gold, most likely," his secretary added.

Samson cocked his head to one side. "Gold? What gold?"

"My sister works at the pub across the street. Said some priest gave the captain a sackful of gold. She'd never seen so much. Even got a silver for a tip."

Samson's heart sank in his chest, and the color drained from his face. "What did you say?"

His secretary looked up from her reading material, a collection of magically created images showcasing this year's fashion trends in Hogkarta, and stared at Samson with a blank expression. "My sister saw some priest give the undead captain gold. She said the priest said, 'Payment in full,' or something."

"No, no... It can't be true!"

She shrugged. "Well, it is. My sister is known for telling me tall tales, to be sure, but this one is true. I know because she promised to pay for lunch on the week's end. She never does that. So, she must have gotten silver."

Samson slammed his fist on the desk. "No, no, no! I have to stop this!"

"Can you be quieter? It's my break."

"It's *my* office!" he snapped.

"Yeah, but we don't have an official break room, do we?"

Samson leapt from his desk and grabbed his satchel. He threw several magilurgical books inside and ran out of the room. "It's all yours! School is closed until further notice!"

He sprinted through the corridors and out of the

building to the docks. Those funds were to pay for Jonathan and William. The church was funding the expedition! Samson's entire world was in jeopardy. Jonathan succeeding would be terrible. Jonathan succeeding and holding a grudge would be disastrous. At all costs, Samson knew, he had to stop Jonathan from reaching the source—by any means necessary.

ARCHBISHOP SANTOS BURST through the door of Administrator Streckenbach's office. Both Ludwig and Streckenbach turned to him in shock. The administrator was halfway through a rather sad-looking pastry, while Ludwig faced the window, his hands clasped tightly behind his back. A large cup of bumble brew, made from the honey of the bumble bee, sat on Streckenbach's desk.

"What is the meaning of this?" Ludwig demanded, taking a step towards Santos.

"It's fine, Ludwig."

"Are you certain? I wouldn't think it would be advisable to have an audience with the church."

"Nonsense. What is there left for me to accidentally reveal, anyway?"

Ludwig nodded once, smiled, and moved behind Santos to shut the door. He took up his position inside the room and clasped his hands in front of him. Santos regarded Ludwig with suspicion, but also respect. It was for that reason that he positioned himself so that Ludwig wasn't fully out of sight.

"What can I do for you, Archbishop Santos?" Streckenbach asked.

"Oh, please, Alfred. We can dispense with the pleasantries."

The administrator raised his eyebrows and smiled. "I wasn't aware that using your title was a pleasantry. But fine, Philip. What's on your mind? Would you like a pastry? They are quite stale."

Archbishop Santos shook his head and sighed. "No, thank you." He took a seat opposite Streckenbach's desk. "I'm not sure you've thought through your choices, Alfred."

The administrator shrugged. "Oh, I have. Or rather, Ludwig has. We discussed the potential of the empire establishing a presence here when we first learned of their coming."

"Did you, now?"

Administrator Streckenbach nodded. "Ludwig is quite the planner."

The archbishop nodded. "He is. But I fear you underestimate the empire."

"And you underestimate the constables. And your own Magi. Do you really expect either group to just divulge spells to the empire? They didn't even know Hogkarta existed!"

"That's because they used the True Religionists as spies." Archbishop Santos allowed himself a quick chuckle.

"Even if they learned a few spells, our people are far more adept at casting," the administrator pointed out. "Granted, any fool can cast a simple floating spell, but getting complex spells just right—now, that takes practice. I truly don't believe they are a threat to Dressa. If I did, we wouldn't have invited them."

Archbishop Santos shook his head several times. "I don't think I believe you, Alfred. Or at least, I don't think you know the empire as well as I do. I've lived in the Riverlands.

The empire is everywhere. Except in the interior, where democracy rules."

"Democracy? What is that?" Streckenbach asked.

"A form of government. They cover the interior of the continent. They vote, Administrator. On everything," Ludwig said.

"Vote?"

Santos sighed. "Yes, they vote. Their citizenry votes on matters of state."

The administrator huffed a laugh. "Madness. Their citizenry *votes*? Sounds worse than the kingdom. At least the kingdom had good pastries ... historically speaking, of course. Being as the kingdom is cut off, you know."

"You are underestimating them, Alfred. The empire—they will take over. They will want to rule this place."

"This is a boon, Philip. Our coffers will fill with Riverlands gold. Tourism. Payoffs... I mean, donations. Not to mention, the School of Comedic Thought and the School of Gastronomy will be coming." Administrator Streckenbach looked up at Ludwig. "Make sure we make that a point of contention, Ludwig. We must have both schools. The empire should sponsor them."

"Yes, of course, Administrator."

"Gold isn't the only thing that matters, Alfred. Nor is food. Or comedy."

The administrator shrugged. "Gold matters quite a lot, though. And who doesn't like to laugh? Or eat?" Streckenbach took a bite of his pastry, wrinkled his nose, and threw the remainder in the bin. "I'm rather more concerned about this mission to the Wizard and the Dragon, aren't you?"

Santos shrugged. "Less so. Why?"

Streckenbach huffed. "Do you think they'll succeed in whatever it is they're doing?"

"Perhaps. The DemiGod feels this professor may bring something new. A different perspective."

Streckenbach shrugged. "Let him. He'll turn himself into a frog. That will be a different perspective, won't it?"

Archbishop Santos nodded.

"I am more concerned if they fail," Ludwig said.

"Why is that a concern?" Streckenbach asked.

"The True Religionists failed in their last attempt twenty years ago—and look what happened to Bedrich."

Santos shifted in his seat. "We didn't so much *fail* as we didn't exactly succeed."

Streckenbach laughed. "Spoken like a politician!" He turned to Ludwig. "We'll be fine, Ludwig. The magical dams will protect us, as they always have."

Streckenbach's eyes turned to the large pillars that stood like quiet sentinels around the docks. Santos followed his gaze. The dams stretched around the whole of the city and behind into the hills, leading deep into the interior. Those structures had been here before Hogkarta itself. Ancient when the world was young, the magical dams were the only reason the city had survived the moment when the Wizard and the Dragon met a hundred years ago, or the meddling of the Church which created the un-alivers twenty years ago.

Streckenbach sipped from his glass and pointed it at the water. "Besides, maybe that commodore fellow will catch them, anyway. So, the point will be mute."

"I think it's 'moot,'" Ludwig offered.

Streckenbach grunted, nodded, and smiled. "I think you're right."

Archbishop Santos shook his head and set down his drink. "The fact that the empire is in our waters is a bigger concern than you will accept. And that you invited them here... Disastrous."

"Nonsense, Philip. Why don't you join me for dinner, and we can discuss? I believe we're having squid—though I don't like it when they talk to me as I eat them."

Archbishop Santos shook his head. "No. I have to fix this. All of this. I must travel back to the capital city and speak to the admiralty. They have a rogue commodore on their hands making deals with the denizens of Hogkarta."

"Deni-what? I feel that's an insult?"

Archbishop Santos looked at the administrator and sighed. He stood without another word and stormed out. He didn't care if he mentioned traveling back to Swanville in front of Ludwig and Streckenbach. Ludwig already knew about the crystal cubes and the church's ability to travel great distances. Santos had to get to the capital city of the empire and convince them to withdraw from Dressa, then get back here and make sure this commodore got his orders, removed his garrison, and went back where he belonged—without delay.

COMMODORE WILKES RAN up the gangway to *The Crimson Swan*. A dozen soldiers followed him, each immediately running below decks to stow their gear before returning to the deck. Bridgewater, who had already made it back to the ship, ordered the gangway to be withdrawn and for the ship to prepare to leave port.

"She's already undocked," Bridgewater said when Wilkes made it to the bridge.

In front of *The Swan*, farther down the dock, *The Knotted Wood* had already drifted into the harbor and was raising her sails to turn. On her bridge, Wilkes could see Bartolome at the helm. He could even make out a wide smile on her face.

"Prepare to fire on that ship!" Wilkes yelled.

"You will hold your fire in my harbor!" the chief constable yelled from the dock. He put his hands on his hips and looked up to the rigging. A look of surprise crossed his face when he saw that the damage his men had done had already been repaired.

"Sir?" Bridgewater said.

"Hold your fire. We've just made peace with Hogkarta. Let's not throw ourselves into a war that quickly."

Bridgewater nodded. "Raise sails and get us out of dock! Prepare to give chase!"

Men on the deck ran to their positions. Sails were raised to quarter mast, and with it, *The Crimson Swan* moved forward. Bridgewater yanked the wheel to port, but the ship didn't respond. He said a curse in the name of an ancient god and turned the wheel harder, but still the ship didn't respond.

"What's happening?" Bridgewater demanded. "Check the stern. Have they sabotaged us? She's not responding!"

Several men ran to the back of *The Swan* and looked over the edge to see if anything was amiss. Seconds later, one of them yelled, "Squids!"

"What?" Bridgewater said. "What did he say?"

Wilkes ran to the man at the stern and looked over the side himself. A small army of squids was climbing up the rear of the ship. Through the clear waters of Dressa, with the late afternoon sun shining from the sides of Great Lake, Wilkes could see that the squids had attached themselves to the rudder and were preventing it from turning.

"Shoot them off!"

The man nodded and ran for a gun. Below them, several

of the squids waved their tentacles up at Wilkes. One of them even saluted. Wilkes shook his head and looked at *The Knotted Wood*, which was picking up speed as it left the harbor. On her bridge, Bartolome turned and locked eyes with Wilkes. She smiled and gave him a flourish of a wave.

"Until next time," Wilkes muttered. "Until next time."

ARCHBISHOP SANTOS RAN into his office, slammed the door, and paced back and forth across the rug. His mind spun in a dozen directions, and frankly, he didn't know which one to follow. He'd started down this path at the DemiGod's direction, then changed his mind, then flipped back again, and now he found himself confused as to what to do. The whole convoluted scheme had gone south from the beginning and had only grown worse by the second.

"Renaldo!" Santos shouted.

A priest whom Santos didn't recognize popped his head into the office. "Bishop Renaldo is not in the church, Your Grace."

"Where is he?" Santos shouted.

"On church business."

Santos stomped his foot on the floor, his face turning bright red. "I *am* church business!"

"I'm sorry, I'm not sure I understand, Your Grace."

"Out!" Santos lunged forward, pushed the man out, and slammed the door—hard.

Santos nodded to himself. Then he shook his head. Then he folded his arms and nodded again. "Renaldo is working in the interests of the DemiGod," he said to himself. That was fine. If the gods did return, he would be on the side that ruled the world—granted, not in the highest position, but high enough. Perhaps he'd even become a cardinal based on his efforts to date.

But if Renaldo failed, then the gods would not come to help the church push back against the empire. And that would be a catastrophe, especially considering that that fool of an administrator had practically given Hogkarta—and with it, all of Dressa Moore—to the empire with a bow on it. Santos's only recourse in that regard was to travel back to the empire and beseech the admiralty to send a rainbow crow to this commodore and have him leave Dressa at once. Santos could spin this such that the commodore had come under the influence of the magic in Dressa. Yes, that could work. It had to work.

Santos marched to his desk and opened the bottom right drawer. Sitting inside, the third crystal cube on a silver chain glinted in the light from the window. This crystal was shared with the cardinal of Hogkarta to communicate around the globe with church locations on both continents. It also allowed Santos—or anyone with a matching crystal square —to travel to Hogkarta when the need arose.

Sitting next to the crystal cube was a perfectly made marble swan—one that Santos had made months ago as a gift to the emperor. The marble swan was magical and could fly on nights with a full moon. It could also sing lullabies and even play chess. A gift of such magic would thrill the emperor, and he was sure to grant Santos any request. The archbishop had been saving this gift for just such an occasion.

Santos grabbed the marble swan, attached to a silver chain, from the drawer. He then placed the chain on the desk, directly adjacent to the crystal cube that was meant to stay in Hogkarta, brought his hands to his face, and had a think. Yes, this was what he would do. He had to do it. He grabbed the chain from the desk, walked to the center of the room, spun in a circle, and checked to make sure he had everything for his trip. Once convinced, he cast the spell while holding the crystal cube. Lights and colors danced through the room. Santos's body was again transformed into light that swirled into the crystal and vanished.

PART III

THE CHASE

CHAPTER TWELVE

ind whipped the sails of *The Knotted Wood*, pushing the ship onward through the open waters of Dressa Moore. Evening clouds covered the skies, orange and red hues from the setting sun lighting up the grey with color. Captain Bartolome held the wheel lightly as the ship glided through the waters, her eyes fixed on the heavens above. This was perhaps her favorite time of day.

"It's quite lovely," Jonathan said. He moved onto the bridge from the lower decks with William attached to his side, the other professor's nose buried in the Religionists' hymnal.

"Gentlemen," Captain Bartolome greeted them.

Jonathan kept his face turned toward the aft of the boat, a look of worry etched into his eyes. The events of Hogkarta had spooked the professor. Which was to be expected, frankly, Bartolome thought. *Can't expect bookworms to take to outrunning the law.* Interesting, however, that the chief constable had let them walk away rather than forcing them to run—something she'd have to thank the man for one day.

"Don't worry, Jonathan. No one is following us. At least, not as far as the crow's eye can see." Bartolome pointed to the crow's nest above the deck.

"Why not? I don't understand."

Bartolome shrugged. "As a guess, I'd say they ran into magic."

Jonathan laughed. "If it were only that simple."

Bartolome raised her eyebrows and smiled. She nodded her head to the front of the boat. "Well, if you turn your attention to the bow, you may be surprised, Mr. Jonathan, sir."

Jonathan turned around—and his jaw nearly fell off his face. In front of them, the groves of man were coming into view near the edge of the ship. Pools of rainbow water could be seen just off the port side. Birds of a dozen species flew between the branches of the magnificent trees.

"Go have a look," Bartolome urged.

Jonathan nodded like a boy in a toy store and ran to the front of the ship. William glanced up, gazed at the trees, shrugged, and buried his eyes back in his hymnal.

Jonathan stood gaping at the prow. Multicolored birds, large bats, and flying squirrels flew between the branches of trees that towered into the sky. Beneath the waves, where the setting sun still shined enough light to see, the roots of the trees descended through the waters of Lake Connell and popped out from the bottom. The brown tendrils continued downward, over a mile in length, through the open air to the ground below the lake. Countless varieties of fish swam around the roots submerged in the waters, as well as several massive whales.

"Amazing!" Jonathan mumbled.

"Oh, it gets better," Anton said. The chef of *The Knotted Wood* came to stand next to Jonathan by the rail. "And whatever you do, if you ever see one, never touch one of those." He pointed to the left.

Jonathan looked to see a pool of rainbow-colored water that floated in a direction opposite the currents. The prismatic liquid sloshed in ways that made Jonathan's skin crawl. Tiny multicolored hands grew out of the surface of the water and waved at *The Knotted Wood* as it turned away from the enigmatic pool.

"Is that...?"

"Magic?" Anton nodded.

"I've never seen so much! There are gallons of it. Hundreds of gallons!"

Anton shrugged. "That's just a puddle. Some of the local rivers on the islands around here are pure magic."

"Rivers?"

Anton nodded. "Things get a little weird there."

Fish beneath the rainbow water swam through the colored waves. Jonathan noted that several of them instantly grew additional fins, while others vanished into the water, only to appear several yards away in a flash of light. The rainbow of magic moved towards *The Knotted Wood*, but the ship steered away. Behind them, Captain Bartolome shouted from the bridge to her crew to change the sails faster.

"What happens if that touches our ship?"

Anton shrugged again.

The sound of flapping wings filled the air. Jonathan looked up to see a school of fish hovering above the water, each with a three-foot feathered wingspan. As one, the flock shot upward away from *The Wood* and toward the trees that were becoming more distinct as the ship neared. The fish took up roost in the branches of the trees. They put their mouths to the bark of the tree and just sat there.

"Is that the grove Bartolome talked about?"

Anton's gaze drifted toward the grove, and he nodded once. "That it is."

Large brown trunks of the trees rose from the water to tower several hundred feet in the air, where branches billowed out at all angles. Rainbow-colored leaves shaped like fans swayed in the evening breeze. On some of the larger branches, orbs with a soft yellow glow dangled above the water. The light from the tear-shaped fruit—at least, that's what Jonathan thought they were—seemed to grow brighter as the sun continued to set.

"This is where you're from? Isn't that what Bartolome said? Is there a village here? Do your people live in the trees?"

Anton smiled and shook his head. "No, Jonathan. My people *are* the trees."

Jonathan tilted his head to one side and gave his ears a shake. "Sorry, what did you say?"

"Just watch," Anton said.

Movement from the glowing orbs caught Jonathan's eye. Something inside them shifted as *The Knotted Wood* grew closer. Branches from one tree moved toward the ship, with the tips bending backward and forward. If Jonathan didn't know better, he would have thought it was a wave.

"What ... was that?"

The Knotted Wood struck her sails at a command from Bartolome, and the ship drifted idly toward the grove. More than a hundred trees grew there, Jonathan could see, and he suspected from the dense browns that many more stood beyond these. He turned to look for the rainbow pools of water, but none were anywhere near the ship.

"What about the magic?"

"It doesn't come near the trees. Don't know why."

Above them, just a few dozen yards away, something

from inside one bulb pushed outward in the shape of a tiny hand. The light from the orb grew in brightness as the ship passed beneath it, and the clear shape of a small human body with a face could be seen through a thin membrane.

"Is that a *baby*? How did a baby get in there?" Jonathan moved to get a closer look at the orb.

Anton smiled and nodded. His breathing grew in intensity, and his feet shuffled on the deck. Several branches from the nearest trees moved toward the ship, one coming so close as to brush Anton's cheek. He raised his hand and gently caressed a leaf.

"Wait—what is that?" Jonathan pointed to the trunk of the tree above the waterline, where the bark had grown into the clear shape of a human face.

"That's Louis. An old friend," Anton said with a smile.

"An old *friend*?"

More shuffling from Anton's feet caused Jonathan to take a step backward. He nodded once as his mind caught up to the situation. Dressa's magic had altered life in fundamental ways—perhaps none so much as Anton and his people. They *were* the trees. Jonathan shook his head in stunned silence at the implications, pondering what it must be like to live one's life as a very tall plant.

As more trees came into view, more bulbs appeared on their limbs. But these were dark, blackened. As *The Knotted Wood* drifted through the grove, the black bulbs came into better view. Inside the translucent skin of one bulb, a deformed creature twisted and snarled inside. Half of the babe's face was gone. Its teeth were malformed, twisted and long. It turned towards Jonathan and snapped its mouth full of sharp teeth at him as if it he were a tasty treat.

Jonathan gasped. He took a step back from the railing as more blackened bulbs came into view. The trees holding the deformed things also appeared weakened somehow. The bark was a dull shade. Their leaves were mostly grey. Throughout the grove, Jonathan realized he spied more of the blighted trees than the green.

"What is happening here?"

"The grove is sick, Jonathan." Bartolome joined them at the rail and nodded towards one of the afflicted trees. "A disease that started twenty years ago, thanks to a foolhardy quest by the church. It affected both Anton's and my people. Their children will be born undead. But they're different—crazed. I can't control them. I can feel them, but they aren't mindless like my crew."

"What does that mean?"

"My crew are the dead made living. These poor creatures are the living made dead. That's the best I can explain it," Bartolome offered.

"What happens to them when they're born?"

Bartolome pointed into the distance. Several of the blighted bulbs had fallen into the water. Vines from healthy trees reached out to them and pulled them down into the depths. "The trees catch most. There are beasts beneath the waves that make short work of them. Terrible business." Bartolome put her hand on Jonathan's shoulder and turned him to face her. "That's why we came for you in Dressa. That's why we're sailing you to certain doom. That's what I meant in Redbeard's Hall. This is our vested interest in your mission, Jonathan. We—Anton and myself—think we can fix this. We have a spell that should reverse what happened, gods willing. But we could never get through the pass at the Insanity Cliffs. Your passage allows us to reach the source."

Jonathan nodded. "And you must cast it at the source, because that's where the magic is the strongest."

Bartolome nodded. "The very reason."

Jonathan didn't reply. He turned back to the rail and watched as they passed through the grove. More green and healthy trees came into view. The babes giggled and wriggled inside their protective bulbs. Jonathan smiled at them. He even waved.

A sudden thought crept its way up Jonathan's spine. He wrinkled his nose and furrowed his brow as the thought took hold.

"Hang on... If you need us to get you to the source, why were you so insistent on being paid?" Jonathan cocked his head to one side and squinted his eyes. "Did I even need to pay you at all?" His left hand went to his pinky on his right. "Would you really have taken my finger?"

Bartolome's face spread into a wide grin. She held her arms out to her sides and shrugged. "What can I tell you, my good sir? I have appearances to keep up. If I didn't insist on being paid, especially in the middle of Redbeard's pub, rumors would swirl that old Bartolome had lost her edge."

"And my pinky?"

Bartolome shrugged again. "You'd still have nine more fingers. There's a principle at work here."

"What principle is that?"

"Failure to make a payment is a serious offense, Jonathan. Besides, pirates can't be doing things for free. That would upend the natural order of things."

Jonathan scoffed. "Indeed."

Bartolome grinned, patted Jonathan on the arm, and walked over to Anton. "How are you doing, old friend?"

"Are you unwell, Anton?" Jonathan asked.

Bartolome waved him into silence.

Anton wavered backward on his legs. He caught himself on the rail and coughed. "I don't know."

"If you don't know, then that means you're not doing well."

"No, it doesn't." Anton grabbed her hand and shook his head. "I'm fine. I just haven't been here in so long. I've missed their voices."

"You can hear them? Hear the tree ... people?" Jonathan asked, astonished.

Anton nodded. "Yes, and you can't. It's tree-speak."

Bartolome dug her eyes into Anton's. "Are you certain you're okay?"

Anton nodded. He took a long breath and stroked the leaf one last time. "Yes, I'm fine." He beckoned Jonathan to his side and pointed down through the water below. "Down there is a village. The healthy fruit drops children through the water into the open air. The fruit can survive the fall to the ground below. Once they're there, the villagers take them and tend to them until the children are ready to come out. But the sickened fruit, the diseased children—they don't sink. Which is why we must pull them down with vines. On the ground, the children grow up as men and women until we plant ourselves."

"How did this happen?"

Anton shrugged. "Magic. The grove is one hundred years old. We became tree men when the Wizard and Dragon met and battled."

Bartolome lingered for several moments before putting her hand on Anton's shoulder. "Are you sure? If you're feeling unwell, you can go home. I know you have years left to plant yourself, but you don't have to stay with us, Anton. I'll still get there. I'll still do it. You've always had a choice."

"I know that, Marta. But I will see this through. For them." Anton nodded toward several of the blighted trees.

Bartolome, after a long silence, finally nodded. "Fine, then. Onward."

Anton turned back to the rail, with Jonathan joining him by his side. Bartolome left them on the bow to return to the bridge to steer the ship through the grove of trees. Glowing orbs of light, each filled with a child, swayed and bounced in the gentle breeze as the ship passed. Some trees held nearly three dozen orbs dangling above the water.

"The village must be massive below. Do all these drop at once?"

Anton nodded. "With the season. But not all of the healthy fruit makes it to the surface."

"What? That's dreadful!"

Anton shrugged. "That's life—here, anyway. Where's your man? Wouldn't he want to join us to witness this?"

Jonathan huffed and shook his head. "His nose is buried in a hymnal."

Anton let out a small laugh.

"What?" Jonathan said.

"Nothing, friend. I just find it strange to read when we're passing beneath such wonder."

Jonathan could only nod. Anton was right, of course. Though the reason might not be what the tree man thought. Perhaps Jonathan had pushed William into self-imposed solitary confinement. He knew he, and others at the university, had been hard on William for years. And now that William had found something of interest, it was little wonder he sought to explore it. As for how much of that was driven by the constant mocking from his peers, who could say?

With a shrug that carried the silent commitment to talk to William later, Jonathan resigned himself to standing with Anton on the bow and admiring the beauty of the grove they sailed beneath. Trees on all sides waved at them with their branches as they passed. Jonathan wasn't sure, but he thought he saw Anton wipe away a tear several times throughout the journey—which, considering all he'd just learned, was more than understandable.

ON THE FAR side of the world on the second great continent, where Dressa Moore and the Riverlands were mere fables, where magic was nothing more than the rising sun and the cry of a newborn, lived a carefree and simple people in a valley of paradise. It was a place where the weather was always pleasant, the fruit grew in abundance, and the waters ran as clear as air. The reason for such a perfect place in the world was never known to the people who now called the valley home. The ancient magic of a peaceful dragon, now long dead, had crafted this place. The truth of that dragon's act was now lost to the flow of time. Although, if the people who lived there knew of its history, they probably wouldn't have cared.

A simple truth of life in this world was that when people had no wants or needs, where every man and woman had all they could ever ask for, there was a tendency to celebrate. Such celebrations had been the way of the valley people since their ancestors had been invited to the valley by the ancient dragon a thousand years ago. Shortly after they were invited in, they threw a party.

And the party had never stopped.

Music echoed off the canyon walls. Drums made from the fibers of plants pounded a rhythm enjoyed by a hundred people in one corner of the valley. In another area, revelers from the day before lounged on large naturally occurring green leaves that stretched in a U shape between two trunks. In still another corner, on a white sandy beach, crabs emerged from the waves carrying morsels of food to be plucked at by those lounging on the sand.

A man climbed a tree next to the beach. He grabbed a large coconut hanging from a branch. He jumped down to the sand, twisted off the top leaf of the coconut, and poured the contents down his throat. A belch from the man's gut from consuming the magohol produced by the tequi-tree echoed across the beach. Several people laughed.

On the edge of the valley, on a high cliff overlooking the never-ending celebrations, two large crows, with rainbow-colored feathers and bright green feet, sat on a rock and cawed to each other in fast, high-pitched squawks. Both understood each other, but neither had any idea what they were saying. But somehow, despite the odd inability to communicate, they shared the sentiment that they really should do something far more important than they were right now. What it was they should do, they did not know. With a unified shrug—as much as a crow could pull off such a gesture—they both decided at the same time to not worry about it and just enjoy the festivities.

As one, the two crows jumped off the rock of the cliff, landing on a hut-tree—a large wicker tree with natural leaf beds on the inside—and danced. Several people pointed to the two crows that had mysteriously appeared just today. No one in the valley had ever seen crows with rainbow feathers before. They were quite lovely. Both of the crows smiled, somehow. It was quite strange, considering that both had very pointy beaks that were incapable of smiling. But everyone was quite convinced that both crows smiled bright, wide smiles. The crows bobbed up and down to the rhythm of the music. The crowd cheered.

The coconut magahol flowed. The grass burned. And it was a good day.

Archbishop Philip Santos sat in his office in the tiny rectory next to the Great University with his head in his hands and a migraine forming in his skull. Sitting on his desk, two identical crystal squares stared back at him, almost mocking him in his haste to leave Dressa. Instead of grabbing the silver chain around the marble swan that was meant to be a gift for the emperor, Santos had accidentally grabbed the silver chain attached to the crystal cube of Hogkarta. And that simple mistake had ruined his entire morning. Not only did he not have a present for the emperor; by taking the crystal cube that belonged to Hogkarta, he wasn't able to teleport back to Hogkarta using the crystal around his neck.

"Disastrous," Santos moaned.

The empire had refused his request. Santos didn't have a magical gift to offer, and therefore the emperor had refused to see him. Simple as that. The entire mission with the professors was secret, and the empire would deny any involvement. Without acknowledging the mission, the empire had no reason not to pursue the undead captain— the villain of Oyster Piers, as she was becoming renowned to be—into Dressa Moore. That meant Santos's entire reason for coming back to the capital had failed.

And now the church in Hogkarta was furious with him. They had already sent a dozen rainbow crows to the rectory. The first demanded that Santos return to Hogkarta at once. They had sent the other eleven with messages Santos now had to deliver to other churches in the crystal cube network around the world. By taking the crystal that belonged to Hogkarta, he'd effectively cut off Hogkarta from the rest of the church's locations around the world. Suffice it to say, the DemiGod was not happy.

Adding to his mistake, the church now had to pay for the professors' travels a second time. The amount was not trivial, and the church in Hogkarta demanded that the money be returned to the church's coffers. Santos had thought the DemiGod's demand lacked a certain amount of faith in their goals. After all, if the professors were to succeed, the church would never have to worry about funds again.

All of that meant Santos had to return to Hogkarta—and now he had to do it by boat, a journey over a thousand miles. Santos didn't have access to a boat. That meant he had to talk to Chancellor Dunningham. It had been part of the agreement that the church pay for the expedition, but not twice. So, they had to reimburse the church *and* fund a vessel to take him to Hogkarta.

Santos sat back in his chair and sighed. His eyes went to his office. Bookshelves crammed with histories of the world lined the shelves. Several volumes dealt with linguists and language, all of which were authored by William Watts Worthwaddle. Santos took a moment to touch one lightly. He reminded himself of the goal. The professors had to succeed now, as he was powerless to stop the empire from solidifying their presence in Dressa. Santos's hands went to the communication crystal around his neck and cast a new spell.

"Sylvia Santos, daughter of Mateo, heir to the riches of the gods, soon to be queen of all of Dressa Moore. I wish to speak with you!"

Seconds passed, and no response came from the crystal.

"Sylvia. Do you hear me?"

More silence followed. Santos hit the crystal once on the side and shook his head. He wondered if Sylvia had lost her crystal cube. Which, itself, would be disastrous. The crystal cubes were invaluable to the church. Giving one to a teenage girl was bad enough but if she lost it? Santos wasn't sure he could survive any more disasters.

"Sylvia Santos, answer at once!"

"Hello?" a voice returned from the crystal.

"Yes! It is I! Archbishop Phil—"

"Yes, I know who it is. It's always you. No one else even knows I have this. Why do you keep telling me it's you whenever you call?"

Santos sighed. "Never mind that. They are coming. Are you prepared to fulfill your destiny?"

"To give the people on the boat the book you gave me? Yes, it's not very hard."

Santos huffed in annoyance. "You know, you could be more grateful. You will have power and immortality laid at your feet in the coming days, and all you have to do is hand someone a book."

"I doubt it, but okay."

"You doubt our destiny?"

"Well, yes, obviously."

"How can you have doubts? The gods will—"

"They aren't gods."

"Blasphemy!" Santos sputtered.

"Whatever. Bartolome is bringing the book, right?" Sylvia said.

Santos tilted his head to one side. "How do you know that? Did you tell her anything about our mission?"

Silence stretched for several seconds before Sylvia responded. "... No."

"Sylvia? Are you the reason Bartolome pirated our charter?"

"No."

"Sylvia!"

"I have to go."

"Give them the book! Sylvia! Do you hear me? Hello?"

Santos slammed the crystal down on his desk and cursed. The most crucial portion of his plan was clearly the most dangerous. He had to trust Sylvia, his least-favorite niece from his least-favorite brother. It had to look like an accident that they gave William the book. Anything else, and the professors would suspect the church's true intent, and that couldn't be allowed to happen. But he had no choice; he had to trust Sylvia. She was the only person who could perform this task. Largely because he had planted the book on her when she and her gaggle of friends left in their teenage rebellion to join the Anti-Religionists. Not that Sylvia and her friends cared what the Anti-Religionists said, or did, or cared about. Sylvia just wanted to go somewhere where the church wasn't. At least she was honorable and would fulfill her side of the bargain. Santos's brother had insisted that Santos give Sylvia one of the communication crystals so he could keep tabs on her—which, as it happened, had worked to Santos's advantage. How he was going to get it back from her once she fulfilled her purpose and her father's worries about her safety were calmed, however, was another matter. Santos had briefly thought of using the crystal cube to travel to Sylvia and make sure the final steps were completed, but that was folly. The anti-religionists would recognize him in an instant and throw him at the feet of their hamster. Or was it a pig?

Santos huffed. No, he'd have to rely on Sylvia.

Teenagers. More than his hatred of mankind, more than

his loathing of the empire, more than his distaste for the university and all it stood for, Archbishop Philip Santos detested teenagers most of all.

DANIEL DESUN SAT at the table in the assistants' room, his chest puffed out to its maximum extent, shoulders high and rising more with each second. All eyes in the room focused on him, including, most importantly, the eyes of Vanessa. As a unique twist of fate, she now pursued him with as much vigor as he had once pursued her—a fact that Daniel quite enjoyed.

"Tell us again about the rainbow crows," Ryan said.

"And did you really craft the message?" said another in the room.

"Will you be going to Dressa as a special envoy?"

"I'd love to go to Dressa," Vanessa said, placing her hand on Daniel's hand resting on the table.

Daniel smiled. "I can't tell you about them again. I've already spoken of them endlessly. They are quite beautiful, though. Yes, I crafted the message, and I don't know if I'll be going to Dressa yet." He looked into Vanessa's eyes and winked. "But maybe if I do, I can take someone."

The room hushed with a few knowing giggles. The assistants began whispering in smaller groups around the table while Daniel's and Vanessa's eyes continued to lock onto each other like long-lost lovers across a fast-moving river. Had it been wrong to tell them about Dressa? Perhaps. But Daniel took comfort in the fact that he hadn't told them what was going on there, of the mission itself, and besides, everyone knew there was a university outpost in Hogkarta.

So, what was the harm in discussing crafting messages to send to the outpost?

The door to the room burst open before anyone could say another word, and the chancellor of the university stormed in, waved everyone out of the room, and landed a hand on Daniel's shoulder.

"Now! I need you now! Come with me, Daniel," the chancellor said, beads of sweat rolling down his reddened face.

"Yes, sir, of course." Daniel winked at Vanessa and stood.

"What are you winking at? Just come!" The chancellor turned and ran into an assistant leaving the room. "What are you doing, man?!"

"You said to leave, sir?" Ryan said.

"You're fired!" Chancellor Dunningham pushed past Ryan into the hall, dragging Daniel with him.

Ryan's face had gone from joy, to shock, to despair in the short moments since the chancellor had burst into the room. Daniel tried his best to shake his head and convey that Dunningham would likely forget this incident had even occurred. He wasn't sure if he was successful by the time they rounded a corner, likely on the way to the chancellor's office.

"What happened, sir?"

"Disaster. Utter disaster." Chancellor Dunningham practically threw Daniel into his office and slammed the door behind him. He walked over to his decanter of whiskey and poured a stiff drink. He downed one, and then another, before heaving a long sigh and nodding. "Better."

Daniel nodded and waited. He knew it was best to let the chancellor gather his thoughts.

"That fool Samson... Thinks he can back me into a corner!"

"Did something happen, sir?"

Dunningham looked up from his drink and squinted his eyes. "I can trust you, right, Daniel?"

Daniel nodded. "Of course, sir."

"You would never betray me, would you?"

"No, sir. Never. I owe everything to you."

Dunningham nodded, swiftly drank a third glass, and went to his desk. He pulled out two sacks of coins and threw them on the top of his planner. He then pulled out a third empty sack, placed that next to the other two, and fell into his chair.

"What's this?" Daniel asked.

"The first bag is to repay the church. In Dressa."

"Repay them for what?"

"Samson has taken it upon himself to withhold funds for the expedition."

"He can't do that."

Dunningham laughed. "Oh, he can, and he did. And now we have to repay the church. No idea what he did with the funds."

"Why can't we just give this to Archbishop Santos here?"

Dunningham shrugged. "Something about accounting. I don't know. But they are very adamant. Probably want to watch us squirm, as one of our professors, Samson, has almost ruined the entire expedition."

Daniel nodded. "And the second bag?"

"That's to pay for your travel, and for expenses in the expansion of our outpost school in Hogkarta."

"My expenses?"

Dunningham nodded. "Congratulations, Professor Desun. You're promoted."

"Me?" Daniel's voice rose two octaves, and he twisted his feet as anxiety filled his mind. He had little desire to leave the city, and none to go to Dressa. He didn't even like weekend excursions to the hillside, but he reluctantly went, as Vanessa loved to go. And now he had to venture thousands of miles to an unknown land where magic flowed like water and could turn him into a fish while sailing on a lake miles above the ground?

"Yes, you. Who else can I send? No other professors want to go, so it has to be you."

"But I don't want to go either!"

"Well, you have no choice. And you have to fire Samson."

"What? *Me?* Fire a professor of his stature?"

Dunningham nodded. "Can't have that level of blatant disregard for my authority. You will take over the outpost, fire Samson, and expand our classes to double."

"But how can I fire Samson? He's a tenured professor!"

"Didn't you hear the part about *you* being made a professor?"

"Just to fire him?"

"No, also to be a professor in Dressa Moore, and the head of our outpost."

"So I can teach pig farmers how to not have to shovel dung by using a spell?"

Dunningham shrugged. "Sounds like a handy skill to me."

Daniel spun in a circle and raised his hands over his head. Years of study, and more of assistantship, just to be sent away like some piece of flotsam on the river? He would protest! Take his complaint to the council! Expose the entire mess and have the chancellor fired! Yes, he would, indeed.

"No, you won't, boy," Dunningham said.

Daniel shockingly realized he had spoken all of his thoughts out loud. He took a step back, thinking his best course of action would be to run for it. He could find a nice, quiet village and be a schoolmaster. He'd never see Vanessa again, of course. Disgraced assistants were lower than even poor William the linguist in the pecking order of academia.

"Please, don't make me do this," Daniel pleaded.

"All will be well, my son," said a voice from the shadows.

Archbishop Santos emerged from the darkness, his hands folded in front of him, his cowl covering most of his face.

Daniel screamed at his unexpected entrance. "How long has he been here?!"

Dunningham shrugged. "I stopped trying to keep track of him."

"You shall have the full backing of the church, young man. I shall escort you to Dressa. Together, we shall return to Hogkarta in triumph."

"But—"

"And you can take an assistant with you." Dunningham poured more drink from a bottle he took out from his desk and gave Daniel a wink.

Daniel stopped complaining and tilted his head to one side. "Any assistant?"

Dunningham smiled.

CHAPTER THIRTEEN

*T*he *Knotted Wood* passed through the grove of man through the night, emerging the next day into the dawn. Light from the morning sun cast red hues across the open waters. Bartolome stood on the bridge and commanded her undead soldiers to the rigging. Full sails billowed, and the ship picked up speed towards the Anti-Religionists' home. Below *The Knotted Wood*, in the land beneath the waters of Lake Connell, the peaks of a mountain range jutted upward, some rising high enough to touch the bottom of the floating lake. In a valley of the mountains, between floating boulders and vibrant arching rainbows, a lonely man in a grey cloak stood before a titan of a dragon, both wings of the beast fully raised and spread wide.

"There they are," Bartolome said.

Jonathan ran to the rail, his small black box with a cord and wand attached in his hand. He waved the wand over the waters and yelped in surprise. "The readings are off the charts! This is the source!"

"Isn't that what I said?" Bartolome smiled, but took no

offense. Jonathan was giddy again, and she was getting a feel for his moods.

"This is astounding! We made it!" Jonathan exclaimed.

"Not yet, Professor. First, we must get permission to sail through the strait. The Anti-Religionists picked this spot to prevent anyone from getting to them." Bartolome nodded to the Wizard and Dragon far below through the water.

Of course, Jonathan barely heard her. "I need to write this down." He sat on the deck and took out his notebook—the same one he'd been writing in for most of the journey.

"What are you writing?"

"Magon levels."

"And what's a magon again?"

"A fundamental particle of magic."

Bartolome nodded. "Well, glad you found your ... magons."

Jonathan didn't respond, scribbling furiously.

Far ahead of them, nearly touching the horizon, enormous cliffs rose hundreds of feet into the air. Somewhere along the cliffs they formed a strait through which the waters of Lake Connell funneled. Along the cliffs, Bartolome knew, in caves and artificially constructed walls, canons lined the pass. This was going to get a little risky. Especially considering that the entire reason the Anti-Religionists had colonized the cliffs was to prevent another incident like what had happened on her home island twenty years ago, the now undead island of Bedrich. Though Jonathan wasn't trying to do anything but research, it could spook the locals. Fortunately, they had a soft spot for the undead, considering that the remnants of the True Religionists that caused the event twenty years ago had founded the Anti-Religionist movement.

Water suddenly erupted to the right of *The Knotted*

Wood. Bartolome clutched the wheel and studied the shore and cliffs to see where the cannon fire had come from. Her sense from the undead sailor in the crow's nest told her to look behind her. Behind them, nearly lost in the morning sun, the full sails of a war frigate pushed *The Crimson Swan* forward at a fast pace—fast enough that Bartolome knew they would soon catch her.

"Battle stations! Ready the cannons!" Bartolome shouted. "Get below deck, Jonathan!"

"How did they find us?"

"Doesn't matter. She must have come up on us during the night. No clue how they sailed that fast through the groves. They should have been stuck there for days. The man trees don't allow most ships to sail through. Anton is the only reason we passed through with ease."

Jonathan nodded and ran below deck. Bartolome directed her crew to open the canon doors and prime the guns. No amount of squids would save them today, and *The Wood* was no match for an imperial frigate on the high seas. For the first time in a very long time, Bartolome felt fear creep up her spine.

"FULL SAILS! COME TO PORT!" Bridgewater screamed from the bridge.

"Give them a full broadside, Captain," Wilkes commanded. "Spare nothing!"

"That I will," Bridgewater replied.

Along the deck, the crew of the empire and four-limbed members of the crew ran and swung amongst the rigging of the ship, adjusting *The Swan's* sails to get as much speed out of the frigate as the winds could create. More crew members ran below deck to ready the cannons for a full assault on *The Knotted Wood*. The games were over. Dead or alive, Bartolome and her crew were coming back to Dressa—especially now that Wilkes knew his wife wasn't even on the undead ship.

Cannon fire erupted from the gun on the bow, which had been exchanged for the harpoon system used previously in the Riverlands. Water erupted just off the stern of *The Wood*, and the gunners on *The Swan* were already adjusting the front-facing cannon for another shot.

In front of them and closing fast, *The Knotted Wood* turned towards the port side, all of her gun ports slamming open and her own cannons protruding, which only numbered six per side. It wasn't much, and *The Swan* would win this battle, but every cannon shot from *The Wood* could still hit *The Swan* and kill her crew.

"She's coming around!" Wilkes cried.

"We'll swing to starboard and bring our guns to her rear."

The Crimson Swan cut through the water like a knife. The frigate, though designed to sail the wide rivers below Dressa, took to the open waters in Lake Connell like a fish. Throughout their trip, they'd spotted enigmatic rainbow pools that their four-limbed crew had warned them to avoid. They said it was pure magic, and if touched, it could cast any spell in creation without warning. That was all the warning Wilkes needed.

"Prepare to fire!" Bridgewater yelled.

The Knotted Wood, herself a fast ship, continued to port, but her guns weren't yet aimed at *The Swan*. But something else on *The Wood* started a flurry of motion. Ropes and pulleys whipped around the ship. Wilkes tapped Bridgewater on the shoulder and pointed him toward the activity on the enemy vessel.

"Prepare for boarders!" Bridgewater shouted.

Wilkes ran to the rail and used the spyglass to spot what was on the other end of the rope on *The Wood*. Something flashed, but he couldn't get a good eye on whatever Bartolome was doing. One thing was for certain: there was nobody flinging through the rigging. She was sending something else.

"Fire!" Bridgewater yelled.

Fifteen cannons on the port side of *The Crimson Swan* erupted. The ship shuddered and shook as the explosions ripped across its side. Smoke billowed out as the shots flew toward *The Wood*. In seconds, several of the cannonballs struck the stern and portside rear of Bartolome's ship, while two others blew through her sails.

"Prepare starboard cannons!" Bridgewater commanded. "We'll come around again and give her the other side."

Wilkes ignored the command and focused on the object at the end of Bartolome's sling. He could clearly see a metal bucket soaring between the sails and over the edge of the boat. The sling shot around *The Swan* and released the container—and whatever was inside—toward the mainmasts.

"What is that?" Bridgewater cried.

"Gunpowder? What else could do us harm?" Wilkes replied.

Several of the four-limbers scurried off the masts and shouted for the crew to take cover. They jumped over the side of the boat, clinging to the rail with their extra arms, waiting for whatever was about to happen. Wilkes looked back to the bucket, and his eyes went wide with horror as several large drops of rainbow-colored liquid spilled out and landed in the lake just before the magic-filled metal hit the sails.

"Magic! She's throwing magic! Brace yourselves!"

The white sails billowed out, and then the rainbow liquid struck them. They transformed into massive white-feathered wings. *The Crimson Swan* shook from the strained pressure as the wings flapped in a frantic confusion of not being attached to an actual creature built for flight.

"What? What do we do?!" Wilkes cried.

Bridgewater looked to Wilkes, then back to his sails, and shrugged.

Explosions from *The Knotted Wood* made Wilkes and Bridgewater's heads spin. Shots from her cannon slammed into the hull of *The Swan* just above the waterline, and the ship lurched to port. Bridgewater shouted to his crew to pull on a rope to get the wings under control, but no matter how hard his crew tried to restrain them, the feathered sails just flapped harder.

"We'll sink if we don't get this under control!" Bridge-water shouted as the ship lurched to port from the pressure of the wingbeats.

LAUGHTER BILLOWED out of Bartolome's soul as the magic hit the sails of *The Swan*, her largest sail taking on feathers and flapping wildly in the wind. A brief sense of hope washed over her, as she might just be able to make it out of this mess. The empire did not know anything about magic, and she had to use that to her advantage.

"Faster!" Bartolome called out. "Bring us around, and we'll give her a broadside!"

The undead crew grunted, but moved to the rigging.

Fortunately, *The Wood* had weathered the cannons from *The Swan* reasonably well. There was a large hole in the stern, and one sail had torn, not to mention three crew members had had limbs blown off, but all of that was reparable. As long as the ship didn't sink, they could manage the single salvo broadside hitting the stern. If *The Swan* were to give a full salvo lined up with the full port side of *The Wood*, Bartolome was certain her ship wouldn't survive. So, she had to make sure that didn't happen.

WITHOUT WARNING OR DIRECTION, the four-limbers sailed over the rail from the sides of the ship and climbed the ropes into the sails. One by one, they positioned themselves around the wings and began speaking something that neither Wilkes nor Bridgewater could hear. In seconds, the flapping wings calmed themselves down and slowly transformed back into canvas.

"Well done, lads!" Bridgewater screamed. "Starboard guns, prepare to fire!"

The Swan came under control and began her turn to starboard, her crew rushing below decks to fix the holes caused by *The Wood's* cannons. Wilkes gritted his teeth, but smiled. Dressa had her surprises, but the empire had its resolve. They would win this day and take their prize and the head of Bartolome as a warning. And then he would return with a fleet, find his wife, and bring imperial justice to every village and town on this cursed lake.

Bartolome turned back to *The Swan* and had to clear her eyes. The sails were reverting from wings to canvas. How in name of the Wizard had they managed that? She pulled out her spyglass and saw the four-limbers climbing among the rigging, coaxing the wings to calm down.

"Blasted four-limbers! Since when do they sail with the empire?" But the reason didn't matter. If the empire could handle a bucketful of magic, then she had bigger problems. *The Knotted Wood* groaned under the increased strain as Bartolome spun the wheel. She had to get the ship around fast. If *The Swan* brought her starboard guns to bear, she would be done.

Without warning, a column of water erupted just off her bow, followed by waves that pushed *The Swan* and *The Wood* apart. A quick scan of the area revealed a boat filled with spell-casting Magi. Bartolome looked towards the cliffs in the distance and thought of making a run for it. But it was a gamble. If the empire had four-limbers, they could deal with the Magi.

Wilkes clutched the rail as a column of water exploded out of the waves between *The Swan* and *The Wood* with such force that both ships surged away from each other. A wave formed behind *The Swan*. The pulse of water pushed her away from *The Wood*. Gusts of wind blew the now fully canvas sails away from them even faster.

"What's happening?" Wilkes demanded.

"Magi!" One of the four-limbers in the rigging pointed a hand toward a small boat to the stern. Aboard it, several of the cloaked Magi from the Church of the True Religionists stood together, all of their eyes fixed on the battle.

"Turn us about, and fire on that skiff!" Wilkes commanded.

The guns, still primed and ready to fire on *The Swan*, quickly targeted the small boat nearby. The shifting wind and massive wave had pivoted the ship in such a way that brought the starboard cannons precisely in line with where the Magis' boat sat, something Wilkes chalked up to battle fog. One never could be sure how an attack would be realized in the heat of the moment. Unfortunately for the Magi, it wouldn't be in their favor this day.

"Fire!" Bridgewater ordered.

BEHIND BARTOLOME, *The Swan* pivoted on the wave. The frigate twisted around, and by happenstance, lined her starboard guns up directly in the path of the Magis' boat. If she fired, it would blow the Magi to pieces, and considering that the four-limbers could help them with magical attacks, Bartolome knew she had only one choice.

"To starboard!" Bartolome screamed at her crew.

Her starboard guns were loaded. She had to come about quick, bringing her starboard side to bear and unloading everything. It was her only option. Three of her guns on the starboard side were loaded with sail shot, which would hopefully rip *The Swan's* sails to pieces.

In front of *The Wood*, all fifteen guns on *The Crimson Swan* fired on the tiny boat in an instant. Several Magi jumped, while others vanished. Clearly, they weren't ready for a full salvo. It was nice of Renaldo to send help, but they weren't prepared for an imperial frigate, just as the empire wasn't ready for a bucketful of magic. Except that, ultimately, they were, with the help of the four-limbers. Some part of Bartolome's' mind knew that this did not bode well for the future of Dressa Moore. But that wasn't something she could concern herself with today.

ALL FIFTEEN CANNONS on the starboard side shot at the Magi boat. If even one were to hit, the vessel would be utterly destroyed. The Magi, clearly not prepared for an attack of such magnitude, became frantic on the deck of their tiny boat. Some shifted their attention to the cannons, while others jumped off the boat, realizing the tactical error they had made. The waves and the wind from their spell both subsided as soon as their attention was taken away from the spell.

Several of the Magi on the boat vanished just seconds before it exploded into shrapnel. *The Swan* eased herself back into calmer waters. A line of soldiers ran to the back of the ship at Wilkes's command with orders to shoot any Magi they could see in the water. Several shots rang out as he returned to the wheel.

"Where is *The Wood*?"

Both men turned to port to see that *The Wood* hadn't run when the Magi attacked. Rather, she had pivoted and brought all her cannons to bear on *The Swan*. Wilkes's shoulders sank at the sight. Another broadside from *The Wood* at this range, with the port guns of *The Swan* empty, could be disastrous.

"Incoming!" Bridgewater screamed.

THE WOOD FINISHED its turn just as the crew on *The Swan* turned their attention back to Bartolome. Fortunately, all the guns on *The Swan* had already fired on the Magi and weren't ready. At least, Bartolome hoped they weren't. *The Wood*, however, had positioned herself perfectly to give a full broadside of all guns into the sails and masts of *The Swan*. The four-armers could fix things, but it would take them time. And that was all Bartolome needed.

All cannons along the side of *The Wood* erupted in perfect range of *The Swan*. Shots ravaged the masts and sails, and crew fell from the rigging to the deck with loud thumps. Bartolome gritted her teeth. She couldn't at all stomach the idea of attacking an imperial frigate. But what choice did she have? Four-armers jumped and dove from the rigging. Say what you wanted about them; the four-armers knew how to get out of the way when they needed to.

Soldiers on *The Swan* rushed to the railing, guns raised quickly across the line. Bartolome smiled at the attempt. Those guns wouldn't hurt *The Wood* much, and they certainly wouldn't harm the crew. More important than the soldiers, Bartolome could see into the gun ports along the side of *The Swan*. She was reloading fast.

"Move!" Bartolome shouted.

The Wood turned away from *The Swan* and picked up speed with a small gust of wind into her sails. The frigate turned, but her sails were in tatters. Four-armers were already climbing the rigging to make repairs, but knowing them as she did, Bartolome thought it would take a few hours to fix that much damage.

"Full sails! Get us out of here!" Bartolome stomped across the deck and pushed her undead crew hard. She could visibly see the flesh rotting on several of them as they forced themselves to obey her commands. If her crew weren't eating Anton's dead limbs, then their bodies ate themselves.

Behind them, *The Swan*, resigned to her loss, struck her sails. Four-armers had already started weaving magic into the sails to repair the holes. Bartolome could see Wilkes on the bridge of the ship, but couldn't quite make out his face. That was unfortunate. She liked seeing him scowl.

COMMODORE WILKES GROUND his teeth and balled his fists in absolute disbelief and rising anger. He stood at the rail of *The Swan* and watched as *The Knotted Wood* slipped away from him yet again. This cursed place was filled with the unexpected. If not for the Magi or a flying bucket of rainbow water, Bartolome would be his prisoner, and they would sail back down to the Riverlands. But Dressa had her surprises.

"The four-armers are fixing the sails, Commodore. They said it may be a few hours."

"What did she hit us with? More magic?"

Bridgewater shook his head. "These." He held up what looked like two small cannonballs. Both could have easily fit in the palm of Wilkes's hand, with a chain connecting them. Metal spikes covered the surface of both the chain and the miniature cannonballs. If fired in a volley, these could easily shred the sails of a ship.

"Nasty things," Wilkes said.

"We have nothing like this."

Wilkes nodded. "No actual need on the rivers. But I can see the advantage on the open lakes." He turned back to the shrinking *Wood* and shook his head. "She's bested us twice now."

"Won't happen a third time."

Wilkes nodded.

Bridgewater saluted and walked away to command the men and four-armers on the repairs. Wilkes watched the four-armed men climb the rigging with ease. If not for the quick alliance he had made with the village, *The Swan* would have been in far greater peril and possibly not have made it out of this engagement in one piece. But that also meant the empire might do well in Dressa. Yes, there would be much to learn. But there were alliances to be made. And the empire was very good at doing both.

CHAPTER FOURTEEN

The *Knotted Wood* glided into a small cove beneath towering cliffs. Several wooden piers extended out into the cove from a long strip of rocky land. They were made of twisted wood and lashed together with more rope than needed. Behind the rocks, past the wooden piers, rows of square and sometimes crooked wooden shacks lined the shore. Taller buildings, none more than three stories, stood behind the first row of shacks. The roads were made of seashells and ran from the docks along the shore and back through the rows of buildings.

A procession of people wearing long black robes appeared on the seashell road. They walked in two columns and swayed as they stepped while chanting some unintelligible song. In the middle of the group, four of the black-cloaked people carried a large cage suspended on poles that they carried on their shoulders. One of the robed walkers carried a barrel. A long tube hung out of the top of the barrel, the end of which was carried by a second robed person.

The *Knotted Wood* drifted towards the docks. Ropes were

flung outward from the deck to waiting hands on shore. The two professors emerged from their room, with the magon-meter, or whatever it was called, clutched tightly in Jonathan's hand. He swung the wand around several times, nodding each time, and quickly jotted down new numbers in his notebook. William, his face finally no longer buried in the hymnal, looked out across the tall cliffs and smiled.

"Impressive, aren't they?" Bartolome said.

William nodded. "And tall."

Bartolome nodded back. "The closer we get to the source, the odder the landscape becomes. These cliffs didn't exist before the event one hundred years ago. There's no pattern to them, and they don't go to the surface below the lake. These cliffs stretch to the far side of Drennal, the island continent where Hogkarta lives. It was split in two with the great upheaval of magic one hundred years ago."

"We could have gotten here by land?" William asked.

Bartolome shook her head. "Drennal curves far inland from the cliffs. Only way to get there is by boat."

"This place is just filled with mysteries," William said.

"And we shall uncover them all," Jonathan said confidently.

Bartolome smiled. "That you shall. Welcome to the domain of the Anti-Religionists, my dear professors." She swung her hand out towards the procession that approached.

"They look *very* religious, if I were to guess," Jonathan observed.

Bartolome nodded. In truth, the Anti-Religionists were, to put it lightly, weird. But they were always friendly to her when she came to their small town. She rifled through the papers she'd pirated from the barge captain to retrieve a document with a stamp from the church on the front. The letter was addressed to the Anti-Religionists. That meant the church had somehow secured passage through the straits to the Insanity Cliffs, the only known way to reach the Wizard and the Dragon. That shocked Bartolome to her core, considering that the Anti-Religionsts not only despised the church, but prevented any ships from sailing peacefully through the straits.

"What is our plan here, Captain?"

"Simple. Visit some old friends, give them this letter from the church, which grants us permission, and sail you to the Wizard."

"Can't we just go through anyway?" William asked.

Bartolome pointed to the cliffs. "They've set up cannons all along the cliffs. They could cut a ship to pieces before you make it a quarter of the way though the straits."

Paling, Jonathan nodded. "Yes, permission would be best, then."

"Quite."

Far down the shore, a large wooden wheel nearly ten feet tall and three feet wide rolled along the seashell road. Two men grunted as they walked inside of it, pushing it forward with every step. Behind the docks, deep into the town of the Anti-Religionists, more wheels came into view as they crisscrossed the streets, each of them manned with Anti-Religionists walking inside of them.

"What is that?" William asked, pointing to a rolling walking wheel.

"Ah, yes. Well, I should warn you, the Anti-Religionists are weird."

"It would seem so," Jonathan said.

"And quite fond of guinea pigs."

"Truly?" William's eyes never left the rolling wheel. "I

mean, there's fondness, and then there's … well, something else."

"Yes, well, when I say 'fond,' I should say 'worship.'" Bartolome smiled. "Shall we?"

The gangway extended out from the deck of *The Knotted Wood* and landed with a thud on the dock in front of the contingent of leaders from the Anti-Religionists. Bartolome nodded to Jonathan and William and walked to the wooden plank that led off the ship. Both of the professors' faces seemed to be frozen in stunned silence from the guinea pig revelation. But they at least moved forward at Bartolome's beckoning.

Something in the back of Bartolome's mind twitched when she scanned the faces aligned in front of her. They had a hardness that she wasn't accustomed to seeing. But she decided it could be due to many things that had nothing to do with her. After all, they all felt immensely guilty for Bartolome, her crew, and the entire undead island of Bedrich. It was the Anti-Religionists' fault that it had happened, after all. They were the remains of the excursion by the church twenty years ago that had caused Bedrich to become undead and Anton's people to be born the same. Still, Bartolome harbored them no ill will. The Anti-Religionists had more than expressed their grief over the years.

"Hello, friends!" Bartolome called as she walked down the gangplank to the dock.

"Welcome, undead leader of the undead," said one of the Anti-Religionists, clad in black robes.

"Good to see you all." Bartolome walked down the gangway, with Jonathan and William close on her heels. Every step she took caused worry to creep up her spine. The acolytes weren't being as friendly as Bartolome remembered. "Is everything alright?"

"Yes, everything is fine," the lead acolyte said.

Bartolome nodded. She then pulled from the pocket of her jacket the note meant for the Anti-Religionists. She handed it to the lead acolyte, who sniffed it twice. He then broke the seal, read the note, nodded, and placed it in his pocket.

"Is that a guinea pig?" William pointed to a cage held on top of two long poles carried on the shoulders of four acolytes.

"Yes. This is Max," the lead acolyte said.

"All hail Max," the rest of the acolytes said in unison.

"I think I may want to go back to Hogkarta now," William muttered.

Before anyone could say a word, the guinea pig in the cage squeaked three times and wiggled its tiny nose. Light flashed above the procession holding the poles. A gust of wind followed by a low rumble came to life. Tiny pieces of lettuce and small round tomatoes began falling from the sky. The brief storm lasted no more than three seconds before dissipating. Several acolytes immediately bent down to collect the fallen vegetables. Some were placed in bowls, while others were put inside the cage holding the guinea pig named Max.

"Did that pig just cast a spell?" Jonathan said with shock.

"Well, no, not as such. He can't speak, can he?" one of the acolytes said.

"No, he can't cast spells. But Max is imbued with magic, so he can do magical things. He's a living magical object, Max is," another acolyte said.

Yet another of the acolytes beamed a smile. "And one day, he'll be a god."

The lead acolyte made a shushing sound and shook his head. "Stop it. All of you."

"Come on, Earl, we don't get guests all that often. And we all know Bartolome," an acolyte said.

Bartolome bowed.

The lead acolyte gritted his teeth.

"Sorry, I don't mean to pry, but how did the guinea pig become magically imbued?" Jonathan asked. He waved his magonmeter near the cage. The needles spiked towards the red line.

"He was on the cliff twenty years ago when we botched the mission."

The lead acolyte turned and glared. "Can you all please be quiet?!"

"You visited the Wizard and Dragon twenty years ago?" Jonathan said, with incredulity thick in his voice.

The lead acolyte sighed. "Yes, we did. We were all members of the church. Sent by the god Yelke and his lot to free the Wizard and Dragon."

"Which, by extension, would free the gods from their prison," an acolyte said.

"But we botched it. Bad instructions, really. Anyway, Bedrich became undead, and the tree folk starting birthing the undead, and we decided to commit ourselves to never going near the Wizard and Dragon again."

"Or letting anyone else near it."

"On our way out of the straits, we saw Max here standing by the water. He had nearly buried himself in falling lettuce and cabbage. So, we took him with us."

Jonathan nodded. He waved his magonmeter around everything.

William's face scrunched into a frown. "Why did you do that, exactly? Take the guinea pig with you?"

"Well, we all thought that if Yelke and his lot ever get out, they'd be pretty peeved that we failed," an acolyte said.

"So, we'd best start preparing," another offered.

"And what better way to prepare than to have our own god on our side?"

The lead acolyte nodded with force. "Max will ascend to godhood and protect us from Yelke and the gods of the church."

William shook his head. "I'm just stuck on how you came to that conclusion, exactly?"

The sound of a sword being drawn startled the crowd. Bartolome's hand flew to her rapier as she scanned the acolytes. A flash of steel glinted in the sun, then the sword fell onto the body of the guinea pig named Max. The blade snapped in half the moment it touched his fur. The acolyte who had attacked held up the broken half for all to see.

"Can't be killed," he said.

"Carl! We've told you not to do that!" the lead acolyte snapped.

"Why? Doesn't hurt him. And it makes the point," Carl retorted.

A very large acolyte from the crowd pushed through the black-robed figures. He snatched the sword hilt from Carl's hand, then grabbed the piece of broken blade from the ground. The man gave Carl a very long, hard stare, then marched back down the seashell road until he was out of sight.

"Blacksmith. He doesn't get along well with Carl," the lead acolyte explained.

"Right. But okay, so the guinea pig can make lettuce rain and is impervious to the sword. How does that make him a god?" William asked.

"Well, it's logic, innit?" the lead acolyte said. "The Dragon down in the ravine with the Wizard is the only magical beast on the planet."

"Well, there are those rainbow crows."

"And the fish with three heads."

The lead acolyte cleared his throat. "None of those are the same. They don't cast spells or use magic. Rather they have some magical property about them. Only dragons could use magic without casting spells. Since the guinea pig can do that, it's just a matter of time before Max becomes a god. Then he can protect us from Yelke."

All the acolytes nodded in agreement. "Logical. Very logical."

Bartolome took a step forward and cleared her throat. "Now that we have introductions out of the way, do we have an accord regarding the church? I believe they have arranged for us to traverse the straits in peace."

The lead acolyte nodded. "Yes, they have. But no, you may not."

Bartolome's smile fell. "What's that, now?"

"We know who they are." The lead acolyte pointed to the professors. "And we know what they are going to do. And we can't allow that. Not again."

"We're here to do research, nothing more!" Jonathan protested.

"Sorry, that's not what we have been told." The lead acolyte nodded to the people behind him, and they each marched forward to grab Bartolome and the two professors.

Growls grew along the rail of *The Knotted Wood*. The lead acolyte looked at the ship and visibly gulped. "Keep them still, Bartolome."

"What if I don't?" Bartolome clenched her teeth and fumed. How dare they take her prisoner? Maybe she should release her crew, let them rampage, let them feast on these cursed people. It would be justice.

The lead acolyte's head came up. He snapped his fingers.

One of the acolytes unlocked the cage of the guinea pig. "By all means. But fear our god's wrath."

"What exactly does that mean?" William asked.

Bartolome looked at her crew, then at the professors, and finally back at the acolytes. In her heart, she knew she could never unleash her crew on them. Senseless killing of innocent people wasn't her way. She took a long, deep breath, and the crew on her ship slowly backed away from the rail. Most returned to their stations in the rigging, while others went below deck to feed.

"This is intolerable. I can assure you, sir, we are only here to research. Nothing more!" Jonathan said, his face turning red with anger.

"They're lying," said a voice behind the group.

Bartolome tilted her head as a stranger walked through the crowd, a smug look plastered on his face. His clothes showed that he wasn't with the Anti-Religionists, and possibly was not even from Dressa. In fact, his shirt and robe seemed to be quite similar to Jonathan's.

"Samson? Samson Oswald Sutter? How are you here?"

"I left Hogkarta the moment I realized I need to take matters into my own hands. I beat you here by just over a quarter of an hour. Thankfully, I had enough gold in reserve to pay for a fast charter." Samson winked. "Even fifteen minutes was more than enough time to explain to the locals what you are up to," Samson said with a wide grin.

"You're a worm!" Jonathan sputtered.

"And you're done. I will take over now. I've made agreements with the Anti-Religionsts. All of your equipment will be mine."

"Why would you do this, Samson? We're colleagues," William cut in.

"No, we *were* colleagues. Now we are not." Samson's face opened into a wide grin.

"How did you even get here?" William asked.

"I commissioned a ship to bring me here. How else?" Samson leaned forward. "Using the money meant to pay the pirate." He winked at Bartolome.

"I'll gut you and turn you into my boot-licking undead deck swabber, you backstabbing, small-minded little man!" Bartolome stepped forward, but froze when she heard a voice she recognized behind her.

"No, you won't."

Bartolome turned to see an imperial rowboat sitting by the dock next to *The Wood*. A contingent of imperial soldiers, as well as several four-limbed rowers, sat in the boat. Commodore Wilkes, flanked by three soldiers, walked up to her and stopped just a foot away from her. "Hello, Captain Bartolome."

Marta took a step backward and folded her arms across her chest. "Well, hello, Commodore Wilkes."

COMMODORE WILKES STARED into the undead captain's eyes and smiled. He had won. He'd caught her. Even if it wasn't his ship that had fired the shot that disabled *The Wood*, she was still his prisoner. Now it was just a matter of somehow executing her undead crew, and hauling Bartolome and the two professors back to the empire to face justice. Perhaps Wilkes would even set another garrison in this village as well. Considering that before the events of the last few days, the empire had gone from having no presence in Dressa Moore to forging treaties, agreements, and appeasements with three separate governments, Wilkes was suddenly having a wonderful week.

Now he just had to find his wife.

"How did they catch us?" Jonathan asked.

Wilkes pointed to the rowboat behind them. Four four-armed men waved as he pointed to them. "Turns out, they can row quite fast. We were on your heels the entire way after our skirmish." Wilkes looked over Bartolome's shoulder. "And I'm sure *The Swan* will be here not long after us."

"But we would have seen you," William protested.

Wilkes smiled. "Our four-armed crew cast an invisibility spell. Or, as they called it, a spell that just makes you not look at them. They don't like stares." He turned to Bartolome. "Now, where is she? Where's my wife? And no more games!"

Bartolome lifted her hands in the air and tilted her head to the side. "Parley?"

"Not a chance."

"I told you where she is. And that's not on my ship."

"Where is the island?"

"Don't you remember?"

Wilkes's stare grew hard. "No, I don't know where it is."

The undead captain shrugged. "Guess we're at an impasse."

Wilkes nodded. "Are we, now?"

"Release me, and them, and I'll tell you exactly how to find her."

Wilkes chuckled. "Do you really think I would do that?"

Bartolome smirked. "No, but worth a try."

"I've forged alliances with many in Dressa. If you don't want to tell me where this island is located, I'm sure my new allies can help."

"You'll still never find it. It's hidden by sorcery that not even the church understands."

"Well, I'm sure all the resources of the empire will find a way."

The smirk on Bartolome's face faded, which made Wilkes's shoulders rise. This rat had finally been cornered and had nothing left to offer. He looked at the two professors, one of their faces still buried in a book, while the other looked at him with a mix of fear and worry.

"Nothing else to say?" Wilkes said smugly.

Bartolome stared into his eyes for a heartbeat before turning away.

He nodded with a grim smile. "It's good that you know when you're beaten. My soldiers will dispatch your crew shortly."

"No!" Bartolome cried.

"And you will all be coming with me as my prisoners. This game is over." Wilkes turned to the acolytes. "I am Commodore Thomas Wilkes of the empire." He took out a bag of gold from his inner coat. "This is a gift from the empire to our new friends. As you can see..." He pointed back to the four-limbers in the rowboat. "... the empire likes to make friends, not enemies. Would you like to be friends with the empire?"

"Depends. Will you be attempting to go to the source of magic?" the lead acolyte asked.

"No."

The lead acolyte nodded and took the gold. "Good enough."

"As a return gesture, would you mind putting this captain and her compatriots in irons until *The Crimson Swan* arrives?" Wilkes asked.

The acolytes exchanged a glance. "What's that mean?"

"Prison. Put them in a prison. We'll dispatch her crew once the bulk of my forces are here," Wilkes said.

"We don't have a prison," the lead acolyte said.

Wilkes turned to him. "Do you have somewhere you can put them where you can lock a door?"

One of the acolytes raised his hand. "We could put them in the old wheel hut. No one uses that anymore."

The lead acolyte nodded. "Good idea, Ted."

Wilkes nodded his approval. He gave Bartolome a grin and motioned for her and the professors to follow the acolytes. He ordered his men to remain near *The Wood* and kill any of the undead crew if they set foot off the ship. When *The Swan* arrived, they could set *The Wood* to blaze and sink her to the bottom. And that would be the end of Bartolome and her crew, once and for all.

SAMSON STOOD at the top of a hill that looked down at the docks below. He'd managed to back away when the imperials arrived. No sense in getting mixed up with them. Below, the locals were leading Jonathan and William away, the looks on their faces frozen in priceless fear. How Samson wished he could freeze this moment for all time and look at it again to cherish it. Perhaps he'd investigate the creation of a new spell that could do just such a thing—even capture the event in a picture and save it in a book. He could mass-produce it and issue it as required reading for all first years. The lesson would be simple: never try to backstab your colleagues.

"Oh, Jonathan. Pity you had to learn that the hard way."

The acolytes led all of them and the undead captain along the seashell road, going deeper into the village. Eventually, Samson lost sight of them as they rounded a corner. Above him, the sun was bright and warmed his skin. It would be noon soon, and a grumble in his midsection reminded him that he hadn't had breakfast. The only thing they had to eat here was fish and eggs, but it would have to do. Couldn't go hunting the mysteries of magic on an empty stomach.

But first, I need to inspect the gear.

Part of the agreement with the Anti-Religionists—whom Samson rather detested, actually—was for him to claim ownership of all of Jonathan's gear. That magonmeter was quite spectacular. When Samson had last been at the university, the device was still being developed. To see one working and in use in the field was remarkable. With reluctance, Samson felt he should at least give Jonathan that much credit. What could it hurt?

On the dock, shouts from several dockhands complaining about boarding the undead ship rose throughout the streets. The crew snarled at them and wouldn't let them board. The villagers backed away and shook their heads. He couldn't blame them. Who would want to go into that death trap? But a deal was a deal. Samson was sure that the Anti-Religionists would figure something out. He patted his stomach once and decided against joining the escalating calamity. Instead, breakfast. Perhaps he'd be lucky, and they'd have some bacon and beans. Perhaps even sausage. He'd grown quite used to the sausage vendors in Hogkarta.

BARTOLOME SUNK down on the cold stone floor of the old wheelhouse and folded her arms over her knees. Jonathan and William huddled together on the opposite side of the large space. William, who was really growing on Bartolome for his singular mindset, popped open his hymnal and began flipping through the pages. Jonathan, in stark contrast, just sat down and glowered. He looked like someone had just stolen his favorite pet.

A large wooden wheel, like the one being walked through town, sat in the middle of the large room. Cobwebs covered the top half. A few empty crates and boxes sat strewn about the space. This structure looked to be hardly used. The single door to the room, which led out to one of the seashell roads, was bolted shut from the outside.

Back on the dock, the crew of *The Knotted Wood* wandered around the deck, wondering what they should do. Bartolome could feel their confusion from here. She tried to direct them to some mundane task, but shouts from the dock made the undead jittery. Several men were complaining about not wanting to board the ship to get Jonathan's things. That was probably for the best. Bartolome still had control of her crew, but the farther away she got from them, the more dangerous they became. Throw some fresh meat in front of them, and they would feed. The Anti-Religionists knew that, however, so the professor's gear was safe for now. Until *The Crimson Swan* reached the harbor, that is.

Bartolome huffed and shook her head in frustration. That Samson guy must have terrified the Anti-Religionists. She'd glossed over the fact that the church had managed to bargain with them at all. What could the church have possibly offered them to allow any ship to get near the Wizard and Dragon? It made no sense. Perhaps there was far more going on here than Bartolome knew.

"So, what happens now? Still think we'll make it by nightfall?" Jonathan grumbled, sarcasm thick on his tongue.

"Wasn't my colleague who betrayed us," Bartolome responded quickly.

"No, it was your *friends* the Anti-Religionists, on their own island. Didn't you say these people are friendly to your kind?"

"I did, indeed. But they have their priorities. And it's really more of a peninsula."

"What's that?" William asked, looking up from his book.

"The island we're on. It's more of a peninsula."

"No, I mean, what are their priorities?"

"Preventing access to the source of magic, of course."

Jonathan snorted. "Ridiculous. They have no right to do such a thing."

"No one has any right to do anything, Jonathan. All that matters is who has the biggest gun."

"We're here for research. That's all! Why can't anyone understand that?"

Bartolome turned her attention to Jonathan, her stare growing harder with each second. "You keep saying that. And yet the empire, the church, and your own university have orchestrated your coming here. Why is that, exactly?"

"Why, the pursuit of knowledge, of course."

Bartolome nodded. "The pursuit of knowledge twenty years ago by these very same Anti-Religionists caused the Dragon to breathe smoke. A magical quake that shook all of Dressa and turned my home island into an undead wasteland."

"I'm sure that's not what they intended."

Bartolome nodded. "No, of course not. The church sent them to free the Dragon and kill the Wizard."

"Why in heaven's name would they want to do such a thing?" William asked.

"There's a movement in the church to free the gods. Bring order to the world."

"Why do gods need to be freed anyway?" William asked.

Bartolome shrugged.

"Nonsense." Jonathan stood and paced in the large room. "Utter nonsense."

"Okay, fine. What exactly is the research you want to do there?" Bartolome asked.

"Why should I tell you?"

"Jonathan, please. Our situation isn't exactly ideal," William said.

Jonathan looked at William and then at Bartolome. "In my trunks is a lead suit. With it, and the magonmeter, I can lower myself down to stand just feet from the Wizard. Magon readings that close could usher in a new understanding of the fundamentals of magical decay."

Bartolome let out a hard laugh. "And you think *we're* mad?"

Anger grew in Jonathan's eyes. "And—not that you'll understand—I theorize there may exist anti-magon particles that can only be detected at the source. My magonmeter can see them. If they exist, I hypothesize that they would work in opposition to magic itself."

"You mean...?"

"I mean, any spell cast can be instantly countered by an anti-magon."

A low whistle escaped Bartlome's lips. "No wonder the empire is here."

"Well, it's just a theory."

"But why would the church want to give that power to

the empire? Magic is their thing. And why give William that book?" Bartolome asked.

"It's just a hymnal. Who cares about that blasted book?!" Jonathan snatched the book from William's hand.

"Jonathan!" William's face twisted into utter shock.

"Please. You've had your nose buried in that stupid book of nonsensical symbols ever since you got it. It's meaningless!"

"It's not! It's not just symbols!"

"Then what is it, William? Tell me."

William looked away and shrugged. "I don't know."

"Exactly." Jonathan turned from them both and directed his attention out the window.

William sighed, darted a look at Jonathan, and buried his hands in his pockets. He instantly withdrew his right hand with the hymnal clutched in his fingers. He held it up and gave Jonathan a brazen stare. "Still think it's just a hymnal?"

Blinking, Jonathan looked from his hand, where the book had been just moments ago, to William's, where the book now resided. "... How?"

"Magic?"

Bartolome leaned her head against the wall behind her. "I still can't fathom what the church could have offered the Anti-Religionists to grant us passage in the first place."

"They wanted you to take Max to the source," a voice from the shadows in the room said. "And my book does that too. Follows you no matter what."

A young girl emerged and tossed a similar-looking hymnal into the air.

Bartolome smiled as Sylvia Santos emerged from the darkness. The girl gave Bartolome a nod and came to stand in the middle of the room. "Hi, Marta."

"I wondered when you'd show up, Sylvia," Bartolome said.

WILLIAM LOOKED at the girl who had emerged from the shadows and got a funny feeling that he'd seen someone do something similar before—just walk out of the shadows as if darkness itself were a doorway. Had it been a priest at the university? He also felt he recognized something in her face —the line of her jaw, her cheekbones. Perhaps he'd spied a relative in the past? But where? And what had Bartolome called her? Santos? Then it hit William square in the cerebellum.

"Santos... Are you related to Archbishop Santos?"

Sylvia let out a sound between a groan of pain and a snort of disgust. "He's my uncle."

"Sorry, but who are you? Niece of the same archbishop who sanctioned this trip?" Jonathan asked.

"Well, that can't be a coincidence," William said earnestly.

"Quite," Bartolome said with a sneer. "Proper introductions, yes? This is Sylvia, a friend. Sylvia, this is Jonathan and William, also friends. Though William is friendlier."

"Rude," Jonathan said.

"And true," Marta shot back.

"Excuse me, what did you mean a moment ago? You have a book that follows you?" William said.

Sylvia pulled out a red book from a bag hanging on her shoulder. She held in the air and tossed it to William. He caught it and turned it over in his hands. The book was bound in red leather and appeared to have some symbols on the cover that matched the ones in his book.

"What is this?" William asked.

"This book has followed me from Hogkarta. No matter where I leave it, the book always finds its way back to me. It's creepy. It works just like yours."

William flipped through the pages in the book, his eyes growing wide with curiosity. It was indeed the same script as was in his book. But he couldn't read it any more than he could his own.

Jonathan approached and brought his face close to Sylvia's. "Can you get us out of here?" he asked. "The same way you came in? Through the shadows?"

Sylvia took a step back. "No, I can't do that. The shadow walk spell only works for me." Sylvia held up her wrist and shook a bracelet wrapped around her arm. "Besides, the whole town knows you're in here. They don't mean you any harm, though. They'll likely just let you go, eventually."

"Right into the empire's prison hold," Bartolome said.

"The empire is here?" Sylvia said.

Bartolome nodded. "All the red coats on the dock."

"So, that's what the commotion was this morning." Sylvia shook her head. "I'm sorry, there's nothing I can do." She looked at Bartolome and shrugged. "What could I even do? I know a handful of useless spells."

Bartolome smiled and shrugged. "Don't worry, Sylvia, we'll be fine."

Jonathan cursed. "I can't believe my research is going to be thwarted by some backwater town fearful of the sky falling!"

"It won't be," Sylvia said. "That other professor— Samson, I think his name is— I overheard he's going to take your things and proceed himself. He has an agreement with the locals that he won't do anything other than look. No spell-casting."

"We don't even know how to cast a spell!" Jonathan roared.

"Why would they agree to that? Makes little sense that they would prevent us, but allow this Samson to move forward with it?" Bartolome said.

"One of the acolytes said Samson is too stupid to do anything bad. And he agreed to take Max to the source."

"Why doesn't one of the acolytes just take the guinea pig themselves? They're right here."

Sylvia smiled. "None of them will ever go near that place again. This lot are the ones who made it back in one piece. A lot came back in pieces, and aren't very happy to this day."

"Well, this is just great." Jonathan kicked the wooden wheel and sighed.

William flipped through Sylvia's book until he sat down on the floor and began comparing it to his own.

Bartolome watched William for a long second before shaking her head. Sylvia gave her a quick shrug and withdrew back into the shadows. Bartolome gave her a nod as if to say it was okay. Sylvia was young. Bartolome didn't want any harm to come to her. The fact that Sylvia had tipped off Bartolome at all to this whole sorted mess in the first place was quite the risk.

A loose nail on one of the walls drew Bartolome's attention. Before she could walk over and examine the nail, a sudden and sharp pain shot up her arm.

CHAPTER FIFTEEN

Bartolome stomped the floor and screamed. She closed her eyes and brought her hands to her temples. Someone had stabbed one of her crew. She could feel their pain as if it were her own.

Bartolome extended her awareness. Images swirled in her vision. The shape of *The Knotted Wood's* hull formed in her mind—as did the large and grinning face of Anton, holding a knife that was jammed into her crewman's arm.

"Sorry, Mum, but I needed to get your attention," Anton said to the undead crewman. "I know you can't talk through the crew, but I just need to make you aware, the imperial ship is nearly here, and the soldiers on the dock are looking ready to board. Fight or flee, Mum?"

"Just hold the line, make a fuss at the entry gate. I'll have the crew snarl. Try to pretend to be undead, yes?" Bartolome tried to say. But since none of her crew could form words, the gurgle and growls that echoed from the undead crew only made Anton frown.

"Can't say I understood that. How about just point, yah? Left flee, right fight. Go." Anton smiled.

Bartolome grunted in frustration. She didn't want him to do either. She really did need to work out a spell to allow her to speak through her crew one of these days. Of course, finding new spells was harder than a days-old kingdom baguette, if the rumors were true. Bartolome forced the crewman to point forward. Then she shook the crewman's head, snarled four times, and crossed his arms into an X.

This caused Anton to only frown deeper. But he soon recovered and smiled. "I can only imagine you're suggesting a third option. Right. Well, I've no idea what that could mean, so I'll just wing it." He patted the crewman on the head and walked away, out of view.

Bartolome released her grip. Her sight returned to the empty room of the old wheelhouse. All eyes were on her, as she'd just growled, pranced, and acted a fool for seemingly no reason. Bartolome waved them off. She sat down against the large wooden wheel and leaned backward. Her head hurt. Her arm hurt. And more importantly, her pride hurt. Wilkes was moments away from taking her ship, permanently killing her crew, and probably imprisoning Anton or taking him back to the Riverlands to put on a show for *The Swan's* emperor. All told, Bartolome was not having a good day.

"We need to get out of here. Now," Bartolome said.

"What do you mean? This is it. We've lost. *I've* lost," Jonathan said. "Samson will claim victory, the university will grant him anything he wants, and I shall retire to a pig farm."

Bartolome huffed a laugh. "At least you'll live. They'll burn me, stake me, shoot me, drown me, and when none of that works, probably just bury me in a hole a thousand feet deep."

Jonathan tilted his head to one side and looked at Bartolome with wide eyes. "You're undead as well?"

Bartolome shook her head. "How did you miss that?"

"I don't know. Why aren't you like the others? Mindless and grunting."

Bartolome shrugged. "No idea. When it happened on Bedrich, some of us turned into mindless undead things, and some of us didn't. Pretty soon, we figured out that we could control them."

"So, you're an undead lord or something?"

Bartolome smiled. "I suppose."

"And there are more of you? Who can control the undead?"

Bartolome nodded. "But they are stuck on Bedrich. I managed to get off, obviously, but the rest of the undead lords, as you call them, or me, are still there." Bartolome let out a long sigh. "As is Wilkes's dear wife, Abigail."

A silence settled over the room. Jonathan sat on the cold stone floor and buried his face in his hands. Bartolome watched the man slowly fall apart as tears fell down his face. She honestly couldn't imagine the pain Jonathan must feel at having come so close to his dream, only to be thwarted by someone he thought he could trust.

Next to him, his fingers flying through both books opened on his lap, William seemed to have heard nothing that had happened in the last few moments. Ever since Sylvia had thrown him that book, his attention was locked and focused on the pages. Bartolome couldn't quite understand that. It simply drove her mad—perhaps out of frustration that William wasn't sharing in she and Jonathan's angst at everything going to absolute ruin—and just when they were all so very close to getting what they wanted. And they were so very close to succeeding. Just moments. Bartolome could have dealt with Samson. But how in the bloody blue blazes was she supposed to know that the four-armers could row that fast?

"What in the name of the gods are you doing, William? Why are you still reading those? Going to sing at church?" Bartolome snapped with frustration rippling through her voice.

William looked up and shook his head in confusion.

"It's a hymnal. What is so bloody fascinating about a stupid hymnal?" Bartolome demanded.

William nodded once, shook his head again, and smiled. "Oh, it's not a hymnal. And neither is this one from Sylvia."

Bartolome let out a long sigh. "Well, what is it then? A guide to escaping from a wheelhouse?"

"They are spell books."

Bartolome felt like a she'd been hit by the butt of an imperial rifle. "What?!"

Jonathan lifted his head and twisted it to look at William. "A spell book? How can you know that?"

William grinned in a manner that Bartolome was more accustomed to seeing on Jonathan's face. "The book Sylvia gave me, it's written in the common tongue. But it also has headings throughout. And symbols that match those in my book. When I open to the same page in both books, the symbols align."

"So? How is that significant? And what is Sylvia's book about if it's written in common?" Jonathan asked.

"Oh, I don't know. I didn't read it for the content. I told you, there's a pattern in the symbols in both my books that seems to match some pages in Sylvia's. I'm now fully confident that these symbols aren't just scribblings."

"You translated it that fast?" Bartolome said.

"I've been studying the patterns in my book ever since

we left Hogkarta. Once I know the patterns, I can propose some rough guesses on what the words mean. But now that I have Sylvia's book and can see the pages lining up, I believe it's a translation—a hidden translation of my book of symbols. That's how I know it's a spell book. The first pages of both have the same symbols. From there, it's a simple translation. This is a language—an actual language!"

"This again." Jonathan sighed. "There's only one language in the world, William. Why can't you just accept that?"

"And why can't you accept that my work is just as important as yours?" he demanded. "They have belittled me for my entire academic career, and yet no one can answer why there is only one language. Why are peoples separated by thousands of years, continents apart, still speaking the same thing? It makes no rational sense."

"It's just the way the world works, William."

"Nonsense."

"Cast a spell, then," Bartolome said. "If it's a spell book, just do it."

"Yes, William. Splendid idea, Captain." Jonathan turned to William with contempt in his eyes. "Cast a spell, prove me wrong, and let's walk out of here. Go on, do it!"

William looked at both Bartolome and Jonathan. He gave a long, deep sigh, but then his face folded into a smile. "As it happens, to answer your first question, Captain, this spell book is meant for those who don't speak the language. It's not enough to read it. Meaning, I know what the symbols in my book mean in the common tongue. But that's not how spells work. You have to speak them in the language of spells. Pronunciation and enunciation would be critical."

"So, you can't do that. Splendid way to tell us you have nothing." Jonathan huffed and folded his arms.

"No, I didn't say that. It's strange, but when I set both books on the right page, and match the symbols in each, consciously matching them in my mind, the pronunciation just pops into my thoughts, as if I know it. Technically, I don't know if it's a spell book at all, but I know that the pronunciation of words from my book sounds exactly like spells being cast. It has to be the same language."

Jonathan leaned forward, his face tight and his eyes hard. "Then do it."

William blinked. He looked down at his books, his finger running over the words until he found something he liked. He looked up at one of the walls and closed his eyes.

"*Walla walud*," William said.

Seconds passed, and nothing happened. Jonathan let out a stifled laugh, while William dug his face back into the book with a sense of panic.

Then, without warning, a shimmering grew over one of the wooden walls. Bartolome tilted her head to make sure she was really seeing this as one piece of lumber vanished. Another piece of wood fell. The second piece rolled over, extended eight legs, and ran off. Three seconds later, a thousand spiders fell from the wooden wall in waves until the wall was gone. The seashell road outside lay waiting for them to simply walk out.

"Gods!" Bartolome cried.

"Spiders!" Jonathan screamed. He jumped to his feet and tried to climb onto William's shoulders. "Why is it spiders?!"

Bartolome couldn't be sure, but she thought she saw a smirk appear and vanish on William's face.

～

BARTOLOME KNELT behind a stack of figs, Jonathan and William behind her. Several of the locals walked by on the seashell road. None of them seemed to notice or care about Bartolome or the professors. That suited her just fine. She had scanned several faces as they casually walked out of the wheelhouse that had inexplicably lost a wall. Bartolome looked for Sylvia, but she had already gone. A smirk flashed across Bartolome's face. Twice now, she'd been hunkered down behind stacked food in two separate towns, and each time, she had been chased there by the same man.

"Well, our situation has improved little since Hogkarta, hasn't it?" Jonathan said.

"Seems like it," Bartolome said.

"What do we do now?"

"Well, I don't think running through the streets like last time would work."

"Why not?"

Bartolome shrugged. "Doubtful that Wilkes would leave *The Wood* unattended a second time."

"We can't surrender," Jonathan said, his voice rising in panic.

"Calm down. No, we can't. Disgrace for you, and likely repeated attempts to end my life for me."

"Where is your friend Sylvia? Could she help?"

"Possibly, but I didn't spot her." Bartolome looked at William, who hadn't spoken. A calm smile rose across his face as he returned her stare. "What about you, linguist? Any more spells in there?"

"As a matter of fact..." William raised his hand and said some strange words again. Fire erupted in his fingers. He chuckled and shook his head as he threw flame onto Bartolome's shoe.

"What are you doing?!" She stomped on her shoe frantically, but no matter how hard she did, the fire didn't die out —but it also didn't hurt in the slightest.

"It's an illusion. Like the one you used on us, and for the faces of your crew, to make them look alive. But this illusion can be thrown. More than that, it spreads."

Bartolome whistled. "That's not bad, Professor. That would be quite the distraction."

"Amazing, William! I'm sorry I ever doubted you. Truly, I am," Jonathan raved. "This is groundbreaking! The implications are staggering."

"We'll go to class another time. Start throwing, William." Bartolome pointed to one of the buildings.

William nodded, rose, then sat back down. "You can too, you know."

"What?"

"Give your foot a toss."

Bartolome looked at the fire on her foot. She kicked out once at the stack of figs. The flames leapt from her boot to the wooden crates and burned. The realness of the illusion was stunning. She couldn't feel any heat, but her brain told her to flee nonetheless. She tried her best to remember the words William had spoken, but they had already left her. No matter; once on her ship, he could teach her that spell, and possibly many more. A new realization formed in her mind. She'd questioned this trip from the start, but now, after William's discovery, she could very well become spell-rich. She could sell them for enough money to buy her own fleet of ships and retake her island, regardless of whether the undead were cured. Her entire world had been turned upside down in the best possible way.

"I think we're going to become fast friends now, William."

"Sure. After Jonathan conducts his research," William said.

The two exchanged looks and pecked a kiss. A warm spot in Bartolome's cold, dead heart sparked for half a second before fading. She wondered what it would feel like to be alive again. Perhaps, with their help, she could find out.

"Alright, enough. Start throwing!" Bartolome grabbed more of the fire with her hands and tossed it onto nearby buildings. The fake fire spread even faster than the real thing. In seconds, the building next to them was engulfed, and soon the flames spread to others. All that they had to do was wait for the town to explode with fear, and they could walk right onto her ship.

Commodore Wilkes marched his way to the docks of yet another town on the supposedly barren floating lake of Dressa Moore. With each step, he furthered his belief that the empire not only belonged here, but would flourish. Of course, there would be the matter of dealing with the church. The empire had hired church spies—clearly a major mistake—and they had done nothing but spread lies to the emperor about what awaited them here. The truth was obvious: the church wanted these lands for themselves.

The Crimson Swan was just pulling into port. Ropes flew from the crew to the docks. The gangway was lowered, and Wilkes's soldiers walked down. More soldiers—the ones who had accompanied Wilkes here on the rowboat—had gathered around the gangway to *The Knotted Wood*. They yelled and pushed at the locals. Some of his men had their guns drawn. As long as they didn't start shooting, that was fine as far as Wilkes was concerned.

"Commodore, is she here?" Bridgewater asked as he walked down the gangway.

"Aye. She's ours."

"What's all this commotion?"

Wilkes nodded. "We want onto the ship, but the locals are denying us. They say we shouldn't hurt the undead."

"And why is that?"

Wilkes shrugged. "I haven't the faintest idea. But you'll find this is a very strange village."

Bridgewater nodded.

Wilkes walked before the soldiers and raised both of his hands. The crowd calmed a little, but didn't give any ground. Several people emerged through the masses, clearly of some level of authority, and approached Wilkes. They all wore long black robes, and each carried the look of being devoutly religious. Wilkes recognized several of their faces from earlier when he first arrived.

"Commodore," one of them greeted him.

"Chief Acolyte," Wilkes responded.

The man nodded. "Just Acolyte. We are all equal here."

"But you can call him Earl," another acolyte said.

Earl, or just Acolyte, frowned and turned. "No, he can't. We don't use names."

"You called Carl, Carl," a third acolyte pointed out.

"Well, Carl is special. And not in good ways." Earl, or just Acolyte, turned back to Wilkes and smiled. "Now, where were we, Captain?"

Wilkes grimaced. "It's Commodore. Please, tell your people to move back."

Earl shook his head. "Well, that's the thing. The undead people are under our protection."

"They aren't people," Wilkes said.

"Now, I realize their current state is distasteful. However—"

"Stop. This ship is the property of the empire. The crew and captain are prisoners of the empire. They sailed into our waters and attacked one of our towns. I am taking this ship, Captain Bartolome, and the professors back to the empire. And I am executing the undead crew. It would be a mercy. Clear?"

The chief acolyte shook his head. "Look, friend, we agreed to put Bartolome in the old wheelhouse in exchange for you and your ship not going to the source of magic. You never said anything about killing the undead. I don't think we can allow that." He frowned for a moment. "What happens if we don't allow it, exactly?"

Wilkes smiled. "That's the wrong question. The correct question is, what happens if you get in our way? Because, you see, you can't stop this. All fifteen guns on our starboard side are primed and loaded to fire into your town. And I will give that order if we come under attack. Do I make myself clear?"

Shouts from the seashell road deeper into the village briefly grabbed Wilkes's attention, but he quickly disregarded them. He stared into Earl's eyes beneath the black hood and forced himself to not blink—something he always found both necessary and quite difficult. His eyes always hurt afterward, but the effect was dramatic. Most men squirmed, just as Earl was doing, and averted their eyes, which Earl had done twice already, and eventually capitulated under the strain of Wilkes's stare. It was a practiced skill, and one he had honed for just such occasions.

"You see, Commodore, we have always found ourselves to be responsible for the undead. It would create great pains in our society if we allowed you to kill Bartolome and her crew. It would strain future relationships."

Wilkes nodded once. "Your terms are accepted." He turned away and motioned for his men to board *The Knotted Wood.*

"But I didn't give you any terms?"

"No, you did." Wilkes turned back to Earl. "Strained relations with the empire. Fine. Although, you'll find that is not an enviable position for your town to take."

"We're more of a village," Carl offered.

Screams from the streets surrounding the docks rose in pitch, replacing the shouts from earlier. Wilkes sighed once and turned to see smoke and fire spreading through several of the buildings nearest the docks. He cursed under his breath and ordered his men back.

"But Earl, you seem to have a calamity here. Would you care for imperial help, or shall we retire to our ship until you've sorted out your fires?"

Earl fumbled with his hands. He looked back into the village to see the fire spreading with ease between the buildings. He gave orders to his men to help. "Yes, please. We would love to accept help."

Wilkes smiled. "Excellent. Captain Bridgewater?"

"Right away, sir."

Wilkes took a step away from *The Wood,* but stopped himself. He turned back to the ship that was once his quarry, and then turned to look at the fire. The coincidence bothered him. The fact that a fire would erupt moments before he was about to claim full victory was just too convenient.

"You three, with me!" Wilkes and three soldiers took off at a run back to the wheelhouse. He didn't know why, but this felt like more than a fire. It felt like another distraction, courtesy of the great Captain Bartolome. Best to double-check whether his prisoner was still imprisoned.

COMMODORE WILKES RAN across the docks through the seashell streets of the town. Fire raged all around him. Buildings seemed to catch the flames with a breeze and became engulfed in moments. One man burst out of a building, half his arm on fire, and ran to a large drum of some liquid. He plunged his arm inside, and a look of relief crossed his face. If the buildings here were so prone to fire, then this town could be consumed quickly.

With increased urgency, Wilkes pulled his men forward through the burning buildings to the wheelhouse, where he had left Bartolome. The door to the building was locked tight. The flames hadn't yet reached this far up the street. Wilkes opened the door, ran inside, and stopped as soon as he saw the missing wall. The undead captain, in her utter depravity, had obviously broken out using magic, and had set fire to the entire town to afford her an escape.

"Back to the streets!" Wilkes commanded.

Outside, more of the buildings caught fire and burned. The man who had run out into the street before Wilkes entered the jail had already caught himself back on fire and run down the street screaming in terror. Dozens more citizens of the town, some with flames covering their bodies, ran through the streets. At least four children were among them.

"Help them! Get some water!" Wilkes commanded his men.

Laughter several feet away drew the commodore's attention. A small child sat on the ground, her body covered in orange and red flames, her hands waving the fire wildly in the air, a bright, wide smile on her face. Wilkes walked over to the girl and knelt, only to see her giggle as the fire raged on her skin.

With his finger, Wilkes touched a spot of flames and steeled himself for the pain, but none came. He brought his finger close to his face and immediately noticed that there was no heat from the fire. He looked back down at the little girl, who had stood up and was currently dancing in the street and twirling beneath a coat of flames.

"Bartolome!" Wilkes ground his teeth and reached for his sidearm. "Soldiers! To the docks!"

BARTOLOME RAN onto her ship with the professors on her heels. Behind them, the docks, the town, and many of the acolytes were engulfed in flames that they could not put out. Several of the townspeople had figured out that the fire was an illusion and were now playing with the flames, tossing it between themselves. Children played a game of kickball with a flaming ball, their feet catching fire along with the ball. Several floating pigs joined the flame-kicking game. Max, the guinea pig god, squealed in fear at the fire on the shoulders of four acolytes. A constant rain of carrots and lettuce fell from darkening clouds above. This turned out to be a boon to the floating pigs, which ate heartily as they sailed across the seashell streets.

"I've never seen an illusion of this strength, nor one that could be spread. This is astounding," Jonathan said.

"I didn't expect this," William agreed.

"You need to be careful with that book," Jonathan said.

"We can discuss it through the straits." Bartolome ran to

the bridge. Her crew was already at work, pulling the gangway back. Both of the professors followed her. "Maybe the distraction will let us pass through without the Anti-Religionists' permission."

"How long does this illusion last, William?"

"I'm not really sure."

"What?"

"I am new to casting a spell, Jonathan."

"Just dispel it, like I do mine. Here, try it on us." Bartolome lifted her leg, which was still on fire.

William looked at her and nodded. Bartolome had taught him the spell she used to remove illusions. William echoed the spell and pushed his intentions towards the flames. The fire on all of them vanished instantly. But on the docks and throughout the town, the fire still raged.

"What about the town? How do you stop it over the whole town?"

William shrugged. "Let me read the book. Give me a moment. I need to find the right word."

"What do you mean?"

"I mean, it's not really a spell book. My hymnal is just written in the language of spells. So, speaking the spell is all it takes. I just need to find the translated word for 'town' or 'village.' The problem is that not every page is a translated page, and most do not share the heading symbol."

"There's Wilkes. He's onto us." Bartolome pointed to the dock just as Wilkes and several of his soldiers ran down the street. Half of the commodore's body was covered in flames, but he didn't react to the faux fire. He barked orders for his soldiers to aim the guns at the deck.

"Never mind the flames. Can you stop bullets?" Bartolome looked up to see the sails from her ship unfurling. They would have to take cover—no chance that they could get the sails down and at sea before the imperials opened fire.

"Oh, wait... Actually, yes. I saw a phrase that may work. Let me try this..."

"Shouldn't we be more cautious?" Jonathan said.

"Not now, we shouldn't," Bartolome replied.

William spoke some words from his book that had not been uttered in several thousand years. He crafted a full sentence in the ancient tongue. A shimmering spread around the entire *Knotted Wood*, but quickly dissipated into the air. Bartolome shot William a look, but he only returned a shrug.

On the dock, a line of five soldiers, with more running to join them, had raised their rifles and pointed them at *The Wood*. Wilkes instantly ordered them to fire. The collective boom from the rifles jolted Jonathan and William, and both dove to the deck. Bartolome gritted her teeth and stepped over them both, hoping to take the shots before they could hit the professors. To her great surprise, more than a dozen rose petals flew across her face and body and settled onto the prone forms below her.

"What just happened?" Bartolome said.

"Are these flowers?" Jonathan asked, bewildered.

"It worked!" William leapt up from the deck and tossed the flowers in the air. "I can't believe that worked!"

"What did you do?"

"Anything fired on this ship will turn into roses."

"Why roses?" Bartolome asked.

"It's all I could find in the translation. And I like them."

More shots rang out from the docks as more soldiers joined the initial line of five. As their guns erupted, more multicolored rose petals fell onto the deck. Wilkes, along with his soldiers, looked at one another in confusion. One soldier flipped his rifle around and peered down the barrel. Others began reloading their weapons to fire another salvo.

"Well done, William."

"I have more!" William recited more of the ancient words. Suddenly, wind swirled around *The Knotted Wood* and filled her sails. A constant breeze that seemed to start just behind the sails rose from nothing and pushed *The Wood* forward.

"You're going to come in very handy," Bartolome said. "Anything you can do to prevent them from following us?"

William smiled. He turned to look at *The Crimson Swan* and again uttered words from his red book. The ship swayed back and forth before an explosion ripped through the rear of the vessel. Bartolome watched in stunned silence as a whale's tail grew out of the back of the ship. The new appendage flapped once in the water and shook *The Swan*, straining the ropes that held her to the dock.

"William?"

A look of surprise crossed William's face. He dove back into his book and flipped pages wildly. His eyes went wide as he darted looks at *The Swan*, Bartolome, and Jonathan, then back to the spell book in his hands. "I have no idea. I didn't mean to do that. I must have mispronounced some part of the word."

"It's alright, don't worry." Bartolome stifled a smile as *The Crimson Swan* flopped in the water, her crew leaping from the deck to the dock or running down the gangway. "The crew seems fine."

The wind from William's spell picked up in intensity. The sails, some still being set, flapped in the growing breeze. The bow of *The Wood* came around, away from the dock. Bartolome aimed the ship to exit the harbor. More flowers rained down on the deck from the soldiers. That meant that together with the magical wind, they were actually going to get out of this in one piece. On the dock, Bartolome saw several of the townspeople clutch at their eyes. The fire had engulfed their heads, and the brightness of the flames, however illusory they were, had blinded them.

"William, turn the flames off. End the illusion."

"What about *The Swan*?"

"You're blinding people, William. Turn it off!"

William nodded. He frantically flipped through a dozen pages, sweat beading on his brow in large drops. "I don't ... I don't know how."

"William!"

"Stop yelling at me!"

Jonathan knelt by William and put his hands on his shoulders. "Calm down. Just take a breath."

"I didn't mean to blind anyone!"

"We know that. You already dispelled the fire on us. Clearly, the ancient tongue has magilurgical influence. Is there a word you've found for 'all,' or 'everything,' something broad?"

William shook his head, looked at the book, then nodded. "Yes, I believe so."

"Then try that. Come on, I'll help," Jonathan said. He moved William to the rail of the ship facing the dock.

"We need to hurry. This wind is getting stronger," Bartolome said.

"Not helping," Jonathan replied.

William took a deep breath.

"Imagine that you want to see the flames dissipate," Jonathan suggested.

"Do you think that matters?"

Jonathan shrugged. "We're in uncharted waters here, William. I don't study how to cast spells. It's meaningless to me. I only understand the deeper principles—the magon, how it interfaces with the real world."

"Alright, okay. Imagine the fire going out," William clarified.

"Will you just do it?!" Bartolome barked.

William said the ancient words and shouted them across the entire town. The flames instantly died down. People on the docks uncovered their eyes and breathed a deep sigh of relief. They at least seemed to still be able to see, which Bartolome felt was a splendid thing. The last thing she needed was to blind the Anti-Religionists.

"Now that that's over, can I have my book back?" Sylvia emerged from below deck and marched her way onto the bridge. She crossed her arms and gave Bartolome a sideways glance.

Bartolome smiled at Sylvia. "Anton!" she called. "We have another mouth to feed!"

CHAPTER SIXTEEN

The flames that had erupted over the Anti-Religionists died down. The citizens of the village began to calm down as well. Several still batted at their arms, even though the flames were gone. Many were soaking wet from dunking themselves in water. There had been a great sense of terror in the town, as the water in the barrels, instead of putting the flame out, had itself caught fire, which was shocking on many levels. No one had ever seen water catch fire before, and yet it had done that very thing just moments ago.

"He has the book. Both books," Renaldo said.

"How do you know?" a Magi asked.

"The magic being cast is stronger than anything the Magi could do," Renaldo said.

"No, it's not," a second Magi said.

"Will you stop? You can barely cast a floating spell," a third Magi said.

"Magnificent," the first Magi said next to Renaldo.

"It's only magnificent if the end goal is reached. If not, we may have unleashed our undoing," the second magi said.

"No, we can control him. He doesn't even understand what he possesses," said the first Magi.

"We don't understand what he possesses either," the second Magi countered.

"I understand it," the third Magi said.

"No, you don't."

"Do so."

"Enough, all of you!" Renaldo snapped. "The linguist will fulfill his destiny. He has no choice."

"Isn't that naïve, brother? He could just choose to not read the inscription left by the gods," one Magi said.

Gunshots continued to erupt along the dock before Renaldo could answer. He tightened his lips and scanned the bridge of *The Knotted Wood* for the linguist.

"Did you see flowers?" the first Magi said.

"Whatcha mean?" the third Magi asked.

"I saw flowers," the second Magi said.

"Where did you see them?" the first magi asked.

"On the deck, just after the soldiers fired."

More shots rang out, followed by more rose petals raining on the deck of *The Wood*.

"That's an impressive spell," said the first Magi.

"More than impressive," said the third.

"Are you sure it's a spell?" asked the second.

"Of course I'm sure," said the third.

The rear of *The Crimson Swan* flopped in the water. The entire aft of the ship had transformed into a living whale's tail. The massive flukes flopped several more times, sending the crew of *The Swan* diving overboard and running for the docks. It only took moments before the ropes holding the ship to the dock broke free from the strain.

"You're right, we need to get that fellow under control," said the second Magi.

"I didn't think magic could do that," said the first.

"I suspected it," said the third.

"That man holds the power of the gods in his hands, and he does not know how to control it," said the second.

"None of us could control such power," said the first Magi.

"I could control it," said the third.

"Shut up, all three of you! We'll follow them to the cliffs. He'll read the inscription. That's why we chose him in the first place. Curiosity is the professor's greatest weakness." Renaldo turned from the three Magi and took out the rainbow crow he carried with them in a cage.

"What are you telling them?" the first Magi asked.

"Why didn't he just give us a crystal cube?" said the third Magi.

"They don't trust lowly bishops with crystal cubes," said the second Magi.

"Shut up, all of you. I'm telling the church our status. And asking for prayers that the world won't crack in half if we fail."

Samson walked out of the tiny inn and patted his belly twice. He pulled out a long cigar from his back pocket and lit the end with a match strike. The smoke filled his mouth with the taste of charcoal and success. Mostly charcoal. Frankly, he didn't understand the habit, but he also couldn't find the desire to cease.

Several people ran by him on the street, one rubbing her eyes and crying. Two more men walked by, talking about a fire. Samson looked at the sky in all directions, but found no black smoke rising into the heavens. He took several steps into the street, only to be bumped by more of the locals running away from the docks.

"Watch where you're going!" Samson yelled after them.

"Apologies, sir. There was gunfire! And a whale!"

"A what? Did you say a whale?" Samson threw his cigar on the ground and turned toward the docks farther down the street. Water splashed high in the air from something thrashing in the harbor. A sense of dread grew in the pit of his stomach.

Samson jolted himself forward and took off at a slight jog toward the docks. If this was Jonathan's doing, or the doing of that undead thing with him, then once again, he was in jeopardy. More people ran away from the docks, and Samson did his best to dodge them.

Once on the wooden platform that surrounded the harbor, he came to a full stop, his eyes growing to twice their size at the unbelievable sight in front of him. The imperial frigate had grown a tail on one end and massive fins on both sides. The ship spun in the middle of the harbor, clearly not either a frigate or an actual whale.

"That's not possible," Samson muttered. His mind simply did not allow him to believe what he was seeing.

"That's him!" someone on the dock cried.

Samson turned to see Earl walking towards him, a contingent of imperial soldiers and local armed men at his side. They approached him in a way that suggested that they weren't here to discuss rental terms for a new university in town. Two soldiers walked to either side of him and placed their hands on his arms with force. One of the imperial men, not dressed like the other soldiers, walked within inches of him and huffed in anger—an act that Samson felt was quite rude.

"What is the meaning of this? We had an agreement!"

"I believe that may no longer be in place," Earl said.

"Not to mention, that was before my ship became *that*." The not-quite-a-soldier pointed to the ship with a whale's tail in the harbor.

"I had nothing to do with that!"

"You were on the docks when Bartolome first arrived, yes?"

Samson nodded. "I came to warn the Anti-Religionists of Jonathan's dangerous experiment."

"And how would you know to warn them?" Wilkes asked.

"I'm a university professor, one of Jonathan's colleagues. I came to stop him from meddling with the source of magic."

"None of that matters now. I am Commodore Wilkes of the empire. I am chasing the fugitives who set this town on magical fire."

Samson looked around. "Nothing appears to be burned."

"Didn't I mention it was magical?" Wilkes turned to Earl. "We mean to give chase. Your biggest ship."

"Mary?" Earl asked.

"What? Who's Mary?"

"That's the name of our biggest ship. *The Mary.*"

Wilkes nodded. "Yes, fine, whatever the name. It's commandeered."

Earl tilted his head back and forth. "Well, are you sure?"

"Yes, I am. Is there a problem?"

Earl shook his head. "Oh, no. It's just that ... we spend all of our resources on cannons and protecting the straits to the falls that lead to the Wizard. We don't really have a budget for ships."

"But you have a ship?" Wilkes asked.

"Oh, yes, of course. It's just... Well..."

"What, man? Out with it!"

Earl pointed to the harbor. The only ships sitting at the dock were fishing trawlers. None of them were even a quarter of the size of *The Knotted Wood*. Commodore Wilkes took a step towards the harbor and ran his hands through his hair.

For the first time in many years, Samson truly wondered about his own safety. He had picked up a few spells during his stay in Dressa, but would they be enough to help him escape these soldiers?

"This can't be all you have?" Wilkes said, mortified.

"Oh, yes. But not to worry. Our cannons—and there are over four hundred of them—are in the cliffs and all pointed at the straits. That ship will never get through that. It'll be torn to pieces."

"Did you miss the part where our rifle bullets turned into flowers?"

Earl's smile disappeared, and he brought his hand to his face. "Did they?"

"They'll sail through your guns without a scratch!"

Earl turned to the acolytes, who all shrugged and shook their heads. "Well, that could be a problem. Are you certain? I've never heard of a spell that could do that. Perhaps it was another illusion?"

Wilkes turned to Samson. "What about that? You said you were a professor. Is this all some experiment to increase the power of spells?"

Samson shook his head. "No, not at all. They're going to the source of magic through the straits. I was trying to prevent them from doing so."

"Why?"

"Because they don't know what they're doing! Look at

that!" Samson pointed to *The Crimson Swan* in the harbor, its tail flopping wildly.

"Perhaps it was on purpose?"

"Who would do that on purpose?" Samson said.

"So, how can they cast such powerful spells? Neither the admiralty, our four-limbed allies, or the acolytes here had ever heard of spells so powerful!"

Samson noticed a group of four-limbers and tried to take a step backwards, but the soldiers prevented him. He detested them, like most people of Dressa did. Not that they had ever done anything to deserve such hatred, but having four limbs was just *odd*—so odd that they were typically shunned. Not exactly banned, but not welcomed—except, it would seem, by the empire.

"I have no idea how they've done it."

"Then you're not much use to us." Wilkes nodded to the soldiers, who dragged Samson away.

"No, wait! I can help you!"

"How? And don't waste my time. I'm not in the mood," Wilkes snapped.

"I am colleagues with Jonathan. He must be responsible for this. I don't know what he's done here, but given time, I can understand it."

Wilkes took a step towards Samson and locked his eyes on the professor. A long silence stretched into an uncomfortable moment, in which Samson looked away several times from the commodore's stare. The soldiers around him remained motionless, while Earl, the lead acolyte, seemed to be equally unsure of what to do and shuffled his feet several times.

"Fine. You're coming." Wilkes turned to Earl. "The largest trawler, then. The four-limbers will stay here, as will most of our crew, and Captain Bridgewater."

"Yes, sir," Bridgewater said.

"The four-limbers will fix *The Swan* and get her ready for a return voyage to the Riverlands."

All the four-limbers shook their heads and shrugged.

"Just try, yes?" Wilkes turned towards a group of five soldiers, two of whom were holding Samson. "Bring him. Let's end this chase once and for all." He marched away from the group toward the largest trawler at the dock.

One thing was certain for Samson: he had better figure out something to appease this commodore, and fast. Wilkes seemed to be coming unhinged, thanks to his chase of Jonathan and William. And Samson didn't want to be in his way if he lost his temper.

Archbishop Philip Santos lowered the communion crystal around his neck and smiled. Sylvia had sent him a message that she had given the linguist her book. At last, things were proceeding as they should be. And judging by Sylvia's account of the magical illusion tearing through the Anti-Religionists' village, it was clear that the linguist could translate the text. The church had tried, of course, and they had met with some success, but something was always missing—a veil of subtlety that apparently William could pierce and understand. Now he just had to read the word inscribed on the stone near the Wizard, and the gods would be freed. Theoretically, at any rate.

For years, he had suspected a correlation, some likeness between Sylvia's book and his own. Why else would there be symbols of the gods written throughout her text? But try as he might, he could discern nothing but squiggly lines and strange artwork on every single page of his book. When word had come of someone studying the intricacies of language itself, Santos took that as an omen from Yelke.

It was Yelke who had set the inscription there, without question. This had been revealed during the last successful communion with the gods, when the church last attempted to free the Wizard and the Dragon. But what the inscription said, and what the intent of the words actually was remained a mystery. In truth, the reason why the gods wanted the church to kill the Wizard as soon as the spell was lifted was a bit confusing. What sense did that make? Dragons were the ancient enemies of wizards, after all, and this Dragon was the last. Wouldn't it make more sense to kill the Dragon? But who was Santos to question the will of the gods, after all?

Giggling distracted Santos from his thoughts. That fool Daniel and his girlfriend assistant stood at the bow of their ship, their hands clasped together, their smiles filled with ideas of adventure and childish love. Not that Santos didn't like youthful exuberance; he just didn't want to be anywhere near it. But he was now on a voyage that would take several weeks, and every moment of this trip would be spent listening to those two mooning over each other. Even hiding in the shadows wouldn't protect him from their constant swooning.

But no matter. Santos took a deep breath and kept his mind focused on the goal: just move forward. Renaldo and the Magi would guide William to his goal. He would speak the words and free the Wizard, and then the Magi would kill him. Then the gods would be free once and for all, and the church would rule the world as the new empire of man! Santos shook his head at the unbelievability of the Demi-God's plan coming to fruition.

"Oh, you're so cute!" the girl said.

"You're cuter," Daniel Desun replied, his cheeks bright red.

Santos sighed, withdrew into the shadows, and quietly waited for the longest voyage of his life to be over.

YELKE ROARED. Bolts of lightning erupted from the top of his palace on the mountain of the gods and struck the barrier holding his people prisoner. He smashed a dozen statues, and with one stomp of his foot, cracked the marble steps leading to his luxe patio. The entirety of their work—thousands of years of planning—was about to be destroyed by the miscommunication of the crystal communion sphere operated by his idiot sister. He should turn her into a toad for a thousand years and let her eat flies and maggots.

"Well, at least there are no statues left to break, husband," Neltzy said testily.

"You realize that if those fools kill Finnian while the Dragon still lives, we shall never be released from this place? We shall spend eternity in this prison!"

"And yet Selke and Fjorn made it out."

"As birds! Do you want us to descend from the mountain and forget who we even are?"

"Where are they?"

Yelke shook his head. Fire shot out of his eyes and began burning the bushes nearest them. "At that insufferable party."

Neltzy shrugged. "It may be nice to visit, once we're free."

"Do you not hear me? The church thinks they should kill Finnian!"

"Then we must make sure they don't, husband."

Yelke turned to his wife and put his hands on his hips. "And how do we do that? We have no reach beyond this mountain keep."

"Selke and Fjorn."

Yelke laughed. "They don't remember who or what they are."

"They will."

"My patience is already wearing thin, wife. If you have an idea, then out with it!"

Neltzy smiled. "When they speak the words from our inscription near the Wizard, the spell will unravel. The magical forces unleashed will wake Selke."

Yelke nodded. "And we may communicate with them."

"We'll have less than a second."

"And they'll need to traverse ten thousand miles in the blink of an eye."

"It is good fortune that they are rainbow crows," Neltzy said with a smile.

"We'll have to be quick. We'll need the power of every god to send even the briefest of messages to Selke." Yelke nodded to himself as the plan unfolded in his mind. If they could work fast enough once the words were recited, then Selke could be told what needed to happen. She could reach the Wizard, protect him from the church, slay the Dragon, and end the great spell on the world. Then Yelke and the gods would finally be free to rule all the cosmos.

PART IV

INSANITY CLIFFS

CHAPTER SEVENTEEN

Cliff walls rose around *The Knotted Wood*. The ship entered the straits only minutes before the cannons, set in nooks and caves throughout the granite cliffs, opened fire. Thankfully, just like the soldiers' bullets, the cannonballs transformed into roses, though in considerably greater numbers. William marveled at the effectiveness of his spell. He marveled that he could even cast spells, and that the strange contents of the book were in fact spells. But what he marveled at most of all, in this moment, was why Sylvia wanted the book back.

"So, you've been reading your book as well?" William asked.

"Of course."

"Then why give it to me?"

Sylvia folded her arms. "I told my uncle Philip that I would. And I keep my word. But I didn't think it would matter. There was a binding spell on the book. Someone from the church planted it on me when we left Hogkarta. No matter where I left the thing, it would follow me. So, I finally started reading it."

"There was a binding spell on mine as well," William said.

"It's one of the church's favorite spells. Hard to steal anything from them when half their valuables are bound to someone at the church," Sylvia said.

"But now the book is no longer bound to you?"

"Let me show you. Give them to me," Sylvia said.

William handed the books to Sylvia, who pocketed both in her coat. She walked to the other end of *The Knotted Wood* and waved for William to walk to the stern. Seconds later, she thrust her hands into her jacket, only to pull them out empty. Behind Bartolome, William pulled out both the spell book and Sylvia's book. He shrugged.

"You can still read it, you know," William called out from the stern.

"Argh!" Sylvia screamed back.

"We'll be at the falls soon." Bartolome nodded at a growing roar at the end of the straits. There, directly above the Wizard and the Dragon on the ground below, things were off—more so than anywhere else in the world. "Play your book games later. We need to get Jonathan ready."

Almost on cue, Jonathan stomped his way on deck, his body encased in a metal suit that resembled paintings of ancient knights of the forgotten kingdoms fighting battles in the vast open fields of the second continent. But this suit, unlike those of legend, didn't appear to be made for fighting, as Jonathan could barely take a single step.

"How are you going to walk in that?" Bartolome asked. "Let alone descend the falls to the ground?"

"Part of our original arrangement, the original charter, was for you and your crew to lower me down. The weight was noted in the original contract."

Bartolome laughed. "I don't think that's going to be possible. How much does that suit weigh?"

"With my equipment, and piping for communication, nearly four hundred pounds."

"Are you counting yourself? So, another two hundred?"

"Excuse me, madam, but it's one eighty-five," Jonathan snapped.

"We'll call it two. And how do you expect me to lower six hundred pounds over a mile?"

Jonathan shifted in his stance. He tried to raise his arms, but could only grunt. Eventually, he shook his head and sighed. "I don't know. It wasn't my concern."

"Well, it's your concern now. Did you bring a mile's worth of rope capable of holding that much weight?"

"No, why would I?"

Bartolome sighed, lowered her head, and laughed. She'd taken these two all over Dressa, on a stolen charter, and now, at the end, when their goal was almost in sight, they would fail—spectacularly. Why hadn't she even thought to ask about how they were getting down there?

"Why are you laughing?" Jonathan demanded.

"We're done, that's why. I can't get you down there, Professor. Unless you have a bright idea?"

"My sling that I installed on your ship is elastic," Sylvia offered. "If we really push it and use the extra ropes I stashed in your cargo hold, we could make it hit a mile. But it'll be stretched to the extreme."

"Can it hold six hundred pounds?"

Sylvia shook her head. "No, but he can fix that." She pointed to William at the back of the ship.

⌇

COMMODORE WILKES GRIPPED the rail of the trawler and leaned into a light fog. Ahead of them, Bartolome was sailing her ship and crew through a small passage between two massive cliffs, each at least half a mile high. Cannons erupted not long after *The Wood* entered those waters, but Wilkes doubted they would be effective. Whatever protected that ship was no minor spell.

"Raise that flag, quickly," Wilkes commanded his men.

A large red flag rose to the top of the trawler. The colors and size marked this ship as friendly to the Anti-Religionists who manned the cannons along the cliffs ahead. If Wilkes and the soldiers didn't announce themselves, the cannons would shred them to pieces.

"Commodore, look!" a soldier said.

Wilkes looked toward the front of the boat to see rose petals drifting in the water. Red, yellow, and white roses drifted by the trawler in increasing amounts. Soon, the sea was carpeted in a thin layer of roses, confirming to Wilkes that *The Wood* was still magically protected. Their only choice was to fight them on land.

"You're certain that they're going over the falls to the ground below?" Wilkes asked.

Samson nodded. "Without question. Jonathan's goal is to reach the Wizard."

"And do what once he's there?"

"I can't be sure of his research goals, Commodore, only that that's where he's going. However, on the last expedition there by the True Religionists, they reported a glowing inscription near the Wizard. They believe it was left there by the gods."

"And?"

"If Jonathan deciphers the meaning of the inscription, then the results could be fantastic."

"You mean it's not written in plain words?"

Samson shook his head. "No, it's just symbols. Like these." He pulled out a piece of paper with several symbols he had copied from the church walls over the years he'd spent in Hogkarta.

"Why would the church send a professor to translate these? I would think they would have more knowledge than anyone," Wilkes said.

Samson nodded. "Yes, I know. But I also don't know. It makes no sense. Unless Jonathan has uncovered something new."

"You think he can do it?"

Samson shrugged. "I am more knowledgeable about magilurgical principles than anyone on the planet. I wrote half the textbooks. Why not send me? I was invited by the church to come to Dressa to lead the university. Why was that done? Perhaps to get me out of the way, because they really wanted Jonathan all along."

"What could he know?"

"I just don't know, Commodore."

"So, what do we do with this information?"

Samson shrugged. "I'm not really sure ... yet. One thing I know, Commodore, is that if Jonathan reads that inscription successfully, everything in our world will change—instantly."

Wilkes looked into Samson's eyes and could see his conviction. If he was even half right, stopping Bartolome from following through with this would mean more than just revenge for the events at Oyster Piers, or finding his wife. It would mean saving the world itself.

BARTOLOME GRIPPED the wheel of *The Wood* and fought against the increasing currents. William had already stopped the magical wind, and her crew had struck the sails. They had wound through several tributaries and side channels through the straits, the directions given to them in the original charter that Bartolome had stolen. The cannons in the cliffs had finally subsided, either because *The Wood* was out of range, or they were running low on ammo. Either way, as long as the Anti-Religionist cannons weren't firing, that was a good thing, considering that Bartolome and her two professors would have to leave the *The Wood* and lose their protection of William's magical roses.

"There's a dock ahead!" Sylvia shouted from the side of the ship.

Just beyond the bow, a wooden dock came into view, jutting out into a small natural harbor just to the right of the waterway. Though the current was getting stronger, Bartolome was confident she could catch the wind in her sails and leave easily enough. The biggest risk was the additional cannons that likely encircled this small spot of safety outside of the fast-moving water.

The closer she came to the harbor, Bartolome could make out a walkway carved into the rock. The path wound around the harbor toward the straits and disappeared behind a bend in the cliff ahead. Without question, this was how the church must have made it down to the Wizard two decades ago.

"Sylvia, do you see the path along the cliffs? It must have been carved by the church. It has to lead us to a point where we can descend."

"I see it. Bring our bow perpendicular to the dock. Our starboard side will cover us as we descend. And it will allow the sling to work."

"Are you certain?"

"I am."

Bartolome spun the wheel and turned *The Wood* per Sylvia's instructions. They wouldn't be moored to the dock, but there was a jetty that would protect them from the current. But if enough guns fired on them, even though their ammo would be rendered harmless, the sheer volume of rose petals against the hull could twist the ship and expose the path ahead to attack.

"We'll need to drop anchor," Bartolome said.

"Yes, perfect!"

On the deck below the bridge, Jonathan leapt into the air and ran three steps forward, then backward again. With Sylvia's help, William had crafted a spell that reduced the weight of the lead suit to be no heavier than a feather. When all this was over and done with, Bartolome wondered what those two could come up with if they sat together long enough. Regardless, she was glad they were both on her side.

"Are we ready?" Bartolome asked. Her crew had moved the anchor to the stern and sent it overboard. This way, no amount of rose petals would shift *The Wood*. She hoped not, anyway.

"Ready as we can be. Let's go make history!" Jonathan cried.

"Wait. Just wait," Sylvia said.

"What is it? Did we forget something?" Bartolome asked.

"Yes. It's urgent. We can't move forward without this." Sylvia reached into her pocket and pulled out a small container. She unscrewed the lid, dipped her index finger into a yellowish cream, and smeared some just beneath her nose. Her face twisted in horror, and she let out a sound of disgust.

"What in heavens is that?" William asked.

"Each of you, take some and dab it under your nose. It's wretched. But required."

"And why is that, precisely?" Jonathan asked.

"Haven't any of you wondered why they call this place the Insanity Cliffs? Trust me, use the salve."

"THERE THEY ARE," Wilkes said. Ahead, in a small harbor, *The Knotted Wood* sat moored to an old dock, an anchor line extending out from her stern. No one was on deck or in the rigging. That could mean many things.

"Where are they?" one soldier asked.

"There are steps on the other side of their ship. They lead straight down to the falls several hundred feet below, and then down to the Wizard," Samson informed them.

"How do you know that?" Wilkes asked.

"I've been in Dressa for years. I know. The Religionists carved out the steps to get access to the Wizard," Samson said.

"No other way down?"

"None. The cliffs surround the waterfall. Gravity doesn't work right here ... but then, nothing does."

"And the walkway goes all the way to the surface?"

Samson shook his head. "No, it stops, as do the falls, at the top of the mountain. The Wizard and Dragon are in the valley."

"How did they get down from there?"

"They walked."

"And it's safe?"

"Not at all. Well, it can be. Apparently, since we're at the source of all magic, the forces are subdued. Like the eye of a hurricane, it's quite calm. But there are eddies, sudden bursts. Several members of the expedition by the True Religionists didn't come back in one piece."

"Killed?"

"No, just not in one piece. You don't want to know."

Wilkes nodded. His options weren't spectacular. There was only one way in, and it ended at a waterfall that fell a straight mile through magical waters into a zone of insanity. Short of turning around and leaving the safety of the world in the hands of Bartolome, Wilkes could charge forward, outmanned ten to one, and likely be cut down in moments by her, her undead crew, or newfound powerful mages. Or he could do the unexpected.

"Raise the sail," Wilkes said. "Full mast."

"What? But sir, we're already being dragged forward!"

"We can only hope to sail past the bulk of her crew to those in front. You two!" Wilkes grabbed two soldiers and dragged them to the back of the ship. "Take the anchor and rope. We'll only have one chance. We'll try to run aground after the harbor, and surprise them in the front. It's our only choice."

"We're going to do *what*?!" Samson cried.

Wilkes ignored him. The soldiers exchanged concerned looks. They all nodded once, but Wilkes could see the worry on their faces. This was practically a suicide mission. But if they failed, it could threaten the empire.

"I know, lads. This is as dangerous as it gets. Trust your training. Trust me. If we don't prevent them from doing whatever it is they're going to do—"

"Read the inscription. They are going to read the inscription."

Wilkes glared daggers at Samson. "We have to stop them from doing it. The last time anyone tried, an undead army rose on an island in Dressa. We can't let that happen again."

The soldiers nodded.

"But how are we going to stop them? Are you going to shoot Jonathan?" Samson asked.

"That's why you're here, Professor. Figure something out —or I'll shoot every professor down there."

Samson gulped.

JONATHAN STOOD at the edge of the cliff. Sylvia's elastic rope was attached to a hook near his neck, and he wondered about that being the only thing saving him from falling to his death. Above him, water from the falls inexplicably turned around in midair and flowed upward at exactly the point where the cliffs ended, hovering a hundred feet above the ledge of a mountain. An old wooden ladder hung down from the spot where Jonathan stood, reaching the top of the cliff below.

"Are we sure this is the best method?" Jonathan asked through a tube connected to his helmet. Another of Sylvia's experiments, the tube allowed speech to be transferred over distance with another tube. There was some amount of magic between the two tubes, of that Jonathan was certain, but now wasn't the time to press the matter. Though Sylvia had said the idea came from her Uncle and some sort of crystal cube.

Moments later, a muffled response returned. "Unless you want to climb down that ladder and then spend days hiking down the mountain, then yes. But it's your choice," Bartolome's voice said through the tube. "But we don't have nearly enough provisions for that."

"Your armor is light as a feather! All you have to do is jump," William shouted.

"But this rope isn't like normal rope. It's stretchy! What even is stretchy rope?"

Jonathan wasn't sure how, but he could hear Sylvia sigh through the tube. "Just trust me," she said. "Everything will work. I've added the exact amount of rope. You'll bounce a few times and then be gently lowered to the ground."

"And how did you do that?"

"Math."

With a huff of fear, Jonathan nodded once to himself. This was it. This was his moment. He could back out now, blame some faulty piece of equipment, and go home. He was alone here on the edge of the carved stairs that jutted down along the cliff. Everyone else remained above the natural landing along the path of the stairs. Bartolome's crew had dismantled and reassembled Sylvia's contraption, and they now stood ready to reclaim Jonathan once he jumped. At least in theory, the mechanical device would do that. The girl had claimed knowledge of this from the book, written in the common tongue, that she'd given to William.

But none of that mattered. Rescue or not, there were discoveries to be made.

Jonathan looked over the edge to the valley below. There, a Dragon three times the size of *The Crimson Swan*, the last dragon in the world—at least, the last that anyone knew about—stood in front of a tiny figure with a raised staff. The great worm's maw was open wide, and even from this distance, Jonathan could see wisps of smoke frozen in time. This was the source of all magic in the whole world. When these two had met one hundred years ago, their sudden encounter and subsequent battle had unleashed so much magic that it froze time around them and forced Lake

Connell and much of the land to rise into the heavens. Many speculated that the land and the lake had just tried to get out of the way.

"I suppose it's now or never," Jonathan muttered. He checked the magonmeter at his side and the filter and pieces that would check for anti-magons. If he found them, it would be his seminal work in magical studies and cement Jonathan as the greatest scientist of the magical arts in the world, for centuries to come. He imagined the banquets, the praise, the accolades that would be showered upon him for the rest of his life. He might even become chancellor of the great university for this effort.

"I'm ready. I'm jumping!"

"Be careful, Jonathan!" William said through the tube.

"Into destiny!"

Jonathan leaped from the ledge and fell through the eye of the magical world.

CHAPTER EIGHTEEN

Commodore Wilkes hunkered down behind a rocky outcrop near the water's edge. The small trawler had sped past *The Knotted Wood* without being spotted by any living being. The carved steps identified by Samson did indeed follow the water, but also curved backward into the cliffs, which allowed the small ship to find a spot along the edge of the fast-moving water and moor up. Ahead of them, though out of sight, the roar from the falls filled the air.

"Alright, gather round. You too, Professor." Wilkes stood on the rocks next to the boat and faced his crew. "We know what we're going to encounter. This crew isn't alive. If they are protected by our bullets turning into rose petals, then retreat. We can't beat them in hand-to-hand combat. Too many of them."

"But if we retreat?" Samson asked.

"Easy, Professor. Retreating isn't surrendering. You two soldiers will attack *The Wood*. If the ship is empty, and it looks like it did when we passed, pull the anchor up and lower her sails. See if you can point her to the river. We'll send the cursed ship over the falls." Wilkes turned to the other soldiers. "The rest of you, with me. These undead only have one weakness. When you aim, shoot or thrust your swords into their heads. It's the only way to kill them."

"Where do I go?" Samson asked.

"You stay by my side at all times. Understand?"

Samson and the soldiers nodded.

"Good. We may only have one chance at this. Let's go."

Wilkes turned from the soldiers and climbed over the rocks to the carved steps that wrapped around the cliff wall. His soldiers jumped over the rocks with ease, two of them nodding once and running back down the path toward *The Knotted Wood*. The rest, including Samson, followed Wilkes around the bend in the path.

Voices and grunts soon filled the air. Wilkes held his fist up and peered around the edge. Ahead and below, the path led around the cliff to a large landing. From his position, Wilkes could see several of the undead crew carrying large boulders and working around what appeared to be a sling-shot mechanism similar to what Wilkes had witnessed on *The Knotted Wood* in Oyster Piers.

"They lowered him down already," Wilkes said.

"Are you certain?"

"Yes, that cable is elastic. I saw it used once before. An ingenious contraption. Like a slingshot, but on a massive scale. With all of Bartolome's crew here, they can just pull him up in minutes."

"What do we do, then?"

Wilkes turned to his men and nodded. "What else? We attack." He pulled out his sidearm, took a long breath, and charged.

∼

Bartolome stood on the cliffside, looking down toward the Wizard with his staff held high against the great and last Dragon of the world. She could hardly believe she was standing at the edge of the world, ready to reclaim her island home. The only thing she needed was the confidence to do it, and perhaps a great deal of luck.

Magic was, even in Dressa, poorly understood. The one thing known throughout Dressa Moore, however, was that if someone recited a spell in reverse order, saying it backwards, and they were near a powerful pool of magical energy, not a random spot on floating Lake Connell, the effects of the original spell could be reversed. Of course, it could also be enhanced, or doubled, or a frog could appear and insist it was a prince... Magic could be quite unpredictable if it wasn't done with precision. But it was a chance Marta would take. She only needed the spell originally cast by the church. She had searched for years for the spell. She'd pirated, lain with, stolen from, and paid for information from a hundred officials of the church all over Dressa Moore and beyond. Fortunately, with the help of Sylvia, the niece of the archbishop, who was not at all a fan of the church, Marta had finally found the spell and was at last ready to reverse the magic that had chased her out of her home.

From her satchel, Marta pulled out a magic-imbued repeating stone. The artifact could repeat out loud a phrase after being thrown. Objects like these were easy to craft with spells and had been used often during the Great Insult Wars of Dressa Moore a half century ago. Marta had always thought the wars were silly. She had infused her repeating stone with the original spell spoken backwards. She'd spent months perfecting the phrase, emptying the repeating stone only to fill it again with her voice a dozen times over. Only once she was satisfied that her intonation was perfect had she stopped tinkering.

Marta lifted the repeating stone and smiled. At long last, she would return home and reclaim her rightful place. Shouts erupted from behind her, but she paid them no mind. Not now, being this close. She pulled her arm back to throw the rock over the cliff, so it would repeat the spell backwards and reverse the curse of Bedrich Island.

Just then, rifle shots rang out from behind her. A bullet pierced her arm, causing her to drop the repeating stone and scream in pain. She turned to see the commodore and his men charging their encampment. Several of them had already stopped their charge and begun arguing with their feet, or a tree, which meant the commodore's men were being affected by the magical spores of the Madness Fjords.

"To arms! Protect the ropes!" Marta ordered her crew.

The undead snarled. Marta reached down for the repeating stone, which had already started repeating the spell, and whispered the command to make the stone stop and reset, but not erase the message. Imperial soldiers charged her. She drew her sword to fend them off.

"Fire!" Marta shouted.

The soldiers stopped and looked around. One of them turned, pointed, and yelled, "Fire!" as well. Marta looked to where the man pointed to see shrubbery and rocks. Good to know the Madness Fjords were living up to their name. Both soldiers turned and ran back the way they had come.

"You!"

Marta looked up to see the commodore himself standing in front of her. He had his revolver pointed at her head.

"Commodore. I see you're not making a social call."

"Where is she?" Wilkes demanded.

Marta sighed. She was tired of this game. Besides, she had no more crew to throw at him. "On Bedrich."

Wilkes shook his head and blinked. "Lies! Our spies have told us for years that Abigail sails with you."

Marta shook her head. "And who do you think told that to your spies?"

Wilkes fired his revolver at a spot on the ground and kicked at the dirt. "Why are there bloodthirsty cats with scales pawing the earth?!"

Marta stifled a laugh. "This place is called the Madness Fjords for a reason. There are mushroom spores here that create a hallucinogenic effect. I've heard that some teens from the Anti-Religionists come here to have parties. Must be a blast."

Wilkes shook his head and spat. "Where is my wife?!"

"Abigail is on Bedrich," she repeated wearily. Marta raised both hands in the air and bent down. She picked up the repeating stone and showed it to Wilkes. "We want the same thing, Thomas. We really do. I want her off my island, and so do you. All we have to do is throw this over the cliff, and it's all reversed."

Wilkes squinted his eyes and looked at the rock. "What is that? Some kind of magical bomb?"

"It's what we both want. An end to this."

Behind him, the soldiers were being routed—half were screaming about a fire that was engulfing the rocks, and the other were being pushed back by Bartolome's crew. Marta had full control of her crew, however, and stopped them all from biting any of Wilkes's men. The last thing she needed was more ill will from the commodore. And something deep in her soul told her she would one day need him to deal with his wife, Abigail, who was still on her island.

"Decide. Shoot me in the head and have your

vengeance, but you will never see your wife again. Your men will die, as I won't be here to stop my crew from savaging them. Or go, live to fight another day, and trust that I'm telling the truth. Either way, decide. Now."

Wilkes looked at the repeating rock in Marta's hand and then into her eyes. She saw something there that believed her, that trusted her. Perhaps it was the desperation that Wilkes would see his wife again, or maybe he actually believed Marta. Whichever was the truth, Wilkes holstered his gun and gave the order for his men to retreat.

Marta nodded to him.

Wilkes nodded back. "Throw it." He turned and ran back toward his men.

At that moment, Marta considered the quality of the commodore's character. He was just a man trying to save his wife. Considering that the woman had been lost to him for two decades, it gave Marta a newfound respect for the man.

Behind Wilkes, over the cliff, the form of Professor Samson from Hogkarta shouted something unintelligible as he fell down toward the ground. Bartolome hadn't seem him jump. Had Wilkes thrown him? Or one of his soldiers? An interesting tactical choice, to be sure.

Marta lifted the repeating stone above her head one more time, drew her arm back, and let it fly towards the ground. She watched it sail through the air for half a second before turning to secure her crew. She smiled to herself as she reinforced for them not to bite any of Wilkes's retreating soldiers. She'd done it. Now she had to trust that the magic spell would be reversed.

⁓

JONATHAN MARVELED at the sights in front of him. He stood on ground where no man had stood for decades—not since the True Religionists' expedition. Several hundred yards away, the great Wizard stood frozen in time, his staff held high, a crystal on top glowing with the fire and ferocity of pure magic. Standing a few hundred feet away, the great Dragon towered over the landscape, wings extended, head high in the air to stare down at the lone Wizard. The beast was readying itself to engulf the Wizard in the flames from its belly. Oh, what a battle it would have been! Or would be...? Maybe someday. Yes, that seemed right, considering that they were frozen in time. Eventually, time here would restart, and they would battle.

"Now, let's have a closer look at you." Jonathan reached for his magonmeter and switched the device on. But the small needle at the top of the device showed nothing—not even a drop of magic in the air. Jonathan shook and smacked the device, but still, no reading at all.

"That's curious." With the wand of the device held firmly in his hand, Jonathan took a step forward, swinging the detector over the land. The indicator still showed nothing. He wandered around for a moment, Sylvia's cord attached to his back stretching, allowing him to walk. He took three more steps in the Wizard's direction and then turned to the left to walk perpendicular to his destination. His device nearly exploded with alerts as the needle jumped to the right and buried itself beyond the maximum detection level.

"Amazing. Simply amazing!"

Bands of rainbows bent and twisted a few feet away from Jonathan. Swirls of colors floated through the air, only to collide in mini bursts of magical energy. Roses bloomed from the ground and promptly died, only to regrow from their own remains and repeat the process. Jonathan took several steps backward, and the magical display around him faded from view just as his magonmeter went silent.

"Are you alright, Jonathan?" William asked through the tube attached to his suit.

"Yes, fine. I made it! The magonmeter needle is fully in the red! But there are spots where no magic exists at all. It's amazing!"

"Splendid. Now, do what you came to do, and let's get out of here!" Bartolome urged.

"You can't rush science!" Jonathan insisted.

He was met by a sudden silence, followed by several shouts and what he thought sounded like gunfire. He looked up, but at this distance, he couldn't make out anything but the floating cliffs and the reversing waterfall above him, which were marvels in their own right.

"Well, back to it, then." Jonathan attached a filter to his device and began walking toward the Wizard.

Without warning, a thick band of rainbow energy blasted out from the ground and wrapped around his lead suit. The magic created a swarm of insects the size of apple pies that burst into existence out of thin air. Hands formed within the magic and tried to wrap around his suit, only to give up moments later when they couldn't find a grip.

"It's working!" Jonathan shouted in delighted relief. "The lead suit is working! The magic can't touch it!"

One of his many theories, which he had lightly tested in his lab, was that lead was the antithesis of magic, the one substance that magic had no power over. No spell could be cast on it, which made him, in this moment, perfectly protected. Although, it would seem, since his lead helmet came from the Church of the True Religionists, that this was knowledge they had held for decades.

"I'm coming for your secrets!" Jonathan screamed at the Wizard as the magical storm around him finally died down.

He took another step forward, only to stop almost at once. Just ahead of him, about half the distance to the Wizard, a large rock stood to the side of where he walked. Glowing symbols of the same type as those in William's spell book covered its face. Jonathan immediately took out a notepad. With his pinky finger, which had a special writing utensil attached to the end of his armored gauntlet of a glove, he began to copy down the symbols.

A scream from above him drew his attention away from what lay ahead. Jonathan froze and looked upward. He couldn't see anything, but he was sure he had heard it. He squinted his eyes and could have sworn he could make out a bird or something high above, near the cliff. The bird grew in size, and he heard a scream again.

In only seconds, what Jonathan thought was a bird grew to the shape and size of a man. The screaming intensified as he fell, his legs clutching at the rope attached to the back of Jonathan's suit.

He's going to hit me! Jonathan realized with alarm, but then he remembered he was wearing a suit of lead armor. Would he be hurt?

The man wrapped his legs tighter around the rope and slowed his fall. Jonathan deftly jumped to the side and yanked the elastic rope attached to his back. The force caused the man, whomever it was, to flop in the air and bounce without hitting the ground. On closer inspection, someone had tied a second rope around the man's torso and attached that rope to Jonathan's.

Jonathan took several steps forward. The man had finally landed on the ground with a few more flops and lay with his face turned away. Slowly, he sat up, shook himself, hugged his knees, and whimpered. Recognition came to Jonathan in an instant, and he could hardly believe his eyes.

"Samson? Are you mad?! What in the worlds are you doing here?"

"Jonathan! For the love of all things good, please don't let me sprout something!" Samson cried.

SAMSON ROLLED himself into a ball and whimpered. If he could, he would curse that commodore to the end of his days. They had stormed the landing, dispatched half the undead crew, and pushed on to the crazed contraption— and Samson had been flung over the edge with barely any warning. And now what? At any moment, a stray arc of magical energy could engulf him entirely and turn him into a frog, or worse.

"Samson? Can you hear me?" Jonathan said.

"Yes, of course I can!"

"Why are you in a ball? And why did you fall from the sky? And why are you even here? And how did you get here? And what in the university's name is going on up there?!"

"I can't answer all those inane questions, Jonathan! That commodore from the empire kidnapped me, attacked the landing, and threw me over the edge!"

"Oh... I see. I suppose you answered all the questions, didn't you? Except for why you're in a ball?"

"I don't want to get hit by magic!" he cried, trembling.

"Oh, yes, of course. Well, don't worry, there's none in this spot, according to my readings. But don't walk that way, or that way, or really any way... Just stay put. Perhaps it's best to stay in your ball. Good thinking."

Samson looked up. He saw that Jonathan was clad in

full-body armor, which Samson reasoned must be made of lead. Jonathan took a step forward and bent down with ease, and Samson inspected the suit more closely. Moving that easily shouldn't be possible.

"How...?" Samson motioned to Jonathan's body.

He grinned. "William."

Jonathan cocked an eyebrow. "The linguist?"

"He's discovered how to read the symbols of the church. It's the language of spells. Amazing discovery, Samson. It truly is."

Samson's eyes went wide—and in a flash, he instantly realized the church's true motives. They hadn't truly sent Jonathan for research at all. They had never cared about him. He was nothing to them. Their actual target was William. Unable to translate the magical symbols themselves, they must have reasoned, who better to decode this mystery than someone who studied language? They had pushed Samson out of the way by inviting him to Dressa, then arranged for Jonathan to go to the source of magic, all so that he would bring his linguist lover.

A deeper fear grew in the pit of Samson's belly. If all that was true—and it clearly was—then William could translate the inscription on the rock. The threat was genuine. Samson scanned the area, and in seconds, his eyes fell on the golden glowing symbols in a large rock not far ahead. His mind raced as he weighed his options. No chance that he'd be able to take on Jonathan with that armor he was wearing. But since William wasn't here, then he couldn't see the symbols—unless Jonathan wrote them down and brought them back up. Then he could return and read them aloud. Or William could read them from the landing above. Would that matter, if William wasn't physically here when he read them? Could Samson take that chance?

"Hello up there! William? Are you hurt?"

Samson looked up to see the tube connected to Jonathan's helmet, carrying his voice to the landing above. Cutting it or damaging it wouldn't do a thing. Samson knew a few spells by heart, and he rapidly sifted through them. A simple movement spell, a writing spell, an illusion spell, a spell to stop something from floating...

He stopped at once, and his eyes went wide. He knew exactly what he would do.

"Oh, thank goodness you're safe! Where is Wilkes?" Jonathan asked inside his helmet.

"What's going on up there?" Samson asked.

Jonathan listened for a moment. Samson could see that he was hearing something through the tube. After several seconds, Jonathan nodded. "Your commodore went insane. As did his crew. Sylvia said there are hallucinogenic mushroom spores up there that can cause madness. He's not there, and Bartolome and William have retaken the landing."

Samson nodded.

"Now, stay there. I have to examine things, and then they can pull us both up. But do not move. The magonmeter is showing this spot to be devoid of magic, but it's all around us."

Samson nodded again. He looked at the inscription on the rock and cast the only spell he thought would make a difference. He could just barely see the symbols on the face of the granite shifting.

JONATHAN TURNED from Samson and faced the Wizard and the inscription again. He took several steps forward and checked his equipment another two times. Arcs of magical energy burst into existence over the rock and the Wizard and shifted to the Dragon, only to disappear and reappear seconds later.

"Jonathan, did you say there's an inscription?" William asked.

"Yes, symbols carved into a big rock. Just like the ones in your book."

"Can you describe them?"

"I don't think I can do that."

"Why not?"

Jonathan sighed. "Because my brain doesn't work like that. They're just symbols. Some are round, some are straight with squiggly lines... How do I even describe them?"

"Didn't you just?"

"Oh, not now, William! I've attempted to copy them on paper. I will try my best to describe them as a I transcribe."

William sighed through the tube as Jonathan did his best to describe the symbols. After only a few moments, Jonathan teetered on giving up the endeavor. How does one describe a left leaning squiggly versus an oval shape with any level of accuracy? Yes, he knew the importance of the symbols, but there were many priorities here. Discovering anti-magons, for instance, would define his career. They could always send William down in the suit afterward to look at the symbols himself.

Jonathan stopped describing the symbols and walked beyond the rock to get within just a few yards of the Wizard. He could see the long whiskers on the old man's face and a permanent look of surprise in his eyes. Turning, Jonathan nearly fell backwards at the sight of the Dragon standing over him. The towering beast, thankfully still frozen in time, could crush the entire empire with salvos of fire from its belly, Jonathan was sure.

"Thanks be to the gods. You're the last," Jonathan whispered to the Dragon.

From his belt, Jonathan removed several lead-lined glass test tubes. They were specially constructed, according to his theories, to both attract magons, having been exposed to magic in his lab, and to keep the magons stable with a thin layer of lead on the outside of the glass. He uncorked the tops and set them on the ground in a straight line next to the Wizard. The two outermost tubes shifted as tiny rainbows curled around their edges. The rainbows arced between the first and third tube, but left the second tube unaffected. His first theory was accurate! The level of magons relative to the space could allow for free capture of magons by a substance previously treated with magic. Put simply, the glass, having been exposed to magons, attracted magons, and the lead coating kept them stable.

"Now, is there anything peculiar...?" Jonathan lifted his magonmeter and adjusted the filter. If anti-magons existed, he hoped, and theorized, that they would show on his magonmeter as cold spots. The indicator on the auxiliary device should fall into the negative as anti-magons passed. If anti-magons were detected—again, in theory—the lead tube between the two arcing tubes, which had never been touched by a spell and was lined with lead on the inside and outside, should attract them and allow Jonathan to capture them. Admittedly an improbable outcome, but this was scientific research on the fringes of understanding. He knew he must take a chance and see what the results were!

"Jonathan, the inscription—are there any full circles?"

"Not now, William!" Jonathan shouted. He turned his attention back to his device, but the needle never budged. It sat stubbornly between zero and one, which meant that enough magons were present for spell casting, but too many for anti-magons to be present.

"What am I missing?" Jonathan said. "They must be here!"

"JONATHAN, the inscription—are there any full circles?" William said into the tube.

The answer was filled with anger—a tone that William knew well.

William walked to the edge of the landing, his hand gripping a rope tied around a large boulder, and tried to locate Samson, whom the commodore had just flung over the edge moments ago. He couldn't see a thing.

Behind them, several of the now completely dead crew of Bartolome lay on the ground, victims of Wilkes and Samson's sudden attack. They hadn't even realized that the crazed military man was following them, let alone preparing an attack. And yet he had. The soldiers had burst onto the landing, firing, sometimes at point-blank range, at the heads of the crew. Bartolome had realized exactly what was happening and retreated from the remaining undead. After Wilkes had tossed poor Samson over the edge of the cliff with a rope wrapped around his waist, Bartolome pulled Sylvia and William with her to a series of boulders on the edge of the landing.

Wilkes had then confronted Bartolome. William hadn't been close enough to hear, but they had a conversation that ended with Wilkes retreating off the landing to the path below, where he probably still waited in ambush. That meant they had precious little time, especially considering that Anton was alone on *The Knotted Wood*.

"William, be prepared to run. We need to get Jonathan up here," Bartolome said.

"Do that, and he'll hate us for eternity. This is his life's work."

"Then why won't he help you read the bloody inscription? It must mean something! Maybe it's the key to everything!"

"Yes, of course. But I'm only able to translate the symbols that Jonathan has described to me. I can't see them." William flipped open his spell book, looking for a translation of the symbols that would help their situation. "If only I could see what he sees." The symbols weren't easy to find, considering Jonathan's poor descriptions. Once he found a symbol, however, he could translate by reading the equivalent text written in plain words in the second half of the book, the pronunciation of the words popping into his head as he read each symbol and its definition. How, he did not know. The spell book itself must be imbued with some kind of learning spell.

"See, yes, this symbol means 'see.' And this symbol is 'want.' And here, I'm sure this means 'what is written.'"

"What are you babbling about, William?" Bartolome said. "Just cast a spell! You're constructing an entire diatribe!"

William whispered the words together in a sentence, his mind fixed on the rock inscription below. He imagined the glowing symbols, even though he'd never seen the inscription. He felt the smoothness of the rock in his mind, and he let his desire to understand the words rise in his chest.

"William, what in the name of gods is this?!" Bartolome cried.

William looked up and gasped. Floating in the air, just near the tube system to communicate with Jonathan, a rectangle of light had formed out of nothing. Inside, William could clearly see Jonathan standing on the path next to the Wizard, with Samson lying prone on the ground to his rear. Beyond them both, the glowing inscription on the rock was clear as day, as if William were standing right next to it.

"I can see it!" William shouted in excitement as he ran up to the floating image depicting the events unfolding far below.

His mind hungrily wrapped around the symbols on the rock. He knew at least three of them; they were simple enough. Without wasting a moment, he flipped open the spell book and found the remaining symbols in the first section. He held his finger on the spot, flipped to the second half of the book, and found the equivalent words. After a few moments of flipping back and forth, he nodded, feeling confident in the full translation.

William raised his head from the book and spoke the translation of the symbols aloud. Immediately, he wondered if that was a bad idea. But science was about discovery, not hesitation, as Jonathan always said. Besides, how dangerous could a spell be? Perhaps this would just free the Wizard? Or the Dragon? Although those were not preferable outcomes, they would still lead to a virtually unlimited amount of new discoveries. How could any professor or scientifically minded person turn their back on such things?

"WHAT? See what? What can you see? What are you talking

about, William?" Jonathan said after William shouted about seeing something.

The strange words of a spell echoed through the tube into Jonathan's ear. William had just cast a spell. But why?

It didn't matter. Jonathan turned back to the Wizard—and his heart nearly stopped in his chest. Just moments ago, the Wizard's head had been facing the Dragon, his eyes staring into the maw of the splendid beast. But now, without question, the Wizard's eyes were fixed on Jonathan, a look of quizzical confusion plastered on the Wizard's face.

CHAPTER NINETEEN

Dressa Moore was an ancient land. Composed of five massive land-locked lakes, each large enough to be considered a sea, and one land mass nearly large enough to be considered its own continent, where the city of Hogkarta lay, as well as uncounted islands both large and small. The entirety of Dressa, a country ruled by kings and queens before the magical convergence of the Wizard and Dragon, wasn't quite its own continent, though it's people often referred to it as such out of a sense of pride. The complex series of tributaries and waterways of the Riverlands separated the northern lands of Dressa Moore from the rest of the great continent to the south, but only so much as the width of a single river. The old Kingdom of Dressa Moore, the seat of power cut off from the rest of Dressa from the magical tsunami one hundred years ago, was thought to be greater in military might than all the empire and the Democracy of the great interior of the true continent to the south, which the Riverlands belonged.

When the storm of sorcery had exploded into the world, the magical quake that came with it elevated the largest of the five lakes, Lake Connell, nearly a mile into the air, as well as a quarter of the island continent. This had also created a natural barrier between the remnants of the ancient kingdom and the empire in the Riverlands to the south.

The empty lakebed on the ground below, after the water of Lake Connell had fled to the skies, had become full of vast valleys and long open plains. Powerful magic at the ground had twisted and pulled the newly emptied land in fantastical ways, creating the villages of the tree-man, the lairs of the gater-people and the rather silly towns of the bouncy folk. As for the peoples of the former kingdom of Dressa Moore, they had counted themselves quite lucky. They were spared from the magical storms on the ground by being carried upward a mile into the heavens. The ruling class of the kingdom—kings and queens who had ruled Lake Connell and the sister lakes for centuries—had been cut off not only from Lake Connell, but from the Riverlands and the expanding power of the empire.

That is, until the second great magical explosion, caused by the casting of a spell by William Watts Worthwaddle, who read the not-quite-accurate inscription of said spell on a stone near the Wizard, the words having been changed by Samson Oswald Sutter III just moments before William had read the words, just erupted on Dressa Moore.

A bubble of magic that had once extended only to Lake Connell grew in the blink of an eye. In an instant, the expanse of magical forces engulfed two more of the lakes of Dressa Moore and half of a third. The entire island continent came under the power of the growing tide of magic, as did the immediate portion of the Riverlands, nearly all the way to Oyster Piers. Cliffs that once separated the island continent reformed with the land they had fled from a century ago, reforming open roads and vast plains. Ancient forces, the origins of which were long forgotten in the world's history, scooped up nearly three times the amount of land and sea, shoving it high into the air to rest at the same level as Lake Connell.

All the result of the spell spoken by William Watts Worthwaddle, slightly changed from Yelke's, lord of the gods, original inscription by Samson Oswald Sutter III.

Jonathan fell backward onto the ground, his lead suit creating a dent in the dirt. Before him, moving as slow as a snail, the great Wizard shifted his eyes from Jonathan's now prone form to the Dragon in front of him. Smoke rose from the nostrils of the magnificent beast, sending Jonathan scrambling backwards. He bumped into Samson, who curled himself into an even tighter ball.

"What's happening?!" Samson screamed.

"They're moving!" Jonathan's eyes stayed fixed on the forms of the Wizard and the Dragon. To his shock and dismay, both were reanimated. Neither had moved in over a hundred years, save for the feeble flicker of smoke twenty years ago, and yet both of them, in this moment, were shifting.

Samson looked up and screamed again. "That can't be! I changed the inscription!"

The wings of the dragon unfurled to their full height. The light from the crystal in the Wizard's staff grew in brilliance. Whatever epic battle these two ancient enemies had been in the middle of before they became frozen in time was about to finally unfold.

Arcs of magic the size of mountains erupted along the

landscape as a rolling thunder shook the earth. Red and blue bolts of lightning from the heavens struck, and a fountain of scorpions suddenly came to life, spilling out of the ground only to dig themselves back into the dirt and sprout flowers from their tails.

"This is madness!" Samson cried. "We have to get out of here!"

Alarms sounded on Jonathan's instruments. He looked down at his magonmeter, and the needled jumped to maximum, only to retreat to zero, then dip below zero, which shouldn't even be possible ... unless whatever had caused this magical storm had also unlocked a flurry of anti-magons. Could they be here?

Jonathan looked at his three tubes lying next to the Wizard. A small cloud of blackness hovered over the one in the middle. A smile erupted on his face, and he lunged forward, crawling on his hands and knees, Samson scraping at his feet and following him.

"What are you doing? Tell them to pull us up!"

"Not yet. It's happening, Samson! Anti-magons are being collected in the tubes!"

"Jonathan, please! I'm unprotected here!"

Jonathan didn't even hear his colleague's pleas, his attention riveted to his experiment at the feet of the great Wizard. He scrambled over to his tubes and watched as a black substance dripped into the middle container. Without question, that had to be a concentration of anti-magons, repelled by the arc between the two tubes on the ends. It was working! His experiment had defied all odds and actually produced the outcome he had theorized it would produce.

"Jonathan!"

Behind them, the light at the tip of the Wizard's staff glowed brighter. As for the Dragon, a building storm of fire was lighting in the beast's breast. Jonathan was suddenly and grimly certain that being in this spot right now was probably not the best idea. He turned back to his tubes, corked all three of them, and shoved them into a pouch at his side. He then wrapped an arm around Samson and tugged on the rope attached to his suit.

Nothing happened at first, but he remembered Sylvia's instructions. *"Don't just tug; pull hard. One powerful tug will release the counterweight system and pull you up with force. Another pulley system will wind the elastic rope in a drum and lock it off on the landing. The result will be you dangling two feet above the ground on the landing near the contraption."*

"You have to hold on tight, Samson. There's only one way up."

Samson nodded. He pulled on the rope tied around his waist, still attached to the rope connected to Jonathan's back.

With one arm around Samson, Jonathan gave the rope leading up toward the landing a strong pull. A second later, the rope went taut—but nothing happened. Next to them, the Dragon and Wizard continued to move at a snail's pace, both inching closer to unleashing what could be a world-ending amount of magical energy.

RENALDO SAT at the front of the tiny skiff and grinned a mile wide. They were so very close. The surrounding skies were lit with fire and magic. He could feel the force entering the world from the source, from the Wizard and Dragon. William had done it—or done something, at any rate. Whatever he did, it was working. Well, something was working. And that something was enough for Renaldo to give the command he'd waited his entire life to give.

"Magi, take us over the edge. Take us to the Wizard. We shall kill him in the name of the gods!"

The Magi at the back of the small boat unmoored them from the rock a few hundred feet away from the harbor where *The Knotted Wood* sat. As they passed the undead ship, a tall man with an enormous belly waved to them from the deck, with two imperial soldiers wrapped in his additional arms, something Renaldo found to be quite curious. But not so much that it mattered.

"Onward!"

"Are we sure this is the best way down?" one of the Magi said.

"Well, it's the fastest way," a second Magi said.

"And you're sure that spell works?" a third Magi asked.

"All of you, be quiet! Yes, of course it will work! This is destiny!" Renaldo's eyes were wide with the hunger to finally be vindicated before the gods.

The surrounding water picked up speed as they sped past the cliffs. The roar of the waterfall filled their ears as they rapidly approached the drop. Renaldo clutched a rope tied to the boat and nodded to himself. This would work. This had to work. Soon, the Wizard would be dead, and the gods would be released from their mountain prison.

"Forward!" Renaldo cried.

"Where does he think we're going?" one Magi whispered under his breath.

"Don't antagonize him," the second Magi whispered in response.

The boat flew over the waterfall, the front pitching downward toward the depths of the falls and the Wizard far below. Renaldo prepared a spell in his mind that would create a massive cushion of air just above the ground. Their bodies, after leaping out of the boat, would bounce on the invisible pillow of air, and then they would safely land on the surface. Their only task then would be to kill the Wizard and rule the world.

MUSIC BLASTED onto the beach from nearby crickets and clams. Notes from each combined to create a thumping rhythm. The high-pitched cooing of doves perched on thatched roofs added to the melody. Throngs of dancers swayed and jumped to the beat. Cheers went wild when a light show from the fireflies created intricate designs in the sky. The revelers drank coconut cocktails and burned the local grass in clouds of smoke, which had the added benefit of creating a collective euphoric trance.

On a nearby branch, two rainbow crows hopped up and down and tried to match the rhythm of the music. Several of the locals pointed to the crows and waved. The rainbow crows waved back and made loud cawing noises, not in tune in any way with the music coming from the other flora and fauna of the valley. Several of the partygoers thought this was odd, but not every animal could sing, so the rainbow crows were still welcomed with cheers and salutes of good wishes and happy party times.

One rainbow crow turned to the other and cawed. The other turned its head to the first, nodded, and cawed back. Neither had any idea what they meant, nor what the other had said.

Red lightning erupted in the sky over the beach, causing the local population to cheer. Nothing that happened in the valley of the never-ending party had ever done anything other than contribute to the joy of the ongoing festival. Thus, it was with great concern, surprise, and the experience of a new sensation the local population would later discover was fear that all the people then witnessed a blue lightning bolt streaking across the sky, hitting the branch where the two rainbow crows sat, and exploding into a maelstrom of feathers and bark.

The music on the beach died instantly. Stunned faces and shocked people turned to the source of the sudden commotion. They approached the smell of burning wood with knots in their stomachs—another new feeling that they would learn was anxiety. Lying on the ground, the two rainbow crows flopped in spasms.

"Never seen that before," a woman on the beach said.

"Do you think it's a new dance move?" a man ventured.

"Must be," said the woman.

With a collective nod, everyone on the beach immediately flopped to the ground and began gyrating wildly. After several long minutes, the woman stopped, sat up, and shook her head. Several others followed suit, until it was silently agreed that the ground dancing was not a good thing.

"Doesn't seem very fun," said the man.

"I have this strange feeling of un-festiveness in my stomach," said the woman.

"I have that too!" said someone in the crowd.

"Same."

"Me too."

"I don't think I like this," said the man. "It doesn't seem very fun."

"What should we do?" the woman wondered.

In that moment, the rainbow crows on the ground, hearing every word the locals said and suddenly realizing that they recognized the words and meaning, remembered that they were both gods sent to save the ancient spell from destruction. They promptly got to their feet and tested their wings.

"*Caw?*" said one rainbow crow.

The second rainbow crow heard the sound, but also felt the meaning behind it. "*Caw*—What did you say?"

"*Caw*—Is that you, Selke?"

"*Caw*—Yes. I am Selke. I remember that now. You're Fjorn, right?"

"*Caw*—Yes. I think that's my name. Yes, it is!"

"*Caw*—You realize we're not actually speaking, Fjorn?"

"*Caw*— Yes, I'm just cawing. So are you. But I understand what you're saying, Selke."

"*Caw*—This is quite strange, Fjorn."

"*Caw*— Yes. Yes, it is, Selke."

"*Caw*— So, what do we do now?"

"*Caw*—Wait... The lightning! It also said something. Do you remember? I think his name is Borke."

"*Caw*—Oh, I quite liked Borke. Nice man."

"*Caw*— Yes, Selke. Very nice. But he said we have to do something."

"*Caw*— Oh... Oh, my. The spell! We have to save the spell! Yelke sent us! Remember it all now, Fjorn?"

"*Caw*—Right! Yes, we have to go, Selke!"

"*Caw*—Do you think we can come back, Fjorn?"

Fjorn shrugged his feathered wings. "*Caw*—Don't see why not."

Both rainbow birds cawed their thanks to the locals for the party, and said that they would be back one day to continue the dance. They also apologized for Borke's lightning bolt and the damage it had caused. But not a single person on the beach heard anything but two crows cawing madly back and forth, which caused increased feelings that they weren't at all accustomed to to grow in the pit of their stomachs. The people of the valley of the party had only known animals to sing or provide food from the ocean, or a nice thumping beat to dance to. Whatever the two rainbow crows were doing was clearly none of those things, which created no small amount of apprehension as to the meaning of what had just happened.

Confident that their thanks had been met with a kind welcome—which they hadn't been—Selke and Fjorn flapped their wings, rose into the sky, and soared high into the air. They disappeared from view in an instant—another thing that no one in the valley had ever witnessed. Among many things, it seemed to carry the message that the party was over—which, as it happened, was a concept that no one in the valley of the party was quite equipped to understand.

YELKE, lord of the gods, master of magical forces, and king of all ran to the edge of his patio and cursed the entire universe. Decades, centuries, eons of planning, of a never-ending war with dragon kind, all thwarted in an instant by a fool misreading a spell. They had unlocked nothing. They hadn't freed Finnian or the Dragon. But they had made Finnian the Wizard vulnerable. And if he died, then the grand plan was thwarted, and all was lost.

"No!" Yelke screamed at the heavens. Rainbow bolts of lightning exploded from his fingertips and scorched the newly manicured lawn.

"Husband," Neltzy said.

"The humans have done the unthinkable! They botched the inscription! They miscast the spell! All is lost!"

"You are always the pessimist, Yelke."

Yelke turned to his wife, rage in his eyes. "The True Religionists are about to kill Finnian! We've lost!"

"Borke and Fulte have sent word to Selke and Fjorn. They've woken from their slumber."

Yelke's eyes went wide. "Selke and Fjorn are awake?! Have them fly to the Wizard! Have them speak the spell! Tell them to do it now!"

Neltzy bounced her head back and forth several times. "Well, there's a slight issue there, husband."

"What issue?"

"Last time I checked, dear husband, crows can't speak. Even the rainbow kind."

Yelke threw his head backwards and sighed, exhaling a whirlwind of force into the air. "It just can't be simple, can it?"

"There's still hope, of course. Borke has sent them a message. And they remember. But they can't act on it—at least, not on their own."

Yelke looked at his wife. "What exactly did Borke tell them?"

COMMODORE WILKES KNELT by his remaining soldiers behind a boulder near the path that led back to their trawler. He'd trusted Bartolome in those final moments. He wasn't sure why, but he knew she was being honest. He felt it in his gut. Just before their confrontation, Wilkes had sent Samson over the edge to deal with Jonathan. Admittedly, it wasn't the best of plans, but Wilkes's head wasn't quite clear at the moment. It had seemed like a good idea at the time. But as the world around them exploded into a magical maelstrom, it was clear that Samson, or Bartolome, or both of them had failed.

Wilkes took out his looking glass and pointed it at the floating rectangle next to one of the professors. It appeared to be like a window showing the events unfolding on the ground far below, where the other professors from the university stood. Behind them, through the magical window, Wilkes could also see the Wizard and the Dragon slowly moving. The light from the Wizard's staff glowed brighter, while flame burned deep in the dragon's belly.

"This is the end of the world!" one soldier cried.

"Be still, men, nothing's ended yet." Wilkes peered through his looking glass. The lead-encased form of Jonathan lay prone only inches away from the Wizard. Arcs of magical energy ricocheted off his armor, which seemed to leave him perfectly protected, as if the magic had no ability to affect anything inside the suit.

"Now, that's interesting," Wilkes muttered.

"Sir, what should we do?"

Wilkes turned to his men. They were tired, beaten, and more outnumbered than when they had taken the landing the first time—and that had been by surprise. Wilkes looked back to see a line of Bartolome's undead crew facing the path where he and his men stood. They were ready for them if they charged. Not to mention, nearly half of the rocks on the cliffside had started shifting, and large flowers were blooming from several of his crew members' oral cavities. And there was also the matter of the pelican on Wilkes's shoulder that wanted to argue about the risks of something called colonialism.

"We go home," Wilkes declared. "We need to get as far away from Dressa Moore as we can."

"And just let the criminal go free?"

Wilkes shook his head. "If she survives the next few moments, and if we do too, we'll come back to these waters and find her. We're not giving up on anything, lads. We're regrouping."

The men nodded. Wilkes took one last look at the landing before leading his soldiers down the path and back towards the trawler. Getting his men as far away from whatever was happening below as he could was his number one priority. Bartolome would have to wait. Wilkes could only hope she would be true to her word.

Wilkes stopped and turned to one of his soldiers. "Is there a pelican on my shoulder?"

"No, sir. Is there an enormous snake with large wings wearing a top hat perched on my skull?"

Wilkes's eyes shifted to the soldier's head. Two chipmunks were busily burying a stash of muffins in the man's brain. They both looked up, waved at Wilkes, and immediately got back to work.

"No, nothing. But we should get out of here soon."

SELKE LANDED on a wooden beam that was part of some contraption on the cliff above Finnian and the Dragon. She and Fjorn were headed straight toward the Wizard, but the sight of a floating magical window drew their attention, and they changed course. Creating a viewing window required powerful magic, not the simple trinket tricks often deployed by the church and most humans. No, the window of viewing called for a firm understanding of casting spells.

"*Caw*—Who's that?" Selke asked.

"*Caw*—Don't know."

"*Caw*—Well, whoever he is, he made a window of

viewing and probably botched unlocking Finnian, don't you think, Fjorn?"

"*Caw*—Yes, I quite think that's what happened, Selke."

The man below them turned to look at Selke and Fjorn, his head tilted to one side, his eyes squinting into slits. The woman beside him, a half-undead creature, pulled him back and yelled at him to fix the world.

Selke turned her beaked head towards Fjorn. "*Caw*—You don't seem to care."

"*Caw*— Not really," Fjorn said. "*Caw*—Do you?"

Selke turned to the window of viewing and the man standing in front of it. "*Caw*—I think I do."

"*Caw*—Really? Why? I mean, even if those two blow themselves up, we'll be fine."

"*Caw*—Will we? Yelke doesn't think so."

"*Caw*—Selke, he's full of it. Let's just go back to the party."

"*Caw*—Why did you come here at all, Fjorn?"

"*Caw*—I don't know. I'm sorry, Selke. I think I'm just tired. We did just fly five thousand miles in a few minutes."

Selke bobbed her head up and down several times. "*Caw*—Yes, that was exhausting. Was it five, or ten?"

"*Caw*—I don't know. I think I'm just not sure about living in a world where Yelke controls everything. He has his moods."

Selke bobbed her head a second time. "*Caw*—I do agree with that."

"*Caw*—Why don't we just lock Finnian and the Dragon back up and call it a day? We'd be back at the party before sundown," Fjorn offered.

The man below them looked back up at them again.

"*Caw*—Yelke would be mad."

"*Caw*—Yes, but we won't see him for a few thousand years. He'll forget by then."

Spending a thousand years or more in the valley of the party sounded like a splendid idea to Selke, even if it meant doing so as a rainbow crow. She bobbed her head up and down several times in agreement, but then tilted her beak to one side in confusion. "*Caw*—How do we cast a spell?"

"*Caw*—What do you mean? Like this..." Fjorn sat on the wooden beam for several seconds before shaking his head. "*Caw*—I can't form the words. I can only caw."

"*Caw*—That's all we've been doing. We're not speaking, we're cawing. We just understand each other."

"*Caw*—And why is that, do you think, Selke?"

"*Caw*—Not really sure, Fjorn."

"I can cast a spell! Tell me what to do!" the man below them said, looking directly at Selke and Fjorn.

"*Caw*—Who's he talking to?" Fjorn asked.

"*Caw*—He's looking at us."

"*Caw*—He can't understand us. And he looks too stupid to cast an understanding spell."

"I'll have you know, I'm a principal scholar at the university of the Riverlands—and I would very much like to save the world now!" William called to them.

WILLIAM STOMPED his foot and cursed at the talking birds sitting above him on the wooden beam of Sylvia's contraption. He did not know how he understood them, but he did. Perhaps whatever he had cast also allowed him to talk to animals, or perhaps rainbow crows could speak all the time anyway and just chose to do so now, or lastly, perhaps these were special rainbow crows kept at the university to communicate with Samson in Hogkarta, and somehow the chancellor had gotten them to come here and help. Regardless of the reason, they were here now, and William desperately needed help.

"What are you doing, William?" Bartolome asked. "We need to flee, and fast. All is lost!"

"I'm not leaving without Jonathan." William spared a glance at the floating rectangle window. Jonathan was loading his tubes into his satchel and preparing to return. At least, William hoped he was. If he didn't get up here fast, then even his suit wouldn't be able to withstand the magical storm. Samson, poor soul, already had flowers blooming on his skin and what appeared to be antlers growing out of his skull.

"*Caw*—What did you do to cause all this in the first place?" one crow asked.

"I read the inscription on the rock." William pointed to the symbols still visible through the floating rectangle.

"*Caw*—Didn't Borke put that there?"

"*Caw*—No, I think it was Fulte."

"Who are they? True Religionists?" William asked.

"*Caw*—No, they're gods. So are we."

"William, why are you talking to those birds?"

William looked at Bartolome. "Can't you hear them? They're speaking. They say they're actually gods."

Bartolome nodded once and looked at the birds, then back to William, then to Sylvia. "I think we need to put more smelling stuff under his nose."

"*Caw*—Do you think Fulte got the inscription wrong? I don't think this is what she intended."

"What did she intend?" William asked.

"*Caw*—Finnian's magic and the Dragon's are opposites.

When they touched, they froze time around them and unleashed a tsunami of magical forces. It was very unexpected."

"Who is Finnian?"

"*Caw*—That's the Wizard. Nice fellow, really. Loved pastries."

Thunderclaps filled the air as rainbow-colored lightning flashed across the sky. William turned back to the floating rectangle to see Jonathan yanking hard on the rope attached to his back. But nothing was happening. He turned to the mechanism Sylvia had created. Bars, wheels, and pulleys came to life as Jonathan's pull untethered the machine's systems, but there was a locking mechanism in place. William pointed at it and then at Sylvia. She raced over to the machine and swung a piece of metal to the side. A series of twisting arms flew down with enough force to yank Jonathan off the ground and send him sailing skyward.

"We have to do something!" Bartolome said above the rising storm. "We're not in a good place if those two really wake up!"

"*Caw*—Oh, they won't. You botched the spell casting. Said the wrong thing."

"*Caw*—Yes, Fjorn's right. But it still won't be good."

"*Caw*—Oh, no, didn't mean to say it would be good. Things will just happen slowly."

"Can we stop it?" William asked.

The crows exchanged looks. "*Caw*—We can't, but you can."

"*Caw*—You have to stop time again."

"I don't know how to do that!"

"*Caw*—It's a conundrum. We can't actually speak, so we can't tell you the spell."

"William, we have to go!" Bartolome cried, just as Jonathan and Samson reached the top of the machine. A lever attached to the spot where they touched instantly untethered them both from the elastic rope. They tumbled into a heap next to Bartolome and Sylvia, Samson kissing the ground and crying as the flowers fell off his arms.

"What happens if we run?" William asked the birds.

"*Caw*—Oh, you'll likely die. Can't outrun this. You're far too close."

William turned in a circle and ran his hands through his hair. Lightning continued to rage around them as Finnian and the Dragon edged closer to having their opposing magic touch. He looked at Jonathan, who huffed on the ground, trying to keep Samson calm as one of his antlers got stuck in a piece of Sylvia's machine.

In the rectangle showing the Wizard and the Dragon, four Magi of the Church of the True Religionists landed on the ground with a soft thump. William ran to the floating viewing window and recognized Renaldo immediately. The four Magi nodded to themselves and walked toward the Wizard, each drawing a knife.

"How did they get here?" William demanded.

"I saw a boat fly over the edge, but I didn't see them on it," Bartolome offered.

"Whatever they're doing, it can't be good," William said.

"*Caw*—Oh, it's not. They're going to kill the Wizard."

"Why would they do that?!"

"*Caw*—It's a mistake. They're operating on bad information."

"What?"

"*Caw*—It's a long story. They misunderstood the message. They're supposed to kill the Dragon first, not the Wizard. Lost in translation."

"How could that happen? What kind of gods are you?!"

"*Caw*—We often ask this question ourselves."

"Wait, just wait... You said you can't speak the spell, but I can understand you," William pointed out.

"*Caw*—Yes, but we aren't really speaking."

"*Caw*—We're cawing. Can't you hear that annoying high-pitched sound?"

"*Caw*—I find it tranquil, Selke."

"*Caw*—Well, you're weird, Fjorn."

"But if I can understand you, can't you just tell me what to do?"

"*Caw*—Whatcha mean?"

William sighed. "I don't need to know how the spell sounds. I need to know the intent; then I can translate it. Just say the intent of the spell."

"*Caw*—Intent of the spell? Is that a thing, Selke?"

"*Caw*—No, I don't think so. I don't think it works that way, Fjorn."

"How do you not know this?" William demanded. "Aren't you both gods?"

"*Caw*—Very minor ones."

"Just tell me!"

The rainbow crows exchanged tilted looks. One of them shrugged. Then the one William thought was named Selke explained the intent of the spell and what it should do. Most of the words William had already found, except one. The concept of locking or freezing time wasn't something he'd yet encountered in the text.

Waves of energy from the magical storm rose above the cliffs and threatened to crash down on them like a tsunami of rainbows. William didn't have the time to find the reference. If only he'd spent more time with the book!

"Sylvia!" William shouted.

"What?" Sylvia sat on the ground, her legs tucked beneath her, her hands resting on her knees. She seemed quite content to allow oblivion to crash into her.

"I can stop this. I can reverse this! But I haven't found a reference in my spell book to freezing or locking something."

"You mean my scientific research book?" Sylvia said, sarcasm dripping from every word.

"Yes-wait, that's what your book is?"

"How do you think I created the talking tubing system or the slingshot and stretchy rope? Though, tiny chipped off shards from uncle's crystal cube he gave me makes the tubes work, to be fair."

"Yes, fine, your research book. Please, or we're done for!"

Sylvia sighed. She tossed her head backward and looked at the sky. "Page two hundred and sixteen, second paragraph, third sentence."

William took a stunned step backward. "How could you know that so quickly?"

Sylvia shrugged. "I remember things."

"Right." William opened the pages in both the first and second section of the book. He found Sylvia's reference and the corresponding symbols. He nodded once to himself. This had to do it. He aligned the words in his mind with how they should flow. Then he focused his thoughts on the symbols, the pronunciation of them flowing into his mind.

William took a step toward the floating rectangle and fixed his eyes on the Wizard named Finnian and the Dragon. He took a deep breath and shouted the spell into the world, with a desperate mental plea for it to work.

The wave of magical energy above them stopped moving. A single thunderclap cracked through the world around them, followed by a torrent of wind that knocked everyone off their feet. The rainbow waves around the cliff dove toward the waterfall, pouring all of their energy downward. The floating rectangle portrayed the colors surround the Wizard and Dragon. Twin jets of rainbow separated and hovered over both of the forms below. The rainbows broke apart into different colors, spun at impossible speeds over their heads, and then quietly vanished without a sound. In the floating viewing rectangle, William could now see four statues standing around the Wizard, each in the likeness of a Magi of the church.

A quiet calm descended on the group. Bartolome picked herself up off the ground and looked around. Most of her crew did the same. William followed suit and looked at the floating rectangle. Orange flame was just barely peeking out of the dragon's maw, while the Wizard's staff glowed nearly as bright as the setting sun. William ran to Jonathan, who nodded and smiled.

"*Caw*—Well done, young wizard!"

"*Caw*—Yes, indeed! Very nice."

"Thank you, but I'm not a wizard," William said.

"*Caw*—Aren't you?"

William shook his head and pulled Jonathan and Samson to their feet. "I'm a linguist."

"*Caw*—What's that?"

"I study language, little birds."

"*Caw*—You mean a grammatist?"

"*Caw*—Sounds silly."

"Who are you talking to, William? And how did you defeat Wilkes and the imperial soldiers? They aren't exactly pushovers," Jonathan said.

"Most went insane, ran off on their own." Sylvia touched the dried paste under her nose and shot Jonathan a wink.

William smiled, ripped Jonathan's helmet off, and shook

his head. "Doesn't matter." He kissed Jonathan hard on the lips. Jonathan kissed him back, and together, they forgot about the world around them.

CHAPTER TWENTY

Daniel Desun, the new chancellor of the university at Dressa Moore, stepped onto the docks of Hogkarta with a bright, wide smile, and the most beautiful assistant holding his arm. Vanessa looked at the buildings and the people and could only marvel at the sights.

"This is a city that could rival ours, Daniel!"

Daniel nodded. "No wonder Samson wanted this all to himself. We could build something great here!"

Archbishop Santos, who had remained quiet throughout the journey, except to huff and grunt whenever Daniel showed affection or when Vanessa giggled, pushed past them and walked with angry purpose toward the center of town. That suited Daniel just fine. He didn't seem to be a delightful man.

"Where do we go?" Vanessa asked.

"There's an office." Daniel led Vanessa through the docks and into the streets. He only had to ask for directions three times—though the last didn't count in his mind—

before he found his way to the university building in Hogkarta. The outside looked nothing like a university building should look. There was only a small square sign showing that this was a place of higher learning. There were no flags signifying the great minds of their age, no sign that this was a place to foster enlightenment, nothing to show the citizens of the town that they could better themselves—something Daniel decided to fix immediately.

He opened the door to the building and stepped inside. A woman looked up at him, shook her head, and looked back down at a newspaper that she continued to read. The room itself was small and dark, with a single door leading to a hallway behind her.

"Excuse me, I'm here to see Samson Oswald Sutter the Third, if you please."

"No, you aren't."

Daniel glanced at Vanessa, who smiled awkwardly. "Excuse me? I most certainly am."

The woman looked up and shook her head. "He's indisposed at the moment."

Daniel sighed, removed a piece of paper from his pocket, and handed it to the woman. "You see, ma'am, I am now the dean of this school, as ordered by the chancellor of the Great University itself. I am to take ownership of all buildings and monies, and take responsibility for all things related to this school. Immediately." Daniel turned to Vanessa and nodded.

"I see. In that case, he's in his office. Through there, turn right, and listen for the scraping sounds. He's trying to shed."

Daniel took a step forward, but stopped. "I'm sorry—he's what?"

"You'll see."

Daniel turned to Vanessa. "Wait here. No sense in embarrassing him."

"You're so very kind," Vanessa said with a smile.

"One must be." Daniel turned and walked through the door.

Once out of her view, he let out a silent cheer of triumph. Things were going swimmingly with Vanessa—as well as they could. He calmed himself down and nodded.

Three more turns, and he found the door to Samson's office. The strange sound of wood scraping against something hard came from inside the room. Daniel knocked twice and put his hand on the knob.

"I asked you to please leave me alone," Samson's voice said from inside.

Daniel entered the office—and let out a gasp of shock. Samson sat at his desk, with large antlers sticking out from his skull and tiny blue and purple flowers blooming along his arms and hands. He took one look at Daniel and spread his arms wide.

"Take a good look, whoever you are. Go giggle about me to your friends. Then get out!"

"Sorry, I can't really do that."

"And why is that?"

Daniel took a long, deep breath and stilled his nerves. "I am here to replace you. I am Daniel Desun, the new dean of this branch of schools from the university. I officially relieve you of all duties, and you are to return to the Riverlands to face tribunal." He nodded, reached inside his coat for the letter, then remembered he had given it to the secretary, and he swore under his breath. "I have a letter of confirmation and can present it to you upon request."

Samson locked eyes with Daniel for a long minute. Then

a smile spread across his face, and he first nodded, then shook his head. "No."

"Sorry? You don't have a choice, sir."

"Well, in that, you are correct." Samson reached into his desk and pulled out a note with the chancellor's seal. "This is for you."

Daniel broke the seal and tore open the letter. His heart sank at the first apologetic word, and it continued to fall as he read the whole thing. He stomped his foot on the floor three times and shook his head. "Gods, no, please..."

"Rainbow crows fly quite fast. I've already had it out with Chancellor Dunningham. Even offered him two cases of magical wine. It's all politics, you know."

"But, no, I can't—"

"You'll stay here as my new assistant. And we have a lot of things to do, dear Daniel. The Chancellor says you come highly recommended."

"But I'm a professor now!"

"Rescinded. Sorry. Actually, I think he never even submitted it. He likes the drink, you know."

Daniel twisted in his shoes and looked at the ceiling. He slapped his leg three times before nodding once. What choice did he have? If he went back to the university, they would fire him for insubordination. This was a direct order from the chancellor himself, which meant if he didn't follow it, his academic career was over. But at least he could spend the time with Vanessa. He could spin this to make it sound good. Yes, he could do that.

Samson heaved a large box onto his desk. It slammed down on the wood with a thud. "This needs to go back to the chancellor, along with his wine. The other assistant— what's her name? She's to return at once."

"What?!" Daniel was sure he hadn't heard him correctly.

"She's to return at once, with the wine and this chest. Someone has to deliver it. Can't be me, can't be you, so who else is there?"

"But, she's my girl—I mean, my assistant."

"Assistants don't have their own assistants, Daniel. That breaks the logic of the system."

Daniel moved his mouth, but no words came out. He stood mutely for several seconds as Samson moved his head back and forth to scrape his antlers on the wooden wall behind him, picking flowers off his arm, only to have them bloom again seconds later.

"And can you find me a back scratcher or something? I can't reach with these head horns."

Daniel could only nod.

ARCHBISHOP PHILIP SANTOS paused inside the cathedral of the True Religionists as the doors closed, the forgotten but well-recognized echo bouncing off the walls, sending a smile to his weary face. He hadn't heard that sound for the last few weeks. But even the sound of the echo couldn't ease Santos's mind. A maelstrom of magic had erupted over the world. There were now three floating lakes in the sky of Dressa Moore and the rest of the island continent of Hogkarta. More importantly, no gods had shown themselves. That meant that ultimately, Philip Santos had failed.

"This way, Archbishop," said a woman Philip didn't recognize.

"Where is Renaldo?"

"He is no longer."

Philip nodded. That was a loss. Renaldo had been a good priest. The new assistant—Philip didn't bother asking her name—led him through the familiar corridors and stairwells of the headquarters of the church. He looked fondly at the tapestries and carvings on his walk. At one point, he could see over the edge of the upper levels to the carved wall of the central cathedral, where the inscriptions of the gods listed every deity in existence. He frowned at the image, sorrow in his heart for having failed.

"Philip, do come in," Cardinal Rossi said. The cardinal sat in a red leather chair that matched her red hair. She held a glass of red wine in her hand and sniffed the contents.

Philip nodded once to himself and turned to enter the cardinal's office. To his surprise, only the cardinal sat in the plush room. Rossi raised her wine glass in the air and waved for the archbishop to sit in the chair across from her.

"How was your trip, Cardinal?" Santos asked.

"Fine, fine. The DemiGod sends her regrets about your failure."

Santos nodded. "I see."

"Do you? You used the travel stones to pop around the continent, failed to bring the emperor his gift, failed to release the gods, and failed to keep the empire out of Dressa. Quite a lot of failing for one month, wouldn't you say, Philip?" Cardinal Rossi said.

"It was a difficult task to begin with."

"Clearly. Have you heard of the outcome of the events?"

Philip nodded and lifted the crystal around his chest into the air.

"Who told you?"

"Sylvia. After a good amount of insistence."

Cardinal Rossi smiled. "How is your niece? Doing well? Ready to convert back to the church?"

Philip's lips curled into a tight smile. "I'm afraid not."

Cardinal Rossi nodded. "Well, I'm sure you only know the half of things, then."

Here it comes, Philip thought. Banishment, excommunication, disavowed and forgotten... Perhaps he could join Sylvia with the Anti-Religionists. Or he could return to the empire to be a chief spy—though considering how much he'd lied to them, the likelihood there was quite low. No, his fate most likely would be in the gutter, broke and destitute, begging for coins from sailors or soldiers, considering that the empire was already set up in the warehouse given to them by the administrator. Perhaps he could work for the city itself, become an accountant or some such thing.

"What are you brooding about, Philip? We have work to discuss," Cardinal Rossi said.

"Your Grace?"

"Your eyes are drifting to the wall, and your face couldn't be sadder. Did you not hear a word I said? The kingdom is back, Philip. The old kingdom that ruled all of Dressa Moore for a thousand years is back. The magical upheaval that your two professors caused lifted the remaining island continent into the sky. Runners have already come across the broken road to Hogkarta. Do you have any idea how aggravating the kingdom was? Their royal class is the absolute worst. They all have at least five names. Five! They weren't content to have fewer names than any others. How self-important must you be to have five names?"

Santos shrugged. "I've heard their food is quite nice."

Rossi nodded. "There are strong rumors of their pastries being delicious, yes."

"And they were well known for their breads," Santos added.

"Yes, well, perhaps there may be some benefits to the kingdom being back. But the empire is declaring this an official port, and they are bringing those annoying four-armers with them. And now half of the Great Lakes of Dressa are floating along with Lake Connell. Not to mention, there's now a linguist out there casting spells stronger than those of the most skilled Magi. It's utter madness, Philip."

Philip nodded, then shook his head. "What does this have to do with my excommunication?"

"Your what? Who said anything about excommunication? Yes, of course, the DemiGod is disappointed in you, but summoning gods to walk among men is no small task. And the empire was going to come here sooner or later. Rather glad we got it out of the way, and now we deal with keeping them in line. The complexity is the kingdom. Now that they've joined us in the skies and have access to the Riverlands, there is little doubt that trouble will come with them. I need you here, Philip. There is suspicion among the church council that the king could ask for reparations."

"For what?"

Cardinal Rossi huffed and leaned forward. "For causing the first and now the second great upheaval. And as I understand it, that fool Renaldo and his Magi are now stone statues surrounding the Wizard—all of them with daggers drawn. Not something we can exactly explain away."

Philip's mind rolled onto itself. He took three quick breaths and nodded. Not only would he not be leaving the church, it sounded as if he would inherit a mountain of troubles. The cardinal wanted someone else out front besides herself. She wanted someone to take the front role and be easy to blame if things went south. A smile grew on Philip's lips. This was something he knew how to do well. The church might have failed to bring the gods back, but from another perspective, they might have opened a door to claim greater power in the world. Who better to stand at the convergence of the kingdom, the empire, and the return of true magic via the linguist?

Yes, Philip thought, things were looking very good, indeed.

COMMODORE THOMAS WILKES pushed past several soldiers and citizens and a few officers. He marched through Oyster Piers with a singular mission. After making his necessary reports and recommendations to the admiralty, he had been given instant and complete authority to carry out his proposal. What else could the empire do? If the early reports were accurate—and there was no reason to think they weren't—the remaining half of Dressa Moore had just popped off the earth and floated up a mile to join the rest of the lake and lands already there. The amount of magic released into the world could probably be measured in metric tons. But at the very least, there was still a world in which it could be measured.

"You." Wilkes walked up to a young sailor sitting on his bunk in the barracks of the Piers. "Are you the one who rigged that spear contraption on Bridgewater's vessel? The webbed foot or whatever it's called?"

The boy, his face blooming into a bright red patch, sat up straight on his bunk, and then immediately tried to stand. He banged his head on the wooden bed frame above him, gripped the back of his skull, then stood and nodded once. "Yes, sir. I made—"

Wilkes waved him into silence. "Your commanding officer says you've quite the mind."

"Yes, sir. I suppose I—"

"Good. If you aren't already aware, things have taken a

dramatic turn in the world, and the empire is in a dangerous position. Do you know your history, boy?"

The sailor nodded.

"Then you know that the empire and the kingdom didn't get along. The magical storm that erupted over Dressa has reconnected rivers and the island continent. We don't know yet the state of the kingdom, but they knew more about magical principles and history than anyone in the world. If they know how to wield magic, then we're in trouble."

"I don't know what I can do, sir. But whatever it is, I will do my best."

"Good lad. I was on the cliff when those fools unleashed this storm. I witnessed something there. A man encased in a metal suit—it looked like lead—walked freely around the Wizard, and magic did not touch him."

The sailor's face instantly changed from one of fear to curiosity. "Not at all?"

Wilkes shook his head. "I saw bands of rainbows bounce off his armor as if they were mere rain."

"How?"

"Well, that's what I need you to figure out, young man. Actually, I need more than that."

"You want me to create a lead suit of armor?"

Wilkes smiled. "No, son. I want you to make a ship—an imperial frigate. And I want you to clad it in iron and line it with lead."

YELKE SAT ON A MARBLE BENCH, half broken from a single strike of his hammer fists, and brooded over the events of the last few hours. A dozen minor deities ran among the grounds of the palace to repair statures, replant bushes, and fix the lawn. None of them dared look at the king of the gods, or really even get that close to him. That had a secondary effect: none of the lawn near him had been repaired.

"Yelke, are you going to brood all day?" Neltzy asked as she sat down next to her husband.

Yelke looked up to see Fulte and Borke standing next to the bench. Each held a bottle in their hands, and both waved when Yelke looked at them. Borke held a bottle out, and Yelke took it, uncorked the top with his teeth, and drained the contents in a single pull.

"That should have been allowed to breathe. It would have been better," Borke said.

Yelke belched and grabbed the bottle held by his sister, Fulte.

"You shouldn't drink so much, Yelke," Neltzy said.

"Why not? We're not getting out of here any time soon."

Neltzy nodded. "That may be true, but we're running out of marble to make new statues."

"I don't care." Yelke shook his head and gritted his teeth. "Selke and Fjorn... They betrayed us at the last moment."

"We don't know that," Borke said.

"Don't we? How else did the remaining lakes rise, but Finnian and the Dragon remained frozen? How?"

Borke shrugged. "It is a conundrum."

Yelke threw his hand in the air and pointed. The great spell, as written and agreed to by the wizards and dragons thousands of years ago, scrolled in midair. Yelke pointed to one spot in the spell that mentioned Finnian's loophole for the nesting habits of the rainbow crows. "See that?"

"Yes, Yelke. Of course I do. I showed that to you originally."

"You found that, Borke."

Borke looked to Neltzy and Fulte. "Yes, didn't I just say that?"

Yelke nodded. "Find a way for a god to use this—to enter the world of men as a rainbow crow, and then transform themselves back into a gods."

Borke shook his head. "It's not possible. Walking in the world below as gods and being able to speak would violate the great spell. They must remain as a rainbow crow, or all would be lost."

"Selke and Fjorn seem to have gotten around that."

Fulte shrugged. "We don't know how, or what they did, brother."

Yelke burped, stood, uncorked Fulte's bottle, and took a long pull. "I don't care what either of you has to do. You need to find a way, Borke, and you need to send a communication to the church, Fulte. Or I'll turn you both into frogs." Yelke smiled, kissed his wife on the cheek, and stumbled his way back to the castle. A wave of deities followed in his wake to fix the marble bench and the surrounding land-scaping.

"Well, this is a fine mess," Neltzy muttered.

"He's turned me into a frog once before. It's actually not as bad as it sounds," Borke said.

"I worry about his health," Fulte said.

Both Neltzy and Borke turned to her and tilted their heads.

"Well, not his health, exactly... Clearly, none of us needs to worry about our health. You two don't need to be so literal all the time. But he's not in a pleasant state."

Neltzy nodded. "Well, that is true."

Blue lightning shot out from inside the palace. Shouts and the sound of shattering glass soon followed. Neltzy frowned and let out a long sigh. "I may have to find a new house if this keeps up." She turned to Borke and Fulte. "Do try to find something, anything to appease him. For my sake?" She nodded once, smiled, and ran to calm her husband down.

"Well, I have no ideas. Do you?" Borke asked.

Fulte shrugged. "None. Perhaps we can figure it out together?"

Borke nodded. Together, they walked back toward the palace to fetch more wine and try to avoid their impending transformations.

JONATHAN STOOD on the dock of the port of Hogkarta. He had his packed bags at his feet, his luggage packed with more notebooks than clothing, and the tubes of magons and anti-magons were jiggling in his coat pocket, doing everything they could to get as far away from each other as possible. There would be mountains of experiments, research... The entire university would be turned upside down in a single day upon his return. And yet, what would be the moment of his total triumph was actually the saddest day of his life.

"Are you sure you won't come?" Jonathan asked.

"Are you sure you won't stay?" William replied.

Jonathan turned and stared William in the eyes. "It's because of the teasing, isn't it? The constant ridicule? I can fix that. What you have achieved is as great as my research."

William nodded. "Perhaps partially. But the books..." He held up the red-bound spell book he and Sylvia used to translate the symbols. "They won't leave Dressa."

"You don't know that."

"But I feel it. And Sylvia believes it as well. The books belong here. And I need to study them."

Jonathan nodded. He wiped his nose with his handkerchief and coughed once in the frosty morning air. "I may not be back here for some time."

"And I may not leave here for even longer." William's voice broke slightly as he spoke.

"I can't stay. The equipment, the resources, the researchers back at the university... I need them, William. We have years of work to study."

"I know, I know. And I'm not asking you to stay. I know you can't. But I can't go either. The book is filled with more than just symbols. The contraption that saved you—Sylvia found the design in this book. There's mathematics here, and something they call calculus, and science that we know nothing about, and there are even references to other languages! I just can't abandon such a treasure, Jonathan."

A soft silence stretched from seconds to minutes. Jonathan and William stared into each other's eyes, but both soon looked away almost at the same moment. Neither knew the right way to say goodbye, as neither wanted to. But both were driven by their research, which was now pushing them apart.

"Well..." Jonathan grabbed his bags and turned.

"Have a safe trip," William said.

Jonathan didn't reply. He walked onto the boat that would take him back to the Riverlands. William blinked, and in an instant, Jonathan was gone from view on the deck. Crowds moved around William, but he didn't notice their passing or the odd stares he received for standing still in the middle of the dock.

"You're better off," Sylvia said.

"No one asked you."

"Opinions can be given regardless of whether they've been requested or not. And he's too stiff for you."

"Maybe," William said. "But I love him."

Sylvia patted William once on the shoulder. "No sense in just standing here. I'll find you an inn."

William nodded and turned. "You sure you're safe here?"

"Oh, I'm sure my uncle will smooth things over. If he doesn't, we can always run to the Anti-Religionists."

William let himself laugh. "I think they want to kill us even more than the church would."

Sylvia shrugged. "Eventually, in Dressa Moore, everyone wants someone dead."

Together, they walked into the streets of Hogkarta and soon blended in with the citizens of the town, as if each had always been one of them.

SELKE FLEXED her wings and settled on a tree branch at the beach of the valley of the party. Fjorn settled next to her and cawed several times without actually saying anything. He was finding it pleasing to caw for no reason, which worried him to no end. Settling into the body of a rainbow crow was a dangerous road to take. One never knew if he'd just forget being Fjorn and start being the crow.

Greater than the shock of being a bird for the rest of his life was the silence that greeted Selke and Fjorn when they landed. On the beach, standing in rows, the citizens of the valley looked at the two birds with apprehension and fear. The music had been silenced, and not a soul on the beach was dancing.

"*Caw*—What's happening?" Selke asked.

"*Caw*—Not really sure. Where's the party?"

A scream sounded on the beach. Fingers pointed to the two rainbow crows, and the crowd erupted in terror. Voices shouted for everyone to run, that the omens of despair and *un*-joy had returned. Another voice cried to the heavens to remove the creatures and let the party reign. A rock sailed past Fjorn's beak, thrown by a child whose mother immediately grabbed him and ran for one of the palm tree huts.

"*Caw*—I have a bad feeling, Selke."

"*Caw*— I have a worse feeling, Fjorn."

"*Caw*—Are we...?"

"*Caw*—Yes. We've become the omen that the party's over."

Fjorn shook his wings and moved up and down on the branch. "*Caw*—How did that happen?"

"*Caw*—Must have been when we awoke."

Angry shouts came from behind them. The birds turned to see a dozen men and women from the village, each carrying spears that they unskillfully thrust forward violently. One of them pushed their spear so hard that it flew out of their hand and impaled the ground. The villager shrugged, grabbed the spear, and waved it at the birds in a manner in which spears were simply never intended to be used.

"*Caw*—At least they know little about fighting."

"*Caw*—Yes, but what do we do? Can't stay around here forever. Eventually, one of them will figure out how to throw a rock."

As if on cue, a rock flung from someone on the beach sailed by the birds nearly three feet away.

"*Caw*—Though it may take some time."

"*Caw*—Still, this is terrible. It means we can't be part of the party anymore, Selke. I was very much looking forward to the coconut drinks and the smoking grass."

Selke bobbed her head up and down. "*Caw*—And I wanted to eat those mushrooms. But if we tried to land now, I don't think it would go well. They can at least kick."

"*Caw*—So, what do we do?"

"*Caw*—I think it's rather obvious. We have to go back to Finnian and put Yelke's plan into action."

"*Caw*—Selke, are you certain? Yelke won't be happy with us. And his leadership style is something I take exception to."

"*Caw*—What choice do we have? Do you want to spend the next thousand years sitting on a branch, watching cows in a field on some farm somewhere?"

"*Caw*—No, Selke. I don't think I do."

Selke raised her wings and gave them a flap. "*Caw*—Well then, I suppose we'd best find that new wizard and convince him to do it."

"*Caw*—Do you think he will?"

"*Caw*—If not, we'll sit on his window and recite the history of the valley of the leopard people."

"*Caw*—That's a terrible thing to do, Selke... I like it!"

The birds flapped their wings and took off from their perch. Cheers erupted on the beach and throughout the valley as they left. Both Fjorn and Selke could hear the unmistakable sound of music, dance, and song erupting—which made their mission even more important.

Captain Marta Agnese Rhia Bartolome stood at the wheel of *The Knotted Wood* and smiled. They'd done the impossible. She'd done the unthinkable. Bartolome had navigated the waters between the Church of the True Religionists, the Anti-Religionists, the Magi, the constables, and even the empire. And she'd come out not only unscathed, but successful. She'd thrown her repeating stone over the Insanity Cliffs and reversed the spell that had cursed she and Anton's people so many years ago.

Well, partly, anyway.

The Knotted Wood drifted lazily through the groves of Anton's people. Every blighted tree showed signs of new growth. Green leaves grew on brown bark. All of the diseased fruit had withered and fallen into the water. New bulbs could already be seen on branches everywhere. The reversing of the curse of Anton's grove had worked. Many trees in the forest waved cheerfully as *The Knotted Wood* glided beneath the branches.

Anton himself had almost joined them when *The Knotted Wood* entered the groves' waters. It wasn't his time though; he wasn't yet meant to plant and join the forest. Tears streamed down the big man's face, making Bartolome smile. She was so very happy that she could give him this moment.

A loud grunt from one of Bartolome's crew caught her attention. They were all still undead, as was she. She could still feel them and control them; it was as if nothing had changed. That meant the reversing spell had only partially worked. Anton's people were thankfully healed, but her own crew was not.

What, then, was the fate of Bedrich? For two decades, ever since the True Religionists had cast their spell at the foot of the Wizard, Bedrich had been lost to the world, forever living in a perpetual night. Bartolome had only escaped her island because she was already on *The Knotted Wood*, heading to Hogkarta, but not before the effects of the spell had made her like the others—undead. Even now, she could feel the pull of the island. She could feel the strength of other undead lords there. One in particular, the strongest of all, who could likely even command Bartolome's actions, scared her to her core. But something was different now; Bartolome was sure it. What if the reversing spell had worked on Bedrich, but not on Marta and her crew? There was really only one way to find out.

Marta gave the command to her crew to set sail for her home, Bedrich, the isle of the dead.

EPILOGUE

William slammed the large tome closed. His wide smile, now covered with long whiskers, edged higher as his eyes fell to the children around him. Each of them leapt to their feet once the reading was done. Some of the boys drew mock swords to swashbuckle across the carpet. Two of the girls donned hats and tried to pirate the boys' bagged lunches. A flock of parents came to collect them, each of them thanking William for the story.

"Well, that was well told," Jonathan said as he sat down next to William.

"Did you think so?"

"Indeed. Though, I'm not sure that's how I remember Samson at the end. I thought he had a horn or something?"

William chuckled. "No, I quite recall the antlers. Remember, he rubbed them against your knitted sweater before your trip back to Hogkarta?"

Jonathan nodded. "Ah, yes, now I do. He ruined the wool."

"That scoundrel."

Jonathan opened a bottle of port and poured two glasses. He handed one to William and sipped the other, smacking his lips in satisfaction. William followed suit, his eyes going wide at the taste. Wood crackled in the fireplace just to their right. William didn't even remember Jonathan stoking the fire.

"Well, now that that's done, will you have it copied? Sent throughout the empire? The kingdom? The Democracy?"

"Perhaps. Or perhaps just a simple retelling to the local children will suffice," William said. "Although, of course, I shared a more truncated version than the entire tome. We'd have been here all day and into tomorrow if I'd read the entire book."

"And I'm sure their parents thank you for removing the scary bits."

William winked and sipped his port.

Jonathan nodded. "That's not all that happened, of course. I'm sure I remember much more."

"Oh, there was. Much more."

"Didn't have room for it, then?" Jonathan asked.

William set his port on the side table, heaved the tome he'd been reading to the children, and placed it on the floor next to him. From the other side table, he lifted another tome, this one filled with blank pages, as well as a pen and a jar of ink.

"What's this, then?" Jonathan asked.

William smiled. "Volume two."

ABOUT THE AUTHOR

George Allen Miller lives in Washington D.C. with his wife, children.

ALSO BY GEORGE ALLEN MILLER

McGilliVerse Series:

Eugene J. McGillicuddy's Alien Detective Agency

Alice Pemberton's Bureau Of Scientific Inquiry

The PepperJack Online Sleuthing Service

Fringe Space:

Life on the Fringe: Tales from the Frontier